As Lily pushed her son on the swing, Michael noticed there was an edginess to her movements. And that her eyes were continuously moving, searching, watching. When she stared over in the direction of the trees where he was parked, Michael held his breath a moment and wondered if he had been spotted. Then her gaze moved past him and seemed to search some spot beyond. Had that been fear in those green eyes? he wondered.

The notion that she was in trouble—and not just for robbing her husband and kidnapping her son—gnawed at him, stirring old feelings and protective instincts he thought he'd buried a long time ago. Yet even as he tried to shake these feelings, he struggled once again with the image of the calculating woman Webster had described. He wanted to believe Lily was a coldhearted female and not this seemingly delicate woman playing with her child.

"Metsy Hingle...will delight readers with her skill at storytelling in this charmer."
—*Romantic Times* on *The Wager*

Dear Reader,

For those of you familiar with my work, you know that many of my books are set in my own hometown of New Orleans. As you've probably guessed from the title, *Behind the Mask* takes place in that magical city during the height of the Mardi Gras season. I hope you enjoy reading this book as much as I enjoyed writing it.

One of the best things about being a writer is hearing from readers, and I'd love to hear from you. In fact, as a special thank-you, I've had a commemorative bookmark created just for *Behind the Mask* and, while supplies last, I'll send one to each reader who writes and requests one.

I look forward to hearing from you.

Best wishes,

Metsy Hingle

P.O. Box 3224
Covington, LA
U.S.A. 70433

www.metsyhingle.com

METSY HINGLE

Behind the Mask

MIRA

ISBN 1-55166-926-9

BEHIND THE MASK

Copyright © 2002 by Metsy Hingle.

Visit us at www.mirabooks.com

Printed in U.S.A.

For the very special friends who bless my life:

Sandra and Michael Brown,
Brenda and Jim Gelpi, Mary and Fred Dummett,
Mary Ann and Louis Lahners,
Nancy Wagner aka Hailey North,
Linda Kay West aka Dixie Kane
and Karen Young.

And my very best friend—my husband, Jim.

ACKNOWLEDGMENTS

While my name as the author is listed on this book, the finished product in your hands would not be possible were it not for the help of many people. My heartfelt thanks go to the following people for their help in bringing *Behind the Mask* to life:

Valerie Gray, my editor, whose guidance and patience were invaluable to me in the writing of this book.

Dianne Moggy, editorial director of MIRA Books, for her belief in me and this project.

Karen Solem, my agent, for her continued guidance and support.

Ricardo Coštales, Lancôme makeup artist and genius at finding the beauty in all women.

The incredible MIRA staff for their support.

Tara Gavin and Joan Marlow Golan at Silhouette Books for their continued support and enthusiasm.

My fans, who enable me to live my dream because they allow me to entertain them with my books.

And, as always, very special thanks go to my children and family, whose love and support enable me to spin my tales of love, hope and happily-ever-after.

One

"I'll pay you one million dollars to find my wife."

"All right, Webster," Michael Sullivan replied from the other end of the phone line. "You've got my attention."

Adam Webster smiled in satisfaction at the ex-cop's change in attitude. "I'm glad to hear that," he said as he gazed at the view of the Miami skyline afforded him from his penthouse suite of offices. He was glad, but he wasn't at all surprised. He'd learned a long time ago that money talks—even to a man like Sullivan. A man who, according to his sources, had been among Houston's best and brightest police detectives until five years ago when he'd resigned abruptly following his partner's death. Now he hired himself out as a detective, bodyguard or bounty hunter—whatever the situation called for. The man was said to be as mean as a rattlesnake and twice as dangerous. He also reportedly had the instincts of a bloodhound when it came to tracking down someone who didn't want to be found. It was Sullivan's latter skill that he needed now. "You've been a difficult man to get in touch with, Mr. Sullivan," Adam said, making no attempt to hide his displeasure. "My assistant tells me she's left you several messages."

"I've been out of town handling something for a client. The truth is, the only reason you caught me now is because I had to swing by to the office to pick up some reports."

"I see," Adam said tightly. "I'm not accustomed to being ignored, Mr. Sullivan."

"No one's ignoring you, Webster. But since I'm pressed for time, why don't we dispense with my lack of good manners and you tell me why you're willing to pay me a million bucks to find your wife."

"Because she's missing," Adam said sharply, angered by the man's insolence. Biting back his temper, he reminded himself that he needed Sullivan to find Elisabeth and the disk she'd stolen. With his temper making him edgy, he turned away from the sweep of windows and stalked over to his desk. Sitting down, he picked up the framed photo of Elisabeth. "I understand your expertise is in finding people. And, as I said, I'd like to hire you to find my wife."

"How long has she been missing?"

"Six months." And after six months it still gnawed at him like a festering sore. He detested mistakes, refused to tolerate them. Yet he had made a mistake in underestimating Elisabeth.

Never in a million years would he have believed that sweet, docile Elisabeth—the girl he'd fed, clothed and molded into a woman worthy to be his wife—would have had the guts to defy him. To steal the disk from his safe. To actually drug him and run away. Even more infuriating was that she'd not only gotten away from the idiots he'd hired to guard her, but that he'd doled out a considerable sum of money for private detectives, and some not-so-reputable business associates, to find her. And though they'd come close to grabbing her twice, she had still managed to escape. But not for much longer, Adam promised himself. If Sullivan was half as good as the reports on him indicated, Elisabeth's rebellion was about to come to an end.

"Webster? You still there?"

"Yes. Yes, I'm here," Adam repeated, dragging his thoughts back to the present. "What did you say?"

"I asked if you've filed a missing persons report with the police?"

"No," Adam advised him. "I don't want the police involved."

"Why not?"

"Aside from the fact that I can do without the publicity, I don't want any charges filed against my wife."

"Last I heard, it wasn't a crime for a woman to leave her husband," Sullivan informed him.

"No. But stealing cash and jewelry from my safe and kidnapping my son *are* crimes. If I had brought the police into it, they would have issued an arrest warrant for her. I prefer to handle things myself."

Sullivan swore.

"My sentiments exactly," Adam told him.

"Why didn't you say up front that she stole the kid?" Sullivan demanded.

"I was about to," Adam lied, surprised that a man who was reportedly a real hard-ass should care about the kid. *He* certainly didn't give a damn about the brat. As far as he was concerned, his problems with Elisabeth all began with the kid. Not insisting that she terminate the pregnancy had been a major screwup on his part—one he would make sure didn't happen again. But first...first he had to get Elisabeth back—and that damning disk. Did she even know what was on it? Or the damage it could cause him if it got into the wrong hands?

"How old's your boy?"

Adam frowned at Sullivan's question and quickly calculated how old the kid would be now. "Almost three."

"Man, that's got to be rough, him being so little and you missing all that time with him."

"It is," Adam said, because it was obvious that Sullivan expected it. "I want you to find my family for me, Mr. Sullivan. And I'd like you to start looking for them right away. If you'll come by my office, I'll provide you with any other information you need, and give you a retainer for your services. I'll expect you within the hour."

"I can't make it today."

Adam scowled. "Why not?" he demanded, unaccustomed to having his requests denied.

"Because I'm in the middle of another job."

"And is this other client offering to pay you a million dollars for your services?" he countered.

"No."

"Then I don't see the problem. Tell your client to find someone else to handle whatever it is you're doing."

"That's not the way I work," Sullivan said, his voice cool and hard. "When I make a commitment, I honor it. I've got to go. I'll give you a call when I get back and, if you're still interested in hiring me, we'll talk."

When the dial tone buzzed in his ear, Adam slammed down the receiver. "Arrogant bastard," he muttered, clenching his fists. Sullivan would pay for that, he promised. As soon as the man found Elisabeth, he would make Sullivan regret his insolence. Shoving back from the desk, he headed to the bar and poured himself a shot of bourbon. He tossed it back, felt the sting as the drink slid down his throat like liquid fire. After pouring himself another one, he grabbed the crystal tumbler and stalked across the ultramodern office on which he'd spent a small fortune. Ignoring the polished finish on the black marble desktop, he set down his glass and picked up the silver-framed picture of Elisabeth. He stared at her—the pale delicate skin, the silky blond hair, the long slender neck. Never taking his eyes from the photo, he reached for the bourbon and tossed back another swallow.

She belonged to him, he reasoned, and felt that violent punch of lust that always came with thoughts of Elisabeth. From the moment he'd first set eyes on her he'd wanted her. Even at fifteen and still an innocent, she'd left him breathless and aching. She'd been worth ten of her mother. It was the reason he'd saved her. Were it not for him, she'd have probably hooked up with some two-bit punk and been selling herself on the streets of Miami before she'd turned sixteen.

Instead he'd rescued her from her wretched life. He'd provided for her education, showered her with gifts, and when she'd been a legal adult, he had married her. Any number of women would have killed to be in her position, just for the chance to be in his bed. He knew he looked good. He took care of himself, kept his body in shape and could easily pass for a man twenty years younger. Hadn't he heard a woman in one of his clubs call him a stud just last week? He could have had his pick of women, but he'd chosen Elisabeth.

Elisabeth.

So sweet. So soft. So young. His breath turned to a pant as he thought of taking her that first time, of thrusting himself into her warm tender flesh. And the memory made the throbbing in his groin even more painful.

He slapped down the glass and reached for the phone. "Kit, it's Adam," he said when the line was answered at his Miami nightclub. "How's that new girl working out, the young blonde with the southern drawl you introduced me to last week?"

"You must mean Annabelle," Kit said, her voice

warm and sultry. "She's working out fine. A little shy, but the customers seem to like her. She's a fast learner and very eager to please. She should be here in a few minutes."

"Send her up to the penthouse when she gets there," he said, already anticipating the feel of the pretty, young girl beneath him. "And Kit, get someone else to take her shift tonight. She's going to be busy."

After hanging up the phone, he reached for his glass and started toward the bedroom adjoining his office to wait for Annabelle. But his gaze fell on Elisabeth's photo again. He lifted his glass in a mock salute. "It won't be long now, darling," he whispered before downing the remainder of the whiskey. He would use Sullivan to find her, and once he had her and the disk back, he'd see to it that she never dared to defy him again.

As for Sullivan, the man was in need of a lesson in respect—which he personally intended to deliver.

"According to the APB on him, his name is Bill 'The Bull' Dozier and he's wanted in three states for robbery, rape and murder," the broad-shouldered state trooper told Michael.

Michael took in the scene before him—the flashing lights of the police cars and ambulance, the brightly lit front of the all-night store advertising drinks, food and gas, the dark, lonely stretch of road with cops and paramedics at a crime scene. He couldn't help feeling a sense of déjà vu. When he saw three curiosity seekers make their way over to the storefront to look inside, he had to fight the itch to tell them to stay clear and to let the cops do their jobs. But he was no longer a cop, he reminded himself. He was a bystander and a witness.

"Man, he is one big mother," the trooper said as two Florida state police exited the convenience store with the bald, tattooed piece of scum. Michael had interrupted him in the middle of raping the store's female clerk.

"Yeah. But you know what they say. The bigger they come, the harder they fall." But this one hadn't gone down easy, Michael admitted. It had taken him more than a dozen vicious blows and two bullets to finally bring the man down. And even with two slugs in him, shackled and bleeding, the guy was still able to walk out of the store to the second ambulance that had been called to the scene. As Michael watched him being loaded into the ambulance, he thought of the terrified young woman whom he'd rescued a short time ago. Remembering her battered face and the way her clothes had been torn from her body, he clenched his bruised fingers into a fist and wished he could ram it down the monster's throat. "How's the girl?"

"Alive, thanks to you. She's lucky you came along when you did. According to his rap sheet, he took a knife to the last woman when he was finished. A remote spot like this and this late at night, chances are no one would have found her for hours."

"That's probably what he was counting on," Michael said. And if he hadn't been so determined to make it back to Miami tonight, he never would have pulled off the interstate and come to the all-night store in the middle of nowhere in search of a jolt of caffeine to keep him awake. For the first time in the four days since his temper had caused him to mouth off to Webster and blow off what was a once-in-a-lifetime fee of a million bucks, Michael cut himself some slack. Had he taken Webster's job instead of tracking down the deadbeat who'd wiped out a widow's savings, he wouldn't have been here to save the girl. If he were a man who believed in such things as fate, he might even think that something besides the need for coffee had made him choose this particular exit on this particular night.

But if he'd learned nothing else since seeing his partner die before his eyes five years ago, he'd learned that he, and he alone, was responsible for his choices.

"Like I said, she was lucky you decided to stop for coffee."

But he doubted the woman was feeling particularly lucky at the moment. "What did the paramedics say? She going to be okay?"

"He did a number on her with his fists, but nothing that shouldn't heal eventually."

Maybe physically she would heal, Michael thought. Mentally, it would be another story. She'd probably carry the scars for the rest of her life. "She had a picture of a baby propped up by her cash register."

"Yeah, the local police say she had a little girl about six months ago. Apparently her husband got laid off from his job, and she decided to go back to work to help out. She took the graveyard shift because it paid more money and allowed her to be home with her baby during the day. Poor kid only started working here about two weeks ago.''

''Too bad I didn't put a bullet between his eyes and saved the state, and her, the trouble of going through a trial.''

''You won't get an argument from anybody here on that one,'' the trooper told him. ''That cut by your eye looks pretty nasty. You might want to have the paramedics take a look at it until you can get to a hospital.''

Michael tested the tender spot with his fingertips and when they came away bloody, he pressed a handkerchief to the wound. ''It's just a scratch,'' Michael informed him. As it was, he'd probably be tied up for hours while the cops took his statement and filled out the paperwork. The last thing he wanted to do was get bogged down with even more red tape by going to the hospital.

''Suit yourself. But I'm going to need you to come down to the station and make a statement about what went down here tonight.''

''I know the drill,'' Michael told him.

''Yeah? I thought you private dicks did your best to avoid dealing with the law.''

''I was a cop for twelve years before I decided to go out on my own,'' Michael informed him.

''Here in Florida?''

''Texas,'' Michael told him, eager to end the conversation. Rehashing his career as a police detective wasn't high on his list of priorities—especially at one in the morning. He also didn't want to remember how his own stupidity had caused the bust he and Pete had worked on for months to fall apart. Stupidity that had cost his partner his life and his father his pride. Not to mention the black mark on the entire Houston Police Department.

"Good thing the perp didn't know that or you'd have a lot more than that gash on your head."

"Let me guess. He's a cop-hater."

The trooper nodded. "Word is he did a real number on the two prison guards he escaped from last month. According to the reports, one of them may lose an eye and the other one is still in a body cast."

Michael had no trouble believing it. As a fourth-generation cop, he'd heard plenty of stories about cop-haters and had encountered his fair share of them during his years with the Houston P.D. One look at the monster-size guy with the gold teeth and the ugly scar down one side of his face would have been enough to set off alarms in most cops. But it had been the lack of emotion in the man's dark eyes that should have told the fools at the prison just how dangerous the guy was. He'd seen that look before. And each time he had, he'd been faced with a cold-blooded killer without a conscience, without a soul.

A long black sedan pulled into the busy parking lot. A tall man in a dark suit with a cap of silver hair exited the vehicle and sought out the officer in charge.

"Wonder who that is?" the trooper remarked.

''His name's Hennessey, he's a federal agent,'' Michael told him.

''You know him?''

''Our paths have crossed a time or two,'' Michael replied. But even if he hadn't known Hennessey, he'd have pegged him as a fed right off. The nondescript car, the somber suit, the steely look and calm demeanor. There had even been a time when he'd actually wanted to leave the Houston P.D. and join his brother Travis at the Bureau. So had Pete. Only Pete had flunked the tests. And when his friend had accused him of breaking their childhood pact to be partners, Michael had passed on the Bureau's offer. Later that same year, after Pete had been killed, he'd abandoned any thoughts of becoming a federal agent. He'd walked away from his badge, too.

''The feds must want this guy pretty bad if they sent an agent out here this quickly.''

''It's more a question of covering their asses before the press gets wind of what went down here,'' Michael said. At the trooper's puzzled look, he explained, ''The Bureau takes a lot of heat in the media. Bringing in a killer like Dozier will play well in the headlines.''

''But the feds had nothing to do with this. You're the one who caught him,'' the trooper pointed out.

Michael shook his head. ''That won't play as well as saying that I assisted the FBI in taking him down. Look, here comes Hennessey now to try to sell me on the idea on what happened here tonight.''

And after dispatching the trooper, the federal agent

did his best to convince Michael about the official story that the Bureau wanted to give the press. "Since you've worked with the Bureau before, we'd like to say you were working in conjunction with us to track down Dozier and that you followed him to the convenience store where you apprehended him during the assault on the woman. You okay with that, Sullivan?"

"Would it make any difference if I wasn't?"

"No."

"Then why bother asking for permission?"

"Don't be such a hard-ass, Sullivan.

"You did a good thing saving that girl tonight. Taking that animal down couldn't have been easy. You did a hell of a job."

"Thanks."

"It's a shame that a man with your talents is wasting his time chasing cheating husbands when he could be doing something worthwhile."

"I like what I'm doing."

"Bullshit. I've told you before, you'd make a damn good federal agent, Sullivan."

"No thanks. I know what you guys earn, and it's not enough."

Hennessey made a dismissive sound. "You expect me to believe that money is all that motivates you?"

"You should, because it's the truth."

"That's a load of crap. You were a cop. A man doesn't become a cop or an agent for the money. You do it for times like tonight—because you want to be able to help people. You can't make me believe that saving that woman tonight wasn't a lot more gratifying than tracking down some deadbeat,'' Hennessey pointed out.

''I don't give a damn what you believe. As for gratification, I got a hell of a lot of gratification when the last jerk I tracked down was thrown in jail for fraud after he bilked an old lady out of her life savings. And I got paid a fat fee for doing it.''

''You can cut the act, Sullivan. You and I both know that if you really liked hiring yourself out as a P.I. you wouldn't have offered your services to the Bureau pro bono when they were hunting that serial killer a few months ago. And from what I heard, it wasn't the first time you've done that.''

Michael shrugged. ''Just trying to be civic-minded,'' he said, not wanting to admit that while the money was good and some of his cases left him with a feeling of accomplishment, many of them didn't. He did it for the money. Money for Janie and Pete's boys.

As for the work he occasionally did for the feds, in a roundabout way, he did it for his brother Travis. After all, Travis was a federal agent. Besides, it was also a way for him to keep his skills sharp and his contacts strong. And if that sounded a bit too pat, he could live with it. What he didn't want to do—refused to do despite his brother's prodding—was examine his motivations too closely. He couldn't afford to—not with Janie and Pete's boys depending on him.

''That's a line of bull, and you know it,'' Hennessey told him.

''Listen, believe whatever you want,'' Michael

said. "But if we're through here, I'd like to wrap this up so I get on my way."

"Hot date?"

"No, a hot client. One who's offering me a big fat fee to find his runaway wife." Or at least Michael hoped Webster would still be offering him that fat fee—if he hadn't already hired someone else.

"All right. But you'll need to come into headquarters and make a statement about what happened here tonight, and you'll need to be available to testify at Dozier's trial."

"All right."

"Make sure you give my people a number where they can reach you."

"Will do," Michael said, and started toward the state troopers in order to finish with them before heading to police headquarters.

"Sullivan?"

Michael stopped, turned and looked over at Hennessey. "Yeah?"

"When you get tired of playing bloodhound for the rich and overprivileged, give me a call."

"I keep telling you, you're barking up the wrong tree, Hennessey. I like being my own boss—and I like making a lot of money."

"Money isn't what made you tackle that gorilla in that store tonight and risk getting your brains beaten out. You did it because at your core, you're still a cop. You believe in protecting the weak and fighting for justice."

Michael scowled at him. "I hate to rain on this

parade of yours, but I did what anyone would have done if they'd walked in on that monster and seen what he was doing to that girl.''

''Most people would have called for help—not taken on a guy who was armed and outweighed them by at least a hundred pounds.''

''That's because most people have more sense than I do.'' Not at all happy with the tenor of the conversation, Michael added, ''I'm no hero, Hennessey. Don't make me out to be one. I acted on instinct. Taking down Dozier was part stupidity, part dumb luck. If I'd failed, he might have killed that girl.''

''And if you hadn't stepped in, he would have killed her for sure.''

Michael let out an exasperated breath. ''Is there a point here?''

''Yeah. The point is that when you stop running from whatever demons are chasing you, let me know.'' He stuffed a card in the pocket of Michael's chambray shirt. ''You could make a difference.''

Michael removed the card from his shirt pocket, crumpled it in his fist, and walked away. Regardless of what Hennessey thought, saving that girl tonight had been dumb luck, just as he'd claimed. He'd gotten out of the hero business when he'd turned in his badge. From now on, he was in it for the bucks.

Two

"No," Lily murmured as she tossed and turned in her sleep. "No," she repeated, her heart beating faster and faster, her head moving from side to side in denial. "Adam, no!"

Suddenly she jerked upright in the bed. Breath heaving, she scrambled back up against the headboard and pulled her knees up to her chest. Still shaken by the nightmare, she buried her face against her knees and waited for the trembling to stop. But try as she might, she couldn't seem to stop shaking.

It was a dream. Just a dream.

She repeated the words like a litany in her head until the worst of the terror had passed. Despite the coolness of the room, sweat beaded her forehead. Fumbling for the lamp on the bedside table, she switched it on. A whimper slipped past her lips when light spilled across the room, chasing away the shadows and darkness to reveal her surroundings.

She wasn't in the massive king-size bed with the ornate mahogany scrolls. She was in the small, plain bed with a simple pewter headboard. There was no damask duvet stretched across the foot of her bed, only a colorful comforter with a bright rose pattern. Following the familiar ritual that enabled her to shake off the paralyzing fear that always followed the nightmare, she curled her fingers into the sheets. White, bargain-priced cotton sheets, she assured herself. No colored satin, no rare eight-hundred-count Egyptian blend that was softer than a sigh against the skin, but had cost more than it would take to feed a family of four for a month.

Clutching one of those plain sheets in her fist, Lily closed her eyes, breathing deeply. She and Timmy were safe. They were in New Orleans—not Miami. They were in the rented shotgun house they'd lived in for more than two months now—not in the palatial prison that had been their home. And she was no longer Elisabeth Webster, wife of wealthy Florida nightclub owner/businessman and philanthropist Adam Webster. She was now Lily Tremont, a widow with an almost-three-year-old son who worked as a waitress at the River Bend Diner. They were safe, she reminded herself. She and Timmy were safe. Adam didn't know where they were.

Finally, when her heartbeat and breathing were almost normal again, Lily opened her eyes and glanced at the clock on the bedside table. She sighed. Dawn was more than four hours away, but she knew from experience that she wouldn't be able to sleep anymore tonight. Not when the memories remained so close to the surface.

And just as she always did whenever the nightmares came, she slipped out of bed and went to check on Timmy. Easing open the door to his bedroom, she tiptoed over to his bed and looked down at the sandy-haired little boy who was her life. Clad in his favorite Spider-Man pajamas, Timmy lay curled on his side, clutching his ever-present teddy bear in his arms. Satisfied that he was safe, Lily adjusted the covers he'd kicked off with hands that were still unsteady. Annoyed with herself for the weakness, she pressed a kiss to the top of Timmy's head and exited the room.

Now that she knew Timmy was safe, the worst of the panic was over. But not the memories that always came flooding back whenever she had the dream. Retreating to the bathroom, she closed the door and turned on the shower. When the water was as hot as she could stand it, Lily stripped off her nightgown and stepped under the steaming spray. And in the shower where she had no fear that Timmy would hear her sobs, she allowed herself to cry as she relived the events of that terrible night six months ago...

Elisabeth sat up in bed, unsure what had awakened her. Then she heard it—the sound of rain slapping against the windowpanes. Must have been the rain, she decided as she pushed the hair out of her eyes and switched on the lamp. Glancing around the elegantly appointed bedroom, it took her a moment to orient herself.

And then she remembered. She'd had a monster headache all day, and after she'd put Timmy down for the night and complained of not feeling well, Adam had given her something to take for her head. To her surprise, he'd suggested she go to bed without him and told her not to wait up because he had a business meeting that would run late.

Relieved not to have him make love to her that night, she'd taken the pill he'd given her and gone to bed alone. A check of the silver-framed clock with diamond and onyx numerals revealed it was after three o'clock in the morning. She couldn't remember the last time she'd gone to bed without her husband and been able to sleep for a six-hour stretch without Adam waking her to make love. Even when she'd been in the final stages of her pregnancy, with her belly swollen and her back aching, Adam's desire for her had never lagged. He had refused to be denied access to her body, reminding her of the many women who would gladly service his needs, but how it was only her that he wanted.

She should be grateful, Elisabeth told herself. After all, how many women had a husband like Adam who remained passionate about his wife even after seven years of marriage and a child. But she didn't feel grateful, Elisabeth admitted. She felt trapped.

Irritated with herself, she reached for the flimsy robe of the expensive black peignoir—one of dozens that Adam had bought her and insisted she wear for him. And as she slid her arms into the whisper-sheer fabric, she wondered why she'd even bothered to put it on since it provided little in the way of covering or warmth. After she slipped on the matching high-heel slippers, she walked over to the huge windows that looked out over the gardens.

Wrapping her arms around herself, Elisabeth

stared out at the rain. A movement in the tree caught her eye, and she looked closer, smiled as she saw the little wren flap its wings and bravely fly through the raindrops to the neighboring tree. Pressing her fingers against the cool panes of glass, she wished she were that wren. Wished she had the courage to break free of this beautiful cage where Adam kept her— wished she could escape with Timmy.

Immediately ashamed of her thoughts, Elisabeth silently chastised herself. She had no reason to be so unhappy. Adam was a good husband. He adored her, lavished her with jewels and expensive clothes. He provided her with everything a woman could possibly want.

And, because of Adam, she had a beautiful little boy, she reminded herself. Her eyes misted as she thought of her son, still unable to believe that something as perfect and wonderful as Timmy had actually come from her. From her and Adam, she amended, realizing she had to stop thinking of Timmy as only being her son. He was Adam's child, too. While Adam may have been unhappy about her pregnancy and had been angry with her for hiding it from him until she was well into her second trimester, he was becoming more accustomed to them being a family now, she assured herself. He just hadn't been prepared to become a father. But now that Timmy had turned two and was becoming more of a person, Adam would begin to enjoy his son more. Surely he would learn to love Timmy as she did.

A father shouldn't have to learn to love his child.

Elisabeth tried to shut off the nagging voice in her head, told herself that Adam hadn't planned on them having a family. Learning to share her had been a big adjustment for him. But he would come around.

And what about those accidents Timmy keeps having? What would have happened last month if you hadn't come out to the pool when you did and saw Timmy floating facedown in the water?

Elisabeth shivered at the memory of coming out to the pool to surprise her two fellows with a pitcher of lemonade only to discover Adam on his cell phone and Timmy's unmoving body floating in the pool. Clutching her throat, she could feel the terror clawing inside her as she recalled dropping the tray and diving into the water—even though she couldn't swim.

Would Adam have saved Timmy if you hadn't been in danger of drowning, too?

Elisabeth put her hands over her ears, tried to block out the questions that had been plaguing her for weeks now. She had to stop doing this to herself. She had to stop suspecting her husband of such horrible things. Even more restless now than she'd been before, she knew there was little chance of her going back to sleep and decided to go check on Timmy.

As she made her way down the massive staircase, Elisabeth tried to make as little noise as possible. Adam hated that she was so protective of Timmy, she reminded herself. It was one of the reasons he had insisted Timmy's room be downstairs and away from their suite. When she reached the bottom of the stairs, she listened carefully, trying to determine whether

Adam was still at work in his study or if perhaps he'd gone out. She'd learned early in their marriage not to question him about his late-night trips to the office or to the clubs he owned.

As she passed his study, she noted the light from under the door and hurried in the opposite direction toward Timmy's room. When Elisabeth reached the door to Timmy's room, a smile was already forming on her lips. She eased it open and saw Adam standing over Timmy's crib with a pillow poised over the little boy's face.

"What are you doing?" she screamed.

He swung around. "Elisabeth!"

She lunged at him. "Get away from my baby!"

"What in the hell's the matter with you?" he demanded, gripping her wrists so tightly she thought the bones would snap.

"My baby! You were going to smother my baby!"

"Don't be ridiculous. I was just picking up his pillow."

"You're lying," she accused him as she fought to free herself from his ironlike grip. Adam was lying and she knew it. Just as she'd known he'd lied to her when he'd told her Timmy must have fallen into the pool when he'd gone to answer his phone. Just as she'd known deep in her heart that all those little accidents Timmy had had since he was an infant hadn't been accidents at all. She just hadn't wanted to believe Adam was capable of trying to kill his own son.

"You're hysterical," Adam told her.

"No, I'm not. I'm not," she fired back and continued to struggle.

"Mommy! Mommy," Timmy cried, awakened by their shouting. He stood up in his crib, held his arms out to her.

"Adam, please let me go. He needs me," she pleaded.

"Shut up," he yelled at Timmy who huddled down into the corner of his crib against the bed railings, his brown eyes wide and terrified as deep hiccuping sobs escaped his lips.

"You're scaring him. Let me go!" She fought wildly to break free and get to her son, but her efforts proved useless. *"Please, Adam, he's crying."*

"Let him cry. You're making a ninny out of that kid fussing over him the way you do," he said, and began dragging her from the room. *"I've been patient long enough, Elisabeth. Your days of coddling that kid are over. Tomorrow I'm hiring a nanny to take care of him, and you're going to be a real wife to me again. Beginning now,"* he told her.

As Adam pulled the door closed on Timmy's heart-wrenching sobs, and forced her up the stairs to the bedroom, something broke inside her. She knew then that she had to escape.

So when he kicked the door shut behind them and she recognized the lustful glint in his eyes, she shut off her mind and her heart, telling herself she would get through this. She would bide her time and she and Timmy would escape.

"Take it off," Adam told her.

Not wanting to enrage him any further and risk hurting Timmy, she began to unbutton the peignoir. By the time she'd removed the robe and started on the buttons of the low-cut nightgown, Adam had already shed his own clothes and now stood naked and fully aroused. He was a handsome man. He worked hard to keep his six-foot frame trim, and showed not an ounce of flab. With his dark hair and year-round tan, Adam had reminded her of movie-star George Hamilton the first time she'd seen him. On the surface, he'd been a perfect gentleman. But behind the mask he wore, she now knew there lurked a monster— a dangerous monster.

"Come here," he commanded.

Elisabeth did as he said. And when she stood before him in the flimsy gown, his eyes darkened. "So beautiful. So perfect," he said as he reached for the bodice of the gown. He lifted his eyes to hers and she caught the flash of triumph just before he ripped the delicate fabric in two. "And mine."

Adam filled his big hands with her breasts, squeezed them so hard that she whimpered with pain. "Adam, please. You're hurting me."

But her pain only seemed to excite him. He shoved her down to her knees in front of him. Knowing what he expected, how he'd trained her to pleasure him since that first night when he'd married her on her eighteenth birthday, Elisabeth took him in her mouth.

She wanted to gag, but she thought of her baby downstairs, and knew that if she did so, it would only enrage Adam. So she blocked out the feel of his fin-

gers digging into her scalp, the sound of the grunting noises that came from him. Suddenly he jerked her up, pushed her onto the bed.

"Adam, wait—"

But he was already shoving himself inside her. Unprepared, she gasped at the painful invasion. Heedless of her discomfort, he continued to thrust himself into her. "You were made for this," he told her, his voice a guttural pant, his dark eyes gleaming madly. "For me," he said as he slammed into her again. And again. And again. Finally, when she thought he might never stop, his body went rigid and he shouted out in triumph before he collapsed on top of her.

She didn't know how long she lay there, crushed beneath Adam's heavier weight. Not until she thought he was asleep did she begin to ease out from under him, intent on slipping away to go check on Timmy. She'd almost made it to the edge of the bed when Adam demanded, "Where do you think you're going?"

"I was just going to see—"

"No." He yanked her by the hair and pulled her back down to the bed. She scrambled to sit up, but he shoved her back down and straddled her. "I told you, this is what you were made for. Not to take care of some squalling brat. I'm through sharing you, Elisabeth. You and I are going back to the way things were before you got yourself knocked up. Understand?"

"Adam, please. I realize now that I've been neglecting you," she hedged, trying to bide her time. "I

*promise to be a better wife in the future, but please,
I don't want a nanny. I'm Timmy's mother, I—"*

*He shoved his hard shaft into her again. "It's a
nanny until I can find a boarding school to take him.
This mother fantasy of yours is over, Elisabeth. Accept it, or I'll get rid of him permanently."*

*His words sent a chill through her because she
knew he meant it. She could no longer delude herself.
Adam was insane, and unless she got Timmy away,
he would kill her son. Even as he mauled her body,
and poured his seed into her, she began planning
their escape...*

They had escaped, Lily reminded herself as she sat
huddled on the floor of the shower, shivering beneath
the spray of water that had long since turned cold.
While Adam had come close to finding them twice
now, she had managed to get away. For now at least,
her son was safe.

"Thank you Chantal," Webster told the statuesque
secretary who ushered Michael into his office.

"Sorry to have kept you waiting, Sullivan," Webster told him from behind the massive marble desk
that gleamed like a black diamond. After shaking
hands, he gestured to the pair of chairs positioned in
front of the desk. "Please, have a seat."

Michael sat down in the cushy leather chair. With
the same swiftness he'd employed as a cop to size up
a suspect, he took in the other man's two-hundred-
dollar haircut, the manicured nails, the pricey Italian
suit. Rich. Powerful. Sophisticated. A well-connected

player. And according to his sources, a dangerous enemy.

"May I offer you something to drink?"

"No thanks. I'm fine," Michael replied.

"Very well. Chantel, have a check cut for the congressman's campaign fund and include this note with it," he instructed the secretary as he handed her an envelope. "That'll be all for now."

"Yes, sir," the woman said, and then quickly exited the room.

Michael didn't doubt for a minute that the reference to the congressman, as well as the hour he'd been left to cool his heels in the reception area, was Webster's way of showing him that he was the one in control.

"Cigar?" Webster offered, opening the ornate box and sliding it toward Michael. "They're Cuban."

"No thanks. I don't smoke."

"How wise of you. These are one of my vices, I'm afraid." He chose one for himself, sniffed it appreciatively. And before he could put the thing in his mouth, the hired muscle at the door was beside him with a light.

The guy must be one hell of a poker player, Michael thought as he observed the ritual. Despite Webster's pleasant expression, Michael had no doubts that the man was still pissed at him for not jumping at his offer a week ago. Unfortunately, Webster had caught him fresh on the heels of an argument with Pete's widow over the money he'd had deposited into her bank account for the kids. On his best day, he didn't go out of his way to charm a potential client. On that particular day he'd made no attempt to sugarcoat his feelings about the million-dollar carrot that Webster had dangled in front of his nose. Of course, he'd spent the better part of the next four days kicking himself for his short temper and stupidity. Not until he'd interrupted that perp in the convenience store had he cut himself some slack. While he might hate losing a shot at that million-dollar fee, he didn't regret that he'd been able to help that girl.

After several puffs on the cigar, Webster sat back in his chair. "I must say that I was rather surprised to hear from you, Sullivan. When we spoke on the phone, you didn't seem particularly interested in my offer."

"I was interested. But like I told you, I had another commitment."

He took another puff of the cigar, blew out a ring of smoke. "So you said. I understand you proved to be quite the hero, saving that young woman's life and apprehending an escaped felon."

Since the incident had occurred in a small town and both he and the FBI had made sure that his name was not listed in the press, Michael couldn't help wondering about Webster's contacts. "You're well informed."

"I make it my business to know who I'm dealing with," Webster replied.

Which meant Webster probably also knew that he'd walked away from his job as a cop after Pete had been killed. What Webster didn't know—what few people knew—was that he had been the one responsible for Pete's death just as surely as if he'd pulled the trigger, because he'd been the one to introduce his friend to Giselle.

"I hope that doesn't offend you."

Michael shrugged. "It's your business."

"Yes, it is. And I'm sure you can understand the need for a man in my position to be careful."

"Of course." He understood all right. Besides, he had done some checking, as well. He'd learned that the fifty-six-year-old self-made millionaire had made a killing with a string of high-end restaurants and nightclubs across Florida. Seven years ago he had married his ward, the former Elisabeth Jeffries, with whom he had one child, a son named Timothy. The man was touted as a generous patron of the arts and, reportedly, gave huge sums of money to charity. He also supported the current regime of politicians in office. The lavish parties he hosted were legendary for attracting Florida's business, political and social powerhouses. And, according to Michael's sources, not all of Webster's millions had been attained by legal means.

"I'm glad we agree on the importance of being careful because, *if* I hire you, you'll find that I don't tolerate mistakes," Webster said.

Not liking the veiled warning, Michael told him, "And *if* I take the job, you'll find that I don't make mistakes."

Webster's eyes went flat for a heartbeat. "Then we should have no problems."

Deciding he'd had enough of the pleasantries and

veiled warnings, Michael said, "You mentioned on the phone that your wife and son had been missing for about six months."

"That's right."

"Then I assume the first detective you hired failed to find her."

A look of annoyance crossed the other man's face. "You assume correctly. They found Elisabeth, but she managed to give them the slip before I could get there. A mistake on the agency's part, which led to their dismissal. That's why I contacted you."

"Speaking of contacting me," Michael began. "I'm curious why you did. I mean I'm a one-man agency, and there are any number of bigger agencies with more manpower. So why me?"

Webster smiled, and there was something about that sly twist of the man's lips that had the hair on the back of Michael's neck lifting. "Most men in your business would simply be grateful that I called them."

"I'm not most men."

Webster laughed. "Obviously. But in answer to your question, you came highly recommended by my chief of security, Bernie Pavlovich. I understand the two of you once worked together."

It had been ten years since Bernie had been booted off the Houston P.D. on charges of police brutality. Big, brawny and a bully, it didn't come as a surprise to find out that Bernie was Webster's hired muscle. What did surprise him was that Bernie would recommend him to Webster, since they hadn't exactly been friends.

"Bernie told me you earned quite a reputation for yourself with the Houston Police Department, and that you were their 'go to' guy in tough situations."

"I was lucky to have good people working with me," Michael told him.

"Come now, Sullivan. There's no reason to be modest. I know you were the unnamed private agent who led the authorities through the swamps in Louisiana a few months ago, enabling them to recapture that trio of escaped convicts."

Michael didn't bother denying it. But he couldn't help wondering again how Webster had obtained the information, since no one outside the police departments and several federal agents involved knew of his role in the affair. It had been a black eye to both the law enforcement agencies and the FBI that the cons had not only managed to escape a high-security prison facility, but that they had been able to take a prominent businessman hostage in the process. His participation in the venture had been on a need-to-know basis only. Even his fee had been paid out of a private fund. The fact that Webster knew about his role in defusing the incident spoke volumes about the man's connections.

Webster took another puff on his cigar, then ground out the hot tip in the ashtray. He sat forward. The genial expression disappeared from his face, replaced by something hard and ruthless. "You have an impressive record, Sullivan. Both as a police detective and as a private agent. It's the reason I agreed to meet with you when you called—despite your attitude last week. I want my wife back, and I think you're the man who can find her for me.''

''For one million dollars.''

''That's right,'' Webster replied.

''That's a lot of money,'' Michael pointed out. ''No offense, Webster, but I find it hard to imagine any woman being worth that kind of money.''

''But then you don't know my wife,'' Webster informed him in that smooth, cultured voice that went hand in hand with the man's thousand-dollar suit, gold cuff links and perfect white teeth. He reached for the photo of an attractive blonde that sat on the credenza and handed it to Michael. ''Stunning, isn't she?''

Michael had noticed the picture when he'd first come into the room. There was no question about what the man had seen in her, Michael concluded. Despite the demure smile and wistful look in her green eyes, everything about Elisabeth Webster screamed 'hot sex'—from the long blond hair that tumbled past her shoulders, to the figure-hugging black dress that showcased her curves. Michael allowed his gaze to follow the slashing neckline of the dress to an emerald the size of a baby's fist nestled between her breasts. At his body's sharp response to the pale, creamy skin, Michael swallowed hard.

He dragged his gaze away from the photograph, warning himself not to forget how another knockout blonde with an innocent smile had impeded his judgment, wrecking four lives in the process. He shoved the framed picture toward Webster. "She's beautiful."

"Yes, she is," Webster told him, his eyes going hot as he stared at the photo once more. "And believe me, she's worth every penny I'm offering and more."

"And your son?" Michael countered, still irritated by his own reaction to the woman and unable to resist prodding the other man from his lustful musings. Besides, except during their initial phone conversation, Webster hadn't mentioned his son again. "I assume you want him found, too."

"Of course," Webster replied, a trace of annoyance in his voice. "I want you to find both Elisabeth and Timothy."

Michael was puzzled by the lack of emotion in Webster's eyes and voice when he spoke of his son. "Tell me what happened on the day she left."

Webster told him about his wife's depression after having the baby, her mood swings, the tiff they'd had the day before she'd left, and how she'd laced his morning coffee with a sleeping pill and then had run away. According to Webster, the woman had had an emotional breakdown—one which had caused his sweet, gentle wife to flee her husband and home.

Michael reasoned that chances were, Elisabeth Webster was simply a bored young woman who had grown tired of her rich older husband and had run off. But something about the whole scenario, along with Webster's story, nagged at him like a pesky mosquito bite. While he might have turned in his badge five years ago, his instincts remained strong. And those instincts were sounding alarm bells now.

Telling himself that it was Webster's questionable dealings that had set off his sensors, Michael tried to shake off his misgivings. "What about family or friends? Could they be hiding out with them?"

"Elisabeth has no family. Just me. As for friends, my wife has always been somewhat of a loner."

"You said the other detective had managed to locate her."

"Yes, about two months ago in a small town in Arkansas."

"And since then?" Michael asked.

"Nothing. It's almost as though she's disappeared from the face of the earth. I'm worried about her. About both of them. It's the reason I've set the reward so high. My wife has led a very sheltered life. She's not used to dealing with things on her own."

"You said she took a lot of cash and jewelry with her when she left. How much?" Michael asked.

"Nearly fifty thousand in cash. The jewelry was worth probably ten times that amount."

Michael whistled through his teeth. If she managed it wisely, that kind of money could keep the missing Mrs. Webster and her son in Happy Meals and modest digs for a long time. "Has any of the jewelry surfaced?"

"No. The truth is, I doubt Elisabeth would even know how to go about selling it. As I said, she's led a sheltered life and, because of that, she's far more innocent in the ways of the world than most women her age.''

Michael checked himself from pointing out that while Mrs. Webster may look like a fragile flower, the woman obviously had enough grit to rob her husband's safe and leave him. But then he knew firsthand how deceptive a beautiful woman with a sob story could be. She'd also had enough savvy to elude his detectives for six months. Either that, or she and her son hadn't been found for another reason. He lifted his gaze to Webster's. ''You know, there's always the possibility that no one has seen them for another reason.''

''I'm not naive, Sullivan. I know what you're suggesting and you're wrong. Elisabeth is alive. I know it.''

''If she is I'll find her. And your son,'' Michael added firmly.

Webster tipped back his head and laughed. ''I'll say one thing for you, Sullivan. You certainly don't lack chutzpah.''

''As you said, there's no need for false modesty.'' And there wasn't, Michael reasoned. Since leaving the police department, he'd earned more than five times his salary as a cop by working as a bounty hunter, a detective, a bodyguard or whatever the occasion called for. Maybe the jobs weren't all that satisfying or noble, but the money had been good enough to pay his living expenses and provide him with extra cash to help out Janie and the two boys.

And a million bucks would enable him to see to it that Janie and the boys' futures were secure.

"I'm going to need copies of everything you have on them—including the other detective's reports."

Webster removed a manila file folder from a drawer in his desk and handed it to Michael. "I think you'll find everything you need in there. Photographs, fingerprints, background information on Elisabeth and copies of the other reports."

After quickly skimming the contents, he closed the folder and stood. "I'll need a retainer."

"Of course," Webster told him, and reached inside his top desk drawer. He drew out a black leather checkbook. "I'll pay you fifty thousand dollars now and the balance when you find Elisabeth and Timothy."

"You'll pay me two hundred fifty thousand dollars now and the balance, plus my expenses, when I find your wife and son."

The smile died on Webster's lips. "You're out of your mind if you think I'm just going to hand over that kind of money as a retainer."

"That's the deal, Webster. Take it or leave it." Though Michael hadn't seen the bodyguard move, he sensed the big man come up behind him. Lightning quick, he whirled around, kicked the gun from the bruiser's hand and sent the other man to his knees howling.

"Why, you son of a—"

"That's enough, Otto. Leave us alone," Webster ordered.

"You can count on payback for this, Sullivan," Otto muttered as he left the room.

When the door closed, Michael asked, "So what's it going to be, Webster? Do you want me to find your wife and son or not?"

"Why should I believe you won't just skip town with my money?"

"My word," Michael said softly. "You said you checked me out. If you did, then you know I never go back on my word."

Again, all the gentlemanly charm and refinement disappeared. Rage distorted Webster's urbane expression. There was a coldness, a ruthlessness in Webster's dark eyes that made Michael feel almost sorry for Elisabeth Webster. He'd seen enough evil in his thirty-three years to recognize it when he saw it. He was looking at evil now. And, in the space of a heartbeat, Michael considered walking away from the job.

Webster scribbled out a check and slid it across the desk. "Here's your money," he said, keeping his fingers atop the check until Michael met his gaze. "But there's a condition that comes with it. If you haven't found my wife in thirty days, I pay you nothing. You return the retainer and eat your expenses."

"The last detective had six months," Michael pointed out.

"But as you pointed out, you're better. It's thirty days or nothing."

"All right," Michael said.

Webster released the check and sat back in his

chair. ''Don't disappoint me, Sullivan. Find my wife and son for me.''

''Don't worry, I intend to,'' Michael assured him, and tucked the check into his coat pocket. ''You just get ready to write another check.''

Three

"Lily, your order's up."

"Thanks, May," Lily told the short-order cook who'd slapped down the BLT with extra mayo and fries for table six. Grabbing the order, Lily juggled it, along with the two salads and a sandwich plate, and began weaving her way through the crowded diner.

She dropped off the salads and made her way to table five, where she served a roast beef po'boy, then turned to table six and delivered the BLT order. "Would you like another root beer?" she asked the guy who'd been in every day that week for lunch. He'd told her two days earlier that his name was Joe and that he was working with the construction crew down the block. Lily figured him to be in his midtwenties. With his blond hair, sun-bronzed skin and a body that sported muscles from hard, physical labor, he'd caught the eye of her co-workers.

"That would be great," he told her in that odd drawl that sounded like a combination of Old South and Brooklyn, New York. But the smile—the smile was pure southern charm—something she'd discovered these New Orleans boys had in abundance. Since arriving in the city two months ago she had witnessed it again and again.

"Be right back," she promised, then stopped to take another order before making her way back to the counter. After turning in her new orders, she headed for the fountain where she joined Amber and Gina, the other waitresses at the diner, to load up her drinks.

"I see Brad Pitt's twin is back," Amber commented as she lined up her tray with glasses and began filling them with Coke, tea and ice water. "And why am I not surprised that he sat at one of *your* tables again?"

"I guess mine was the only one open," Lily suggested.

Amber rolled her eyes. "Lily girl, wake up. Anyone with eyes in their head could see the guy's got a thing for you."

"Don't be silly," Lily said, taken aback by Amber's comment. "He's just a boy."

"Right. And I suppose you're old enough to be his mother."

Gina chuckled. "She's right, you know. That fellow's got to be at least twenty-five. And if you're older than that, it's not by much."

She wasn't. She'd turned twenty-five on her last birthday. Yet, she felt a lifetime older. "I guess I just feel older because I'm a widow and I have a child."

"Aw shoot, honey, I forgot," Gina said. "I'm sorry."

"It's all right," Lily told her, uncomfortable that

her fib had generated sympathy from the other woman.

"Listen, I know how hard it is to lose a man you love. I've buried three husbands myself. But, trust me. It gets easier with time. You'll see."

"I'm sure you're right," Lily murmured, eager to end the conversation.

Gina gave her shoulder a pat. "In the meantime, don't go ruling out Construction Joe over there. At least the guy's got a job, which is more than I can say for my last husband. Besides, you're still young. You have your whole life ahead of you."

But she didn't feel young, Lily thought as she finished loading her drink orders. Probably because her life had been filled with so many changes in the ten years since her grandmother had died, and she'd gone to live with her mother. Those first two years in Florida had been frightening, living with the stranger who'd given birth to her, trying to fit in at a new school, in a new city. The one bright spot had been Adam. She'd been an awkward, shy girl, but he had treated her like a real person. He'd been sweet and kind to her, listened to the things she had to say. He'd made her feel special. And when her mother had accidentally overdosed on her insulin and died so suddenly, Adam had rescued her. He'd sent her to a Catholic boarding school, and when she'd graduated, he'd made her his wife. A shiver raced down her spine as she thought back on all the little things that had pointed to a sick, dangerous man. How could she have been so blind for so long? And what would have happened to Timmy if she hadn't gotten him away from Adam when she had?

"Hey, Lily." Amber nudged her. "Your order's up."

Shoving away thoughts of the past, Lily went back to work. She dropped off two more orders, four glasses of tea and brought Joe his root beer. "There you go. How about dessert? We've got apple pie, bread pudding and, since it's Mardi Gras time, king cake."

"I'll pass on the dessert but, speaking of Mardi Gras, I was wondering if you might like to catch a parade with me this weekend."

Oh darn, Lily thought. Amber and Gina had been right. "I'm afraid I can't. But thanks for asking."

"Already have plans, huh?"

"Yes," Lily said, thinking of Timmy.

"Maybe another time when you're not busy?"

Lily hesitated, not wanting to lead him on, but not wanting to bruise his ego, either. "Actually, another time wouldn't work, either. I have other commitments that demand most of my time. I'm sorry."

Joe's hazel eyes lost some of their spark. He shrugged. "Can't blame a guy for trying, huh? I suppose it was dumb of me to think you wouldn't already have a guy in your life."

Regretting that she'd failed to read his interest properly, Lily tried to explain, "I do have a guy in my life. But not the kind you mean. He's my son. And he takes up just about all of my spare time."

"You've got a kid?" Joe asked, clearly surprised.

"Yes. He just turned three and he's a bundle of energy."

"What about his dad?"

Lily immediately wished she hadn't opened the discussion. "I'm a widow," she said and, because she couldn't bring herself to look at him directly after the lie, she began clearing the remains of his lunch from the table. She'd never been very good at lying—something to do with her Catholic-school upbringing most likely—yet for the past six months she'd told more lies than she'd ever dreamed of telling in a lifetime.

"Geez, I'm sorry, Lily. I didn't realize, I mean you're so young."

"It's all right. You had no way of knowing."

"Well, maybe you could get a sitter—"

"The truth is, I don't date," she told him as she picked up her tray. "But you might want to ask Amber. I think she'd really enjoy going to the parade with you, and the two of you would have a great time."

Not waiting for a response she turned away, more eager than ever for three o'clock to come so she could end this day and head to Gertie's to pick up Timmy.

After she'd finished scrubbing down the counters and refilling the napkin holders, Lily stripped off her apron. She retrieved her purse and jacket from the office out back and started toward the table where Amber, Gina, May and Nancy Lee, the owner of the River Bend Diner, were gathered around Ricardo.

One of the diner's regular patrons, Ricardo was known only by the singular name, and was reported to be a maven of fashion. Because he was always impeccably dressed and well groomed, Lily likened him to a young Ricardo Montalban. With his neatly styled black hair, laughing dark eyes and olive skin, he was a favorite among the ladies at the diner who didn't seem to mind that Ricardo preferred men to women. Probably because Ricardo neither apologized nor flaunted his sexuality, she mused. It was part of who he was. Just as his talent for making a woman beautiful was part of who he was.

"Excuse me," she said, interrupting the chatter. "Nancy Lee, if there's nothing else, I'm going to head out."

"But you haven't heard what Ricardo's got planned," Amber exclaimed. And, with the enthusiasm of a twenty-year-old who lived for the next party, Amber began to explain. "You know that Ricardo here has this really rad store with all kinds of clothes and makeup and stuff, right?"

Lily nodded. She'd heard about the specialty shop that carried exorbitantly priced costumes, wigs and ladies' apparel.

"Well, he says we can pick out any outfit we want for Mardi Gras Day from his store and he'll let us have it at half-price. And get this, he's going to help us do our hair and makeup. Isn't that major cool?"

"That's very kind of you," Lily offered, even though she had no intention of taking the man up on his offer. The month of parades leading up to the big celebration was more than enough for her. She certainly had no intention of dressing up for the city's big party day. Aside from Mardi Gras sounding a bit wild for her, she couldn't imagine spending her hard-earned money on a costume that she'd wear once and never use again.

"Lily's right. That's real nice of Ricardo," Nancy Lee said as she shifted the ever-present gum in her mouth. A well-preserved woman in her late-fifties, Nancy Lee eyed her employees. "Just make sure you girls don't bankrupt me by plying Ricardo here with free food and drinks to show your appreciation."

"You wound me, Señora Nancy," Ricardo said in a voice that still held the thick accent of his native Spain. With a hand pressed dramatically to his heart, he continued, "This offer is merely to show my gratitude to you and these ladies for making this foreigner welcome."

Nancy Lee let out a bawdy laugh. "Ricardo, you faker you. You're no more a foreigner than I am. Why, you've been living here for twenty years that I know of."

"Ah, but were it not for you and your lovely ladies, I would have returned to Madrid long ago. It is your friendship that keeps me here."

"Along with all those rich ladies uptown who spend a fortune on the clothes and makeup you sell in that shop of yours," Nancy Lee added.

"What can I say? I have been blessed with an eye for beauty, and it is a gift that I share with my friends. That I wish to share with you. You need only to tell

Ricardo who you wish to be, and I will make it happen.''

Lily listened in amusement as Ricardo went about describing how he would transform each of them in outfits ranging from Britney Spears to dance-hall queens to European royalty. It was like being a little girl and playing dress up—only on a much grander scale than the dress-up games she'd played as a youngster.

''And what about you Señorita Lily? Whom do you wish to be?''

Lily blinked, caught off guard by the question and at becoming the center of attention. ''I...I don't know,'' she said.

''You do not have a secret fantasy to be someone else for a day? Perhaps a movie star or a famous figure from the past?''

''No,'' she said honestly, because since escaping from Adam six months ago, her total focus had been on erasing any trace of Elisabeth Webster.

''Then perhaps you would like to be Scheherazede, the sultan's wife, or Princess Jasmine in the tale of Arabian Nights. Or maybe Shakespeare's Juliet.''

Lily laughed. ''No. I don't think so.''

Ricardo made a frame of his hands and positioned it around her face, as though he saw her as a canvas and was trying to determine what shades of paint he wanted to use. ''With your cheekbones, the green eyes and mouth, I could turn you into Faith Hill or perhaps a young Marilyn Monroe.''

''I don't know about the Marilyn Monroe gig,''

Amber chimed in. "But you might be right about the Faith Hill thing. Lily's got that pale skin and delicate-looking thing going that Faith has."

Ricardo tipped up her chin and examined her face from several angles. "The hairdresser who's responsible for this mess should be shot. You should let it grow. But since Mardi Gras is only a few weeks away, we will lighten the color and work with some hairpieces."

Lily took a step back, smoothed a hand over her hair. She wasn't about to admit that she was the one responsible for chopping off the long blond hair and dying it the dark honey shade. It had been one of the many steps she'd taken in the past six months to disguise her appearance in order to distance herself from the woman she had been. "Thanks, I'll think about it," Lily said, but she had no intention of doing so.

"Very well. You come to Ricardo when you decide."

"Well, I've already decided. I want the Britney Spears look," Amber declared. "In fact, how about I follow you back to the shop now?"

"That sounds like a good idea," Gina added. "You want to come with us, Lily? Maybe you'll see something you like."

"Thanks, but I can't," she said. "I need to pick up my son."

Assuming a karate stance, Michael faced the two serious-looking Crenshaw boys. "All right, guys, prepare to go down," he told them and swiped at the air dramatically, making the appropriate *hi-ya* sounds before he lunged at the two giggling towheads.

Seven-year-old Petey kicked out his leg. His six-year-old brother, Micky, did the same. When Petey kicked out again and his foot came within a few inches of him, Michael pretended to go down. He lay on the carpet unmoving, with his eyes closed, and waited until the two boys came to stand over him.

"Uncle Mike?" Petey nudged him with his toe.

Michael opened his eyes and grabbed them both around the middle. "Gotcha," he cried out and fell back, pulling the two boys on top of him.

"Say uncle or die," Petey demanded as they climbed on top of him.

"Uncle," Michael said, much to their delight.

"All right, boys. It's time for bed. Let your Uncle Mike up."

"Aw, Mom," the boys whined in unison.

"Don't 'aw, Mom' me. Tomorrow's a school day," Janie Crenshaw told her sons. Dressed in green cords and a sweater, she stood with her hands on her hips and attempted to appear stern. Michael grinned to himself. With her petite frame and honey-colored hair pulled into a ponytail, Janie looked like a kid herself.

"But Uncle Mike needs us to show him the rest of the new moves we learned in karate so he'll know how to defend himself against the bad guys. Don't 'cha, Uncle Mike?" Petey asked hopefully, with the laughing hazel eyes that reminded Michael so much of the boy's late father.

"Yeah, I do. But I think you guys have given me enough new stuff to work on for now. You can show me the rest the next time I come over."

"Tomorrow?" Micky asked.

"Gee, partner, I wish I could. But I'm afraid I've got this really big case I'm working on and I'm going out of town tomorrow."

"For how long?" Petey asked.

Michael rubbed at the back of his neck. He loved the kids, and didn't want to disappoint them. "It could be a couple of weeks, maybe even a month." The truth was, he didn't know how long it would take him to pick up Elisabeth Webster's trail. With a six-month head start, the woman could be just about anywhere by now. But wherever she was, he intended to find her within the thirty days specified so he could collect the rest of that fee from her husband.

"I bet it's a robbery case like the ones you and my dad used to work on," Petey offered. "And you're going to catch the bad guys and lock them up in jail. Then you'll be a hero just like my dad was."

Michael felt that hitch in his chest again as he listened to Petey describe what he believed to be the way his father had died. As Pete Crenshaw's partner and the man indirectly responsible for his death, Michael had felt an obligation to shield the boys from the ugly truth. Unfortunately, he had been too late to shield Janie. She'd already found out about Pete and Giselle.

As long as he lived, Michael would never be able to forgive himself for destroying the Crenshaws' lives the way he had by introducing a viper like Giselle into their midst. And while Janie had argued with him, threatening to tell the department that it had been Pete who had been guilty of the pillow talk that had led to the botched drug bust and Pete's death, she had gone along with him in the end. She had allowed him to protect her boys with an edited version of what had happened that night five years ago when their father had been killed. While the boys had been too young to understand at the time, Michael had known that as they grew older they would want to know how their father had died. He owed it to Pete to let his sons believe their father had died a hero. So he stuck to the story he'd given to the Houston Police Department, to Pete's sons and to his own family. Doing so had cost him a great deal in terms of career, family and friendship. But the way he'd looked at it, he'd paid a much smaller price than Pete had. He was still alive and watching Pete's boys grow up. Whereas Pete was dead and would never know his sons.

"Only you're not going to get shot and have to go to heaven the way Daddy did, will you, Uncle Mike?" Micky asked.

"Are you kidding? With all these fancy karate moves you and your brother have been teaching me, nobody better mess with me," Michael joked, hoping to lighten the mood.

"Okay, boys, kiss Uncle Mike good-night."

"Kissing is for girls," Petey informed his mother. "Us men don't kiss."

"Yeah, us men don't kiss," Micky parroted.

Michael bit back a grin. "Trust me, guys, someday you're going to change your mind about that. What do you say we shake hands?"

"I guess that would be okay," Petey said solemnly.

Michael held out his hand. And when Petey offered his smaller hand, Michael took it and hugged the boy close. Then he did the same thing with Micky.

"Well, I'm a girl, and I want a kiss," Janie told her sons.

Both boys looked to him. "It's all right for us guys to kiss a girl—especially if the girl happens to be a mom."

Satisfied with the answer, both boys kissed and hugged their mother. "You going to kiss Mom goodnight, too, Uncle Mike?" Micky asked him.

Janie flushed. "I'm not Uncle Mike's mom," she informed her son.

"But I saw Jason's mom kissing that guy Eric she's supposed to marry. Jason said Eric's going to be his new dad," Micky argued.

"But your Uncle Mike and I aren't married, and he isn't your dad," Janie explained.

"But Petey and I want him to be our dad. It's not fair. Jason's going to have two dads and we don't have any. So maybe if you kissed Uncle Mike, you and him could get married and then Uncle Mike could stay with us all the time and be our dad," Micky offered.

"Oh, Micky," Janie said. "It doesn't work that way, sweetie."

Oh man, Michael thought, feeling as though he

were dancing in quicksand. From the stricken look on Janie's face, she felt the same. "Your Mom's right, partner. That's not how it works."

"Then how does it work?" Petey demanded.

"When two people get married it's because they love each other and they want to spend the rest of their lives together," Janie explained.

"Well, Uncle Mike loves us and we love him," Petey reasoned. "Don'tcha, Uncle Mike?"

Michael felt as though someone had just reached inside his chest and closed a fist around his heart. He stooped down so that he was eye level with the two boys. "Yeah. I do love you guys. And I love your mom, too—but not the way a man loves a woman he marries." Perhaps if he and Janie hadn't both loved Pete, things between them might have been different. As it was, Pete would always stand between them. Pete—and his own guilt for the hand he'd played in destroying their marriage.

"What your Uncle Mike is trying to say is that he and I love each other like a brother and sister," Janie clarified.

"But brothers and sisters can't get married to each other," Petey said in that what-a-yucky-idea tone that only a seven-year-old boy could pull off.

"And that's why your Uncle Mike and I could never get married," Janie said. "Do you understand?"

Petey shrugged. "I guess so. You're saying you don't love him the way you loved my dad, because he's like your brother or something."

"Or something," Janie conceded.

"But it sure would have been cool to have Uncle Mike be our dad," Petey said with disappointment.

Michael ruffled the two blond heads. "And it would have been cool to be your dad. But since I can't, how about Uncle Mike the Karate King?" And to lighten the moment, Michael made the ridiculous *hi-ya* sound again and began chopping at the air— sending both boys into fits of giggles.

"All right," Janie said, clapping her hands. "Let's get those teeth brushed and hit the sack. I'll be there in a few minutes to tuck you in."

"'Night, Uncle Mike," Petey said. Evidently forgetting about guys not kissing, he wrapped his arms around Michael's neck and kissed his cheek.

"'Night, partner," Michael said, and hugged both boys in turn.

Once the boys had left the room, Janie said, "I'm sorry they put you on the spot that way. I hadn't realized they might misconstrue things."

"They're just kids, Janie."

"I know. But maybe I haven't been fair to them. I mean, after what happened with Pete, and that mess with you in the department...well, leaving Houston and starting over here in Florida seemed like the right thing to do. Maybe it wasn't."

"You did what you felt was best at the time."

She looked up at him out of those big doe eyes. "We both know I left Texas because I needed to get away from the memories of what Pete had done to me, to our family."

"Pete loved you, Janie."

"Is that why he betrayed me? Is that why he broke his oath as a police officer and tried to double-cross those drug dealers so he could get money to run away with Giselle?"

Michael went to her, took her in his arms. "He was confused. The thing you have to remember is that Pete realized he'd made a mistake. That's why he called me that night. He wanted out. He wanted to fix things, make them right with you."

As long as he lived, he'd never forget that night, that phone call from Pete telling him that he'd planned to leave Janie and the boys for Giselle. He had told Giselle that the buy with the Russian was a sting. The two of them were supposed to take the money and run, only now he was having second thoughts, but he'd left things too late. Not even Michael could fix it for him this time.

Michael could still hear himself insisting Pete tell him when he'd set up the exchange. He should have known Pete had lied, but by the time he'd figured it out, and arrived on the scene, things were already out of control. Pete had gone down trying to save Giselle. It didn't matter that he'd managed to take out the dealers, he hadn't saved Pete. He'd let Giselle get away—on the condition that she kept her mouth shut about Pete's involvement—and with the promise if she ever said a word he would kill her. "He wouldn't have gone through with it, Janie."

She looked up at him, pressed a sisterly kiss to his lips and stepped back. "You're a good man, Michael

Patrick Sullivan. But you and I both know that you're lying.''

"Janie—''

"Stop making excuses for him!''

"I'm not,'' he argued.

"Yes, you are. Michael, you've made a career of covering for Pete. Even back when the three of us were in college, you were covering for him. When Pete broke team curfew and almost got kicked off the football team. And when Pete partied too hard and missed his English final, you were the one who sweet-talked the professor into letting him take the makeup. And then you locked yourself up with him all weekend to cram.''

"He was my friend. Friends look out for each other.''

"Don't you see?'' Janie said. "From the time you two were kids, you've been bailing Pete out of trouble. Well, Pete's dead. He doesn't need you to cover for him anymore.''

"That's not what I'm doing,'' he insisted.

"Isn't it?''

"No,'' he told her. "That night…that night he wouldn't have gone through with it. I knew Pete, Janie. He wouldn't have gone through with it.''

Janie sighed. "I knew Pete, too. He was funny and sweet and lovable. And he was also weak, irresponsible and a little selfish.'' She held up her hand, cutting off his protest. "It's true. I may have loved Pete, but I wasn't blind to what he was, Michael.''

"You think I am?''

"I think you don't want to believe that the kid you took a blood brother's oath with at ten grew up to be less honorable than you did."

"I'm not a saint," he fired back, annoyed by the implication.

"No, but you have a sense of honor that Pete never had. If things had been the other way around and you'd been the one who'd been killed that night and had left a wife and two babies behind, do you think Pete would still be hanging around, trying to take care of your family for you?"

The Pete he'd known wouldn't have hung around. Not because he didn't care, but because he'd always found it difficult to deal with other people's problems. Feeling the need to defend his dead friend, he turned around and said, "Pete was a good man."

"I'm not saying he wasn't. But he's dead, Michael. You need to quit blaming yourself for his mistakes."

"I should have seen what was going on, that Giselle was using him," he argued, and stalked over to the window to stare out at the dark street.

"He didn't want you to see. Just like he didn't want me to see. He knew what he was doing was wrong. The mistakes were Pete's. Not yours. I never blamed you, and you need to stop blaming yourself."

"I don't know if I can," he told her.

She came up behind him, touched his back. "You have to. It's time you moved on with your life, Michael. It's time we both did. I didn't realize until tonight how selfish I'd been until I listened to the boys ask you to be their father."

"They're just kids. Besides, you couldn't be selfish if you tried."

"It was selfish of me to encourage you to leave your job and move here away from your family when things were so strained between you and your father."

"My decision to leave the Houston P.D. had nothing to do with you. Neither did my problems with my father."

"But you might have stayed in Texas and worked things out with him if it hadn't been for me and the boys. We both know the real reason you moved to Florida was so you could look out for us—the same way you were always looking out for Pete. I shouldn't have let you do that. It was selfish."

"It wasn't your choice. It was mine. I wanted to be near you and the boys. And the only selfish thing you've done is not offer me some more of those chocolate chip cookies you made."

Janie hesitated a moment, then said, "All right. Go on into the kitchen and find yourself something to drink while I make sure my little monsters are in bed. Then I'll see if I have any cookies left."

As much at home in the Crenshaw house as he was in his own, Michael put the teakettle on for Janie and a pot of coffee on for himself. While he waited for the water to heat and his coffee to brew, he piled a half-dozen of the chocolate chip cookies onto a plate.

When Janie joined him a short time later, she smiled at the sight of the tea fixings. "It's kind of late for coffee, isn't it?" she asked as she selected her tea and poured the steaming water into the cup to steep.

"I could use the caffeine. I've got a lot of prep work to do tonight if I hope to leave in the morning."

"More corporate espionage? Or another one of those millionaire investors who skipped town with his clients' money?"

"A runaway wife."

Janie arched her eyebrow as she added sugar to her tea. "I thought you'd sworn off those types of cases and were sticking with the corporate stuff."

"I did, and I was. But the lady's husband made me an offer I couldn't refuse," he said in his best Brando/godfather imitation.

Janie laughed and passed him the milk for his coffee. "That was terrible. I hope the guy didn't actually sound that bad."

"He didn't. But he might as well have. I didn't like him."

"Then why'd you take the case?" she asked.

"The money primarily. He offered me a million bucks to find her."

Janie nearly choked on her tea. "Who is this guy?"

"You know I can't tell you that." And the truth was, he suspected Janie would be better off not knowing. "Let's just say, he's someone with deep pockets who desperately wants his much younger wife back."

"You said money was the primary reason. What's the other one?"

"The woman swiped the guy's kid. A little boy who's three. I may not have liked the man, but he has a right to see his child. And the kid has a right to know his father.'' He couldn't help thinking once again how Petey and Micky hadn't had a chance to know their own father.

Janie reached across the table, patted his hand. ''See what I mean about that honorable streak of yours?''

''It's a job, Janie,'' he said.

''It's more than a job. You're doing it for the little boy.''

''And the money.''

''All right, for the money, too. But something tells me you could have said no to the money, but not to helping that little boy.''

It was true, which made him feel like a sap. He didn't even know the kid, but the photo he'd gotten from Webster had shown a brown-haired little boy with serious dark eyes. ''Maybe,'' he finally conceded. ''But the money was a big factor, too. Speaking of which, I want you to have this for the boys.'' He slid a bank book across the table to Janie. He'd opened an account in her sons' names into which he'd deposited the bulk of the retainer.

Janie's eyes widened as she stared at the bank book. Then she shoved the book back at him. ''I can't accept this. I can't believe you actually thought that I would. It's bad enough that I allowed you to pay for their karate lessons. But this…this is going too far.''

''Come on, Janie. You've been worried for months about being laid off from your job. That money will take some of the pressure off and even allow you to plan for the boys' futures.''

''They're my sons, Michael, and my responsibility. Not yours.''

''I'm their godfather. What's wrong with me wanting to help?''

''What's wrong is that you're working at a job you hate. You've cut off ties with a father you adored, out of some misplaced sense of guilt. You have no close friendships outside of me and the boys, and I can't even remember the last time you had a woman in your life.''

''There are tons of women in my life,'' he said defensively.

''I'm talking about a serious relationship—not one that consists of a casual dinner followed by casual sex.''

Because she was hitting some sore spots, he fired back without thinking, ''And what about you, Janie? You're pretty, smart and one of the best women I know, but I don't see you letting any guy get close to you.''

''I'll admit I have been gun-shy for a long time because of what Pete did. But there is someone I'm sort of seeing.''

''There is?'' he countered, stunned by the news. Immediately protective, he asked, ''Who is he?''

''No one you know. Besides, it's nothing serious. Not yet anyway. But at least I'm willing to take a chance again. You need to, as well.'' She let out a breath. "Look, I really appreciate this," she said, indicating the bank book. "But I can't accept it."

"Listen, I know it seems like a lot of money, but it's just the retainer I got for this case. When I find the woman and her son, I'm going to collect the rest of my fee." He saw no point in telling her that if he didn't find Mrs. Webster and her son, he would have to return the money.

"But it's your money. You should use it to do something for you."

He grinned at her. "When I collect the balance, I plan to. I'm going to buy that sailboat I've had my eye on, take some time off and spend it sailing." He caught her hand, placed the bank book in it. "But right now, I want you to have this. For the boys."

"But suppose you can't find this woman?" Janie asked.

"Oh, I'll find her all right." Elisabeth Webster didn't have a prayer at remaining hidden from him. "You can count on it."

Four

"Yeah, that's her. That's Beth," the woman named Susie, working behind the drugstore counter, told Michael as she studied the photograph of Elisabeth Webster he'd shown her. "Only she wasn't wearing any diamonds like those when she worked here."

Excited to have finally come across someone who had actually been able to identify the Webster woman, he asked, "Can you remember how long ago that was?"

"Gee, probably two—no, two and a half months ago. I remember because she quit right after Thanksgiving weekend without giving Mr. Perkins any notice. He was pretty steamed, it being the holidays and all."

At least he was getting closer, Michael told himself. After spending the past ten days retracing Elisabeth Webster's path through Florida and Mississippi, he'd ended up in the small, quiet town of El Dorado, Arkansas, population twenty-five thousand. Not exactly a hot spot like Miami and West Palm Beach where she'd lived and partied with her husband for the past seven years. It certainly was an odd choice for a woman who was used to the nightclub scene. "Your boss mentioned she left because of a family emergency." Which, in itself, was interesting, Michael decided, since he'd been able to find no family whatsoever for Elisabeth Webster other than her husband and son.

"Susie, how about a piece of that pie?" a burly-looking guy called out from the end of the counter.

"Be right there," the girl replied, and hustled down to the other end of the old-fashioned counter to serve the fellow a thick slab of pie.

While he waited for Susie to return, Michael tried to reconcile the Elisabeth Webster described in the file to the woman who had worked at a day-care center in Mississippi before moving to the sleepy little Arkansas town where she'd worked behind the counter in a drugstore. It simply didn't make sense.

"You want me to freshen up that coffee for you?" Susie asked, breaking into his thoughts.

"Sure." He shoved his cup toward the waitress and allowed the woman to pour him the coffee that he neither wanted nor needed. "Did Beth happen to mention what the family emergency was?"

"She *claimed* her grandmother was sick."

Michael added sugar and milk to the coffee. "You didn't believe her?" he prompted.

The gum-smacking redhead looked around then lowered her voice conspiratorially and said, "Let's just say, I don't think it was a sick grandmother that made her pack up and leave here quick like she did."

"Then why do you think she left?" Michael asked.

"I think she was hiding from someone, and she took off when she thought they were getting too close."

"What makes you think that?"

"Because she was scared."

"She told you she was scared?" Michael asked.

"Didn't have to. I could tell." When he arched his eyebrow in question, Susie continued, "First off, Beth was real quiet. Most women with looks like hers do everything they can to play up their good looks and draw attention to themselves. But not Beth. She didn't seem to like people noticing her. Of course, they did notice her and that only seemed to make her more uncomfortable."

"Maybe she was shy," Michael offered, wanting to get back to the point of the discussion—which was why this young woman had believed Elisabeth Webster was afraid.

"I know shy when I see it. My cousin Penny is shy. The girl gets tongue-tied and blushes six shades of red when a man gets within ten feet of her. Beth wasn't shy. She was scared. You could see it in her eyes."

"See what?"

"Fear. I saw that same look in the eyes of a stray kitten I once rescued when a neighbor's dog cornered it under a porch. After I ran the dog off, I tried to coax the kitten out, but the little thing spit and hissed and clawed at me for all it was worth. The poor thing was starving, but for the longest time it wouldn't come out to eat the food I brought. When it finally came out to eat, it watched me the whole time like it expected me to turn on it at any minute. Beth had that same look. Like she wanted to trust you, but she was afraid to let her guard down even for a second.''

Michael frowned, disliking this image of a frightened Elisabeth Webster. He didn't want to feel sorry for the woman. The last thing he needed was to see her as some damsel in distress instead of a meal ticket. Hardening his resolve, he recalled the data he'd collected on her. She was a young woman who had married a man more than twice her age. And when she'd grown unhappy in her marriage, she'd probably asked for a divorce. Only Webster, being the macho prick he was, had most likely tightened the leash on his wife. So she'd drugged him, stole his money and took off with the kid. If anyone was frightened in the whole mess, it was probably the little boy. ''What about her son? Did you ever meet him?''

''I saw him a couple of times. A cute kid. But Beth was real protective of him—didn't let anyone get too close. Except for Miss Margie, of course.''

''Miss Margie?'' Michael prompted, suddenly alert.

''Margie Schubert. She owns the boardinghouse where Beth stayed while she was here in El Dorado. Miss Margie watched the little boy for Beth when she was at work. As far as I know, she was the only person Beth trusted him with.''

''Thanks, Susie. You've been a big help,'' Michael told her, leaving a generous tip on the counter before going in search of Margie Schubert.

Finding Margie Schubert proved to be easy. Getting the lady to talk was a different story. Unlike the people at Perkins's Drugstore, Margie Schubert was far less forthcoming about the woman who had resided in her boardinghouse. Finally, after nearly an hour, during which time Michael had done his best to convince the woman that he meant dear Beth and her baby no harm, the woman finally relented and agreed to answer a few questions.

"Let me see that ID of yours again," Ms. Schubert demanded, and Michael handed over his photo credentials, identifying him as a private investigator. She eyed him warily. "You know you're not the first one to come around here asking questions about Beth."

"So you've told me." Michael knew from Webster's reports that two detectives had located Elisabeth in this small, rural town. But the former cop in him suspected it had been two of Webster's enforcers who had been dispatched to bring back the wayward Mrs. Webster. And given Margie Schubert's attitude, he was fairly sure that neither of the men had endeared themselves to the older woman.

"They said they were trying to locate Beth to tell her about an inheritance, some rich uncle who'd left her a lot of money."

Having learned long ago that it was better to stick as close to the truth as possible, he said, "As far as I know, Beth, or rather, Elisabeth, didn't have any living relatives other than her son and her husband. And, as I told you, I'm searching for her and her son on behalf of her husband. He's feeling very bad about the spat they had, and he wants her to come home.''

The older woman frowned, her ample jowls giving her a forbidding expression. ''Still can't believe Beth was lying about her being a widow.''

''If it's any consolation, I suspect she told you that to spare you from becoming involved in any kind of legal action.''

''What kind of legal action?'' she asked sharply.

''Well, since Elisabeth…Beth,'' he amended. ''Since she took her son out of state without the father's knowledge, it's considered kidnapping. And since you were helping her, you could be considered an accessory.''

''How can a mother be charged with kidnapping her own child?'' Ms. Schubert demanded, apparently not pleased by the accusation. ''I've never heard such a thing. The poor girl would have spent every cent she earned on day care if I hadn't kept the little one for her.''

''And it was kind of you to help her.'' Michael saw no point in scaring the woman. As far as she was concerned, she'd helped out a friend. ''I'm sure her husband will be glad to hear she has a friend like you.''

''You say her husband is rich?''

''Yes, he is,'' Michael assured her.

The woman shook her gray head. ''The girl sure didn't act like she was married to money. Why, when I got sick, she was in this kitchen fixing up supper for my other tenants, washing dishes and changing the linens. Never once acted like it was beneath her the way rich folks usually do.''

"She was apparently very fond of you."

"And I was fond of her," Ms. Schubert countered. "The last thing I'd want to do is add to the girl's troubles by talking to you."

"But you do want to help her, don't you?"

"Of course."

"Then, by helping me find her, you would be," Michael assured the woman. "Even if she decides she doesn't want to go back to her husband, he would be obligated to help her financially. I'm sure it can't be easy for her being on her own and having a child to care for, too."

"She never complained. And she took real good care of Timmy. Why, anyone with eyes in their head could see that as far as Beth was concerned, the sun rose and set on that little boy of hers."

"Her husband said she was a good mother," Michael said, although Webster had indicated just the opposite. "I'm sure Mr. Webster would be happy to pay a reward to anyone who could help me find his wife and son."

"I'm not looking for any reward," the woman informed him. "And if Beth ran away from the man, she must have had her reasons."

He was beginning to wonder if the lady was right, but immediately cut off that line of thought. "From what I understand, he and his wife had a nasty argument, and the next thing he knew, she and the little boy were gone. I'm sure you can understand how worried Mr. Webster is, not knowing where they are.''

"I suppose so,'' Ms. Schubert told him.

"There are a lot of crazy people out there in the world. Because of Mr. Webster's wealth, he's afraid that if the wrong person were to find out that she's his wife, she and her little boy could be in danger. Maybe even held for ransom.''

"Oh my,'' Ms. Schubert said in alarm. "I guess being rich isn't all it's cracked up to be.''

"Doesn't seem like it to me,'' Michael told her. And because he suspected she was weakening, he added, "If you can think of a place or the name of someone that Beth might have mentioned, anything that might help me locate her, you'd be doing her and her little boy a favor.''

"And if Beth doesn't want to go back to this Webster fellow, she doesn't have to?''

"No. Not unless that's what she wants. My job is to make sure that she and her son are safe, and to let her know that her husband would like to see her. What she does after I tell her is up to her.''

"Well, I don't know for sure, mind you,'' Ms. Schubert began, "but she did mention going to New Orleans. She said her grandmother had an old friend who'd moved there years ago.''

"Did she happen to tell you the name of this friend?''

Margie Schubert shook her head. "And I didn't ask.''

"Thank you, Ms. Schubert. You've been a tremendous help.'' Michael stood and shook the woman's hand.

''If you find Beth, would you give her something for me?''

''Sure,'' Michael said.

The older woman disappeared into a back room of the sprawling house. When she returned, she handed him a photograph. It was of Elisabeth Webster and her son, Timmy. Only, the woman in the snapshot didn't look anything like the glamorous creature in the studio photo Webster had given him. This woman wasn't wearing diamonds. Nor was her hair a curtain of long blond silk that fell to her shoulders. Her lips weren't pulled into a sexy pout and painted a bold red. And she wasn't wearing a strapless gown that revealed milk-pale shoulders and cleavage that would make a man's mouth water for a glimpse of what lay beneath the sheer black lace. Instead, the woman in the snapshot was wearing a pair of faded jeans and a sweatshirt that only gave a hint of the curves that lay beneath. Instead of looking sexy, she looked wholesome seated in the center of a pile of leaves. Her hair was pulled up into a lopsided ponytail strewn with leaves in various shades of orange and gold and brown. Her lips were bare and the smile on them totally lacking in artifice as she clutched the laughing little boy in her lap.

''I took that the day before she left. She and Timmy were raking the yard for me, and they were having such a good time. I remember thinking how happy they looked that day,'' she said, her expression softening with the memory. "I thought Beth might like to have the picture, to remember her time here with me."

"I'll see that she gets it," Michael promised, and tucked the photo into his pocket.

Later that night in his hotel room Michael made a series of calls and planned a trip to Elisabeth Webster's grandmother's old neighborhood, then he stretched out on the bed. Pulling the snapshot out of his shirt pocket, he stared at the woman whose green eyes had haunted him from the moment he'd first seen them in the framed photograph on Adam Webster's desk. While he'd found the sexy Elisabeth Webster appealing, it was this softer version of the woman that intrigued him. "Who are you?" he murmured to the fragile-looking woman in the photo. Was she the calculating, coldhearted gold digger who'd drugged her husband and stolen his child? Or was she this innocent-looking creature who pitched in to help a sick old woman in need?

The sound of his cell phone ringing pulled Michael from his disturbing thoughts. He tossed the photo onto the nightstand and snatched up his phone. "Sullivan."

"I got your message. You said you had some news for me. Have you found Elisabeth?"

Michael gritted his teeth at the sound of Webster's voice and reminded himself that the man was paying him to do a job. "Not yet. But I'm getting closer. I talked to some people in Arkansas who knew her as Beth. She left here about two and a half months ago."

"I'm not interested in where my wife was, Mr. Sullivan. I want to know where she is now."

"The best way for me to find her is to retrace her path so I can get an idea of where she was headed. Thanks to the bozos you sent after her, getting people to talk hasn't been easy."

"If finding my wife was easy, I wouldn't be offering you such a large sum of money to find her, now, would I?" He paused. "Of course, if you don't think you can find her—"

"I'll find her, and the boy, too. I talked to the owner of the boardinghouse in Arkansas where they stayed and was able to get a more recent photo of her and your son."

"I want to see it," Webster demanded.

"I've already overnighted a copy to you. I'm headed for Alabama in the morning to check out a lead."

"What kind of lead?"

"The lady who ran the boardinghouse said your wife mentioned visiting one of her grandmother's old neighbors."

"But Elisabeth's grandmother has been dead for more than ten years. She's had no contact with any of those people," Webster told him.

"Like I said, I'm checking out a lead." What he didn't tell Webster was that the lead would take him to New Orleans.

"It sounds like a waste of time to me. Just be aware that the clock is ticking on our agreement, Sullivan.

You said you could find my wife within thirty days. Don't disappoint me.''

''I'll deliver on my end of the bargain. You just make sure you have the rest of my money ready,'' Michael said, then he cut the connection.

Tired, Michael lay back down on the bed. But when ten minutes had passed and he was no closer to sleeping than he'd been when he'd lain down, Michael sat up. Might as well get a head start for Mobile and then get on to New Orleans, he decided. And after grabbing his bag and jacket, he picked up the snapshot. He took another long look at it, then shoved it into his pocket and headed out the door.

''Mommy, I no feel good,'' Timmy whined to Lily as she settled him into the big, comfy bed at Gertie's house.

''I know you don't, baby,'' she soothed, and pressed her hand to his forehead. ''It's because you have chicken pox. But the shot and medicine Dr. Brinkman gave you is going to make you feel all better real soon.''

''I'm going to fix you a special treat this afternoon,'' Gertie Boudreaux promised as she came into the spare room and joined the pair.

''Cookies?'' Timmy asked hopefully.

''Something better than cookies,'' Gertie assured him. ''But you need to be a good boy and take a little rest now while your mama goes to work.''

''I not seepy,'' Timmy informed her.

''I know you're not, sweetie. But if the medicine

is going to work and make you feel better, you need to rest,'' Lily told him.

"You bring me 'prize?'' Timmy asked her.

"All right. Mommy will bring you a surprise.'' Lily kissed his forehead. Then she planted a kiss on his teddy's forehead, as it was her custom.

"And 'prize for Teddy, too,'' Timmy added.

While she knew Timmy was pushing it, there was no way she could refuse him. "All right. Two surprises. One for you and one for Teddy. But that means you need to be a really good boy, and do what Gertie tells you until Mommy comes back.''

"'Kay,'' Timmy told her, and hugging his teddy close, he snuggled beneath the covers and closed his eyes.

She sat on the edge of the bed a few minutes longer until his breathing had settled into the steady rhythm of sleep. But even when he'd dozed off, Lily found herself reluctant to leave him.

As though sensing her thoughts, Gertie placed a hand on her shoulder. "Come on, child. What he needs now is to rest.''

With leaden feet, Lily stood and followed Gertie out of the room and into the kitchen of the small cottage. But her thoughts remained with her son. "The doctor said it's a mild case, but he looks so sick.''

"If you ask me, you look a lot worse than he does.''

"I'm all right.''

"Uh-huh. That's why you look as though a strong

gust of wind could knock you over. I bet you didn't sleep a wink last night. And you were probably too worried about that boy of yours to bother eating anything this morning, weren't you?''

Lily saw no point in telling her that when Timmy had awakened her saying that he didn't feel well during the wee hours of the morning, she'd panicked upon discovering he had a fever. When she noted that what she'd thought was a rash during his bath had spread to his belly, she'd been terrified. The emergency call to the pediatrician, and his diagnosis by phone that it sounded like chicken pox, did nothing to ease her worries. She'd been unable to sleep a wink after that and had sat beside her son's bed until morning, when she'd taken him to the doctor.

''You better sit down before you fall down, and let me fix you something to eat.''

''Thanks, but I'm not hungry. And I need to get to work.''

''Work isn't going nowhere, and you're not leaving here until you have something in your belly,'' Gertie insisted.

Knowing there was little point in arguing with Gertie Boudreaux, Lily sat down at the small kitchen table where she'd sat, for the first time, two and a half months ago and poured out her troubles to her grandmother's friend. To this day, Lily hadn't figured out how old Gertie was because she had the same white hair and plump figure now that she'd had all those years ago when she'd lived next door to Lily and her grandmother in Alabama. And just as she had done when Lily had first shown up on her doorstep with Timmy in late November, scared and desperate after narrowly escaping Adam's men, Gertie had set about calming her with food. Gertie served up two cups of coffee, placed a plate with steaming biscuits in the center of the table. A dish with real butter, not margarine, followed. She plopped a plate, napkin and utensils in front of Lily.

"I still can't believe I let Timmy catch chicken pox."

"And what makes you think you had anything to do with it one way or the other?" Gertie asked as she took the seat next to her. She picked up the dish and peeled back the cloth to reveal the hot flaky biscuits and held them out to Lily. When Lily selected only one, Gertie added a second one to her plate, then served herself.

"The doctor said Timmy probably came into contact with someone, maybe one of the children at the playground."

"Or he might have picked it up from someone in the grocery or at that hamburger place he likes to go to," Gertie informed her. "He's a child, Lily. Children get chicken pox. Nothing you do or don't do is going to stop that."

"But did you see his eyes? How pitiful he looked?"

"Looked like he was laying it on pretty thick so you'd agree to bring him a surprise, if you ask me," Gertie replied. "The little scamp's got you wrapped around his little finger, Lily, and he knows it."

"I wasn't the only one who promised him a surprise."

She dismissed the comment with a wave of her hand. "Us honorary grandmothers are allowed to spoil grandchildren."

Lily leaned over and kissed the older woman's wrinkled cheek. "Thank you for loving him."

"Hard not to. That boy of yours is a charmer. Mark my words, he's going to steal a lot of hearts."

He'd certainly stolen hers. From the moment she'd known she was carrying him, she had loved Timmy. If only Adam had been able to get beyond his obsession with her to love his son. And just as she'd done so often during the past seven years, she questioned her own blindness to what Adam was. Lily thought of her grandmother, remembered how she'd told her the reason her mother didn't live with them was because of the choices she'd made. Her mother had wanted to be famous, see her picture in fashion magazines, go to fancy parties, her grandmother had explained. Having a baby girl didn't fit in with the lifestyle she'd craved. So when she'd been three months old, she'd left her with her grandmother and had never come back. It had been her mother's choice.

And while she might not have felt she'd had a choice about marrying Adam since he had supported her following her mother's death, she could never regret having done so. Because had she not married Adam, she wouldn't have Timmy. No matter what had happened or would happen, she would never regret her son.

"Child, you going to butter that biscuit and eat it or just admire it?"

"Sorry," Lily said, and smoothed butter onto the warm golden bread. Her eyes strayed toward the bedroom and she thought of her son asleep in the next room, how warm he had been.

"Lily, you need to stop worrying about him. He's going to be fine."

"I know. It's just…he's so little to have chicken pox already."

"No littler than you were when you got them," Gertie told her.

"I had chicken pox?"

"Sure did. Only yours were a lot worse than Timmy's. Your poor grandmother, God rest her soul, worried something fierce you were going to have scars on that pretty face of yours. But you didn't. Not a single one. And your skin's still just as pretty now as it was when you were a baby."

"I don't remember," Lily admitted.

"And Timmy probably isn't going to remember getting them, either. Now eat," she instructed.

Lily ate—more to appease Gertie than because of hunger. But fifteen minutes later, both biscuits were gone. So was the coffee. And she was feeling a great deal better—until she saw the time. Lily groaned. "Nancy Lee's going to kill me. I've missed the breakfast crowd, and by the time I get there, the lunch rush will be starting. Let me help you clear these dishes and—"

"I'll handle the dishes," Gertie insisted, and took the plate and cup from her.

"All right. But only if you let me pick up something for your dinner."

"You don't need to be wasting your hard-earned money on me," Gertie told her.

"Gertie…"

"We'll see," the older woman said, which was her way of saying no without using the word. "Now go check on that boy of yours like you're itching to do and then get yourself out of here."

Lily hurried from the kitchen to the bedroom where Timmy was sleeping. Her heart swelled with love as she looked at him. He was the one thing she'd done right in her life, Lily told herself. And to keep him safe, to protect him, she would fight a thousand Adams.

Gertie came up behind her, touched her shoulder. "He's going to be fine," she whispered. "You go on and stop worrying about him."

After adjusting the blanket around him, she pressed a kiss to the top of his head and exited the room. "Okay, I'm going," Lily told her as she glanced around the kitchen for her keys and sunglasses. She spied her keys, but no sunglasses, and decided she must have left them in the car.

Gertie handed Lily her purse. "Thanks," she said, and kissed the older woman's cheek, hugged her close. "I don't know what we'd do without you."

"You'd do just fine, child. Now, where's your coat? Did you leave it in the car?"

"I didn't wear one. It's nice outside. I think the winter's finally over and spring's arrived a little early."

"Not according to the groundhog. He saw his shadow a couple of weeks ago, which means we've got ourselves another six weeks of winter. Bob Breck says a front's coming through with some rain and that we're going to have a light frost tonight. You'd better stop by your place on your way to work and pick up your coat and Timmy's."

"I thought New Orleans was known for its warm weather," Lily grumbled.

"It is. But not in February. In February you're liable to have the air conditioner on in the morning and the heater on by evening. Of course, come July, you'll be wishing for the cool weather again."

As Lily waved goodbye and slid behind the wheel of her car, she wondered if she and Timmy would still be around in July to wish for the cool weather. She'd already stayed in New Orleans longer than she had planned—and she'd involved Gertie far more than she should have. But she'd been so tired and scared when she'd arrived, just being with someone who knew who she was, feeling the freedom to at least use the nickname her grandmother had called her and not another alias had made her feel more sane. Gertie had been a godsend, a link to her grandmother and a time when her life had been simple. The time before she'd become a burden to her mother and then Adam Webster's possession. As much as she hated the idea of leaving Gertie and uprooting Timmy again, she doubted that Adam had stopped looking for her.

Unless he had other things to worry about—things like the police discovering Adam had been involved in the murder of federal agent. She thought about the disk she'd found in Adam's safe, taking it, along with some cash, the morning she'd escaped. Her hands shook each time she remembered drugging his morning coffee and then lying to the servants that he was sleeping in. To this day, she wondered how she had managed to act normal when she'd had Otto drive her and Timmy to the pediatrician's office for an appointment she didn't have, and how she had exited through the rear door with Timmy after asking to use the rest room.

Lily pulled her car to a stop and raced up the stairs of her house. After retrieving their jackets, she headed for the diner. As she did so, she recalled seeing the Miami newspaper two weeks after she'd escaped and recognizing the photo of a dead man named Carter she'd seen with Adam in his study. Only then did she remember having taken the disk from the safe, deciding it must be important if Adam kept it there. As long as she lived, she'd never forget finally accessing the disk and discovering it contained the names, photos and data on federal agents working on an undercover sting in the Miami area. And Carter had been one of the agents. Had the FBI connected Adam to the man's death yet? she wondered. She'd left an anonymous message for them from a pay phone. She should make time to swing by the library this week and see if any of the newspapers had reported anything more about the agent's death or an investigation of Adam as a suspect. If they had, then perhaps she wouldn't have to worry about running anymore. She could begin planning a future for her and Timmy— one that went beyond simply staying alive.

Five

He was going to cut out the lying weasel's tongue and feed it to him, Michael vowed silently as he nursed the cup of coffee at the diner's counter. Pretending to work the newspaper's crossword puzzle, he studied the waitresses. He'd paid one hundred bucks to a supposedly reliable informant who had sworn that the woman he was looking for worked in a place called the River Bend Diner. Well, he'd check out all three women, as well as the cook, and no way were they Elisabeth Webster. The bottle blonde who seemed to be in charge of the place was at least twice the Webster woman's age. The thirty-something brunette was too tall, too dark and way too Italian-looking to have ever been a natural blonde. The only one who might have come close to fitting the description had been the stacked redhead who'd been sizing him up like a side of beef since he'd walked in the door. He looked at her again now. She was young and sexy enough, he supposed, and if she lost the bright hair maybe, just maybe, she could pass for Elisabeth Webster.

Yeah, maybe in the dark. And on a good day, he

amended upon closer inspection of the woman. Anyone with eyes in his head could see that the redhead, although attractive, lacked the fine-boned features and arresting beauty of Elisabeth Webster. Besides, the fact was her eyes were blue, not green. There was excitement and expectation in the redhead's eyes, not that hint of innocence and sadness that had been in the portrait of Elisabeth Webster. And not the genuine delight he'd seen in the snapshot of her with her son.

Dammit. He really thought he had latched onto something when he'd tracked down the grandmother's neighbor to New Orleans. But who'd have thought the name Boudreaux would be as common as the name Smith. So far, he'd found no listing for anyone with the name Gert or Gertrude Boudreaux. He still wasn't sure if that listing for G. Boudreaux he'd called had been answered by a man or a woman. But since whomever it was had sounded as if they'd put away one too many cocktails, he'd ruled them out as being the elderly lady who had once lived next door to the young Elisabeth Webster, née Elisabeth Jeffries, more than a dozen years ago.

After wasting another thirty minutes dialing people named Boudreaux, he'd placed a call to an old contact in the Jefferson Parish Police Department, one of the major suburbs of New Orleans. Although it had been more than five years since he'd worked as an undercover detective with the Houston P.D., he'd taken a chance the deputy he'd once worked with was still employed there. He really thought things were looking up when the guy was not only still there, but remembered him and provided him with the name of a snitch who was supposedly reliable.

Reliable my ass, Michael thought, and scowled at the amount of time he'd lost on this wild-goose chase.

"You want me to freshen that up for you, hon?"

Michael looked up at the brunette behind the counter. "Thanks, ma'am. I'd appreciate it," he said, and shoved his cup toward her for a refill.

"Haven't seen you in here before," the woman whose name tag read Gina said. "New in town?"

"Yeah. I just got in last night."

"That a hint of Texas I hear in your voice?"

"Sure is," Michael told her. "I'm from Houston originally."

"Nice city. And big. I visited it about ten years ago with my second husband. So you just passing through, cowboy? Or are you here for the Mardi Gras."

"Haven't made my mind up yet," Michael said. "I've been working offshore for a while and decided to take some time off. I thought I'd check out sin city. In fact, you might be able to help me. A buddy of mine said his sister lived here, but so far I haven't been able to find her."

"Well, we may be a big city, but New Orleans is pretty small when it comes to people. Everybody knows just about everybody. What's your friend's sister's name?"

"That's the thing. I'm not sure what name she's using. I mean, my buddy calls her Beth—which is a nickname."

"She got a last name?"

"She's married. But I don't remember what he said her husband's name was. He did give me a snapshot of her though. Maybe if you saw it, you—"

"Excuse me, hon. One of the other waitresses just came in and I have a message for her from her doctor's office."

Michael turned and glanced toward the door where a woman wearing a shapeless gray coat and a rainsoaked hat had entered. Gina hurried over to the woman, handed her a note and the stranger's head bobbed up and down as they spoke. A customer motioned for Gina, and when she moved he watched as the woman removed the hat and shook out her hair. Not pale blond and long, he noted, but honey-colored and chopped in some kind of short shag. She removed the ugly coat, hung it on a rack. Right height, a little thin, Michael thought as he skimmed the body clad in the same black skirt and white blouse the other waitresses wore. What he could see of the legs were nice, even if the black tennis shoes were unappealing.

"Lily, Nancy Lee wants you in the office," the redhead called out.

"Coming," Lily replied.

And when she turned around, Michael felt as though he'd been kicked in the gut when he saw her face. Excitement sprinted through him as he quickly drank in the pale skin, the delicate features and those haunting green eyes.

It was her.

He'd found Elisabeth Webster, he realized as he

watched her hurry across the diner and disappear through the doors. Now all he had to do was make sure she still had the boy, and then he'd make the call to Webster.

"Sorry about that," Gina told him.

Michael jerked his attention back at the sound of her voice and realized he hadn't even noticed the woman had returned to the counter. "No problem."

"So, you want to show me the picture of your friend's sister?"

"Uh, it looks like I left it in my hotel room," Michael improvised. Now that he'd located Elisabeth Webster, aka Lily, he didn't want to tip her off. At least not before he notified her husband and collected the rest of his fee.

"Well, if you want to swing by later, I'll take a look at it. My name's Gina, by the way."

"Thanks, Gina," he told her. "And I'm Michael. Michael Sullivan."

"An Irishman? I was hoping that dark hair meant you were Italian."

"Afraid not," Michael said with a chuckle. "Black Irish on both sides."

"Oh well," she said with a sigh.

Gina looked around, leaned closer and said, "Nancy Lee would probably kill me if she heard me tell you this, but you might want to grab yourself a table if you plan to hang around and finish that puzzle. The lunch crowd's starting to come in, and in another thirty minutes it'll be elbow to elbow at this counter."

"I'll do that. Thanks for the tip." Michael stood and tossed down a five-dollar bill for the coffee, then picked up his newspaper.

"I'll be right back with your change."

"Keep it," he said.

"Thanks." Gina beamed and slid the five into the pocket of her apron.

Michael noted Lily coming through the doors again. "Which tables are hers?" he asked with a nod of his head toward Lily.

Gina's smile dimmed. "Should have known she was more your type."

A little taken aback by the comment, Michael studied Gina. Only then did he realize the woman wasn't just being friendly, but that she might have been flirting with him. "I'm sorry," he mumbled, annoyed with himself for hurting the woman's feelings.

"It's no big deal," she told him. "Lily's a real pretty girl, and I'd probably hate her if she weren't so darn sweet."

Feeling worse by the second, he said, "I really am sorry."

"No reason to be. I do all right. Some men actually prefer a woman with experience and a little more meat on her bones."

"And don't forget those smoldering Italian looks," Michael replied, and winked at her.

She smiled, patted her hair. "Lily's tables are the ones in that section on the right."

"Thanks," he said, picking up his coffee cup, and starting to leave.

"Say, Texas?"

He looked back at Gina. "Yeah?"

"Don't take it personal when she shoots you down."

"Got a lot of admirers, huh?"

"Quite a few and, so far, every one of them has struck out."

"She's not married or engaged, is she?" he asked, already knowing the answer.

"Worse. A widow and still in love with her dead husband."

He arched his eyebrow, surprised by the comment. "Kind of young to be a widow, isn't she?"

Gina shrugged. "I was sixteen when I married the first time."

"And you say she's still grieving for the guy?"

"That's my guess, since she hasn't shown a lick of interest in any man who's come through that door. While they're not all hunks, there have been a couple like you who would make a nun rethink her vows."

"But not Lily," Michael replied.

"Not Lily. She's immune."

"Maybe she just hasn't met the right guy yet."

"So, what's the story on him?" Amber asked as she joined Gina behind the counter. Together they watched the big, handsome Texan saunter across the diner and sit down at a table next to the window.

"What do you mean?"

"I mean, like, he's gay, isn't he?" she asked, a petulant expression on her face. "I swear, lately it seems that nearly all the really hot-looking guys are into other men.''

Gina looked at the girl as though she'd lost her mind. ''Why on earth would you think the man's gay?''

''Well, for starters, he's a hottie. Got that David James Elliott from *JAG* thing going.''

Now that Amber mentioned it, she could see the resemblance. ''So?''

''So the man comes in here, gives me the eye. Does the whole once-over thing, you know. And I figure he's interested. Right?''

Gina nodded, waiting for Amber to get to the point.

''So I give him my nicest smile, tell him all about the specials and try to, you know, like, make conversation. So here I am being all friendly-like, ready to give him my phone number, when he asks for it—only he doesn't ask for it. He just orders coffee, then pulls out his newspaper and buries his nose in it.''

''And from that you concluded the man was gay?''

Amber blinked her big blue eyes, rimmed in black. ''Wouldn't you?''

''Amber, honey, I hate to burst your bubble. But believe me, the man's not gay.''

Amber eyed her suspiciously. ''You telling me he hit on *you?*''

Gina had enough of an Italian temper to take offense at the younger woman's remark. Instead, she decided to let it pass, knowing that if Amber thought she'd hurt her feelings, she would be devastated. The little airhead really had a good heart, Gina reminded herself. Unfortunately, the girl had been brought up to believe that her looks were all she had going for her. It simply would never have occurred to the girl that a real man would see beyond a pretty face. "No, he didn't hit on me. But I suspect that's because he's already set his sights on Lily."

"Lily," Amber said with exasperation. "What is it with these guys that they all zero in on her?"

"Oh, I don't know. It could have something to do with the fact that she's beautiful."

"And what am I? Chopped liver?" Amber countered, striking an affronted pose.

Gina laughed. "Oh, don't go getting your panties in a wad, sugar. You give half the guys who come into this place whiplash every time you walk across a room. And I don't even want to think about what you do to their blood pressure. Besides, didn't that fellow who came in here last week say you should be a model?"

"Yeah, he did," Amber acknowledged.

"And I seem to remember that trucker who came in yesterday didn't have eyes for anyone but you."

"No, he didn't. Did he?" Amber said, apparently mollified. "So how come this one and the construction hunk who was hanging around here for a while only have eyes for Lily? I mean, look at her. She's kinda skinny. I've never even seen her wearing makeup. And don't even get me started on that hair."

"Careful, girl. Your claws are showing."

Amber sniffed. "I like Lily. You know I do. All I'm saying is she obviously doesn't put a lot of time in to fixing herself up. Why I bet she doesn't even own a lipstick.''

"Sugar, this may come as a surprise to you. But not everyone's into hair and makeup,'' Gina pointed out.

"But everyone wants to look their best. Or they should. Let's face it. Lily's pretty, but she's not...you know, movie-star gorgeous or anything.''

Gina heard the unspoken words *not like me,* but decided to remain silent. She also decided it was best not to point out that Lily's beauty was softer, almost ethereal, like a young Grace Kelly. Classy, Gina thought, remembering Ricardo's remark last week.

"All I'm saying is that I just don't get it. She's not even interested in men, and the guys still go for her.''

"Maybe they go for her because she's not interested,'' Gina offered.

"Well, that doesn't make any sense.''

"Neither does your theory that that fellow is gay,'' Gina told her, and motioned with her head across the room to where Michael was sitting. "From the way he's watching Lily, I'd say that what the man wants is *definitely* not on the menu.''

"So have you decided what you're going to have, or do you need a few more minutes?'' Lily asked the dark-haired man seated at one of the tables in her section.

"What did you say the special was again?''

"Red beans and rice with sausage and French bread.''

"Is it any good?" he asked, and gave her a warm, friendly smile.

"It's a Monday staple in New Orleans and, May— she's our cook here at the River Bend—fixes some of the best red beans in the city."

He snapped the menu shut. "Sold. Red beans and rice it is," he said, flashing her another smile.

"What can I get you to drink? You want some iced tea or a soft drink? Or are you going to stick with coffee?"

"Iced tea sounds good," he told her.

She jotted down his order on her pad. "I'll be right back with your tea," Lily informed him as she reached for the plastic-coated menu. Only he held on to the menu. She looked up and met his blue gaze. For a moment there was something so intense about the way he looked at her that Lily could have sworn he knew who she was. But then he released the menu and gave her another of those friendly smiles that softened his expression.

"Lily," he said, motioning to the name on her tag. "Pretty name."

"Thanks," she said, averting her gaze.

"I'm Michael. Michael Sullivan."

Lily nodded in acknowledgment. "I'd better go turn in your order," she said, and hurried away. But even as she went to the next table, she could have sworn his eyes remained on her.

She took another three orders, served up teas, waters, cold drinks and coffee, keenly aware of Michael Sullivan seated at the table near the window. While he was no longer watching her and appeared to be engrossed in working a crossword puzzle, Lily couldn't shake the nerves that he'd set off inside her.

She was being silly, she told herself as she filled water glasses and rushed about to accommodate the lunch crowd. The guy couldn't possibly know who she was. He was simply flirting with her. And the last thing she wanted was to find herself facing another situation like the one she'd had a week ago when she'd ignored the signals and ended up shooting some guy's ego to bits. What still amazed her was that any man would want to flirt with her now. She'd done everything she could to distance herself from the woman Adam had created. The long, pale-blond hair, the expert makeup, the sexy, revealing clothes, and even some of the curves were gone now. She couldn't help thinking how furious Adam would be at her appearance. He'd monitored her body and her looks as carefully, more carefully, than he'd monitored his own. She squeezed her eyes shut to blot out the memory of that night when she'd made up her mind to leave him. Of the way he had ripped her clothes from her body, drove himself into her and told her that he owned her—that if she wanted Timmy to go on breathing, she had better never forget that fact.

"Whoops! Excuse me."

At the bump from Amber, Lily yanked her thoughts back to the present. Giving herself a mental shake, she realized she was standing in front of the fountain with a half-filled glass of water in her hand.

"You okay?" Amber asked her. "You seem a little distracted."

"Just a little tired, I guess," she managed to say. "I was up most of the night with Timmy."

"Yeah, Nancy Lee said you had to take him to the doctor this morning. He okay?"

Lily nodded. "Except for the fact that he has chicken pox."

"Ooh, poor baby," Amber said, making a face.

"You talk to the doctor's office yet?" Gina asked as she joined them to unload her tray of dishes. "Nothing else is wrong, is there?"

"No, thank heavens," Lily replied. "They just wanted to let me know that I'd left my sunglasses in the office when I brought Timmy in this morning."

"Girls, get a move on," Nancy Lee ordered as she exited the kitchen with two steaming plates of red beans and rice. "We've got people waiting for tables."

Lily didn't need to be told twice. In the little more than two months that she'd worked at the River Bend Diner, she'd learned to juggle trays heaped with plates of food and drinks like a pro. She'd also learned that for any restaurant to succeed in a place like New Orleans, where good food was as common as mosquitoes, the tables needed to be turned over as often as possible. Not only was it the key to a restaurant's profits, it also made a big difference in how much she would make in tips. And she needed the extra tip money. Timmy's visit to the doctor, along with his prescriptions, had set her back more than a hundred dollars that morning. She recalled explaining to the doctor's nurse that her insurance wouldn't kick in for another month with her employer. She couldn't help wondering again if she dare stick around long enough to take advantage of that employee benefit. She would like to stay, she admitted. Especially with Gertie here. If only she could be sure that Adam wouldn't find her, or that if he did, he wouldn't be able to harm Timmy. Lily thought about the disk again, wondered if there was a way she could use it to protect her son. Vowing to check for any further info on that agent's death, she zipped over to the pick-up counter.

The dinging of the bell and the repeated, "Lily, order up," kept her too busy to dwell on Timmy's bout with chicken pox, the disk or the dark-haired man who went out of his way to engage her in conversation each time she came to his table.

For the next hour, Lily didn't miss a beat. She lost count of the number of orders she took for the special, or of the number of slices of king cake she'd served. With the exception of Michael Sullivan's table, most of the tables in her area had turned over at least once as the lunch crowd zipped in and out of the diner.

"Thanks," she said to the two secretaries who left a couple of ones on the table for her and took the to-go boxes she'd handed them. Slipping the ones into her apron pocket, she began clearing the table and was grateful to see that the worst of the rush was over.

She walked over to his table, cleared away the dish that had been filled with bread pudding. "Did you want some more coffee?" she asked.

"That would be great," he said, and flashed her another smile. "The bread pudding was terrific, by the way. Thanks for recommending it."

"No problem." She glanced over to the counter and noted one of the coffeepots was empty and the other was very low. "Looks like I'll need to put on a fresh pot. It'll only be a few minutes."

"No problem," he told her. "Say, how are you at crossword puzzles?"

"Lousy," she said, even though that wasn't exactly true since crossword puzzles were a favorite of hers. But to tell him so would only encourage him, she reasoned, and encouraging him or any man was the last thing she wanted to do. "I'll go see about that coffee," she told him. Glad to be behind the safety of the counter, and away from all that charm, she unloaded her tray and set out to brew a fresh pot of coffee.

"So, what do you think of Texas?" Gina asked as she wiped down the counter.

Lily wrinkled her forehead. "The state?"

Gina laughed. "The guy at your table. His name's Michael Sullivan, and he's from Texas," she explained. "He sure is a cutie-pie, don't you think?"

"I suppose so," Lily said, looking over at him. Although with his dark hair, blue eyes and that strong jawline, she didn't think the word *cute* was one she'd use to describe the man. *Cute* made her think of soft and cuddly, like Timmy's teddy bear. There was nothing soft or cuddly-looking about him. He was tall, probably a good ten inches taller than her own five foot five inches. And she suspected that every ounce on his lean frame was solid muscle. His hands were like the rest of him—big—but unlike Adam's hands, his showed no signs of regular manicures. She was fairly sure that if she were to examine his hands closely, she'd find them scarred and calloused and rough against her skin. No, *cute* didn't describe Michael Sullivan, she decided. He was handsome and sexy in a rugged kind of way.

As though sensing her scrutiny, he looked up, locking his gaze with hers. And for the space of a heartbeat, Lily felt as though she couldn't breathe. At the beep of the coffeemaker, she yanked her attention back to the task at hand.

"He seems like a nice guy. Says he's been working offshore," Gina told her.

"You talking about Lily's new admirer?" Amber asked as she joined them behind the counter, the pique in her voice matching her expression.

Lily frowned. "My admirer?"

"The hunk with the dreamy eyes," she said with a sigh. "Don't tell me you haven't noticed him. A woman would have to be dead not to notice a guy like that."

"He's all right," Lily replied, uncomfortable talking with the other women about men. Female friends were something she'd never really had—in part because she'd spent her early years caring for her ailing grandmother, and later, when she'd been sent to boarding school, her relationship with Adam had marked her as different. Once she and Adam had married, he'd made it clear to her that her only duty had been to be his wife. Not that she'd had any female friends. Even the wives and girlfriends of his associates shunned her because they, like most people, had believed her to be a bimbo who had slept her way to a cushy lifestyle. The one and only friendship she had formed had been with Emily, a strong-willed and independent young woman who owned and ran a flower shop that she had begun to frequent. It had been Emily who had encouraged her to do something for herself and had offered her a part-time job in her shop. Two weeks later, Emily's shop had burned down. And Lily had never bothered to try to form another friendship after that.

"Lily girl, you better get your pulse checked," Amber told her. "That guy is so hot, he's ice."

"She's right, hon," Gina said. "He could give those movie-star heartthrobs a run for their money."

"You can bet if he'd been looking at me the way he's been looking at you, I'd have noticed," Amber informed her.

Suddenly uncomfortable, Lily offered, "Why don't you bring him his coffee and check?"

"You're kidding, right? You're really not interested in him?" Amber asked, looking at her as though she'd lost her mind.

"No, I'm not. And you'd be doing me a favor. I really want to get back to Timmy, and Nancy Lee said it was okay for me to leave a little early."

"Well, sure, I'd be glad to help out."

"But the tip is hers," Gina told Amber as the girl

took both the check and the coffee and sashayed her way over to Michael Sullivan's table.

"I really don't mind Amber getting the tip," Lily told Gina.

"You need it more than she does," Gina insisted. "I'm guessing that doctor's visit set you back a chunk and I know your insurance hasn't kicked in yet. Besides, Amber would only spend the money on makeup or clothes and she's already got plenty of both."

"Thanks," Lily said, touched by the woman's understanding. She started to wipe down behind the counter, when Gina took the sponge from her hand.

"I'll finish up. You go on home to that baby."

"Thank you," Lily murmured, and stripped off her apron. She hurried into the back office where she signed out and gathered her purse. "I'll see you in the morning," she told Gina when she came back out front.

"I still think you're nuts for passing on Texas, you know."

"I know," Lily said. "But I'm sure he'll be happy to move on to Amber once he realizes I'm not interested."

"Don't count on it," Gina said to her retreating back. "Something tells me that he's one man who doesn't give up easily on something he wants."

Six

"How long are you going to be in town?" Amber asked.

"I'm not sure," Michael said, doing his best to discourage the girl without hurting her feelings and, at the same time, trying to keep an eye on Lily.

"Well you picked a good time to visit with it being Mardi Gras season and all. Most people don't realize the celebrations and parades go on for a month before the big day. You been to any of the parades yet?"

"Hmm? No. No, I haven't," he said as he watched Lily talking with the brunette waitress named Gina.

"If you're going to be around this weekend, there are a lot of parades scheduled. You think you might want to see a couple of them?"

When the girl fell silent, Michael assumed she was waiting for an answer from him. But he didn't have a clue what she'd been talking about. "I'm sorry, what did you say?"

"I was wondering if you thought you might want to, you know, maybe catch a couple of parades this weekend."

"Um, sure. I guess so," Michael said absently. His

attention still on Lily, he tracked her movements, noted she had her purse and was retrieving her coat and hat from the rack by the door.

"Great. We're not open for dinner. So what about Saturday night?"

Michael jerked his attention back to the smiling redhead. "Saturday?"

"Can you make the parade Saturday night?"

Damn! Michael wanted to kick himself for not paying closer attention. "I don't think so. You see, I sort of promised a buddy of mine that I'd help him out with a fishing charter this weekend."

"You're going fishing? During Mardi Gras season?"

"Afraid so. But I appreciate the offer. Maybe another time."

"Sure. Another time," she said, but he caught the note of disappointment in her voice.

"Man, will you look at the time? I had no idea it was so late. I need to get going." He stood, tossed a twenty on top of the table. "Thanks again for the invite. It's not every day a gorgeous woman asks me out. But I guess my loss is going to be some other lucky fellow's gain."

"You've got that right," Amber said, beaming at the compliment. "I usually catch lots of the long beads. They're the best ones, you know. If you're still around next week, I'll bring you a few."

"Sounds great." He dropped another five on the table before snagging his jacket from the back of the chair and exiting the diner.

Michael walked slowly across the street toward his truck and scanned the area in search of Lily aka Elisabeth Webster. Damn, where had she gone? he wondered as he unlocked his Ford Bronco and climbed inside. Taking his time, he adjusted his mirrors, all the while looking for the woman. Finally, he spied a small, ancient brown Chevrolet traveling up from a side street. The car stopped at the corner across from him to check for traffic.

Bingo!

Recognizing the honey-blond driver at the wheel of the vehicle, Michael started his engine. And when she turned into traffic, he shifted into Drive and followed her.

Twenty minutes later, the little brown car turned onto a street in what appeared to be a modest section of the city. Most of the houses were small and single-storied. The yards were equally small, but the lawns were neatly trimmed and dotted with big oaks or magnolia trees. And nearly every house had rows of azalea bushes, thick with blooms in a range of pinks, reds, and white across the front or around the sides.

When Lily pulled her car into the driveway of a little cottage in the middle of the next block, Michael hung back. Easing his truck to the curb, he parked behind an old Buick and shut off his engine. He watched as Lily exited her car and ran up the stairs. When the door opened and she disappeared inside, he slumped down in his seat and prepared to wait.

While he waited, Michael found himself comparing the woman who called herself Lily to Elisabeth Webster. Like the woman in Ms. Schubert's snapshot, there was a fragility about her. There was a softness, a subtle beauty that had been missing in the glamourous portrait in her husband's office. She certainly didn't look like a woman who would drug her husband and steal his kid.

What he had trouble understanding was why the woman was working in a second-rate diner when she'd reportedly stolen a great deal of cash and jewelry? And why was she driving a beat-up car that looked as if it was on its last legs? If Elisabeth Webster was a gold digger, then why trade her plush life for this? It didn't make sense.

It didn't need to make sense, Michael reminded himself. Just because a woman looked fragile didn't mean that she was. Hadn't he learned that lesson the hard way with Giselle? Whatever Elisabeth Webster's problems were, they weren't his concern. His only concern was to make sure that she had the kid and then bring them both back to Webster. Once he did that, he'd collect the rest of his fee, and somehow he'd convince Janie to let him help her and the boys. Then maybe, just maybe, he'd be able to finally find some peace.

Sitting in the truck, Michael kept his eyes trained on the door of the house Lily had entered. As the hours ticked by, the sun went down and the cold set in. He huddled in his jacket and debated about whether to go off and try to find some hot coffee, but decided against it. All he needed was to see the kid.

Once he knew the boy was still with her, he could call Webster.

At half past eight he decided that the lady was in for the night, and that he might as well head back to the hotel. He could come back early in the morning, and hopefully, he'd spot the boy then. Reaching for the key in the ignition, Michael was about to start the engine when the door opened and out walked Lily. Alone. When she slid behind the wheel of her car and backed out of the driveway, Michael started his truck and followed. A dozen blocks later she stopped in front of another house, this one a double.

Parked halfway down the block on the opposite side of the street, Michael watched Lily climb the stairs up to the porch and enter one side of the house. He could see a red-and-white sign posted on the opposite door of the shared porch and suspected it was a For Rent or For Lease sign. Making a note to check it out later, he settled in and prepared to wait.

Thirty minutes later, when the lights inside the house went out, Michael exited his truck and started down the walkway toward the now-dark house. Like the previous neighborhood where she had spent all afternoon and evening, this one appeared to be an older, residential section of the city. The houses seemed smaller. So did the yards. And the street was just as quiet. Only a scattering of lights glowed from the windows of the nearby homes. Several houses down, he heard the sound of a dog barking and a shout for it to be quiet.

Michael paused in front of the house into which

Lily had disappeared. As he'd suspected, the other half of the double was empty and the sign announced it was for rent. After making a mental note of the number to call, he leaned on the wrought-iron fence and pretended to have something inside his boot. While he made a show of shaking out his boot in case anyone was watching, he tried to make out the name on the mailbox. Even with only the dim light of the street lamp, he could read the name Tremont.

Sliding his foot back inside the boot, Michael continued down the street. After circling the block, he returned to his truck and headed back to his hotel room to make some calls.

"Well, look who's back," Gina said in her husky voice.

Lily wasn't sure how she knew, but she simply knew that the "he" Gina referred to was the man named Sullivan who'd been at the diner on Monday. For some reason, he had made a major impression on her co-workers and his name had come up several times since then.

"Looks like you've got a customer, Lily," Gina said, a teasing note in her voice.

Lily looked up from the pot of coffee she'd been preparing for Wednesday's lunch crowd. Sure enough, it was him, and he sat at one of her tables. "I don't suppose you'd want to take his order for me, would you?"

"No," Gina said firmly but sweetly. "And don't bother asking Amber," Gina told her when she glanced around for the younger woman. "The girl's got her hands full with that trucker she's suddenly gone sweet on. We're lucky she even handles her own tables. Go on, hon. He seemed like a nice guy to me and, you have to admit, he's easy on the eyes."

Nancy Lee chose that moment to come through the doors of the kitchen. "Who's easy on the eyes?"

"The good-looking fellow seated over there by the window," Gina said with a nod of her head toward the table. "He was in earlier this week. He's from Texas. Said his name's Michael Sullivan."

"My, my, they certainly do grow them big in Texas, don't they?" Nancy Lee remarked. "And you said his name's Sullivan?"

"That's what he says," Gina replied.

Nancy Lee's stern expression softened. "Must be Irish then. Incredible lovers those Irishmen. Two of my husbands were Irish." She cut her gaze to Lily. "He say or do something to offend you?"

"No. Not at all," Lily replied.

"So what's the problem?"

"There's no problem," Lily fibbed. The problem was that she couldn't shake the feeling that Michael Sullivan wasn't just a handsome offshore worker. Oh, she could buy the bit about his working offshore. Louisiana's oil business attracted a lot of workers for the rigs. And the man had the sun-bronzed skin, the calloused palms and muscled build that could never be attained by working out in some sterile gym with a physical trainer. But there was something in those laser-sharp eyes of his—something dark and dangerous—that made her think he wasn't quite the harmless cowboy he appeared to be.

Or maybe she was just being paranoid, Lily told herself, wishing she didn't feel the need to suspect everyone. Wishing she could just accept a man's attention without worrying that he'd been sent by Adam to find her. But she couldn't, she told herself. Not if she wanted to keep Timmy safe. Realizing that Nancy Lee and Gina were both looking at her, she grabbed a menu and a glass of water. "I'd better go take his order."

"Hey there." He looked up from his newspaper and gave her one of those wicked smiles. "Lily, isn't it?"

"That's right," she said as she handed him the menu.

When his fingers brushed hers, she snatched her hand back. Her stomach fluttered from the brief contact, and when his gaze met hers, it did nothing to ease her apprehension. There was a time when she might have enjoyed and welcomed these feelings of attraction he stirred in her. He certainly fit her schoolgirl image of Prince Charming. But that had been a lifetime ago. Before she'd gone to live with her mother. Before she'd become Adam's ward and then his wife. Before she'd learned that a handsome face and friendly smile could mask evil.

"Any specials today?" Michael asked.

Yanking her thoughts back to the present, she said, "Stuffed pork chop, crawfish étouffée or beef stew.

Each comes with a salad and May's special bread pudding with rum sauce for dessert.''

''Any recommendations?''

''They're all good,'' Lily told him.

''What's your favorite?''

''I… The crawfish étouffée,'' she confessed.

''Then that's what I'll have.''

He closed the menu and offered it to her. Taking care, she took it from him and tucked it under her arm. ''What would you like to drink?''

''Iced tea's good.''

After jotting down the order, she said, ''I'll be back with your salad and tea in a minute.''

And ten minutes later, when she approached his table with his lunch order, Lily was relieved to see he was absorbed in working another crossword puzzle. Maybe she'd be able to serve him his meal and escape without any chitchat.

No such luck. He looked up just as she reached his table and gave her another one of those knee-weakening grins. ''Boy, does that smell good.''

Lily placed the plate brimming with the thick red creole sauce and crawfish tails over a mound of steaming rice in front of him. She set the basket with hot bread in the center of the table. Scooping up the empty salad plate, she said, ''Enjoy your meal.''

''Whoa! Could I get a refill on the tea?'' he asked, holding up the empty glass.

''Sure,'' she said, chastising herself for not offering in the first place. She cleared the next table and disposed of the dishes behind the counter while she lectured herself for her poor service and even poorer manners. Then she made her way back to Michael's table with a pitcher of tea.

To her surprise he'd really tucked into the étouffée and half the bread. As she poured his tea, she smiled. Michael Sullivan obviously wasn't a man who was worried about his calorie intake, she thought. She couldn't help recalling Adam's obsession with keeping himself fit, his body tanned and an ample supply of Viagra on hand to enhance his performance in the bedroom. Realizing what she was doing—comparing Michael to Adam—Lily's hand shook and she spilled tea on the table. "I'm so sorry. Your newspaper—"

"Hey, it's no problem," he told her as he grabbed the napkin from his lap to help her wipe up the spill.

As he dabbed at the mess, his fingers brushed against hers again. Awareness shot through her like a rocket and Lily jerked her eyes to Michael's face. She recognized the heated look in his gaze and realized he'd felt it, too. Unsettled, she said, "I better go get some more napkins."

When she returned a few minutes later, she had regained her composure and Michael had finished his meal. "I'm sorry about the mess. Did I ruin your crossword?"

"I was finished with it already. So no harm done."

Relieved, she nodded and began clearing away the remains of his meal. "You up for the bread pudding?" she asked.

"Sounds good to me."

"Coffee with cream, one sugar, right?"

He winked at her. "You remembered. Want to get married?"

Lily paled.

"Hey, I was only kidding."

"I know that," she said, forcing a smile to her lips. She was being ridiculous, Lily told herself. The man was just trying to be friendly and here she was acting like some outraged virgin who'd been propositioned. "I'll be right back with the coffee."

By the time she returned to Michael's table to bring him his check, she was over the worst of her embarrassment and feeling more like herself. She'd decided that she was going to swing by the library right after work and see if she could find out anything more about that agent who'd been killed in Miami. And, depending on what she discovered, maybe she could somehow use the disk to ensure her and Timmy's safety.

"This stuff is sinful," Michael told her as he scooped the last of the rum sauce from the dish with his finger.

"I know." She'd never been big on sweets, but since moving to New Orleans, she'd discovered she adored them. She slid his check facedown on the table.

"Lily, hang on a second." He pushed the empty dish aside. "I was wondering if you could help me with something?"

"I'll try," she said cautiously.

"You think you could take a look at a couple of these places I've circled in the classifieds?" He shoved the folded paper toward her, and she noted he'd drawn circles around several boxes in the "for rent" section.

"You're looking for an apartment?" she asked, surprised since Gina had mentioned that he was just passing through.

"I'm thinking about it. That is, if I can find a place that fits my budget. At the moment, I'm not working. But I heard through the grapevine that they're going to be hiring workers for a couple of new offshore rigs next month. So I thought I'd stick around and see if I could get on," he explained. "Only problem is, I've been staying in a hotel and apparently they jack up the rates when it gets close to Mardi Gras time. So I was thinking I might do better renting a place."

"Oh," she said, realizing how inane that sounded. She also wasn't sure why the idea of Michael being around for a while unsettled her. "So what is it you want me to help you with?"

"I was hoping you could tell me about the areas where these places are located," he said, indicating several circled ads. "You know, whether or not it's a decent part of town. Or am I liable to get mugged going out to pick up the morning paper?"

"I'm sorry. But I'm really not the right person to ask. I'm relatively new to the city myself. You might want to check with Gina or one of the other ladies. They've lived here a lot longer than I have." Noting that Gina was clearing the next table, she called out to her and motioned her over.

''What's up?'' Gina asked as she joined them at the table.

''Mr. Sullivan needs some help,'' Lily told her.

''What can I do for you, Texas?''

''Well, ma'am, as I explained to Lily, I'm hoping to get on with one of the oil rigs next month. So I'm thinking about moving out of the hotel I'm staying in and renting a place to save a few bucks. I found a few places in the classifieds I can afford, but I don't have any idea about the areas.''

While Gina scanned the ads he'd circled, Lily began loading his now-empty dessert dish and silverware onto her tray. As she listened to Gina rule out a couple of the possibilities, she couldn't help feeling a little guilty for not mentioning that the other half of the double where she lived was available. It was a decent neighborhood. The rent was reasonable, and the landlady would gladly rent him the place. Yet the prospect of having Michael live next door made her more anxious than ever.

''Sorry, pal,'' Gina declared. ''But I wouldn't put my worst enemy or even that last SOB I was married to in one of these places.''

''That bad, huh?''

''Worse,'' Gina said.

Michael sighed. ''Well, it was worth a shot. I guess I'll just have to let the hotel gouge me with those Mardi Gras rates.''

''Wait a minute,'' Gina said as Lily started to walk away. ''Lily, what about that double where you live? When I gave you a lift to work a couple of weeks ago, I noticed there was a For Rent sign in the other half. Is it still available?''

Michael knew from Lily's expression that she wasn't at all happy that Gina had mentioned the place. He couldn't help wondering why.

''I'm not sure,'' Lily replied, a weariness in her voice that matched the look in her eyes. ''I mean, no one's living there at the moment. But I don't know whether Mrs. Davis has a tenant lined up for it or not.''

He made the lady nervous, Michael realized. Since he'd been careful not to say anything that might tip her off, he didn't think the nerves were because she suspected he was looking for her. Maybe he simply had enough of a male ego to want to believe it was because she was attracted to him. He hadn't missed the awareness in those big green eyes of hers when his fingers had brushed hers. The first time, he'd written it off to wishful thinking. So today, he'd deliberately touched her again. That darkening of her eyes, the slight tremor in her fingers, had told him that the sensual spark between them hadn't been one-sided. What puzzled him was the genuine alarm her reaction seemed to strike in her. If he hadn't known she'd been married to Webster, who'd apparently taken pleasure in showing off her assets, he'd have sworn the lady was gun-shy around men. ''Can you find out?'' Michael asked.

''I suppose so. But I doubt it's the kind of place you're looking for,'' she told him.

"It looked fine to me," Gina countered.

"What I mean is it's not an apartment. It's a house. What they call a shotgun double down here," she explained to him. "But it's a pretty quiet neighborhood, mostly families and retired couples. You'd probably find it stuffy."

She positively didn't want him next door, Michael decided. "I don't know. It sounds pretty nice to me. Unless you object to the idea of me as a neighbor, I'd like to check it out."

"Now, why would Lily object to having you for a neighbor?" Gina said, a hint of mischief in her dark eyes.

"Because she doesn't know me," Michael said, offering the obvious. "But I can assure you that I'm trustworthy. I help little old ladies cross the street and I like animals. And if you want references, I'll give you my mother's phone number," he told her with a smile, determined to win Lily over. "She'll vouch for my good character."

Both Gina and Lily laughed at the absurdity of his remark—just as he'd intended.

What he hadn't intended, what he hadn't been at all prepared for, was the effect Lily's laughter had on him. His gut tightened at the picture she made. That unmistakable thrum of desire that he'd been fighting from the moment he'd set eyes on her exploded like wildfire in his veins. "You know, your eyes light up when you laugh," he said, the words tumbling out before he could stop them. "You really should do it more often."

Lily immediately tensed up again, and Michael could have kicked himself for the remark. "I...thank you," she murmured, the laughter dying on her lips and in her eyes.

"Boy, did that ever sound like a line," he joked. "I'm sorry if I embarrassed you."

"You didn't," she said.

But Michael knew that wasn't true. Maybe he hadn't embarrassed her, but he *had* made her uncomfortable, which was one more part of the puzzle of Lily, aka Elisabeth Webster, that didn't make any sense. Why would having a man compliment her looks—something she'd surely heard hundreds of times—make her so uneasy?

"Now that we've established he's trustworthy, why don't you give him the address, hon?" Gina prompted.

Lily wrote down the address on a sheet from her order pad. She tore the paper off and handed it to him. "I don't know Mrs. Davis's phone number offhand but she's listed. You can call her and talk to her about the place."

"Thanks. I appreciate it," Michael said as he tucked the slip of paper into his shirt pocket. "I'll swing by when I leave here and take a look at the outside then give Mrs. Davis a call and see if I can set up an appointment to look at the inside."

"You know, those old shotgun doubles are really just one big house split down the middle. The layouts are identical on both sides. You could probably take a look at Lily's place if you want to get an idea of what the inside looks like,'' Gina suggested. ''She'll be clocking out of here in another ten minutes or so. Maybe you should just follow her home.''

''Sounds good to me. But I wouldn't want to put Lily out,'' Michael offered.

''Actually, I'm not going straight home when I leave here,'' Lily told him. ''My car has been acting up again and I've made plans to drop it off at the dealership. Sorry.''

Liar, Michael thought, but he decided not to push it. ''Thanks anyway,'' he said, tossing some bills down on the table to cover the check.

Lily scooped them up, along with the check, and said, ''I'll get you your change.''

''Keep it,'' he told her.

''Thanks,'' Lily said. ''And good luck.''

When she walked away, he turned to Gina, who was still standing beside the table. ''And thank you, pretty lady.''

''For what?''

''For letting me know about the rental.''

''You're welcome,'' Gina told him, a twinkle in her dark eyes.

''Why do I get the feeling that you're playing matchmaker?''

''Because I am.''

''Why?''

Gina laughed. ''It's simple. I like you. And I like Lily. I also think the girl's too young to spend the rest of her life mourning a dead man. She needs someone to shake her up, remind her what it's like to be a woman.''

"And you think I'm the one to do it?'' Michael countered.

"Sugar, if you can't, then I'm gonna stop looking for a husband and go enter the convent.''

Michael laughed. He caught Gina by the shoulders and kissed her right on the mouth. "I appreciate the vote of confidence, ma'am.''

"Oh my,'' she said, her eyelashes fluttering when he released her. "You do that, and the girl's toast.''

He grinned. "Let's hope you're right, because I'm certainly going to give it the old Boy Scout try.''

Since he'd never been a Boy Scout, he had no intention of trying to resurrect Elizabeth Webster's love life, Michael admitted. Exiting the diner, he reminded himself that the lady was his meal ticket and nothing more. That meant finding out if she still had the kid. Once he did that, he would notify Webster. And then he'd forget all about Elisabeth Webster.

Seven

Lily sat at the computer terminal in the public library and pulled up a series of newspaper articles. After rereading the initial article she had seen six months ago, recounting the death of a man whose body had been found on the Florida beach and believed to be the victim of a shark attack, she scanned the follow-up pieces.

The man had been identified as Gregory Carter, age thirty-eight, and an employee of the federal government for fifteen years. For the past five years he'd worked in the office of the Federal Bureau of Investigation and had been assigned to an office in Miami at the time of his death. A subsequent article reported the autopsy findings had revealed the man had not died from the shark attack, but from a knife wound to the heart. Other than the obituary and a statement by a spokesperson for the FBI named Bryce Logan, in which a reward had been offered for any information leading to an arrest in the man's death, she could find no further references. Grabbing a piece of paper, she jotted down Logan's name and the number listed in the article and tucked it in her purse.

Lily stared at the photo of Carter again, remembering the night she had come downstairs late to check on Timmy and had heard the sound of arguing coming from Adam's office. She had ventured down the forbidden hall to see if she could determine what was wrong. When the office door had suddenly opened, she'd caught a glimpse of Carter—his mouth bloodied, his eyes wild. She'd gasped, and at the sound, Adam had shut the door at once. He'd been furious with her, refusing to answer her questions and insisting she go back to bed. But she hadn't been able to forget the terror written on Carter's face. When she'd seen the article and his photo in the paper, she'd known immediately that Adam had been responsible for his death.

After another search of the periodicals, she could find no mention of any link between Adam and Carter. Other than a piece detailing the opening of Adam's newest nightclub in the West Palm Beach area, she could find nothing more on either of them.

Not for the first time, Lily wondered if it had been Gregory Carter who had supplied Adam with the disk that contained the information on the federal agents. While she'd suspected that Adam's nightclubs had not been the true source of his income, she'd never known for sure. And Adam had been adamant that she not question him about his business. Now, when she thought back about how she'd blinded herself to Adam's true nature for so long, remaining safe in the pretty cage he'd built for her, she couldn't help feeling ashamed.

As she shut off the terminal and prepared to leave the library, Lily thought about the disk again. She'd known it had to be important. Otherwise Adam wouldn't have kept it in his safe. She'd learned early in their marriage that his study and the safe in it was where he kept his secrets. But what she hadn't realized when she'd taken the disk was that it would contain a list with the names and photos of federal agents working undercover in a sting of some kind, aimed at drug and prostitution traffic in the Florida nightclub scene. It had been her insurance. Her only line of defense if Adam should ever get his hands on Timmy.

Lily thought about the slip of paper with Agent Logan's phone number in her purse. While the authorities hadn't linked Adam to Carter's death, the disk would. After all, she had seen the man in Adam's home and she had taken the disk from his safe. If she were to turn it over to the FBI, it might contain enough evidence for them to arrest Adam. And if he were in prison, then she and Timmy would be safe from him.

But what if Carter wasn't Adam's mole in the FBI office? Or what if he had more than one? What if she were to go to the Bureau, tell them what she knew and turn the disk over only to have Adam find out before they could arrest him? If by doing so, could she and her son finally be free to lead a normal life? Would it be worth the risk?

As Lily came through the library entrance and started down the steps, she noted the row of telephones. She hesitated a moment then, before she lost her nerve, she dug out the slip of paper and placed the call.

"Logan."

Lily held her breath a moment when she was finally connected to the agent she'd requested. She pressed a hand to her throat, tried to steady her fast-beating heart. "Mr. Logan," she finally managed to get out. "I…I'm calling for a friend. She has some information about the death of one of your employees. A Mr. Gregory Carter."

"To whom am I speaking?"

"I'd rather not say," Lily said.

"If you or your friend are interested in the reward, I'll have to have a name."

"I'm not…interested in the reward, I mean. And neither is my friend. I, that is, my friend, just wants to see justice done."

"All right," Logan told her. "Why don't you tell me about this information?"

Lily explained quickly that this man had been seen with her friend's husband and the friend had come across some confidential information that identified a number of undercover federal agents. "If my friend were to send you this information, could you use it to arrest her husband and put him in jail?"

"I'm afraid we'd need more than that. We'd need your friend to testify that she'd seen Carter with her husband, and that her husband had been in possession of the data."

"She can't testify," Lily insisted. The idea of facing Adam in a courtroom, allowing him to know where she and Timmy were, terrified her.

"Then we would have no grounds to arrest him."

Lily hesitated. "If she agreed to testify, could you guarantee her husband would go to jail?"

"That would be up to a jury, ma'am. The prosecutors would certainly do their best to build a solid case against him, and they could place your friend in protective custody."

"But you can't guarantee he'll go to jail, can you?" Lily asked.

"No, ma'am."

"Thank you, Agent Logan."

"Ma'am? Ma'am, don't hang up," Logan said. "If your friend knows her husband was involved in a murder and she has information linking him to the crime, she has to come forward."

"And if she doesn't?"

"Then she could be charged with withholding evidence and possibly even aiding and abetting. If you'll tell me where you are and how to reach your friend—"

Lily hung up the phone. My God, she thought. Not only would turning over the disk not guarantee Adam would be sent to jail, but she could very well find herself charged with a crime. Disheartened, she tore the slip of paper in half and dumped it in the stone ashtray near the entrance to the library. Then she descended the steps and headed toward her car, unaware that she was being watched.

* * *

Michael sat slouched in the seat of his truck and watched Lily as she walked toward her car. He noted that she'd carried no books with her when she'd entered the library nearly two hours ago and that she carried none when she'd left. Since he doubted he could find out what she'd been looking for at the library, he opted to try the phone instead. Exiting his truck, he made his way toward the row of pay phones, stopping en route at the ashtray into which Lily had tossed something when she'd left. He retrieved the torn and crumpled pieces of paper from the sand and cigarette butts and then he went over to the telephone Lily had used a few moments before.

As he'd suspected, the antiquated phones didn't sport redial buttons and the chances of getting an operator to redial the number she'd just called were slim to none. Smoothing out the fragments of paper, he pieced it together. "Logan." he read the name aloud before dialing the number listed.

"Federal Bureau of Investigation."

Surprised, Michael asked, "Do you have an Agent Logan working there?"

"One moment, please."

A few seconds later, a man answered, "Agent Logan."

Michael hung up the phone.

Now, why would Lily be calling the FBI? he wondered as he started down the stairs of the library. Once he was inside his Bronco, he whipped out his cell phone and placed a call to his brother. After getting a voice mail at Travis's office, he tried calling him at home. When the answering machine kicked on, he said, "Hey, Trav, it's Michael. I'm in New Orleans working on a case and came across the name of an agent out of the Florida office. I'd like to run his name by you and see if there's anything you can tell me about him. Give me a call back on my cell phone," he instructed, and left the number.

But Michael didn't hear from his younger brother that day, or the next day or the next. Upon subsequent calls to his office, he'd been able to find out that Travis was away on assignment. Michael cursed himself for not keeping in closer touch or making sure he had Travis's current cell phone number. While he considered calling his parents' home to request it, he decided to wait and continue to track Lily's movements.

Since he'd detected that his presence made her jumpy, Michael hadn't returned to the diner at all that week. He had, however, continued to monitor Lily. But so far he had not seen the little boy. He recalled his last conversation with Webster and still wasn't sure why he hadn't told the man he had found his wife. If he had, Webster could have met him in New Orleans and, once he'd directed him to Lily, he could have collected his money and walked away.

But he still hadn't found the boy, Michael reasoned as he followed Lily from the diner. His agreement was to find both Webster's wife and his son.

Like clockwork, Lily returned to the small uptown cottage she visited each day. Michael had learned that the place belonged to Anna Gertrude Boudreaux, the grandmother's former neighbor. And despite following Lily to the Boudreaux woman's house and then to her own place every day, he had yet to see any signs of the little boy.

Michael parked his truck a block away, making sure that he had a view of the Boudreaux woman's front door. He watched Lily enter the house, and then he shut off the engine. Slouching down in his seat, he pulled his cowboy hat low on his forehead and prepared to wait for the next several hours.

"So what do you say, big guy? You ready to come home? Mommy sure has missed you this past week."

"Miss you, too," Timmy told her, and gave her a big hug.

Lily scooped her son up in her arms, held him close and breathed in his baby scent. When she continued to hug him, Timmy began to squirm. Reluctantly, she put him down and said, "Guess what? Since you've been such a good boy, Mommy has a present for you."

"Present?" Timmy repeated, his facing lighting up.

Lily dug into the tote bag she'd placed on the kitchen table and withdrew the little car she'd purchased for her son. Stooping down, she handed it to him. "Here you go."

Timmy grabbed the bright red car from her.

"What do you say when someone gives you a gift?" she prompted.

"Tank you," Timmy said dutifully and gave her a

smacking kiss before settling down on the tile floor to play with his new toy.

When she stood again, she told Gertie, "I can't thank you enough for taking care of him like this. I know I've said it a hundred times, but it's true. I really don't know what I would have done without you, Gertie. I just wish you'd let me pay you something for helping us."

"Don't go insulting me by offering me money again. Lord, when I think of all the times your grandmother Sara helped me out, I could watch that little scamp of yours for the next twenty years and never repay her."

"She loved you," Lily told her. "Grandma always said you were the sister she never had."

"And I felt the same way about her. Watching after that little one of yours is the least I can do."

"But—"

"No buts. The truth is he's been a joy to have around—even sick with those nasty chicken pox. You've done a fine job with him, Lily."

"Thank you," Lily said, pleased by the compliment. Considering all that he'd been through, it amazed her that Timmy was such a happy and good-natured child.

"The truth is, I've gotten used to having him stay here. I'm afraid this house is going to seem empty tonight without him now."

"I know what you mean. I don't think I've had a decent night's sleep since he's been gone," Lily confessed. The weather had been atrocious all week—

rainy and cold one day, sunshine and warm temperatures the next. The decision to leave Timmy with Gertie while he was suffering with the worst of the chicken pox instead of shuffling him back and forth in the unpredictable weather had been the right one, she conceded. But it hadn't been easy being away from her son. And although Gertie had offered her the couch, she'd known having both her and Timmy underfoot would have been an even greater imposition on the older woman. "I swear, I don't think I'm ever going to let him spend another night away from me until he gets married," she joked.

Gertie frowned. "You're too young a woman to talk like that."

"Like what?"

"Like you don't ever expect to marry again, maybe have more children."

"I don't," Lily informed her. Aware of Timmy playing just a few feet away, she lowered her voice. "I have Timmy. He's all that I want or need."

Gertie shook her head. "You feel that way now because you had a rough time of it with that man you were married to. But not all men are like him. You're still a young woman, Lily. Too young to shut yourself off from the world the way you do. Someday you'll meet someone else."

For a moment, an image of Michael Sullivan's face came to mind, surprising her. Just as quickly she dismissed it. Probably because Gina had asked her whether or not he'd come by to check out the place next to hers, she reasoned. As far as she knew, he hadn't. And he hadn't been back to the diner, for which she was grateful. "I don't want to meet anyone else."

"Well, you should. You deserve more. And so does that boy of yours."

"Timmy and I have each other. We don't need anyone else," Lily insisted. She didn't expect Gertie to understand. How could she? The woman had out-lived two husbands and both of her marriages had been happy. Whereas her own marriage to Adam had left her feeling worthless, nothing more than a pretty bauble to be dressed up and shown off, a vessel for Adam's lust. While she had known others had envied her lifestyle and Adam's seeming devotion, she'd felt like an animal locked in a cage. Never again did she want to experience that feeling.

"If you'd let me help you, lend you the money to hire a good lawyer, you could file for divorce and—"

"Gertie, now's not the time for this discussion," Lily warned. She knew her friend meant well, but there was no way she could ever tell Gertie the full details of why she'd left Adam. She'd already told her more than she should and, in doing so, she worried that she'd exposed the older woman to potential danger.

"All right. But you need to be thinking about the future, Lily. While there's nothing wrong with working at the diner, you're too smart a girl to be content with waiting tables."

"I know," Lily told her. In truth, she had thought more than once about going to school, getting some training and even maybe starting a business of her own. She'd even daydreamed a time or two about being able to buy a house instead of renting. But how she could do any of those things when trying to stay out of Adam's reach remained her greatest concern. She thought again about the disk and the phone call she'd made to the FBI. She'd worried herself sick for nearly a week, fearful they would somehow connect the call to her.

"If you decided to go back to school a few nights a week, I wouldn't mind keeping Timmy for you."

"Thanks, Gertie. I appreciate that and I promise to think about it." Eager to change the subject, she said, "But right now, I'm just going to enjoy having my son with me again. I thought we'd stop at the park on the way home so he can play outside for a while."

"I'm sure he'll like that," Gertie said, her expression softening as she looked at Timmy. "With the weather so nasty and him running a temperature and itching from those chicken pox, the poor little lamb's been cooped up in this house way too long. I'm sure it'll do him good to be outdoors for a change."

"That's what I thought, too," Lily said, and was relieved that her friend had dropped the discussion about divorcing Adam and her plans for the future. She walked over to where Timmy was making racing noises with his new toy and knelt down. "Hey, sweetie, how would you like to go to the park?"

"Park?" Timmy cried out excitedly. He immediately abandoned his new car and scrambled to his feet. "Go to park, Mommy. Go to park."

Lily laughed. "All right. But first you need to kiss Gertie goodbye and thank her for taking such good care of you."

He ran over, hugged the older woman around one thick leg and offered his face to her for a kiss. When Gertie bent over, he gave her a big kiss and said, "Tank you taking care of me."

"Oh, you're welcome, snuggle bug," Gertie told him, ruffling his hair.

"Come, Mommy," Timmy said, tugging on her hand. "We go to park."

"All right, we're going." She pressed a kiss to Gertie's wrinkled cheek and said, "Thanks again. For everything."

Eager to take advantage of what was left of the afternoon, Lily strapped Timmy, along with his teddy, into his safety seat in the rear of the car and stored his suitcase in the trunk. After shutting the trunk, she started toward the driver's side and paused, suddenly alert. She had the strangest sensation that she was being watched.

A shiver raced down Lily's spine as she pulled open the car door. All the while she listened closely. She heard the birds chirping above her in the oak trees that shaded the street, heard the dog bark next door. A cat's yowl and a hiss followed. Unable to shake the feeling that she was being observed, she glanced down the street, noted a woman in her early twenties jogging with her dog. A look in the opposite direction revealed an elderly couple taking advantage of the mild springlike weather, strolling down the sidewalk.

She noted the way the woman's hand was tucked into the crook of the gentleman's arm and was struck by the oneness of the pair.

"Park, Mommy," Timmy demanded from the back seat.

"All right, big guy," she said. And telling herself she was only imagining things, Lily slid behind the wheel of the car and headed for the park.

"Bingo," Michael muttered as he watched Lily from his hunkered-down position in the seat of his Bronco. Only now could he acknowledge that he'd begun to worry that something might have happened to the little boy. And for a moment his excitement at finally seeing the kid had made him less than discreet. It was why, he suspected, that she'd suddenly begun looking around her.

But seeing the boy now, knowing that he was safe, sent relief flooding through his system. He didn't know why the kid had been staying at the Boudreaux woman's house all this time, and the truth was he didn't care. He was simply glad that, at last, she had the boy with her.

When Lily's car pulled away from the curb, Michael started his truck and followed her. When she turned onto the winding road that snaked through Audubon Park, Michael took care to remain far enough behind her so that she wouldn't spot him. After she stopped her vehicle across from the playground and raced with the little boy toward the swings, he parked the truck several hundred yards away beneath one of the moss-draped oaks and shut off the engine. Then he reached for his binoculars.

The kid was small, Michael thought as he watched Lily pushing the little boy on the swing. He'd turned three only a few weeks ago, Michael recalled, remembering the data in the file Webster had given him. The boy was fair like his mother, Michael noted, but his hair was darker, sort of a sandy-brown color. And although he had his mother's nose and mouth, his eyes were brown like Webster's. When the little boy tipped his head back and laughed, Michael recognized the smile immediately. It was Lily's smile, he realized, and he couldn't help remembering that jolt to his system when she had laughed the other day in the diner.

He shifted his gaze to Lily. Sunshine slanted across her face and he was struck once more by her fragile beauty. When she laughed at something her son said, Michael experienced that same one-two punch of desire again and swore.

Irritated with his reaction to the woman, he reminded himself of who and what she was—Elisabeth Webster, Adam Webster's trophy wife. A woman who had drugged her wealthy, older husband and kidnapped his son.

Yet, as she pushed her son on the swing, Michael noticed there was an edginess to Lily's movements. And that her eyes were continuously moving, searching, watching. When she stared over in the direction of the trees where he was parked, Michael held his breath a moment and wondered if she had spotted him. Then her gaze moved past him and seemed to search some spot beyond. Had that been fear in those green eyes? he wondered.

The notion that she was in trouble—and not just for robbing her husband and kidnapping his son— gnawed at him, stirring old feelings and protective instincts inside him he thought he'd buried a long time ago. Yet even as he tried to shake the urges that Lily stirred in him, he struggled once again with the image of the calculating woman Webster had described. He wanted to believe Lily was a coldhearted female and not this seemingly delicate woman playing with her child.

And what about the money? You've thought from the outset that the money Webster was willing to pay to find her was excessive, didn't you?

Michael frowned at the voices playing havoc inside his head. If Timmy and Lily were his, wouldn't he pay anything to get them back? And if Lily belonged to him, wouldn't he be just as tied up in knots over her as Webster apparently was? He knew that the answer to both questions was yes. But Timmy didn't belong to him. And neither did Lily, he reminded himself. Especially not Lily.

Face it, Sullivan. You didn't like Webster. But the main reason you didn't like the man was because you wanted what's his. You wanted his wife, and you're looking for excuses to play hero so you can keep her for yourself.

Michael stared at Lily, forced himself to see beyond the delicate creature that she appeared to be.

Again he went over all the facts of the case: Lily marrying a man old enough to be her father, Lily drugging her husband, Lily stealing cash from her husband's safe, Lily stealing her son. To do any of those things, she would have had to plan, to scheme.

Just the way that Giselle had planned and schemed. Giselle. He recalled her coming into the bar where he had gone for a few beers after work, and remembered how blinded he had been by her beauty. She'd been so fragile-looking and he'd fallen for her hard-luck story, hook, line and sinker. And because he had, he'd unleashed a viper into their midst. Suddenly, as though it were yesterday instead of five years ago, he was back in Houston…

Cursing the rainstorm that had created a gridlock in traffic, Michael slammed his truck into Park and, heedless of the rain that continued to pummel him, started for the warehouse. His boots skidded along a slick spot. He righted himself and prayed that the thundering rain would conceal the sound of his feet slapping the wet surface. He ran past an empty crate, ignored the scurry of rodents and stench of rotting fruit.

Got to save Pete. Got to save Pete.

He repeated the words like a mantra. He'd known something was wrong with Pete for weeks now. He'd felt it in his gut, sensed it in the way his partner had been acting—distracted, secretive, edgy. So why hadn't he listened to his instincts and confronted his friend?

Because he hadn't wanted to believe Pete had

turned. Just as he hadn't wanted to admit that there had been something going on between Pete and Giselle. Giselle, who looked like an angel, and seemed so helpless, so vulnerable. Only now did he realize it had all been an act—that she'd used him to get to Pete.

"What are you doing? That's my money," Pete yelled.

"No, Mr. Crenshaw. It is my money. And these are my drugs."

Michael froze at the sound of Alexi's voice. For the past six months they'd been working a special assignment, setting up a drug sting to nail the Russian who had been dealing in the Houston area.

"But you can't do that," Pete argued.

"Oh, but I can," Alexi insisted. "Did you really think I did not know what you and your partner, Sullivan, were up to? That I would be foolish enough to make a transaction with two Houston police detectives?"

Michael retrieved the gun from inside of his boot and released the safety. Taking care to remain quiet, he kept his back pressed against the wall of the empty warehouse as he edged his way around the corner. He dropped low, made his way over to a set of metal drums near the door to look inside. His blood ran cold as he took in the scene. Alexi stood in front of a table containing an open briefcase stacked with money and a suitcase filled with bags of cocaine. While Alexi trained his gun on Pete, one of his men disarmed Pete.

"But how did you know—"

"That this was a setup? And that you were willing to double-cross your partner and keep the money for yourself?" Alexi laughed. He snapped his fingers and another man came out of the shadows with Giselle. He shoved her toward the Russian.

"Giselle," Pete said.

"I'm sorry," she murmured.

"Such a pretty, fragile little thing, don't you think?" Alexi traced the muzzle of his gun along Giselle's cheek. "I had hoped her charms would work on your partner. But although Detective Sullivan was quite taken with her sad tale and was willing to help her, he was uninterested in becoming more intimate and telling her about his work. You, on the other hand, were not. You were quite willing to share, how do you say, pillow talk?"

"Pete, I'm sorry. I—"

Alexi backhanded her, and when Pete started to go for him, the bruiser cocked his gun.

"Alexi, please. Can't you just take the money and drugs and let him go?"

"You know that is not possible, my dear. Unfortunately, this affection you have for Detective Crenshaw has made you somewhat of a liability. I am afraid we will have to alter our little scenario."

"What do you mean?" Giselle asked, and even at a distance Michael could see the woman was petrified. Only now did she realize what was going to happen.

"I mean, my dear, that you will have to die along with your detective."

"Alexi, please," Giselle pleaded.

He shoved her toward Pete. *"What a pity it will be for the detective's family to discover that he was not only a dirty cop who stole money and drugs, but that he ran away with his mistress. And what could be more fitting than to have the two lovers die in a fiery car explosion in their haste to escape? Of course, the money and drugs will be destroyed in the accident."*

"You'll never get away with this," Pete told him as he held a sobbing Giselle in his arms. *"Sullivan knows what's going down."*

"Unfortunately, your Detective Sullivan won't be able to tell anyone, because when he arrives later tonight for the exchange, you will have killed him with your gun before escaping with the money and drugs. Now enough chitchat. Victor, get the suitcases."

As Victor put down his gun to do his boss's bidding, Michael knew this would be his only chance. With his weapon drawn, he jumped out into the opening. *"Drop the gun,"* he ordered the man holding the gun on Pete. *"Drop it now or I put a bullet through your boss's head."*

"Ah, Detective Sullivan. You decided to join us," Alexi said calmly.

"Tell him to drop his weapon," Michael commanded.

"Come, come, now, Detective. There are three of us, and only one of you. Do you really think you will succeed?"

"Maybe. Maybe not. But I know if I go down, you're going with me."

The smile the Russian gave him had the blood chilling in Michael's veins. "Boris, take them out."

Bullets flew. Alexi went down. Something hot stung Michael's shoulder, but not before he'd taken out Victor. He swung his gun toward the bruiser named Boris. And in what seemed like slow motion, Michael saw the big guy aim his gun at Giselle, heard Pete yell out and throw his body in front of her...

"Mommy, look!"

The sound of Timmy squealing for his mother jolted Michael back to the present. Michael swallowed hard, waited for his heartbeat to slow and picked up the binoculars again.

He watched as Lily laughed and swooped her giggling son from the swing to spin him around in her arms. And he thought of Petey and Micky.

As he looked at Lily again he thought about how the money he'd get for handing her and the boy to Webster would go a long way to making the Crenshaws' lives a lot easier.

Suppose Lily really was in trouble?

Then that was her problem. He was out of the white-knight business, Michael reminded himself. Putting aside the binoculars, he reached for his cell phone. All he had to do was punch in Webster's number and tell the man he'd located his wife and son. Webster would be on the next plane, and this time tomorrow he'd be collecting the rest of his money.

Michael rubbed at his eyes and tried to envision

himself on that sailboat, sailing around the world and not having to take any more jobs like this one for a year, maybe longer. Yet try as he might, he couldn't get the image of Lily laughing out of his head. Irritated with himself for allowing the woman to get under his skin he opened his eyes and punched out Webster's number.

"Webster—"

"This is Sullivan," Michael began, only to have what was a recorded message tell him to leave his name and number.

Irritated, Michael said, "This is Sullivan. I've found your wife and son."

Eight

In the bedroom of his Miami penthouse suite, Adam Webster tuned out the sound of the phone ringing in the adjoining office as he moved between the legs of the young blonde beneath him. With the lights dimmed, and if she kept her mouth shut, he could almost believe that she was Elisabeth.

Elisabeth. His Elisabeth, he thought as he filled his hands with her pale breasts and squeezed. He shoved himself into her, smiled as she sucked in a breath. But when her eyes widened, he saw that they were blue. Not green. And he faltered.

"Close your eyes," he ordered, wanting to re-create the illusion that it was Elisabeth beneath him and not the girl from the club. When she closed her eyes as he'd instructed, he began to move inside her again.

Sweat beaded between his shoulders, along his forehead, above his lip as he pumped into her. Harder. Deeper. Faster. Ignoring her moans and the fingers clawing at him, he thought of Elisabeth. Of how beautiful she was. Of how perfect she was. Of how he had trained her in the ways to please him. Of the envy he saw in other men's eyes when they saw her with him. Of the knowledge that no other man had come before him, and that no other man would ever have her. Only him. Only him. Because Elisabeth belonged to him. Only him. "You're mine," he told the girl as he rammed himself into her again and again and again. Finally he felt the rush that had been building to a peak. His body stiffened. He drove himself into her one last time and shouted, "Elisabeth!" Then he collapsed on top of her.

Adam lay atop her, irritated that the rush that came with sexual relief had been too short and less than satisfying. He considered increasing his dosage of Viagra next time to try to sustain the pleasure.

"Adam, I can't breathe."

At the sound of her voice, Adam rolled off the girl and onto his back. While her voice might have that hint of the South as Elisabeth's had, it lacked the softness and refinement.

"Was I okay?" she asked him, reminding him of an eager puppy.

"Yeah, you were fine," he said, and patted her rear. "Why don't you go get me a drink."

When she climbed out of the bed and moved across to the bar, Adam looked away. Despite having her hair restyled and died the pale shade that had been Elisabeth's, the girl's hair lacked the silky texture and thickness that Elisabeth's had. As he studied her figure, he noted more differences. Elisabeth's waist had been smaller than this girl's. So had her breasts. Elisabeth's breasts had been full and rounded, not the size of grapefruits because of implants. He angled his gaze to the thatch of dark hair between her thighs and as she started toward him he scowled. Elisabeth had been a real blonde.

"Here you go," she said, returning to join him on the bed. "Just the way you like it."

Adam sat up, sipped the martini she'd prepared for him. As he enjoyed the drink, she began to pet him, stroke him, lick him. As her tongue circled his shaft, he could feel himself growing hard again. He finished off the martini, set the glass aside and enjoyed the feel of her mouth working on him.

But when she glanced up at him adoringly, he found the blue eyes disturbing. "Tomorrow I want you to go see an eye doctor and have him fit you for green contacts."

"But my eyes are blue," she protested. "Everyone says they're my best feature."

"I don't care what anybody else says," he said, fisting his hand in her hair. "I like green eyes. Understand?"

"Yes, Adam," she whispered.

"That's a good girl," he said, and loosened the hair in his fingers.

And when she went back to stroking and fondling him, he pretended it was Elisabeth who was kissing him. That it was Elisabeth touching him—just the way he had taught her. Finally, when she had him fully aroused once more, Adam reached for her.

Tossing her onto her back, he spread her legs apart, threaded his fingers through the tight curls. Dark curls, he noted, annoyed that the defect had once again pulled him from his fantasy of Elisabeth. "And when you finish with the eye doctor, go to the beauty parlor and have them dye this little bush blond."

"All right," she said.

Closing his eyes, Adam entered her in one swift thrust. He heard her breath catch as he filled her, and he pretended once again that she was Elisabeth. That it was Elisabeth's sweet body beneath him. That it was Elisabeth's moans he heard coming from her lips as he drove himself into her. That it was Elisabeth's voice that cried out his name. That it was Elisabeth he'd once again mastered and made his own.

Kneeling down in front of the small flower bed in her backyard, Lily used her hand spade to dig a hole for the bedding plants. Satisfied it was the right size, she removed the cluster of red impatiens from the little black plastic container and placed the clump of dirt and roots into the hole. Very gently, she smoothed the rest of the dirt around the blooms.

It was coming together, she thought as she looked at the neat row of flowers she'd planted. A quick glance across the yard revealed Timmy was still occupied with his toy lawn mower and was busily running the green plastic thing over the stretch of grass pretending to cut it. Pleased to see him feeling so much better, she was glad that Nancy Lee had agreed to let her have the weekend off so that she could spend it with him. She knew that Nancy Lee hadn't wanted to agree to her request—not with Mardi Gras only a few days away. But the lady had relented on the condition that Lily agree to work both on Lundi Gras, the Monday before Mardi Gras, and on Mardi Gras morning to accommodate the breakfast crowd. Since she had no intention of participating in the Mardi Gras craziness anyway, she'd agreed.

Thankfully, the weather was cooperating for a change. The sunshine and warmer temperatures were just what Timmy needed after being cooped up with the chicken pox for so long, she thought. Scooting over a few inches, she went back to digging holes for the last of the bedding plants. While she knew it had been foolish to spend money and time planting flowers that, in all probability, she wouldn't be around to enjoy for long, she hadn't been able to resist the delicate blooms when she'd spied them in the store. The springlike weather had also beckoned, as well as her son's eagerness to be outdoors. He was such a good little boy, such a sweet boy. And if pretending that their lives were normal for a little while by planting flowers in a garden and allowing him to play at cutting grass made Timmy happy, then it was the least she could do.

For a moment all the weariness of the past seven months weighed upon her. So did the guilt. Because of her poor choices and her failure to recognize the depth of Adam's obsession with her, Timmy had nearly been killed. He would never know a father's love. He would never have his father teach him how to ride a bike or pitch a baseball or hoist him up on his shoulders. Because of her, he was in danger from his own father. She would have to make sure that he remained safe until Adam was no longer a threat.

And if that meant moving from town to town, telling so many lies that she was no longer sure what was true and what wasn't, then she would do it. She would do whatever she had to in order to protect her son.

"I help you, Mommy?"

Shaking off her somber thoughts, Lily smiled at her son, who had abandoned his lawn mower and now squatted beside her. He stared down at the holes she was digging with serious brown eyes.

"Okay, sweetie," she said. She handed him the plastic yellow spade she'd bought for him and proceeded to show him how to scoop out the earth.

Ten minutes later, when they'd finished with the last of the plants, Lily stood. "Good job," she said as she dusted off her hands and jeans, and was surprised to discover that she was wearing quite a bit of the dirt, while Timmy had managed to remain clean. "Now we need to water the flowers."

"Why?"

"Because flowers and plants get thirsty. Just like you."

"Oh," he commented, watching as she set the nozzle of the hose on mist and began to water the flowering plants.

"I help," Timmy insisted.

"All right," Lily said and handed him the hose.

Very carefully, he watered the tiny garden for a few minutes. Then he turned toward her. As he did so, the spray hit Lily and she shrieked. She held up her hands and laughed as the water got her—much to Timmy's delight. Thinking it was a new game, Timmy began to chase her with the hose.

"Timmy, stop," she said. Continuing to laugh, she made a halfhearted effort to run from him.

At the sound of a man's laughter, Lily froze. She grabbed her son, knocking the hose from his hands. "Be still," she told Timmy when he squirmed, fear-induced adrenaline making her voice sharper than she'd intended.

"Lily?"

Only then did she realize that it wasn't Adam or one of his men. It was Michael. Michael Sullivan. "What are you doing here?" she demanded, that metallic taste of fear still in her mouth.

He appeared somewhat taken aback by the question, but he said, "I tried ringing the bell. But there wasn't any answer. When I heard laughing, I decided to check out back. I'm sorry if I frightened you."

Embarrassed, and knowing she'd overreacted, Lily put Timmy down. "You didn't. Frighten me, I mean," she fibbed. "I just didn't hear you come into the yard. You caught me off guard."

"Again, I apologize. I just finished looking at the place next door."

"Is Mrs. Davis with you?" Lily asked.

"No. She had some kind of Mardi Gras ball to go to tonight and was in a hurry. But she said to tell you hello. I just came by to thank you for telling me about the place."

Feeling foolish for overreacting, she averted her gaze while she turned off the hose. "You don't have to thank me. Gina's the one who remembered the place was for rent."

"But you're the one who referred me to Mrs. Davis. And my momma was real strict about us boys thanking people properly. You wouldn't want me to get in trouble with my momma, now, would you?"

"Something tells me it wouldn't be the first time you were in trouble with your momma. And I imagine you're very good at sweet-talking your way out of it."

"I'm not sure if I should be insulted or complimented by that remark. So I think I'll ignore it." He stooped down, bringing himself to eye level with Timmy. "And who is this?"

Still wary, Lily kept a protective hand on Timmy's shoulder. "This is my son, Timmy."

If he was surprised to learn she had a son, he gave no indication. He simply held out his hand and said, "Hi, Timmy. I'm Michael."

Timmy looked up at her and when she nodded, he shook Michael's hand. "I helped Mommy pwant fwowers."

"And it looks to me like you did a good job."

"They get thirsty just like people," he explained.

"Is that so?"

Timmy nodded. "Are you thirsty? I give you a drink."

"Timmy," Lily said, giving her son's shoulder a

squeeze. "Mr. Sullivan isn't thirsty. He just came by to thank Mommy."

"Why?"

Lily rolled her eyes. "I'm afraid that's his favorite new word."

"Because I'm looking for a place to live and your mommy was nice enough to tell me about the house next door," he said in response to Timmy. "Maybe you'll let me take your mommy and you to lunch so that I can say thank-you."

"That's really not necessary," Lily told him. "You didn't say. Are you going to take the place?"

As Michael stood, he gave her a look that said he knew she'd deliberately changed the subject. "First off, it may not be necessary for me to thank you by taking you to lunch, but I'd like to. And as far as the house goes, I'm not sure if I'll be renting it or not."

"You didn't like it?"

"Oh, I liked it just fine. But I won't know for another week or two if I'll be able to get on with that offshore company. If I do, and the place is still available, I'll probably take it. If I don't, then I'll be moving on and try to get on someplace else. In the meantime, I've managed to convince the hotel manager to let me stay on at the current rate—even if it is Mardi Gras time."

"Then you're lucky. I understand hotel rooms are at a premium here this time of year—especially if the weather holds up like this."

"So how about that lunch?" he asked.

"Really, Michael, I appreciate the offer, but—"

"What do you say, Timmy?" he asked, stooping down to face her son. "Will you let me take you and your mom out to lunch?"

"For Happy Meal?"

Michael laughed. "Sure, if that's what you want."

"Happy Meal," he yelled, and launched himself at Michael, who caught him in a bear hug and scooped him up in his arms.

"Timmy," Lily reprimanded, reaching for her son. Adam had wanted nothing to do with Timmy, had never even held him. To see him now being held in a man's arms left her shaken.

"It's okay," he told Lily. "I have a friend with a couple of boys not much older than him. He's a real cute kid. How old is he anyway?"

"I three," Timmy told him, and held up three fingers.

"Three, huh? That's pretty big. So what do you say, big guy? Can I take you and your mom out for a Happy Meal?"

"We can't," Lily told him.

"Why not?" Michael asked, turning those blue eyes on her.

She sighed. "Listen, I'm just going to be direct. I'm flattered by your interest. Really I am. But the thing is, I'm not interested in going out with you."

"I see," he said solemnly. "Well, since we're being direct, I'll confess that I know you're a widow and that you're not involved with anyone, because I asked. So the question is, is it me in particular that you're not interested in going out with? Or is it men in general?''

''Men in general.''

''Okay,'' he said. ''Now what about that Happy Meal? I think I spotted a McDonald's about five blocks from here.''

Lily squinched her eyebrows together. ''Didn't you hear what I said? I don't date.''

''I heard you. But this isn't a date. It's a Happy Meal thank-you.''

''But—''

''I want Happy Meal,'' Timmy said, bouncing in Michael's arms.

''You going to explain to him why you won't at least let me buy you a Happy Meal?''

Lily looked from her son to Michael, read the challenge in his eyes. ''I'm a mess,'' she told him, and pointed to her dirt-stained jeans.

''You look pretty good to me, but if you want to change, go ahead. Timmy and I will wait. Won't we, partner?''

''We wait,'' Timmy said, delighting in the high five Michael gave him.

''But I'll need to shower, not just change my clothes.''

''Go ahead. From what I've seen, you don't wear a lot of gunk on your face like most women, so I don't imagine it'll take you long.''

Lily weighed her options, and decided lunch at McDonald's would be okay. As sweet as her son was, he'd developed a stubborn streak. And while she didn't want to spoil him, she didn't think giving in to such a small demand would do any real damage to her position of authority. "All right. Come on, Timmy," she told her son, holding out her arms for him.

To her surprise, Timmy tightened his arms around Michael.

"You go ahead. I'll take care of him."

Lily hesitated a moment, not at all comfortable leaving her son with anyone but Gertie.

"It's all right. I really do know my way around kids."

"Okay. But I'd feel better if you came inside with him."

Michael set her son down. "Hey, partner, what do you say you take me inside and show me some of your toys while your mommy gets cleaned up?"

"'Kay," Timmy told him, and taking Michael's hand, he led him into the house.

"Okay, partner, you ready to ride the pony?"

"Ready," Timmy said with a giggle.

"Then hang on tight," Michael told the little boy who sat on his back while he proceeded to crawl around on all fours pretending to be a horse.

"Gitty up, horsey," Timmy said.

Michael pretended to buck, laughed when the boy squealed and managed not to yelp when the kid yanked him by the hair. He circled the small living room a second time, making ridiculous whinnying noises like a horse.

''It looks to me like your horsey needs to rest.''

Michael yanked his gaze toward the doorway at the sound of that soft, smoky voice, and he found Lily standing there watching them. True to her word, she'd only taken a few minutes. The ends of her hair were still damp from her shower. Except for a touch of lipstick, her face remained makeup free. Not that she needed any, he thought. Her skin was pale and smooth and perfect. And damned if she didn't take his breath away.

She'd opted for another pair of faded jeans that skimmed her hips and long legs. The chambray shirt she'd worn earlier had been replaced by a long-sleeved, pale-blue T-shirt that clung to her still-damp skin. The desire to slide his hands beneath that T-shirt and cup her breasts hit him like a sucker punch.

''Horsey, gitty up,'' Timmy demanded.

Grateful this time for the little fists yanking at his hair, Michael circled the room again. He was also grateful to be on all fours with Timmy astride him so that Lily wouldn't notice his all too obvious reaction.

''Timmy, I think your horse needs a rest.''

''Why?''

Lily sighed at the question. ''Because the horse needs to go eat.''

''Happy Meal?'' her son asked hopefully.

''Yes, Happy Meal,'' Lily replied, and lifted her son from his back.

But as soon as she set him on his feet he reached for Michael's hand.

Michael laughed and took the boy's hand. ''Come

on, Lily,'' he said. ''This little cowboy and his horse need food.''

''Looks like the horse really did need food,'' Lily commented as she eyed his tray from her side of the booth at the neighborhood McDonald's restaurant.

''What can I say? Us horses need lots of fuel,'' he replied with a smile and bit into one of the two double burgers he'd ordered, along with a supersize French fries and supersize drink.

''Cowboys need food, too,'' Timmy mimicked and bit into his hamburger.

''They sure do,'' Michael said, winking at the boy.

Much to his relief, Lily had relaxed somewhat. While he occasionally caught her checking out their surroundings and the mob scene of kids, parents and teens in the place, she was less edgy than she'd been when he'd shown up at her place. He thought about that wild-eyed fear that had been in her eyes when she'd looked up and seen him standing in her yard, and he couldn't help feeling a twinge of regret at having frightened her.

Michael reached for a French fry, and when he noted that Timmy once again copied his movements, he smiled. The kid really was cute, he thought. He could understand Webster wanting to get him back. But as the thought entered his head he remembered Webster's lack of concern for his son. The man hadn't been interested in getting his kid back. Only his wife. Only Lily.

And not for the first time since leaving that message the previous day did he regret making that call. It was the reason why, when Webster had called him back last night, he hadn't answered the phone. It was also the reason he hadn't returned the man's call as he'd been instructed to do.

"Is something wrong?"

Lily's question jarred him from his dark thoughts. "Nope. Just debating whether or not to get some dessert. What about you, cowboy?" he asked Timmy. "You think you'd like some ice cream?"

"Ice cream," Timmy squealed.

"Oops," Michael said when he glanced up and spied the frown on Lily's face. "Guess I should have asked your mom first. Sorry. You think your little cowboy here could have some ice cream?"

"I suppose if he finishes his hamburger, it would be all right."

Timmy finished the burger and the three of them dug into the ice-cream cones. He and Timmy both went for vanilla cones, while Lily opted for chocolate. While he made quick work of his own ice cream and Timmy was doing a credible job of getting at least half of the thing inside him, Lily took her time. And as he watched her lick the ice cream, flick her tongue at the side of her mouth to catch a dribble of chocolate, Michael found himself becoming aroused again. Worse, he was actually considering lying to Webster and telling the man he had made a mistake, that he hadn't found them.

Realizing the direction of his thoughts, Michael sobered. He must be out of his mind, he thought. If anyone had told him a week ago that he would be sitting in a crowded McDonald's restaurant with a three-year-old boy and a woman he was being paid one million dollars to find, and that he was seriously considering walking away from a once-in-a-lifetime fee, he would have assured them they were nuts. He'd taken the job for the money—money earmarked for Janie and her boys, he reminded himself.

"Finished," Timmy announced, holding up sticky fingers.

"Wait a second," Lily told her son, and abandoned her ice-cream cone. "We'd better get you cleaned up."

"I'll take him," Michael offered. "You go ahead and finish your ice cream." And because she looked as if she might object, Michael scooped up the boy and headed for the men's room.

He cleaned up Timmy, saw that the little guy used the facilities and made the boy laugh when he splashed water on his face. While a cold shower would have been more effective, at least it helped to cool off some of the heated thoughts he'd been having about Lily.

When he returned to the table, he was surprised to find that Lily had bought him a large cup of coffee. "I remembered you ordered a cup after your meals at the diner," she explained, lowering her green eyes shyly.

"Thanks," he told her, sliding back onto his seat at the booth. "What about you?"

"I think I've had enough caffeine for one day,"

she said with a smile. ''I'm not usually much of a lunch-eater. And today I not only had lunch, but dessert, too.''

''Don't tell me you're one of those women who are always on a diet? Because if you ask me, you could even stand to gain a few pounds.''

''Thanks. I think,'' she said, parroting his earlier response to her at a backhanded compliment. ''And no, I'm not a dieter. But I guess I serve so many breakfasts and lunches at the diner, I must inhale some of the food, because I'm usually not hungry until dinnertime.''

''Mommy, I pway on swide?'' Timmy asked, motioning to the playland outside the window where at least a dozen little ones were enjoying themselves.

''Sweetie, we'll come back another time and you can play. Mr. Sullivan needs to be going.''

''I'm in no hurry,'' Michael assured her. ''Come on, I'll take the coffee outside. And while he's playing, maybe I can convince you to let me take you out for dinner and spring for a real thank-you meal.''

''I'll agree to going outside and letting Timmy play while you finish your coffee,'' she said as the three of them headed outdoors. They'd no sooner gone through the doors when Timmy charged straight for the playland.

''And the dinner?'' Michael prompted once they'd sat down at one of the picnic-style tables.

''I meant what I said earlier, Michael. I'm not interested in a relationship.''

"Who said anything about a relationship? All I'm asking is for you to have dinner with me."

"It isn't going to work, you know."

"What isn't going to work?" Michael asked innocently, flashing her a smile.

"You trying to charm me with that sexy little grin of yours."

"You think my grin's sexy?" he asked.

She shot him a reproachful look. "I think you're very skilled at getting people to do what you want—particularly when it comes to women."

"You make me sound like some kind of Casanova."

"I don't mean to. The truth is, I think you're a really sweet guy."

Michael cringed at the description and glanced around furtively. "Careful, you'll ruin my reputation."

Lily laughed, as he'd wanted her to do. "What I'm trying to say is that I like you, and I appreciate your being so nice to Timmy."

"Why do I think there's a 'but' coming?"

"Because there is. But I'm all that Timmy has. His father...his father died before he was born, and neither of us have any other family. So Timmy has to be my first priority. There's no room in my life for anyone else. And if I were to go out with you, well, it just wouldn't be fair to you. You should be spending your time and money on a woman you might have a chance of developing a relationship with. I'm not that woman."

''What if I were to tell you that you're the woman I want?'' The question tripped off his tongue before he could stop it, and Michael was shaken because he realized that he'd meant it.

Lily lowered her gaze, but not before Michael caught the flicker of yearning in those green eyes. He hadn't remained a single heterosexual male for the past thirty-three years without knowing when a woman was attracted to him. Lily was attracted to him—even if she didn't want to be.

''Then I'd have to tell you that I'm sorry, because I'm not available.''

Her statement hit him like a slap to the face, a slap that brought him back to his senses.

Of course, she isn't available. She already has a man—a husband. A husband who's paying you one million bucks to bring her back to him.

The reminder made him furious. With Webster. With her. But mostly with himself. How in the devil had he managed to let his feelings get all tangled up where she was concerned?

''We should go. It's time for Timmy's nap,'' she said, and went to retrieve her son.

Timmy zonked out within minutes of strapping him in the car seat. And since the drive back to Lily's place was relatively silent, Michael used the short trip to get a grip on his ricocheting emotions. By the time he turned onto Lily's street, he had himself and his objectives under control. But judging by the way Lily's fingers kept curling and uncurling around the strap of her purse, he'd made her more nervous than ever.

When he pulled up to the curb in front of her house Lily jumped out of the truck. "If you'll give me a minute to get Timmy inside, I'll come back and get the car seat," she told him.

"Hang on a second." Quickly he exited the truck and came around to the rear passenger door where she was fighting to unhook the safety belt on Timmy. "Why don't you let me get that," he suggested, and without waiting for her to comply, he shoved her fingers aside. He released the catch and removed the slumbering little boy from the seat.

"I'll take him," Lily told him as she held out her arms.

"Go unlock the door, Lily. I'll carry him in for you."

"That's not necessary. I can—"

"Lily, go unlock the door," he said firmly, using the same tone with her that he'd used when reprimanding Janie's boys.

She gave him a mutinous look, removed the car seat from his truck and shut the door. Then she turned and headed up the stairs to the porch of the house. After she'd unlocked the door and placed the car seat on the floor, he followed her inside. "Timmy's room is at the end of the house."

Holding Timmy in his arms, Michael followed her through the long, narrow house. As he did so, he caught glimpses of the small, neat and sparsely furnished rooms. Lily pulled back the colorful comforter atop the bed and Michael laid the little boy down. She covered him, then pressed a kiss to his head before exiting the room and pulling the door almost closed. Silently she headed back toward the front of the house. Since he knew she was probably eager to get rid of him, Michael stopped at the kitchen. "You've done a nice job in here."

Lily paused, turned to face him. "Thanks. And thanks for the lunch."

When she turned and started to lead him to the door again, Michael walked over to the small two-burner stove and said, "I forgot to ask Mrs. Davis. Is it gas or electric here?"

"Gas," she told him with a sigh. "Most of these old shotgun houses are equipped for gas heat."

"I've been meaning to ask how come they call these houses shotguns?"

"Michael, I really did mean what I said. I'm not going to change my mind. There's no room in my life for anyone but my son."

"Not even a friend?" he countered. When she eyed him warily, he told her, "Listen, I understand what you're saying. I may not necessarily agree with it, or even like it. But I do understand. Remember that friend I told you about? The one with the two boys?"

Lily nodded.

"Her name's Janie. Her husband was my best friend, and he was…he died when their youngest son was less than a year old. That was five years ago, and Janie's been totally devoted to her two boys ever since," Michael explained, opting for the truth and hoping that maybe by doing so Lily would open up and tell him who she really was. He didn't know why it suddenly mattered to him that she be honest with him—especially when he hadn't been honest with her. But for whatever reason, it did matter. "Anyway, a couple of weeks ago Janie told me that she thought maybe she'd been unfair to her boys and to herself by shutting herself off from any other relationship all these years. Maybe you're making the same mistake."

"I'm not," Lily insisted.

"All right. But it seems to me that everybody could use a friend. I know *I* could. I'd like to think that, if nothing else, we can be friends."

"I'm not sure that's possible."

"We could try."

"Michael, it's—"

"Come on, Lily. All I'm asking is for friendship. How much harm can there be in you offering me a cup of coffee and telling me about shotgun houses?"

Nine

Lily didn't know how it had happened. One minute she'd been prepared to kick the man out, tell him she didn't want him as a lover or a friend. And the next minute she was brewing a pot of coffee and sitting across the kitchen table from him, explaining the history of shotgun houses.

"So what you're saying is that the people built these long, skinny houses as a way to beat the tax collector."

"Partially," Lily conceded. "But since the lots were only thirty-by-a hundred feet, it was actually an efficient way to house a lot of people on a limited piece of land. Since this particular house is a double, it was probably built originally to house two families."

"There certainly are a lot of them in this neighborhood."

"Not just in this neighborhood. You'll find shotguns throughout New Orleans. Depending on whether or not you classify the side-halls as shotguns, about forty-nine percent of the housing in the city consists of shotguns."

Michael took a bite of one of the chocolate chip cookies she'd piled on a plate between them. "Shotguns. You think when this place was built, the owner actually shot a bullet through the front door and then dashed around back to see if it went straight through the rear door without hitting anything in between?"

Lily shivered as Michael repeated the explanation she'd given him on how the houses were given their name. "I certainly hope not," she said. After her own experience of finding Timmy with Adam's gun, she didn't ever want to see a gun again.

"How old do you think this house is?"

"It's Italianate in style, and those were most popular during the Victorian period and post-Civil War until about 1900," she told him, caught up in the subject. She'd always adored architecture and had spent countless hours studying houses. "If you noted the brackets on the front galley—"

"Brackets?"

"The fancy millwork," she explained. "It's a hallmark of the late-Victorian style."

"For someone who's only lived here for a few months, you certainly know a lot about the architecture."

Lily flushed. She wrapped her hands around the glass of milk she'd poured herself in lieu of coffee. "I like houses. Ever since I was a little girl, I used to make sketches of homes I liked. And it's become sort of a hobby of mine to study old houses like this one. It's fun being able to find identifying marks like the brackets or the quoins."

"Coins?"

Lily laughed. "It's pronounced coins, but it's spelled 'quoins.' Those are the raised, squarish decorative elements that line the top to bottom at the front edges of facades on some of the houses. Anyway, it's a challenge to try to analyze all the components of a house and be able to pinpoint its age and the era it was built in."

"Maybe you should think about going into restoration work. You know, someone who comes in and takes an old place like this one and restores it to the way it looked originally."

"I could never do that," she told him.

"Why not? You certainly know enough about it."

"You need a degree in architecture and probably one in design or something before you can get a job like that. I never even went to college."

"So? Go now and get your degree," Michael said as though it were the easiest thing in the world.

"I'm twenty-five years old. And I have a child to support."

"First off, twenty-five is young. And there are women a lot older than you are with more than one child to support who go back to college. You can, too. There are all kinds of programs available to help working mothers. Seeing how much you love this stuff, I think you'd be crazy not to consider making a career of it."

"I already have a career. I'm a wi—" Lily caught herself, cutting off the familiar response Adam had given her when she'd told him she wanted to go to college. "I'm a mother," she corrected. "Being Timmy's mother is the only career I want."

Michael narrowed his eyes. "You were about to say you have a career as a wife, weren't you? Is that why you didn't go to college and study architecture? Because your husband didn't want you to?"

Nervous, Lily brought her hand to her throat. "My husband preferred that I be a full-time wife...and a mother after Timmy was born," she added.

"I thought you said he died before Timmy was born?"

Lily paled, realized the slip she'd made. "He did. But when I was pregnant, he used to say how good it was going to be for Timmy to have a mother who didn't work and could be at home with him instead of leaving him with a nanny or sending him to a day-care center."

"It sounds to me like your husband was pretty domineering."

"He wasn't," Lily defended, because she felt that she should. "My husband was older than me. He knew a great deal more than I did, and I respected his judgment."

"Yet you work now, and I assume Timmy's in day care while you're at the diner," he pointed out.

"Timmy stays with a friend of mine while I'm working. And I work now because I'm a widow and I have to."

"Didn't your husband have any insurance?"

"Yes. Of course he did," Lily said. "But his death was unexpected and the coverage wasn't enough."

''You never did say what happened to him.''

Lily's gaze shot to Michael's face. ''What do you mean?''

''I mean, how did your husband die? Was he ill? Or in an accident?''

''It was a car accident,'' she said, wanting to kick herself for being so jumpy. ''I was pregnant with Timmy and he was racing to get me to the hospital. Only there was a nasty rainstorm that night, and the roads were dark and wet,'' she told him, describing the night she'd gone into labor and Adam had taken her to the hospital. She'd been so frightened when she'd started to bleed that night and Adam had talked of miscarriages, had claimed a miscarriage was God's way of correcting a mistake.

''What happened?''

Lily swallowed and pulled her thoughts back to the present. ''He took one of the turns too fast and lost control of the car and hit a median. I was thrown from the car, hardly had a scratch on me. But my husband…he was killed instantly.'' She'd told the lie so often, Lily could almost believe it was true. That Adam had wanted Timmy. That there really had been an accident and that he'd died rushing her to the hospital for Timmy's birth.

''I'm sorry,'' Michael said. ''That must have been pretty tough for you. I mean, having your baby on the same day you lost your husband.''

''Yes, it was.'' Lily closed her eyes a moment, recalled her utter joy and relief when she hadn't miscarried and Timmy had been born a month early, but healthy. And she'd been so sure that once Adam had seen his son, held him in his arms, he would love Timmy as much as she did. Only, Adam hadn't wanted to hold Timmy, and he'd looked at their son as though he were an annoying pet who'd just soiled his Aubusson rug. Adam's only concern had been whether the C-section would leave a scar and how long it would be before she could resume her marital duties.

"Lily?"

She snapped her eyes open at the feel of Michael's hand touching hers. She jerked away from him. "I'm sorry."

He frowned, stared at her out of worried blue eyes. "Are you okay?"

"Yes. I just don't like talking about it." And that was the truth. "I think I'm going to break down and have a cup of coffee after all. Would you like another cup?"

"Sure," he told her. "But why don't you let me get the coffee."

"No. I'll do it," she insisted, needing to move, needing to escape the memories Michael's questions had brought to the surface.

"Timmy? Was that your husband's name?"

"No. Timmy's named after my maternal grandfather."

"You and your grandfather were close?" he asked.

"No. I never even knew him. But my grandmother raised me, and I guess I learned to love him through her memories."

"She sounds pretty special. Does she live here in New Orleans?"

"No. She passed away when I was fifteen," she said as she set out a cup for herself and reached for the coffeepot. "You certainly do ask a lot of questions."

"Sorry. Occupational hazard, I guess. I used to be a cop."

Lily felt the glass coffeepot slide through her fingers. And then suddenly everything seemed to move in slow motion. She heard the glass carafe shatter, could see herself grabbing for it, the shards of glass slicing her hand, blood dripping onto the countertop and floor. Through a haze in which the room had begun to spin, she saw Michael's lips move as he called out her name, saw him rushing toward her.

"Dammit! Lily? Lily?"

Finally his voice penetrated. So did the icy water coming from the faucet at the sink under which he'd shoved her hand. Lily looked at the blood running down the drain with the water. Suddenly she could feel the net closing around her again. And she was back in Miami, trapped once again in the fancy house with Adam. Only this time…this time Timmy was dead.

"Lily, look at me," he demanded.

Lily looked up at him, and when she realized it was Michael her knees went slack.

Michael swore again. He shoved Lily's hand back under the water. He had expected a reaction from her.

Hell, he'd wanted one, he admitted. He wanted to see the guilt cloud her eyes, maybe even a flicker of fear that he was onto her. He'd wanted something, anything, that would make him shut off these tender feelings she kept stirring inside him. Because telling himself that she'd drugged and robbed her husband, then kidnapped her son sure as hell wasn't working.

Still holding her hand under the running water, he kept pressure on the cut for another minute or two until the bleeding slowed. Then he smoothed his thumb over the laceration and was relieved to note it wasn't as deep as he'd initially thought, given all the blood. "It looks like a clean cut," he told her as he shut off the water and wrapped a dish towel around her hand. Because her color was still off and he felt guilty as hell, he said, "I sure hope my telling you I used to be a cop didn't shake you up that bad. I mean, if you've got a string of unpaid parking tickets you're worried about, your secret's safe with me," he added.

"No. I don't have any parking tickets," she said, her voice not much more than a whisper. "It wasn't anything you said. I…I was just clumsy."

He only wished he believed her. "Well, just for the record, I resigned my badge five years ago. Nowadays I'm just an average Joe working the oil rigs and trying to save enough money to buy myself a sailboat and take a year off to sail it around the world."

"That sounds nice—to be able to just go away like that."

"It will be if I ever get enough set aside to actually do it. Okay, why don't you sit down now," he said, and led her to a kitchen chair. "Do you have a first-aid kit?"

"In the medicine cabinet in the bathroom."

"Keep the towel on that cut while I get some bandages." He looked at her ashen face. "Still feeling light-headed?"

"A little," she admitted.

"Try putting your head between your knees," he instructed as he pressed his hand to the back of her head and guided her down. "I'll be back in a second."

Michael raced to the bathroom. It was small like the rest of the house. Clean, neat, utilitarian, he thought as he opened the no-frills white chest and removed the plastic kit. Certainly not the lavish bathroom he would expect for a woman who'd stolen a fortune in cash and jewels. Once again, the image of Lily struck him as a picture out of focus. Either the woman was a hell of an actress or Webster had lied to him about how much money she'd stolen. But the man hadn't been lying about wanting her back. He'd seen that same love-struck look when Pete had told him he'd fallen in love with Giselle.

Giselle had been one hell of an actress, he reminded himself. He'd bought her sob story about the abusive boyfriend, taken her under his wing and even introduced her to Pete and his family. And all the time, she'd been playing him, looking to hook up with one of them so she could tip off her boss about the drug sting on which he and Pete had been working.

Maybe Lily was playing him, too, he reasoned as

he headed back to the kitchen with the first-aid kit. She lifted her head and looked at him as he approached. And Michael's chest tightened at the weariness in her expression, the haunted look in those green eyes. There was a fragility about her, a sadness, that made him think she bore more resemblance to a broken doll than to a conniving female.

He knelt down in front of her and opened the first-aid kit. After removing the antiseptic, he set it aside and unwrapped the towel. As he'd initially thought, the cut was clean and it didn't appear deep enough to have severed any tendons. He doused a cotton ball with antiseptic, then glanced up at her. "This is probably going to sting a bit," he warned. "Ready?"

She nodded.

Michael dabbed at the laceration. When she sucked in a breath, he blew on the cut, hating to cause her pain. Quickly, he tore open a Band-Aid and placed it over the cut. "You're probably going to have a small scar, but I don't think the wound is deep enough to have done any real damage. You'll still probably need to get a couple of stitches—"

"No stitches."

Michael lifted his gaze to her face. "Hey, if you're scared it's going to hurt trust me, once they give you a shot you won't feel a thing. Growing up, I was a regular in the E.R. My mom probably had to take me a dozen times. She blames me for every one of her gray hairs. Anyway, once they gave me the shot, they could have sewn my fingers together and I wouldn't have felt it." He stood, closed the first-aid kit. "Why don't I go get Timmy and I'll take you to the hospital.''

"No," she said firmly. "No hospitals. No stitches.''

"Lily—''

"Michael, I'm fine. You said yourself the cut's not bad.''

"Yeah, but I'm no doctor. And that's more than a scratch you've got there. You should have it looked at. Stitching it would probably minimize the scarring.''

"I don't care about the scar," she told him, and stood. "And I'd just as soon not spend the money if I don't need to.''

"Then I'll pay for it. It's the least I can do since I'm the reason you cut yourself in the first place.''

"I hardly think my clumsiness is your fault," she told him.

"Lily," he began, intent on reasoning with her.

"I mean it, Michael. I'm not going to the hospital," she insisted, the sternness of her expression matched by her voice. "I'm okay. Other than a little sting, I hardly feel it. Besides, I really need to get this mess cleaned up before Timmy wakes up. He might cut himself on the broken glass.''

"All right. No hospitals. But you sit down and I'll clean this up.''

"But, I—''

"This time *I* mean it," he said, tossing her words back at her. "You've got about as much color as that sink over there. Besides, you're better off not using that hand for a while or it might start bleeding again."

Although she didn't argue with him, Michael suspected she wanted to. He could see that combative spark come back into her eyes and was grateful to see it again—especially after seeing that terror-stricken look when he'd told her he'd been a cop. Guilt and regret nagged at him. Worse, the more time he spent with her, the more worried he was that he was getting in too deep. Annoyed with himself, he asked, "Where's your broom?"

"In the utility closet over there," she said, pointing to the tall, skinny, white cupboard in the corner.

Michael retrieved the broom and dustpan and went to work cleaning up the broken glass. By the time he'd finished, Timmy woke up, calling for his mother.

"I'll get him," Michael told her.

"No. I'll do it," she replied, and hurried from the room.

When Lily returned to the kitchen holding a sleepy-eyed Timmy, Michael felt that pang again as he watched them. She loved her son. He didn't doubt it for a second. It was there in every look, every touch. Yet Webster had claimed she'd been a neglectful mother.

Webster had lied. He had to have lied, Michael told himself. And if he'd lied about what type of mother Lily had been, what else had he lied about? Or was he looking for excuses again? Michael asked himself.

"Look, Mommy have boo-boo," Timmy said. "I kiss and make better," Timmy said, and placed his lips to his mother's bandaged hand. Then he held Lily's hand out toward Michael and said, "You kiss, too, and make better."

"Timmy," Lily admonished, color creeping up her cheeks. "Michael's already made it better. He bandaged Mommy's hand for her."

"Him kiss, too," Timmy insisted.

"You're right, cowboy," Michael said. Taking Lily's hand, he pressed a kiss to the bandaged cut.

"Better?" Timmy asked his mother.

"Yes, sweetie. It's better. Now, why don't we thank Michael and tell him goodbye. We've taken up enough of his day."

Reluctantly, Michael allowed Lily to lead him to the front of the house. When she opened the door for him, he turned around and asked, "You're sure you don't want me to hang around, help you with Timmy or something?"

"We'll be fine," she assured him.

"What about dinner? You probably shouldn't use that hand. I could come back later and take the two of you out to get something to eat."

"Thanks. But I have to pass. Goodbye, Michael."

"'Bye, Mikull," Timmy mimicked.

And as he headed for the Bronco and slid behind the wheel, he couldn't shake the feeling that something was really wrong. He retrieved the cell phone that he'd deliberately left out of sight inside his glove box. Noting the slew of messages, he punched in his code and listened to them as he drove away.

After listening to a string of increasingly irate messages from Webster, Janie's voice came on. "Hi, Michael, it's Janie. I know you're busy, but I'd appreciate it if you'd give me a call when you get this message."

How long had it been since he'd checked in with Janie and the kids? A week? Ten days? Closer to three weeks, he realized—before he'd come to New Orleans. With this realization came a wave of guilt for not having called to see if they were doing okay. Janie had been in an odd mood when he'd left Florida. He'd known her company had been downsizing and that she'd been worried about losing her job. It had been one of the reasons he'd wanted her to take the money he'd gotten as a retainer from Webster.

Webster.

The man was a real piece of work, Michael thought as the phone beeped to signal the end of Janie's message and the next one from Webster.

"Sullivan, I don't know what kind of game you're playing. But I had better hear from you. And it had better be soon," Webster added and, given the man's tone, he was one very unhappy camper.

He thought about Lily and Timmy the entire way back to his hotel. And when he pulled the Bronco into the parking lot and shut off the engine, he was no closer to deciding what he was going to do about them. "Dammit!" He smacked the wheel with the side of his hand.

Grabbing his cell phone, he exited the truck and fished out his room key. He made the short walk down the dimly lit corridor of the no-frills hotel until he reached his room. Once inside, he tossed his keys and phone on top of the dresser. Maybe a run would help clear his head, he decided. As he was about to grab some running shorts and a sweatshirt, the cell phone sounded.

He glared at the thing and was about to ignore it when he noted the familiar cell number and snatched it up. "Hey, Janie," he said, smiling. "I just got your message a few minutes ago and was going to call you."

"Hi, Michael. How's the case going?"

Michael's smile died. Janie never called to ask him about a case. "What's wrong?" He sat down on the bed. "Has something happened? Are you all right?"

"I'm fine."

"The boys, are they—"

"Petey and Micky are fine. No one's hurt. No one's sick. I probably shouldn't have even called you."

"What is it?"

"I got laid off from my job last week," she finally said.

"I'm sorry." And he was. He knew that she'd enjoyed her job, had liked the feeling of independence it had given her. Although she did allow him to help some with extras for the boys, she'd prided herself on supporting them. "If it's money you're worried about, I have some put aside. And there's the money in the account I set up for the boys with the retainer I got for this case," he said, and nearly choked because once he used that money, he would have no choice about turning Lily in to Webster.

"I don't need the money, Michael," Janie insisted. "I got a nice severance package. Enough to take care of me and the boys until I find something else. That's not why I called."

"All right," he said, and waited because he knew there was more to come, and he suspected whatever it was he wasn't going to like it.

"I've decided to leave Florida. I'm moving back to Oklahoma. In fact, I'm in Oklahoma City now."

"Oklahoma? You haven't been back there since you and Pete married."

"I know. But maybe I should have. I have family here—a couple of cousins and an aunt. I also have a lot of old friends. I've been keeping in touch with one of those friends for a while now. Actually, he's a guy I used to date before I met Pete. His name is Hal. Anyway, Hal told me about a job opening here in the D.A.'s office for an experienced legal secretary. I flew out for the interview two days ago and they've offered me the job. And I've decided to take it."

"But what about the boys? What about school? Surely you're not going to uproot them right now," he said as he tried to absorb what she'd told him.

"Actually, they're pretty excited about the move. They've just found out they have a mess of cousins around their age here in Oklahoma. It's a lot different from the beaches and sunshine in Florida, but sometimes change is good. I think it's the right thing for us to do, Michael. It's time for me to start looking toward the future. Maybe it's time you did, too."

Until recently, the only thoughts he had of the future were to make sure Janie and the boys were secure, that and to maybe get himself that little sailboat. He'd even convinced himself to take a job he hadn't wanted in order to secure the Crenshaws' future. Only now, it seemed they were moving toward the future without his help and without him.

"Michael? Are you still there?"

"Yeah, I'm here. Just trying to digest all this. Tell me, this old boyfriend of yours. Hal, was it?"

"Yes," she said, and he could hear the smile in her voice. "Hal Phillips. He's a C.P.A. and has his own firm here."

"He a nice guy?"

Janie laughed. "Very nice. You'll probably think he's dull because he's not the daredevil that Pete was, and he's not like you. He'll never be a white knight or a superhero. But he's sweet and he's honest and he makes me laugh. He claims the reason he's never married is because I broke his heart when I left for Texas and married Pete. He got in touch with me after Pete died to offer his condolences, and we've been exchanging Christmas cards and e-mails for a while. A few months ago, things began to change—or maybe I did. Anyway, Hal says he's just been waiting for me all this time. He makes me feel special."

"You are special," Michael told her. "So when are you moving?"

"In about a week. That's why I called. The boys and I are flying home in the morning to pack, get transfer papers from their schools and handle all the personal stuff. Then we're flying back out here next

Friday afternoon. I've already found us a place. It's a wonderful house and I've worked out a deal where I can lease it and apply the payments toward the purchase if I decide to buy it.''

"That's great, Janie."

"But we want to see you before we leave Florida, to say goodbye. Will you be finished the case you're on by then?"

Michael thought about the situation with Lily, knew he could wrap it up now if he wanted to. "I should be," he told her. "But either way, I'll make sure that I see you guys. And I expect to be invited to visit."

"Oh, you will be. You will. What?" she asked, evidently distracted by someone. "The boys want to talk to you, Michael. So hang on."

Michael listened to the two boys chatter excitedly about their cousins and the new place where they were going to be living. And when he ended the call a short time later, Michael felt more alone than ever.

Stretching out on the bed he thought about Lily, debating what to do. She was a job, he told himself. One he needed to wrap up so he could move on. If she was in trouble, that was her problem. Not his. But, try as he might, he couldn't get that image of her terror-stricken face out of his mind.

Don't be a sucker. Take the money and walk away. It's the smart thing to do.

But he wasn't going to do the smart thing. Whatever it was—that sense of responsibility, the belief his father had instilled in him about his duty to right injustices, that thing inside him that had made him want to become a cop in the first place—kicked in again. Maybe Janie was right, he thought, he had some noble streak. Whatever it was, it wouldn't allow him to walk away from Lily and Timmy now. He had to find a way to get her to trust him with the truth and try to help her.

So when Webster rang his cell phone again later that evening, this time Michael answered it. "Sullivan," he said.

"I've been trying to reach you since last night, Sullivan," Webster told him, rage making the man's voice far less refined than it had been on previous occasions.

"I know. I just got your messages."

"You said you found Elisabeth. Where is she?" he demanded, apparently ready to forgo reading him the riot act to find out where his wife was.

"It isn't her," Michael said, the lie tripping off his tongue.

"What do you mean it isn't her? You said you'd found her."

"I made a mistake. I located a woman with a little boy that I thought was your wife, but I was wrong. It wasn't her. In my excitement, I called you before I had confirmation on her identity. I shouldn't have."

"I was under the impression you didn't make mistakes, Sullivan. It's the reason I paid you that outrageous retainer. You assured me I would get results. But so far all I'm getting for my money is excuses.

Need I remind you that you have very little time left to complete your end of our bargain?''

''I'm aware of that.''

''Then you're also aware that you'll return my money in full and eat your expenses if you don't find her,'' Webster reminded him.

''I know what our deal is, Webster. Don't worry, I haven't spent your money. If I don't find her, you'll get it back.''

A lengthy silence followed, then Webster said, ''Considering that my wife is young and not very bright, I find it difficult to believe that she's managed to outwit someone with your abilities, Sullivan.''

Michael's hand closed into a fist as he listened to Webster. ''Believe what you want. But maybe she's a great deal more clever than you give her credit for.''

''Clever enough to elude a man that was touted by sources inside the FBI as having the instincts of a bloodhound?''

Once again, Michael wondered how it was that Webster knew he'd worked with the FBI on some very hush-hush and sensitive cases. ''Evidently so. But since you're unhappy with my performance, why don't I return your retainer now and let you hire someone else.'' And even as he made the offer, Michael told himself he was a fool.

After another long pause, Webster said, ''No. I want you to stay on the case.''

''All right,'' Michael replied, reasoning that at least as long as Webster thought he was looking for Lily and Timmy then no one else would be.

"And you're sure this woman you found in New Orleans isn't Elisabeth?"

"Yeah, I'm sure," Michael lied.

"That's too bad."

"But I got another lead and it looks like she might headed back to Mississippi. I'm going there now to see if I can pick up her trail."

"Be sure to call me tomorrow and give me an update," Webster said and then severed the connection.

But not before Michael picked up something in the man's voice. Something that told him he hadn't pulled it off, that Webster was suspicious of him.

"He's lying," Adam Webster told Bernie after hitting the off button on the speakerphone in his office. "I want you to take a couple of men and go to New Orleans, find Sullivan and find out why he's lying."

"All right. But why would the man lie to you, boss?" Bernie asked him. "If the guy's found the dame…uh, er, your wife, all he has to do is tell you where she is and he collects the rest of the money. A million bucks is a lot of dough."

Adam saw no point in telling Bernie that he'd never had any intention of paying Sullivan a million dollars. As it was, the bastard had managed to get two hundred fifty thousand dollars out of him already—a great deal more than he'd anticipated paying him. "Perhaps Mr. Sullivan believes he can improve his fee," Adam suggested as he sat back in the plush chair and turned on the massage feature.

"You think he's going to try to hold you up for more money?"

"It's a possibility," Adam replied. For Sullivan's sake he hoped greed for more money was the reason the man had lied to him and not because he'd become infatuated with Elisabeth.

"I don't know, boss. Sullivan's a smart guy. Too smart to think he could pull a fast one like that on you."

"Let's hope you're right, Bernie. Sullivan will be making a big mistake if he tries to double-cross me," Adam told him. He picked up the crystal paperweight shaped like a golf club and closed his fist around it as he contemplated Sullivan taking a liking to Elisabeth. Suddenly a red haze came over his vision as he imagined Elisabeth with the other man, of any other man touching what was his. Fury sent blood pumping hot and fast through his veins. Adam hurled the paperweight across the room where it struck the picture of Elisabeth that sat on the credenza. Bernie leaped back as the glass on the fourteen-by-seventeen framed photo shattered. "Because if he does, Sullivan's a dead man."

Ten

Lily sat up in bed, her breaths coming fast. Another bad dream, she realized as she took stock of her surroundings. A glance at the clock told her that it was after seven in the morning. She started to scramble from the bed, worried she'd be late for work, when she remembered she had the day off. She leaned back against the pillows and thought about the dream. This dream had been worse than the others. More frightening. More real.

She'd been running again—this time racing down a dark street searching for a place to hide. She could see herself turning the corner, panting as she tried to catch her breath, trying to decide which way to go. And then she'd heard the footsteps behind her, heard voices shouting...

"There she is! Get her!"

Lily took off running again. Her feet slapped against the damp pavement as she raced through the Vieux Carré, dashing down street after street of the historic French Quarter of the city. She turned down another street, caught glimpses of the old buildings that rose on either side of her, the balconies lined with plants, the secreted courtyards at the rear. She could hear the barkers urging customers to come inside over on Bourbon Street. A street-corner musician wailed out ''Come to the Mardi Gras'' on his sax. She hurried past a mime who'd sprayed himself with silver paint and stood atop a milk crate while people gathered around and dumped coins in his cup.

Moving farther away from the tourists who crowded the streets for the Mardi Gras celebration, Lily dashed past a corner where two boys who couldn't have been more than ten tapped out a lively jig for the onlookers while their father passed a hat for tips. Her legs ached. Her mouth was dry. But she didn't dare stop running. If she stopped running, Adam would find her. And if he found her, he would kill Timmy. The sounds and sights of revelers grew faint as she continued toward the outskirts of the Quarter. The lights and music and laughter dwindled. The whiffs of spicy foods cooking gave way to the dank, sour stench of urine and beer. The voices faded until all she could hear was the sound of her own feet hitting the pavement in a steady rhythm.

Did I lose him back there in the crowd? Oh please, God, don't let him find me. Don't let him hurt Timmy.

She eased her pace a bit, slowed at the next corner, searching for a street sign so she could figure out where she was. She turned around in a circle, unsure of where she was or which way to go. Gertie had warned her to be careful. One wrong turn and she could find herself in a troubled section of the city where even the police were reluctant to patrol.

"Where'd she go?"

The sound of Adam's voice sent fear ripping through her. And Lily didn't care what danger might be around the next corner if she made a wrong turn. Because nothing could be as terrible as what awaited her if Adam found her. She ran, demanded her legs move faster. Her lungs and chest burned with the effort she exerted. Despite the cool temperatures and humidity, sweat beaded her forehead, clung to her upper lip. The muscles in her legs screamed as she pumped faster and cut around the next corner. And she ran straight into a heavy, cloying mist.

Terrified, Lily raced blindly into the shroud that hung over the street. She was afraid to go forward, but even more afraid to go back. When the mist gave way and she barreled around the next corner, she hit something solid and screamed.

"It's me. Lily, it's me."

"M-Michael? Michael," she cried in relief as his arms closed around her. *"Oh my God, Michael. I was so afraid. I thought he'd found me,"* she babbled as she clung to him.

He stroked her head. *"Shh. Shh. It's all right, Elisabeth. I promised I'd always take care of you, didn't I?"*

Lily jerked her head up at the words, and she froze as the mist cleared and she saw his face. Not Michael's face. Adam's face.

He smiled at her, and even in the dim lighting, she recognized that maniacal gleam in his dark eyes. *"You were a naughty girl, Elisabeth. Drugging me*

*like that, running away. You do realize I'm going to
have to punish you, don't you? But first, I need to
take care of the boy. I brought him a new gun to play
with. You do remember how much he liked playing
with my gun, don't you?"*

"Adam, please," she pleaded as he removed a pistol from his pocket and waved it in front of her face.
*"I'll do whatever you want me to do. I'll send him
away. I swear it. I'll send him away. Just please don't
hurt him, don't hurt my baby."*

He grabbed her by the hair, yanked her head back
until she saw stars in front of her eyes. *"I'm afraid
it's too late for that. Sending him away won't work
now. You've become much too attached to him. It's
my own fault really for not being more firm with you
and insisting you get rid of him while you were pregnant,"* he said as calmly as if he were discussing the
disposal of a pair of old shoes. *"But then I've always
been far too indulgent with you, haven't I?"*

*"Yes, and I'm sorry for not being more apprecia-
tive,"* she told him, praying that she could somehow
soften him. *"I'll do better in the future. I promise."*

"Of course you will." He stroked the side of her
face with the barrel of the gun, and Lily shivered.
*"You'll be able to devote yourself totally to being my
wife again without any more distractions—once I've
gotten rid of the boy."*

"No!"

"No," Lily said aloud. Shuddering, she clutched
her throat and tried to shake off the remnants of the
dream. Wide awake now, she tried to make sense of

the dream, wondered why this one had been so much worse than the others. Adam still didn't know where they were. It had been months since his men had tracked her down in Arkansas. So why was she so spooked?

She pushed the hair from her face. And that's when she spied the bandage on her hand. Michael. Suddenly the events of the previous afternoon came tumbling back, and she remembered how shaken she'd been when he'd told her he'd been a policeman. Her first thought had been that Adam had sent him to find her. She'd learned long ago how far-reaching Adam's influence was and that it extended to the highest ranks of law enforcement and politics in Florida.

That's what had triggered the dream, she reasoned. And she was probably being paranoid again. Just as she'd been paranoid that someone had been watching her and Timmy on Friday. But try as she might, she couldn't quite shake the fear that lingered from the dream. Unable to go back to sleep, she climbed out of bed and started toward Timmy's room to assure herself he was okay, when she heard a soft tapping at the front door.

Lily froze, listened again.

Tap. Tap. Tap.

She swallowed. Unsure what to do, she glanced around her for a weapon and was about to go to the kitchen for a knife, when the taps came again.

"Lily?" Tap. Tap. Tap. "Lily, it's Michael."

Michael?

Abandoning thoughts of arming herself, she hurried

to the front of the house before he woke Timmy. Still wary, she pushed aside the half curtain that covered the glass section of the door and peeked out. It was Michael. And he was alone. She unlatched the door, opened it a crack and demanded in a whisper, "What are you doing here?"

"I come bearing gifts," he replied in a matching whisper and held up a shopping bag in one hand and a pastry bag in the other. "I bought you a new coffeepot."

"You didn't have to do that."

"I wanted to," he informed her. When she said nothing, but simply stood there making no move to invite him in, he asked, "Can I come inside?"

"It's a little early for visitors," she said warily.

"I realize that, but I pegged you for an early riser, and I didn't want you to have to start your day without a cup of coffee." He waved the pastry bag in front of her. "I'll give you a beignet if you let me in," he promised.

"Michael, this really isn't a good idea. I—"

"Mommy," Timmy cried out.

"I have to go."

"Wait! At least let me leave you these." He started to put both bags down in front of the door.

"Mommy," Timmy began crying harder.

"I…all right. Oh, you might as well come in. I need to go see about Timmy."

Leaving Michael to himself, she hurried to the back of the house to Timmy's room. "Mommy's here, sweetheart," she said as she went to her son and sat down at the edge of his bed. He clung to her, sobbing. "What's wrong, baby? Did you have a bad dream?"

"Couldn't f-find T-Teddy."

"Teddy's right here," she told her son. She picked up the stuffed bear from the floor and handed it to her son.

"H-him l-left me. And I was s-scared. Y-you wouldn't come."

It broke her heart to hear him cry so hard. Lily thought back to that night when she'd found Timmy missing from his bed. Frantic, she'd searched the house, and when she couldn't find him, she'd gone into the one room in the house forbidden to her— Adam's study. She'd died a thousand deaths that night when she'd opened the door and seen her precious son sitting on the floor with the end of the pistol in his mouth, sucking on it like it was a lollipop. Her heart lodged in her throat as she recalled going to Timmy, taking the gun from him with trembling fingers and discovering it was loaded. When Adam had come back into the room and started toward them, her maternal instinct to protect her child had kicked in and she'd aimed the gun at him...

"What do you think you're doing, Elisabeth?"

"Protecting my son."

"From his father? I was only doing what you're always harping on me to do—paying attention to him. Now put down that gun and come here."

"No," she told him. "Don't come any closer."

He laughed. "You know you're not going to shoot me. Now put down the gun and do as you're told.

Otherwise, this time I won't punish you. I'll punish him.''

"No you won't," she said, and though she'd wanted to shoot him, she hadn't been able to pull the trigger...

She'd known then that she had to get Timmy out of there, and that she'd have to do it soon. So she'd plotted and planned, trying to get Adam to lower his guard, making him believe she was going along with his plans. Then she'd drugged him, taken her son with only the clothes on their backs, some cash from the safe and escaped.

"Hey, cowboy. What's the problem?"

Lily blinked and realized Michael was standing in the doorway watching them with those laser-sharp eyes. "He had a bad dream. That, and he lost his teddy," Lily explained as she stroked her sobbing son's head. Out of the corner of her eye, she continued to watch Michael, waiting for him to retreat, recalling all too well how Timmy's crying had irritated Adam.

But instead of retreating, Michael came into the room and knelt down beside the bed. "Is that right, cowboy? You thought old Teddy here got lost?"

Still sniffling, Timmy nodded and hugged his teddy tighter.

"Tell you what. How about if we give him an ID tag?"

"What's ID tag?"

"Something like this," Michael explained, taking a silver chain and tag from around his neck and handing it to Timmy. "This was mine from when I did a stint in the navy. See these little numbers? If you punch them into a big computer, it tells everyone who you are and where you live."

"Weally?"

"Uh-huh. So how about we give this to Teddy? I'll fix it so the records show it belongs to him. That way if he ever gets lost, all anyone has to do is put the numbers in the computer and it will tell them his name is Teddy and he belongs to Timmy. Would you like that?"

"Yes," Timmy said, his brown eyes, still bright with tears, watched as Michael fastened the silver chain around the bear's neck and handed it back to Timmy.

"Michael, you don't have to do that," Lily objected.

"It's done," he told her firmly.

"Tank you," Timmy said, and launched himself at Michael.

Lily stood, ready to retrieve her son from Michael, but the man shook his head. So she stood there and looked at them, and something inside her shifted, softened, at the sight of her son in Michael's arms.

"You and Teddy hungry, cowboy?"

"Yes," Timmy replied.

"Then what do you say I rustle us up some breakfast while your mom goes and gets dressed?"

At his remark, Lily looked down and realized she was standing there in her nightgown. In her shaken state from the dream and her hurry to answer the door, she hadn't even bothered with a robe. She shifted her gaze back up to Michael's and her breath caught at the desire she read in his eyes.

He grinned at her. "Not that I'm complaining, mind you," he told her. "I like the look of you in that nightgown, but for the sake of my blood pressure it might be better if you put some clothes on before I serve breakfast." Then, hoisting her son up onto his shoulders, he turned and walked out of the room.

As she watched him walk away, Lily felt a fluttering in her stomach, a rush of heat that ran from her heart down her middle. And she realized that for the first time that she could remember, she felt real desire for a man. No, not for just a man, she amended. For Michael Sullivan.

He was running out of time, Michael admitted.

He had made up his mind last night that he was going to help Lily. After seeing her again this morning, he'd known he'd made the right decision. She was in trouble. And he needed to help her. He'd wanted to tell her the truth, came close to doing so that morning. Only she was still too damn wary of him. If he'd confessed that Webster had hired him to find her, she'd run. Somehow, someway, he had to get her to trust him. And he had to do it fast because his gut told him Webster was already suspicious. He rubbed at the back of his neck, unable to shake the feeling that things were going to blow up in his face at any second.

Michael paced the length of his hotel room, checking his watch again. He still had almost two hours before he was scheduled to go back to Lily's. At least he'd been able to convince her, with Timmy's help, to go to the parade that afternoon. Maybe, just maybe, he could get her to open up and tell the truth—who she was and why she was running—and why she had called the FBI.

Thoughts of the Bureau made him think of his brother. Michael frowned. It wasn't like Travis not to return his calls. Picking up his cell phone, he dialed his brother's home number again. And once again, he got an answering machine.

This time he didn't bother leaving a message. After ending the call, he dialed another number—one that he had only called three times a year since he'd left Houston. The last time had been at Christmas to wish his mother a happy holiday. Where the devil was his mother? Michael wondered when the phone began to ring for a fifth time.

"Hello."

Michael hesitated at the sound of his father's voice.

"Hello," he said again.

"Dad, it's Michael."

"Michael," Big Mike repeated and from the sound of his voice, he was as shocked to find him on the other end of the line as Michael had been to hear his dad's voice.

"Is Mom there?"

"No. She took a ride over to Mrs. Cusimano's to bring her some chicken soup. The old gal came down with a late-winter cold, and you know your mother.

She swears by her chicken soup whenever anybody gets sick."

"Yeah, I remember," Michael said, a flood of memories coming to mind of his mother ministering to family, friends and even casual acquaintances with her cure-all chicken soup.

After an awful silence that stretched endlessly, his father said, "Guess your mother told you I retired last year."

"Yes, sir, she did," Michael replied, unsure what to say and still finding it difficult to imagine his father ever surrendering his badge. He certainly hadn't understood his own need to walk away from his shield. "You enjoying it?"

"Most of the time. I miss the work, but things changed a lot after you left. The new recruits needed a different kind of chief. You remember Henderson?"

"Yes, sir."

"He took over for me, seems to be doing a good job." His father sighed. "But I'm sure you didn't call to hear me talk shop. Since your mother's not here, is there something I can help you with?"

Shaking off the melancholy brought on by talking to his father again, Michael said, "I was trying to get in touch with Travis. I've tried leaving several messages at both the Bureau and his home, but he hasn't returned any of my calls. I really need to talk to him. It's important."

"I haven't heard from him for a couple of weeks now. He said he was going on some kind of special assignment. But he gave me a new cell phone number before he left,'' Big Mike said, and Michael could hear him shuffling through papers. ''Must have left it upstairs somewhere. You want me to call you back when I find it?''

''Maybe you could just have Travis call me. I'm in New Orleans right now, but he can reach me on my cell phone,'' he explained, and gave his father the number.

''Got it. Everything all right, son?''

''Yes, sir. It's just a case I'm working on right now. It's kind of complicated, but there's a woman and a little boy involved. They're in trouble, and need some help.''

''Anything I can do?'' Big Mike asked him.

Michael knew the offer hadn't come lightly considering how things had ended between them five years ago. ''I appreciate the offer,'' Michael said. ''And I may take you up on it. But first I need to talk to Travis, see if he can check on someone for me.''

''All right. I'll try to reach your brother. In the meantime, I've still got some pretty decent contacts. You want me to see if I can find out what you need?''

Michael gave his father Webster's name and filled him in on the case, on Lily and Timmy, on Lily's call to the FBI. It was like old times, running a situation by his father and getting his input on the best way to handle things. He hadn't realized how much he had missed doing so until now. ''Son, I suppose you've considered there could be some other reason this fellow Webster's going to such lengths to get her back.''

"You mean that she might have something that belongs to him," Michael offered.

"Yes."

"I've considered it. But I don't think so. She doesn't have anything of real value. And if you met Lily, saw her with her son, you'd understand."

"It sounds like you're very fond of her," his father said.

And maybe you're letting your feelings cloud your judgment—again. Although Big Mike didn't say the words aloud, Michael could hear the accusation in his head.

"I am fond of her and the little boy. But it hasn't impacted my ability to think like a cop," he countered.

"I didn't think it would," his father said, surprising him. "I'll try to reach your brother and see what I can find out. I'll get back to you."

"Thank you, sir."

"Michael?"

"Yes, sir?"

"Be careful, son."

He was going to have to tell her everything this evening, Michael decided as he climbed the stairs and knocked on Lily's door. He just prayed that once he did, he could convince her not to bolt.

"Hi," he said when she opened the door to him. "All set?"

Juggling Timmy on her hip Lily replied, "You know, I'm not sure this is a good idea. I mean, it hasn't been long since Timmy had the chicken pox and I have to work tomorrow…''

Michael sighed, frustrated to see the wariness coming back into her eyes, hearing it in her voice. ''It's a pretty evening,'' he began, and set out a list of reasons to convince her. He needed the time with her, a chance to put her at ease enough so he could tell her who he was, why he was here. ''It's not too cool and there's no rain in the forecast. The start of the parade route is only a few blocks from here, so we'll be catching it right at the beginning. You'll be back here in plenty of time to get Timmy to bed on schedule and for you to get your beauty sleep.''

''Really, Michael, I don't think—''

''Come on, Lily. You'll disappoint Timmy and me if you say no.''

''Pwease, Mommy?'' Timmy said.

''All right. But let me get Timmy's jacket just in case it gets chilly. And I'll bring his stroller in case he gets tired.''

''No stwoller,'' Timmy said to his mother's retreating form. ''I big. I a cowboy,'' Timmy complained to Michael.

Michael stooped down, bringing himself to eye level with the little boy. ''Tell you what, cowboy. We'll take the stroller just in case we need something to hold all the loot you catch.''

Timmy eyed him in that same wary manner that Lily often did, Michael noted. '''Kay.''

''That's my man,'' Michael said and high-fived the boy.

Then Timmy hugged him, kissed his cheek and said, "I wuv you, Mikull."

Everything inside Michael seemed to shut down. He hugged the little boy close. Emotion formed a knot in his throat, and he swallowed hard, knowing if he tried to speak, his voice would be anything but steady. Damn, he thought. It was bad enough that the mother had gotten under his skin. But had the kid gotten beneath his radar and stolen a chunk of his heart, too? Suddenly he knew that was exactly what had happened.

"Ready?" Lily asked when she joined them.

"Yeah," Michael said. He took the stroller from her, carried it down the short flight of stairs.

"Come on, Timmy. Let Mommy put you in your stroller."

"I big boy," Timmy told her. He crossed his arms over his small chest and gave her a pouting look.

"Um, he and I had a little talk, Lily. I sort of told him we'd use the stroller for the loot."

"The loot?" she repeated.

Michael grinned. "The loot we're going to catch at the parade."

"I see," she said, her tone skeptical. "So you think we're going to catch that much stuff, huh?"

"Yes, ma'am," Michael assured her as they started down the street toward the avenue where the parade was slated to pass. While Lily held on to Timmy's hand, he pushed the stroller. But when the little boy held out his free hand to him, Michael guided the stroller one-handed and used his other one to hold Timmy's.

With Timmy walking, they slowed their pace to accommodate his small steps. As a result, what would have normally been a ten-minute walk took them twenty minutes. And by the time they reached Saint Charles Avenue, the marching bands were already passing.

"I didn't realize there would be so many people," Lily shouted to him above the din of the music and noise.

"I suppose everyone had the same idea we did— catch it at the start and get home early," Michael remarked as he maneuvered to find them a spot near the front of the crowd so that Lily and Timmy could see. He settled for a spot where the people were only two and three deep. After parking the stroller next to a ladder that had been rigged with a seat to accommodate a little girl about a year older than Timmy, he reached for Timmy and hoisted him atop his shoulders. "You're going to need your hands to catch," he explained to Timmy when the boy clung to him with one hand and held on to his teddy with the other. "How about we let Teddy guard the stroller?"

"'Kay," Timmy said as he handed his beloved teddy to his mother.

"All right, here comes the first float. Now, hold up your hands and yell, 'Throw me something, mister,'" Michael instructed. "That goes for you, too, Mom."

"I'll just watch," Lily told him, and Michael smiled. He'd already taken in a couple of the parades and knew firsthand that the lure of catching the cheap trinkets was like a fever. It had nothing to do with value. Most of the beads—even the prized long, colored pearls—doubloons, cups and stuffed toys could all be bought for less than a dollar each. But it had everything to do with the game and the frenzied spirit that gripped the city during the pre-Lenten festival.

So Michael wasn't at all surprised when Lily squealed as she caught a fistful of long, shiny white pearls. He also wasn't surprised to see that she was racking up throws at lightning speed, since the parade was an all-male organization. Even in the faded jeans, tennis shoes and pink sweatshirt, and without a lick of makeup, she was beautiful. And when she was excited and laughing happily as she was now, a man would have to be dead not to take notice.

He'd taken notice.

When the couple next to them offered to let "Michael and Lily's son" join their daughter in the seat, Michael didn't bother correcting the mistake. "Looks like I have a free pair of shoulders," he told Lily. "Want to hop on? I'll carry you up to the float and we'll see if we can get them to part with some of those green pearls."

"I can't get on your shoulders," she informed him, her eyes wide with shock at the suggestion.

"Sure you can. Ma'am," Michael addressed the woman on the ladder behind the little girl and Timmy. "Will you keep an eye on him for us while we go up to the float?"

"Sure thing," the woman replied.

"All right. Now come on," Michael told Lily. "Hop on."

"I can't."

"Why not?" he asked. "Look at all the other women on men's shoulders."

"But those are young girls and women with their boyfriends. I'm...I'm a mother."

"You're probably younger than most of them. Now come on," Michael insisted and stooped down for her to get on.

"Go ahead, honey," the mother of the little girl on the ladder told her. "If my Buddy here had shoulders like your husband's, you can bet I'd have him put me on them."

"What's wrong with my shoulders?" the offended Buddy demanded.

"Nothing, lover. I just don't trust them to hold me."

"But I...he..." Lily stammered.

Michael caught her hand. "Come on, Lily. Get on so we can get those beads while the float's stopped."

She climbed on, and Michael couldn't help thinking how light she was as he made his way through the throng of people. He also was conscious of the feel of her bottom against his shoulders, the curve of her thighs around his neck. And just as he'd thought, she had no problem getting the masked riders to part with their stash of long beads.

"Look, Timmy. Look what Mommy got," she told him, laughing excitedly when she returned with her arms loaded with dozens and dozens of beads, cups and two more stuffed animals. "You can put me down now, Michael," she said. He stooped down and allowed her to slide off his shoulders.

When she'd finished dividing her loot between the other couple, Timmy and the little girl, she came to him. "I think you need a pair of these, too, Mr. Sullivan," she said, slipping the beads around his neck. "Thank you."

Someone in the crowd bumped Lily, and sent her sprawling against him. Instinctively, Michael's arms went around her. And in that instant, the loud music, the laughter, the voices and the people faded. The smile slid from her lips. Her eyes, aglow with the excitement of the parade, darkened. Suddenly he no longer cared that she was Elisabeth Webster, another man's wife, a woman he'd been paid to find. He'd stopped thinking of her as anyone other than Lily more than a week ago. And although he knew it was a mistake, he lowered his head and kissed her.

Eleven

Almost immediately Lily stepped back. Michael wondered if he'd imagined the tiny gasp that escaped Lily's lips before he'd kissed her, the sweet softness and slight tremor of those lips when they'd met his. One look into Lily's eyes, and he knew he hadn't imagined it.

By the time the parade was over and he carried a sleeping Timmy inside the house, Lily was as skittish as a filly about to be saddled for the first time. "Poor little guy is out cold," Michael told her after she'd changed the sleeping tyke into his pajamas and tucked him into bed. Placing his teddy in the bed with him, Lily exited the bedroom and Michael followed.

"We both had a wonderful time tonight," she told him, her voice overbright. A sure sign that she was nervous, Michael realized. "Thank you again for taking us."

"It was my pleasure."

"Well, it's getting late, and I have to work tomorrow."

"You going to kick me out without even offering me a cup of coffee?"

She hesitated a moment. "How about hot chocolate instead?"

"Hot chocolate sounds fine." He followed her into the kitchen and searched for a way to tell her who and what he was.

"I still can't believe all the stuff we caught. What am I supposed to do with all those beads?"

He knew it was nerves that made her ramble, but since he was feeling some nerves of his own—albeit for a different reason—he wasn't sure how to put her at ease. "I think people sell them or save them for when they ride in a parade and use them as their own throws."

"That would make sense," she said as she opened the pantry. "I imagine it's expensive to buy all those things just to throw them away." She reached for the canister on the top shelf.

"Here, let me get that for you."

"That's all right, I can get it," she began.

But he'd already moved behind her. And in the small space, his body brushed up against her back. The feel of her bottom pressed against him sent desire racing through him. Her honey-colored hair tickled his mouth. He sucked in a breath, and her scent—peaches and sunshine—filled his head. Michael closed his hands over her shoulders and turned her to face him. When she looked up at him he saw the answering heat in her eyes, and he did what he'd wanted to do from the moment he'd first seen her. No, he amended. What he'd wanted to do from the moment he'd seen her picture. He closed his arms around her and kissed her.

But unlike that barely-there brushing of lips they'd shared at the parade, this time he truly kissed her. His mouth closed over hers. Mouths met, tasted, tempted. He lifted his head, angled for a better fit, and went back for more. When he tested the seam of her lips with his tongue, she opened to him. He groaned and deepened the kiss.

He had known desire before now, Michael told himself. He had known the ache to make love to a woman before now. Yet nothing, nothing in his life compared to the vicious burning inside him now to make love with Lily. He skimmed his hands down her sides, drank in her gasp as his fingers brushed her breasts. He smoothed his palms along the slope of her waist, over the curve of her hips, then cupped her bottom and fitted her against his hardness.

Michael tore his mouth free, breathed in her scent, shuddered at the feel of her against him. Her quickening breath only fueled his need for more. He wanted her. Here. Now. With a fierceness that frightened him. And because he wanted her so desperately, he forced himself to slow down. It wouldn't be fair to take things further with so many secrets between them.

He had thought everything tender inside him had died in that back alley in Houston five years ago when Pete had been killed. Yet it was tenderness he felt when he captured Lily's flushed face in his hands and said, "I want you, Lily. But before this goes any further, we need to talk. I need you to tell me the truth."

She had to be dreaming, Lily thought. A wonderful, delicious dream. How else could she explain all these feelings inside her, this longing for Michael? After that last night with Adam, she had been positive she could never again bear a man's touch. She had been so sure that she would never want a man's touch. Yet she had wanted Michael. She had welcomed his touch. His kisses. Him. Still reveling in the taste and feel of him, it took her a moment to realize he was no longer kissing her, that his hands were no longer touching her. That he was talking to her.

"Tell me the truth, Lily."

Lily blinked.

"You can trust me," Michael told her. He slid his hands to her shoulders and held her. "Tell me what it is you're running from."

Lily stilled as his words penetrated her kiss-drugged senses. She trembled, fearful for a moment that somehow Michael knew about Adam and he'd come to take her back. He was a former cop, she remembered. Adam knew lots of cops. "I'm not running from anything," she fibbed, and started to turn away from him.

Michael held on to her shoulders, not hurting her, but not releasing her, either. "Then tell me who or what it is that you're so afraid of."

"You're wrong," she insisted.

"Am I?"

"This...what happened just now between us was a mistake," she told him.

"You mean the kiss?"

"Yes," she responded.

"It wasn't a mistake, Lily. It was inevitable. We've been leading up to that kiss and a whole lot more from the moment we set eyes on each other."

"You don't know what you're talking about," she insisted. Jerking free of his grasp, she stalked across the kitchen to the counter.

"I know that I want you. And I know that you want me."

Keeping her back to him, she said, "Whether I want you or you want me is immaterial. I should never have let things go this far. I told you before, I'm not interested in a relationship with you or anyone."

"Because of Timmy," he said from behind her.

"That's right."

His hands came down on her shoulders. He turned her to face him. "Look at me, Lily."

She looked up at him, refusing to allow herself to be moved by the tenderness she read in his blue eyes. When he stroked a finger along her cheek, she turned her face away.

"I can help you, Lily. You and Timmy. But you need to tell me what it is you're afraid of."

Only, Michael couldn't help her. No one could. And were she to involve him in any way, she would only put his life in danger. It was time for her and Timmy to move on, she realized. Past time. She'd evidently done or said something that had caused Michael to pick up on the fact that she was on the run. And if he had picked up on it, chances were someone else would, too—if they hadn't already. As much as she hated to admit it, New Orleans was no longer a safe place for her and Timmy.

"Let me help you," he insisted.

"If you really want to help me, you'll leave now and not come back."

He stared at her for a long time, and Lily could have sworn he was going to argue with her further. "I'll leave. For now. Because there's something I have to take care of, some business I need to finish. But once it's done, I'll be back, and you and I are going to talk."

But when she closed the door behind him and watched the taillights of his truck wink and fade as he drove away, Lily knew that when Michael came back, she would no longer be there.

Walking over to the telephone, she picked up the receiver and dialed Nancy Lee's home number. And when the woman who had been her boss and her friend answered, Lily said, "Nancy Lee, it's Lily. I'm sorry to be calling you so late, but I'm afraid I've had some bad news. I just got off the phone with the hospital in Atlanta, my Aunt Sally's had a stroke."

"I'm sorry to hear that," Nancy Lee told her. "I didn't realize you had any relatives."

"Just my Aunt Sally now," Lily said, spinning the tale. "She's actually my great-aunt, my grandmother's sister, and I'm the only family she has. The doctors say it doesn't look good and that I need to come as soon as possible. I hate doing this to you with Mardi Gras the day after tomorrow, but I'm going to have to leave tomorrow morning on the first flight I can get.''

"Janie, I realize it's a lot to ask. You've practically just walked through the doors of the place yourself, and here I am asking you to take in a couple of strangers.''

"Michael, I said it's okay. As along as she and her little boy don't mind sacking out in sleeping bags until those movers show up, the boys and I don't mind.''

"Thanks, Janie. I wouldn't have asked, but Oklahoma's probably the last place anyone will look for them. And you're the one person I feel I can trust,'' he said honestly.

"I'm glad, because I feel the same way about you,'' she told him. "Just let me know what flight they're going to be coming in on, and the two monsters and I will meet them at the airport.''

"I haven't checked with the airlines yet, but I'll let you know as soon as I do. Then I'm going to have to try to convince Lily to go,'' Michael said, and he knew that that would be the difficult part. He still wasn't all that sure how he was going to pull it off— especially considering that the lady in question had just told him to butt out and not to come back.

"Well, my money's on you, Sullivan.''

"Thanks.'' He just wished he felt as sure as Janie

did that he could convince Lily that he wasn't the enemy and to let him help her. Although he'd made up his mind to come clean with her, he had sensed her panic earlier that evening when he had pressed her to tell him why she was so afraid. He'd also been fairly sure if he had confessed to her then—that he'd been hired by Webster to find her, but had decided to help her instead—she probably wouldn't have believed him.

He couldn't blame her. He supposed he wouldn't believe him, either. That's why he'd wanted to set up a safe haven for Lily and Timmy to go to, a place where Webster wouldn't think to look for them. Because unless his instincts were off, she was about to run again. He'd seen it in her eyes last night. He suspected she'd been thinking about it for a while now. He figured he had two, maybe three days at best before she bolted.

"She must be very special for you to do this," Janie remarked.

"She is," he admitted. He'd known that for a while now, but just hadn't been willing to admit it to himself. "And she's probably going to hate my guts when she finds out everything. But I'm going to help her whether she wants me to or not."

"Sounds like I'm not the only one who's making some big life changes."

Michael frowned. "What's that supposed to mean?"

"It means you sound more like the old Michael Sullivan. The one who once told me he became a cop because he wanted to make a difference, and figured the best way to do that was by making sure the bad guys didn't win.''

''Yeah, well. Lily's in trouble, and somebody's got to help her.''

''And she couldn't be in better hands,'' Janie told him.

''Thanks, Janie. I owe you one.''

''No you don't. Now go talk to the lady, and let me know about the flights.''

But the flights were a problem, Michael discovered after he made a call to the airlines. It seemed as many people were leaving the city to escape Mardi Gras as there were people coming in to celebrate the event. ''So when *do* you have a flight going to Oklahoma City that has seats available?'' he asked the ticket agent.

''Right now the earliest availability that I'm showing is Tuesday afternoon.''

''All right. I'll need two tickets. One adult and one child,'' he told her, and gave her Lily's and Timmy's names. ''I'd like to pay cash for these tickets. Can you hold them at the desk and I'll swing by and pay for them tomorrow?''

''I can't guarantee them. It would be better if you could give me a credit card number.''

But he didn't want to risk using his credit card—just in case Webster grew wise to what he had done. Purchasing two tickets to Oklahoma would surely raise a red flag. "I'd rather pay cash. I'll try to get to the airport in the morning."

"Actually, you don't have to come all the way to the airport to pay for the tickets. We have an office located in the CBD, the Central Business District," she explained. "You could go there and avoid the crush at the Louis Armstrong Airport, if you'd like."

"I'd like that," Michael told her, and jotted down the information.

Once he had Lily and Timmy safe with Janie and her boys in Oklahoma, he could settle up things with Webster, Michael decided. Since Lily wouldn't tell him why she was so afraid of the man, he was hoping that either his brother or his father would be able to find out something for him. But first, he had to make another report to Webster and see if he could determine whether or not the man had bought his story last night.

Reaching for his cell phone again, Michael punched in the number to Webster's private line. He answered on the second ring, surprising Michael, given it was after midnight in Miami.

"Yes," he said, a touch of impatience in the cultured voice.

"It's Sullivan."

"Ah, Mr. Sullivan," he said. "I hope you're calling with good news."

"I'm afraid not," Michael began, and went on to explain that he'd hit a dead end. "I realize our agreement was that I'd find her in thirty days. We're almost at the end of that time frame now and I don't think another couple of days will make any difference. So I'm going to return your retainer and cut my losses now.''

''Well, I must say I'm disappointed, Sullivan. I actually thought you were going to collect that million dollars. In fact, I would have taken odds that you thought so, too.''

''I did think so. And if you think it's easy for me to walk away from that kind of money and eat the expenses I've racked up, you're wrong.''

''Then why walk away? I'll give you a short extension,'' Webster offered.

Michael couldn't shake the feeling the man was toying with him—the way a cat would with a mouse it had cornered. ''A few days, a few weeks won't make any difference. I'm smart enough to know when I'm spinning my wheels. Your wife has covered her tracks. My guess is she's left the country, and since I limit my work to the U.S., I'd just as soon cut my losses now and move on to another job that actually pays me something.''

''And to think that a little less than a month ago you seemed so sure you'd be able to find my wife. I wouldn't have pegged you for a quitter.''

Michael gritted his teeth at the barb. ''We both know you hired me because no one else had been successful in finding her. And my guess is that whomever you hire after me won't be able to find her, either.'' At least he hoped they wouldn't. ''As soon as

I get back to Florida, I'll return your retainer,'' Michael told him, and cut the connection without waiting for a reply.

Adam shuddered with rage. Did the man really think he was such a fool that he actually believed him? The man had found Elisabeth. He knew it. Marching over to the bar he poured himself a whiskey and tossed it back.

He grabbed the phone and buzzed for Bernie.

"Yeah?'' the sleepy brute answered.

"Did you send some boys to New Orleans to find Sullivan like I told you?''

"Yes, boss. They're there now.''

"Then what in the hell is taking them so long to locate that son of a bitch?'' he demanded.

"I don't know, boss. They said something about it being Mardi Gras, and how things were kind of crazy down there right now.''

"I don't give a fuck about Mardi Gras. Sullivan knows where Elisabeth is, and I want him found.''

"Sure thing, boss. I'll get right on it.''

"Be sure that you do, Bernie. Because if your people screw up and Elisabeth gets away again, someone is going to pay for it. Understand?''

"Yes, boss,'' Bernie said. "She won't get away. And neither will Sullivan.''

Adam slammed down the phone. He tossed back another whiskey, but the liquor did nothing to ease his fury. He marched back to the adjoining bedroom, stripped off his robe and started for the bed, intent on working off some of his frustration with the girl.

She wasn't in the bed, which only added to his anger. "Now, where did the little bitch go?" he muttered. When he didn't find her in the bathroom, he stared at the door that led to the room he'd kept for Elisabeth. No, he thought. The stupid cunt wouldn't dare go in there—he'd told her it was forbidden.

He opened the door.

"Adam," she gasped, whipping around as he opened the door.

"What are you doing in here? And what are you doing wearing that?"

"M-my clothes were messed up from earlier this evening," she explained, reminding him that he had ripped the dress she'd been wearing from her body. "I thought it would be okay if I…if I just borrowed something to wear for now and returned it later."

Adam went to her, slapped her hard across the face and knocked her to the floor. "Take it off," he commanded.

"Yes," she sobbed, trying to unzip the dress.

But watching her tremble, seeing her body exposed, inflamed him. It made him think of Elisabeth, and of how she'd disobeyed him. Him. The man who had given her everything. Just as he'd given this stupid bitch everything.

"Here," she said, offering him the dress.

Adam took it, tossed it aside. "You know what happens to little girls who are disobedient?"

She stared at him, the eyes that were now green, wide and wet from tears. "But I'm not a little girl," she said.

"You're whatever I want you to be," he told her, and grabbed her by the hair, shoved her to her knees.

"Yes," she agreed.

"Naughty girls need to be punished. And I'm going to have to punish you, Elisabeth."

Twelve

Lily jumped at the sound of the ringing telephone. After the fourth ring, she picked it up. "Hello," she said, but was met with silence at the other end. "Hello?" she repeated, and when she still got no answer, she hung up the phone.

Uneasiness tripped down her spine. She tried to blow off the call as a fluke, a wrong number that someone hadn't wanted to own up to. But now, now, she wasn't so sure. And though she had saved money by declining the caller ID device, she couldn't help wishing now that she'd had it. Feeling a headache coming on, she downed several aspirin and, after checking her watch, she went to wake up Timmy.

As always when she looked at her son, her heart swelled with love for him. My sweet, beautiful baby, she thought as she sat down on the edge of his bed. Smoothing his hair back, she pressed a kiss to his forehead. "Timmy, it's time to wake up, baby."

He stirred, opening sleepy brown eyes. "I seepy," he said.

"I know you are, sweetheart. That's because it's

very early. But Mommy has a special day planned for us. We're going to take a little trip.''

"To pwade?" he asked with a yawn as Lily stripped off his pajama top and pulled on a long-sleeved polo.

"No, not to the parade. Someplace better."

"To see Mickey Mouse?"

Lily sighed as she stood him up and replaced his pajama bottoms with a pair of blue jeans. "Even better. How would you like to go to Texas and see real horses and cowboys?"

"Can Mikull come wif us?"

Her son's innocent question sent pain slashing through her heart. "No. Michael can't come."

"Why?" he asked while she slipped on his socks and tennis shoes.

"Because he needs to stay here."

"Why?"

"Because you and Mommy are a family, and families go on trips together. Michael's not part of our family."

"But I wuv him."

Not only had the man managed to sneak his way into her heart, but he'd also stolen her son's heart, too. "And I'm sure Michael loves you, too," she told Timmy. "But this trip is just for you and Mommy. Understand?"

He nodded, but those sad eyes and the puckered lower lip were a swipe to her heart.

"Tell you what. How would you like a bowl of Mickey Mouse cereal for breakfast this morning?"

"Can I have chocwate milk?"

Lily blanched at the idea of the sweet cereal and even sweeter chocolate milk. But because she'd already disappointed him, she gave in and said, "All right. Mickey Mouse cereal with chocolate milk."

He gave her a kiss and ran to the kitchen.

Once she had Timmy settled at the table, she went into the next room and placed a call to Gertie. "Gertie, it's Lily. I know it's early, but I need a favor. Can I bring Timmy a little early this morning?"

"Of course you can," the generous older woman told her. "Do you have to go in to work already?"

"No. I have some things I need to take care of."

"Lily, what is it? What's wrong? Is Timmy sick again?"

"No, Timmy's fine," she assured her. "I promise I'll explain everything when I get there."

Once she arrived at Gertie's Lily told her they would be leaving.

"I can't believe you're going to run," Gertie told her.

"I have to, Gertie," Lily explained once again, telling her that she believed Adam had found them.

"If your grandmother, God rest her soul, were alive, she'd tell you the same thing I'm telling you—that you need to stop running away because you're afraid. It's not good for that little boy in there," she said, pointing a finger to the next room where Timmy was watching a Barney video. "And it's not good for you. Look at you. You've got circles under your eyes and you look like a strong wind would knock you over.''

"I'm all right," Lily tried to tell her. If she looked like hell it was because she hadn't been able to sleep last night, knowing what this morning would bring.

"You're not all right. And you won't be until you stand up for yourself. Take the man to court, Lily. File for divorce and fight him for custody of Timmy.''

"I can't. If I do, I'll lose Timmy. There's no way I can fight Adam and win," Lily explained.

"You don't know that. Just because he's a big-shot businessman with money doesn't mean that the courts will take a child away from his mother. He would have to prove that you were unfit, that Timmy was better off with him.''

"And he would. You don't know him, Gertie. He would find a way. Adam always gets what he wants." He'd wanted her, and had gotten her by first becoming her guardian and then by marrying her. He'd wanted something from Carter—and the man had been found dead. He always found a way to get rid of what he didn't want—and Adam didn't want Timmy. Lily shivered. "He has lots of friends in high places—even in the governor's mansion. He will find a way," she repeated. And it was the truth. Adam would find a way to take Timmy from her, and when something happened to Timmy, he would play the role of the grieving father for the public, and no one would question him.

"He's not the only one with friends. You have friends, too," Gertie insisted. "That lady you work for, the other people at the diner. And me. I could testify for you, tell them what a wonderful mother you are.''

But it wouldn't be enough. And Lily knew it. ''I appreciate the offer. But I can't risk it, Gertie. I just can't.''

''Lily,'' Gertie began, her voice breaking. Her faded blue eyes filled with tears. ''I don't want you and Timmy to go.''

''Oh, Gertie.'' Lily hugged the other woman close and held her tightly a moment. Then after collecting herself, she stepped back. ''I don't want to leave you, either. But I have to. It's the only way Timmy will be safe. If there's any way for me to come back, any way at all, I will. I promise.''

Gertie sniffed, wiped at her eyes with the bottom of her apron. ''All right. Then go on. Do whatever it is you have to do. I'll take care of Timmy for you.''

''Thank you.'' Lily kissed Gertie's cheek. ''I'll try not to be too long.''

And after kissing Timmy goodbye and explaining to him that when she came back the two of them would be leaving for their trip, Lily began taking the steps necessary to end Lily Tremont's life in New Orleans. To start over somewhere else as someone else—until Adam found her again.

''Hey, Texas. We haven't seen you in a while.''

''Good morning, Gina,'' Michael said to the waitress as he strolled into the diner at half past ten that morning. ''I've been kind of busy lately—some business I needed to take care of,'' Michael informed her as he took a table by the window. He patted his shirt pocket just to be sure it still contained the two ticket confirmations for the flight that would take Lily and Timmy to Oklahoma. He felt good about what he'd done and the decisions he'd made. The only hurdle now was getting Lily to go along with his plan.

Already his thoughts were jumping ahead to how he was going to calmly lay out the facts for her, including his own duplicity. Then he would present her with the airline tickets and a safe haven for her and Timmy. She might hate him for his role in the situation, but she would do what was best for Timmy. He knew that, he was counting it. And while she and Timmy were with Janie and the boys, he would find out what hold Webster had on Lily. If he ruined whatever there was between them, it was a chance he would have to take. She needed help whether she knew it or not. And he intended to provide it.

Not interested in eating, he didn't bother looking at the menu. Impatient, he kept his eyes trained on the doors leading from the kitchen, waiting for Lily to walk through them and come over to take his order.

Gina placed a glass of water, a cup of coffee and a setting of silverware wrapped in a white napkin on the table. ''So, you decided what you want yet?'' she asked him.

Michael looked up at the dark-haired woman who stood waiting in front of him, order pad and pencil in hand, realizing that the table Gina had been clearing had been one of Lily's. "How come you're covering Lily's tables?"

Because she's not here. She called Nancy Lee last night and said she had a family emergency and would be out for a few days."

"Did something happen to Timmy? Her little boy?" He didn't even question the sudden panic he felt at the idea of something happening to the child.

"No. Nothing like that. Her aunt in Atlanta had a stroke. She said she had to fly out first thing this morning because the doctors said it wasn't looking good. Although how she expected to get a flight out of New Orleans the day before Mardi Gras is beyond me."

But Lily wouldn't have to worry about getting a flight out from the busy airport—because she wouldn't be going to Atlanta—since she didn't have any aunt in Atlanta or anywhere else. "Gina, did she come by here this morning to pick up her paycheck?"

She frowned. "She sure did. How'd you know?"

"A hunch," Michael explained. "How long ago was that?"

"A little before seven. I remember because I was just getting ready to unlock the door and put the Open sign out when she came in."

"Did she have Timmy with her?"

"No, at least not that I saw. She was in and out of here pretty fast, but she didn't bring him inside with her. It's possible she left him waiting in the car."

But Lily would never leave Timmy unattended in

a car. Of that much he was sure. Michael stood, tossed some bills on the table. "Thanks."

"Sullivan?"

He paused. "Yeah?"

"Lily didn't look good. You know, like she hadn't slept and maybe had been crying some. But I just figured it was because she was worried about her aunt. Is she in some kind of trouble?"

"I don't know. But I intend to find out."

Knowing she had a three-and-a-half-hour start on him, he had to find her fast. Wherever she was running to she would need money. Which meant she would have to wait for the banks to open at nine o'clock to cash her paycheck and to clear out what money she had, he reasoned. With tomorrow being a holiday, along with the influx of tourists, the lines at the bank would be long. At least, he hoped they were.

He jogged across the street to his Bronco, unlocked it and got behind the wheel. She would have left Timmy with Gertie while she ran her errands—coming to the diner for her paycheck, going to the bank, packing and shutting up the house. Michael started the truck and pulled away from the curb, barely braking for the stoplight. Did he go to Gertie's first or to Lily's house? His gut told him Timmy would be her last stop before she skipped town. Given the time and the holiday crowds, he opted to try Lily's place first. The moment the light turned green, he stomped on the gas and headed south. And as he sped through the streets, dodging Mardi Gras revelers who were gearing up to the big day tomorrow, his heart beat frantically in his chest, and he prayed that he wouldn't be too late—that when he got there, he would find Lily.

She was there. Or at least her car was there, with the trunk open, packed with a couple of boxes, two suitcases and a small box of toys. Michael jumped out of the truck and hit the ground running. "Lily," he yelled, racing through the house. He found her in the kitchen packing an ice chest.

"What are you doing here?" she demanded.

Gina had been right. She did look bad. Her face was the color of chalk. The shadows beneath her eyes stood out like bruises. And her eyes, those damn green eyes that had haunted him since he'd first seen her picture, were wide and filled with fear. "Going somewhere?" he asked her.

"Out of town."

"Where?"

"That's none of your business," she told him as she dumped several packages of cold cuts and juice boxes into the ice chest.

He walked over and stopped in front of the ice chest. "I'm making it my business." Ignoring him, she continued—but he didn't miss the slight tremor in her fingers.

Apparently deciding to abandon the remainder of the refrigerator's contents, she closed the door and reached for the chest top. "Get out of my way, Michael."

"Not until you tell me where you're running to and why."

"I'm not running anywhere. If you must know, I'm going to Atlanta to see my Aunt Sally. She had a stroke last night."

"You don't have an Aunt Sally," Michael informed her.

She slapped the lightweight cover on top of the chest and glanced up at him out of eyes that had narrowed suspiciously. "How would you know?"

He debated how much to tell her, tried to gauge her reaction, decided the timing was wrong. "Because you told me. You said you didn't have any family other than Timmy."

She gnawed on her lip for a moment. "I didn't think about Aunt Sally. She was my grandmother's sister. Now, would you please get out of my way?"

"Here, let me carry that for you," he said when she started to pick up the chest. After some reluctance, she let him take the ice chest and carry it out to the car for her, where he loaded it into the trunk.

"Thanks." She slammed the trunk closed and headed back inside.

"How long are you planning to be gone?" he asked as he followed her into the den where she retrieved her purse and coat.

"A week. Maybe two," she told him as she slipped on her jacket.

"Then how come it looks like you've packed just about everything you own?"

"I haven't," she countered.

"No? Then explain this," he demanded, and

marched into her bedroom, pulling open the closet door. "Tell me why all your clothes are gone."

"I don't owe you any explanations," she shouted, and when she started to turn away he caught her.

"Who are you afraid of? Why are you afraid? Tell me." He knew he was pushing her, hating to do it. But everything inside him said that if he confessed now, she would bolt. He needed her to trust him. It was the only way he could help her. Because suddenly helping her was all that mattered to him. "Don't shut me out, Lily," he said, his voice softening with the tenderness he felt for her. He smoothed his hands down her arms, held her. "Trust me. Let me help you."

For a moment, her body went slack in his arms. Some of the fear left her eyes. Then the phone sitting on the table next to them started to ring. Lily tensed. Her eyes darted to the ringing phone.

Michael knew panic when he saw it, had dealt with it numerous times when he'd been a cop. It was panic he read in Lily's eyes now. "Aren't you going to answer it?"

"No. I have to go," she insisted, and tried to pull away from him.

Michael grabbed the phone. "Hello?"

Silence.

"Hello? Who's there?" he demanded, aware of Lily's terror-stricken expression, the stiffness of her body as he held her against him.

Then the line clicked and the dial tone buzzed in his ear.

"Oh my God! Please, Michael. Let me go, please," she pleaded.

"Lily, what is it? What's wrong?"

"It's him. He's found me."

"Who?" he asked, doing his best to calm her, hating to see her so frightened. "Who's found you?"

"My husband."

Some survival instinct in her—the same instinct that had made her run away from Adam seven months ago—kicked in again now. Adam knew where she was. He had found her. She could feel it in her bones. And she had to get away. Now. Before he got there. Before he found Timmy.

"I have to go. Please, Michael. Don't try to stop me. I have to get Timmy and leave before he gets here," Lily told him.

"All right. Calm down, Lily," Michael soothed. "We're going. He's not going to find you. I promise."

She shook her head, knew Michael couldn't understand. "He will. You don't know him. He won't stop until he gets me back." Distraught, she didn't realize, or even question, that Michael hadn't seemed surprised to find out she was running from her husband—a husband whom she had told him was dead. Some portion of her brain simply stored that fact away, unwilling to examine it now when her only thought, her only goal, was to get her son and escape before Adam closed in on her. "Please, I have to go," she cried out.

"Come on then. We'll take my truck. And on the way to get Timmy, I'll call the police and alert them," he said, pulling a cell phone from his coat pocket. "They'll protect—"

"No!" She slapped the cell phone from his hand, shoved him back against the table and ran.

"Lily, wait!"

But she didn't wait. She couldn't let Michael notify the police. Adam had too many police officials in his pocket, too many lawyers and judges on his payroll. They would just turn her and Timmy over to him. He'd dismiss her accusations as the rantings of a sick young woman. And they would believe him. Terrified, she raced out of the house with Michael's voice ringing in her ears. She didn't stop when she tripped on a rug, nor did she stop when she tipped over a lamp and sent it crashing to the floor. She simply got up and kept running. She didn't even bother to close the door. She flew down the front steps, fought with the catch on the iron gate, and hurried to the street.

He knows where I am. Adam knows where I am. Is he in New Orleans? On his way, even now, to get me? Have to get Timmy. Have to get Timmy and run before he gets here.

She slapped the trunk closed and raced to the front of the car. Fumbling, she managed to get the key into the car door just as Michael came out of the house.

"Lily," he shouted, and charged down the stairs.

Finally the locks released, and she jerked open the driver's door. She threw her purse inside and was about to jump behind the wheel, when Michael yanked open the passenger door. "Michael, please. Don't try to stop me. I have to go. I have to get to Timmy."

"Not without me. I'm going with you."

"You can't. It's too dangerous."

"You think that matters to me?" he snapped. "I care about you, Lily. You and Timmy. You've got to trust me."

Trust?

Oh, how she wanted to trust him, wished that she dare trust him. But she couldn't. Not with Timmy's life at stake. "I can't. I can't trust anyone," she told him, and with the admission came the tears. Scared and exhausted both physically and emotionally, Lily didn't know what to do."

"You don't have a choice. You're going to have to trust me, because you can't do this by yourself. I can help you, Lily. Let me help you."

"You can't help me. No one can."

"You—" Whatever he was about to say, he didn't finish. Instead, he said, "Get in the car."

"Michael, I—"

"Get in the car," he repeated, his voice sharp, his expression fierce. "Now."

She started to protest, but something in his eyes stopped her. She slid behind the wheel. Michael got in and pulled the passenger door shut, but he kept his eyes trained on the side-view mirror.

"What is it? What's wrong?"

"Put the key in the ignition, but don't start the car

yet. Move slowly, act like nothing's wrong, like we're just chatting about something and getting ready to go for a drive. We're being watched.''

Her stomach knotted, but she did as he said. ''Who's watching us? Where is he?''

''They,'' he corrected. ''There are two of them down the street.''

''Where?'' she asked, starting to turn.

''Don't turn around,'' he commanded, and she froze. ''I don't want them to know we've spotted them.''

''Okay,'' she replied and waited.

''All right. Now adjust your rearview mirror. Slowly,'' he cautioned when she started to jerk at the mirror.

Taking care to make her movements more casual, she followed his lead. But all the while she was shaking inside.

''Now look down at the end of the block, on the other side of the street behind that red Mustang. Do you see the dark-gray Lincoln Town Car?''

''Yes,'' Lily told him, her body tensing as she spied the two men sitting inside the vehicle.

''I noticed them when I drove up to your place. I thought at the time that they didn't look like they belonged in this neighborhood, but I figured they were probably visitors in town for Mardi Gras and were waiting for someone. But they're still there. The car hasn't moved, and neither have they.''

Lily's stomach pitched as she listened to Michael. She could feel the color drain from her face. She gripped the steering wheel so tightly her knuckles turned white. How long had they been there? she wondered. Had they been there when she'd left this morning with Timmy? Could they have followed her to Gertie's? No. No, if they had and they worked for Adam, surely they would have grabbed both her and Timmy then.

"The beefy guy in the passenger seat either has a pair of binoculars or some kind of camera. Whichever it is, he's got it aimed in this direction, because I saw the sunlight reflecting off the lens a minute ago."

Oh, God, she thought. What was she going to do?

"Do you recognize them?" Michael asked her.

"No," she said, shaking her head. "But that doesn't mean anything. Adam...my husband has a lot of people working for him. I wouldn't recognize half of them." And if they caught her and found out where Timmy was, Adam would have her son killed.

"If they do work for him, and they haven't grabbed you yet, there's a reason. My guess is they're waiting for instructions."

Or they were waiting for Adam himself, Lily thought.

"Whatever the reason, we're going to have to try to lose them."

Lily looked over at him, recalled those few moments in his arms the previous night. He was a good man, she thought. Too good to drag into this mess. "I appreciate what you're trying to do, Michael. Really I do. But it would be better for both of us if you just got out of the car now and let me handle this myself.''

"How do you plan to do that? We both know the minute you move, those two goons are going to be on you. Do you really think you're going to be able to outrun them in this heap, get Timmy and escape?"

"I've done it before," she defended. "Do you think those two are the only ones he's sent to bring me back? I outwitted the others and got away. I'll do it again." She simply had to. For Timmy's sake.

"Not this time. You can bet they aren't going to let you just drive away. Those two will be on you before you even get to the corner. At least with me here with you, they might not be so quick to grab you."

"Adam will kill you if he finds out you helped me."

"I was a cop, remember? I don't kill easy. Now, buckle your seat belt," he told her. "Damn! This would have been a lot easier if we were in my truck."

"What?" she asked, not following his line of thought.

"We would have had a better chance of outrunning that Lincoln with my truck. But it's too late for us to switch vehicles now without giving them a heads up. So we'll have to improvise. How fast will this baby go?"

"I...I don't know. I don't usually drive faster than the speed limit."

"Great," he muttered. "Have you ever had her out on the interstate?"

"Yes, a number of times. Why?"

"The speed limit's seventy. You had any trouble getting her to hit it?"

"No. In fact, a couple of times I went a little over eighty without realizing it. And I just had it tuned up about a week ago."

"Well, at least that's in our favor," he said, more to himself than to her. "What kind of driver are you?"

"Good. Why?"

"Because in a minute, you're going to start the engine. And then you're going to pull away from the curb real casual like as though nothing is wrong. We don't want Curly and Moe back there to know we've spotted them. All right, go ahead, start the engine."

Lily did as he said. A glance in her rearview mirror and the puff of smoke from the exhaust told her that the driver of the gray Lincoln had started his engine, as well.

"All right. I want you to take your time and just mosey on down the street like you have all the time in the world. Turn right at the corner and head for the intersection. Keep going slow and time your speed so that when you get to the corner, you catch the red light."

She did as Michael instructed, moving slowly, so that as she turned and approached the intersection at the corner where the traffic was thicker, the light turned yellow.

"Don't follow the other cars through the yellow.

Stop and wait for the light to turn red. You want to be first in line at the light.''

Lily followed his instructions—her car was the first in line.

"Okay, you're doing fine. Our guys are three cars in back of us now. Put on your right-turn signal so that our guys know where we're going.''

"We want them to know where we're going?''

"We want them to *think* they know.''

Lily tapped her fingers on the steering wheel impatiently. "I think the light's stuck.''

"It's a long light. Two minutes and fifteen seconds.''

She shot him an incredulous look.

"I timed it," he confessed. "Okay, get ready. When the light turns green, you're going to have one second, maybe two, before the cars across the street start racing across the intersection in this direction. Before they do, I want you to cut a hard left and hit the gas.''

"But it's a no left turn.''

"Exactly," Michael told her. "And by the time Curly and Moe can get through the line of cars whizzing past them to make that same illegal left, we'll be gone. Think you can do it?''

"Yes," she told him. She had to. To keep Timmy safe she could do anything. And she would.

"All right. Six seconds. Five. Four," Michael began to count down. "Two. One. Hit it!''

Lily floored the gas pedal and jerked the wheel to the left. Her tires squealed. Brakes screeched as she barely missed the front end of a Mercedes coming at her. Horns blared all around her. Her car swerved drunkenly for a moment, generating another flurry of blaring horns and slamming brakes. And then she was tearing down the street.

"Up ahead there's a ramp to the interstate. Take it, and drive toward the lakefront."

Lily took the ramp at full speed, felt her teeth rattle as the car hit the slope and sent them bouncing in their seats. Fueled by adrenaline and fear, Lily kept her foot firmly on the gas. She wove in and out of lanes of traffic, aware of passing the much slower-moving cars.

"Take the next exit," Michael told her, and Lily swerved to her right and exited the interstate. All the while, he kept his eyes trained on the traffic behind them. "You can slow it down. I think we lost them."

Lily nearly wept with relief as she eased her foot off the gas. But inside, she was still racing at that breakneck speed. "Do you think it's safe for me to go get Timmy now?"

"Where is he?"

"With a friend. She usually sits him when I'm working. I expected to be back to pick him up by now. She's probably wondering where I am."

"Pull in over there," he said, pointing to the parking lot near the seawall.

Lily parked the car, and not until she pried her fingers from the steering wheel and shut off the engine did she realize how truly frightened she'd been. She rested her head against the steering wheel.

"You all right?"

She lifted her head. "Yes."

Michael handed her his cell phone. "Call Timmy's sitter and see if she has a safe place she can go to with Timmy until we can get there."

Lily made the call and Gertie agreed to take Timmy and go to a friend's house. She gave them the woman's name, address and phone number and agreed to wait to hear from them.

When Lily handed him the phone, he said, "I think they'll be okay for now. Since you don't want me to call the police, I'd like to call my father and ask him to come get Timmy."

"But if Adam—"

"Adam doesn't know where he is at the moment," Michael said. "Mardi Gras is tomorrow, so getting a flight in here will be impossible. But Houston's only about six, seven hours away by car. My dad can come here to keep Timmy safe until we're ready to leave. All right?"

Lily nodded.

She sat in silence as Michael made the call to his father, explained the situation and gave him Gertie's name, her friend's name and address and a phone number. After his father agreed to his plan, Michael ended the call and turned his attention back to Lily.

"All right. Now it's time for you and I to talk. I want to know what's going on. And why you think someone wants to kill you and Timmy."

"Not me. Just Timmy," she told him, and knew

how incredible it sounded. "I know it sounds crazy, but it's true. I swear it."

"Who wants Timmy dead—and why?"

"You're not going to believe me."

"Try me," Michael said.

Lily let out a breath, looked up into his deep-blue eyes. "I'm not sure where to begin."

"Why don't you start by telling me who you really are."

Thirteen

"My real name is Elisabeth Webster. Lily is what my grandmother used to call me," she began, as they walked along the seawall.

And Michael listened as Lily gave him her version of the events that had transpired seven months ago, telling him about Adam's repeated attempts to kill Timmy, about how she had plotted and planned her escape. Sickened by what he heard, Michael remained silent as she told him how she'd drugged her husband, stolen money from his safe, then tricked her guards by claiming to have a pediatrician's appointment and slipped out a back door. She paid cash for the car she had now and had hocked her wedding rings and watch for extra money. She had used some of the money, twice now, to obtain new ID's for herself. He wanted to believe her, but the idea that Webster would actually want to kill his own son just didn't make sense. "So you drugged your husband, stole some money from him and ran away because you were protecting Timmy?"

Lily nodded.

"Why didn't you just divorce the man?"

"For the same reason I don't want you to call the police. Adam is a powerful man with friends in high places. Even if I had been able to divorce him, he would have made sure that he got custody of Timmy. I couldn't take that risk."

Michael didn't miss her shiver, and he suspected it had a great deal more to do with her thoughts of Webster than it did with the breeze that had created the chop on the lake waters.

"I knew that night in his study that if I didn't leave and get Timmy away, it was only a matter of time before Adam found a way to kill Timmy and make it look like an accident."

"But Timmy's the man's son," Michael pointed out.

"I knew you wouldn't understand."

When she started to walk away from him, Michael caught her by the shoulders and turned her around to face him. "Make me understand," he said, wanting to believe her but finding his feelings for her clouding his judgment.

"I was fifteen when my grandmother died and I was sent to live with my mother. My mother was very beautiful. People used to say that she looked like Marilyn Monroe."

And he could believe it, Michael thought as he looked at Lily. Only, Lily's beauty was more ethereal than blatantly sexy.

"A local modeling agency had spotted her in a beauty pageant and got her some small jobs. My mother was just waiting to finish high school and then she was going to head to New York. She figured she would make it big as a model there and parlay that into a singing career.''

''What happened?''

''She got pregnant with me in her senior year and it derailed her big plans.''

''What about your father?'' Michael asked.

''My mother would never say who he was. I'm not sure she knew. From what I gather, my mother wasn't necessarily promiscuous, but she definitely had no qualms about sleeping her way to success. Personally I think he was married, and she'd hoped to use the pregnancy to further her career. Only it didn't happen, and once the agency discovered she was pregnant, the modeling assignments dried up.''

While Michael didn't know Lily's mother, he did know that he didn't like the woman, and she hadn't deserved a daughter like Lily.

''I'm not sure if it was because her pregnancy was too far along, or if my grandmother instilled enough of the Catholic religion in her to make her afraid to have an abortion. Whatever the reason, she didn't. She did want to give me up for adoption, but my grandmother wouldn't hear of it. My grandmother could be really stubborn when she set her mind to it,'' Lily explained, a wistful expression on her face.

''Like her granddaughter, I suspect.''

''Maybe. Anyway, my mother kept me. And when I was three months old, she left me with my grandmother, said she was going to see about getting a job, and she never came back.''

While Lily went on to explain that her mother never did become the star she'd dreamed of being, Michael couldn't help thinking about his own family. Growing up, he had had his share of differences with his father, but even through their estrangement, he'd always known that he was loved and wanted.

"Anyway, after my grandmother died, the courts located my mother and sent me to live with her."

"I'm sure she loved that."

"The truth is, I'm not sure why she agreed to let me come. But she did. And that's when I met Adam for the first time. My mother was working as a singer in one of his supper clubs. He was very kind to me."

"You were just a kid," Michael pointed out, disliking the idea of the man coming on to a young girl.

"A kid who felt a great deal older and probably looked it, too. I was already my full height and had begun to develop a figure." She looked down at herself as though thinking the remark sounded boastful. "Actually, I think I had a bit more of a figure then. I've lost a bit of weight this past year."

"You look fine to me," Michael pointed out. Tired, a little thinner than the woman in Webster's pictures, but every bit as beautiful. Even more beautiful, he amended, because there was a softness and a fragility to Lily now that hadn't been in the photographs.

"Anyway, Adam took a special interest in me. He bought me gifts, took my mother and I to concerts, out to dinner. For a while it was almost like having a father. And when my mother died eighteen months later, he became my guardian.''

''How did he get by with that since he wasn't a relative?''

''Apparently, my mother had drawn up a will after I came to live with her, and she made provisions in it for Adam to be my guardian if something happened to her.''

''Sounds convenient,'' Michael replied.

''In retrospect, I can see that. But at the time, I was just grateful that Adam took on the task. Since he didn't think it would look proper for us to be living together, even if he was my legal guardian, he sent me to a Catholic boarding school. He'd come to visit me on weekends, sign me out to spend the holidays with him. It was lonely, but nice. I certainly didn't have to worry about money or how I was going to support myself. But just before I turned eighteen, things began to change. Adam began to change. His interest in me…it wasn't fatherly,'' she said.

She began to pace along the seawall, staring out at the lake where a sailboat was zipping across the waves. ''Or maybe I just took off the blinders. I'm not sure. I just know that those last few months before I graduated, Adam told me that he loved me, that he'd been in love with me from the moment he'd set eyes on me and that he'd just been waiting for me to grow up. He said I was all grown up now, a woman and not a girl anymore. He said he wanted to go on taking care of me, but not as my guardian—but as a man.

Then he gave me a huge diamond ring and asked me to marry him."

"Did you even love him?" Michael asked, unable to keep some of the bitterness out of his voice.

If Lily noticed his agitation, she gave no indication because she said, "Actually, I did. Oh, not in a sexual way. Not the way Adam felt about me. But I did love him, I guess the way a girl loves her father."

"He wasn't your father," Michael pointed out.

"I know that. But he was the first and only man who'd ever been in my life. I was a shy teenager living with a mother who was a stranger and he paid attention to me. He made me feel special, like I mattered."

"It's a hell of a reason to marry someone," Michael countered. "Why didn't you just tell him no, that you didn't love him in that way? Or was the lure of the money and fancy lifestyle too much?"

She looked up at him, and from the hurt in her eyes, he knew she'd heard similar accusations before.

"Listen, I was out of line. I—"

"It's all right. Why should you be any different than anyone else? I bet if you look up the definition of gold digger in the dictionary, there might even be a picture of me next to it."

"I deserved that," Michael said. "I have no right to judge you. I'm just trying to understand."

"And I'm trying to explain. I married Adam because he was good to me. And because I was lonely. I thought... I hoped that with time, I'd learn to love him the way he loved me."

"Did you?" he asked, and hated himself because the answer mattered so much.

"No. It's one of the reasons I wanted to have a baby. I thought it might make things better somehow."

"I take it, it didn't."

"No. Adam didn't want children. He was very firm about that. He'd already ruled out my going to college or getting a job. I knew he was possessive of me, jealous of anything that took me away from him. So I...I deliberately got pregnant," she confessed. "Only I never thought... I never dreamed he would resent Timmy because I loved him."

"I'm surprised he didn't want you to have an abortion."

"He would have if he'd known."

"Come again?" Michael replied, surprised by her comment.

"I didn't tell him I was pregnant until it was too late for me to have an abortion without there being some risk to my life."

"You expect me to believe a man as jealous and obsessed with you as he was didn't notice you were pregnant?" he asked, not bothering to hide his skepticism.

"I was lucky in that I didn't gain a lot of weight and was able to hide the pregnancy at first. When I started to show, I claimed I'd come down with a bug. So for a week or so he and I...we didn't..."

"I get the picture," Michael said.

"When I couldn't fake being ill any longer without

him insisting I go to the hospital, things went back to normal. He noticed I'd gained weight, but I let him think I'd just been eating too many sweets. Then by the time he realized that I'd laid off the desserts, and the workouts in the gym weren't taking off the weight, I was far enough along that he couldn't force me to get rid of the baby.''

"Jesus! What century are you living in? The man doesn't own you," Michael told her, outraged by her explanation.

"But he does. Or at least he thinks he does. That's what I've been trying to tell you. Adam took care of me. He educated me. He made me who I am."

"You've made yourself who you are."

She shook her head. "Not in Adam's eyes. I *belong* to him, and he doesn't share what's his with anyone."

"Not even with his own son?"

"Not even Timmy."

Edgy, Michael walked away from her. He rammed his fingers through his hair as he looked out at the lake, wishing to hell he were on that sailboat out there. Not here listening to some story about a modern-day Svengali. Angry with Webster and with Lily, because of the feelings she set off in him, Michael whipped back around and marched over to her. "Do you have any idea how sick this all sounds?"

"I know," she whispered, lowering her eyes as though ashamed. "It took me a long time to admit that Adam's feelings for me…that they're not normal. That this obsession he has with me…well, it's just what you said. It's sick. I finally had to accept that. That's when I decided I had to get away from him.''

And now, thanks to him, the bastard knew where she was, Michael admitted. His instincts had been right. Somehow he had managed to tip Webster off—the guy had become suspicious of him. He'd either figured out he was lying about leaving New Orleans or he'd had his goons tracking his movements. It wouldn't be that hard to do, Michael reasoned. Not if someone had the right connections—which, according to Lily, the man had. This also meant that there was no way he could tell Lily now about the hand he'd played in the whole mess—not without her trying to bolt again. And if she did leave, he didn't doubt for a second that Webster would find her. Thoughts of Webster touching Lily or doing anything to hurt Timmy sent a murderous rage through him. He had to figure out a way to keep them safe until he could get them on that plane to Oklahoma tomorrow night. Then he would deal with Webster.

''Listen, now that you know what's involved, I'll understand if you've changed your mind about helping me,'' she said. ''If you want to call your father and tell him not to come, go ahead. I can't take you back to get your truck, because I'm worried those men might have returned to my place to wait for me. But I can drop you off at your hotel or call you a cab.''

Barely listening to what she said, Michael was weighing his options. He couldn't tell her he'd al-

ready purchased the plane tickets—not without revealing his connection with Webster.

"So do you want me to drop you off at your
hotel?"

"What?" Michael asked, unsure of what he'd
missed.

"I asked if you wanted me to drop you off at your
hotel?"

"No. We can't go back there. Chances are they've
run a check of the plates on my truck and know who
I am. It wouldn't be too hard to find out where I'm
staying. I think our best bet is to hide in plain sight
until I can get you and Timmy out of town."

"You still want to help me?"

"Did you think I'd change my mind?"

She nodded. "Adam Webster can be a powerful
enemy. If you help me, he'll be *your* enemy. You
don't have to do this, Michael."

"Yes, I do. I've already told you. I care about
you," he said, brushing a strand of honey-colored hair
behind her ear. "And I like that little boy of yours a
lot, too. I'm not going to let him hurt you."

"I…I'm not sure what to say."

"Say that you trust me," Michael prompted.

"All right," she said, and averted her gaze.

Michael tipped up her chin. "Is that everything,
Lily? Is there anything else I should know?"

She hesitated for a long moment, then shook her
head. "No," she said quietly. "That's everything."

"All right then," he said, and kissed her. When he
lifted his head and looked into those big green eyes,

he wondered how he could ever—even for a moment—confuse her with Giselle. "I think I've come up with a plan. But first, I need to know how much cash you have on you."

"A little over a thousand dollars."

"And I have about twenty-five hundred. That should be enough."

"Enough for what?" she asked.

"To grease a few palms and get us a room in one of the swank hotels during the big Mardi Gras festivities."

"Okay, we've got a room." Michael joined her on the seawall, where she'd been staring out at the boats on the lake while he'd retreated to the quiet of the car to search for a hotel room.

The wind whipped the hair around her face, and she held it away from her eyes to look up at him. "Where?"

"The Saint Charles Court."

At the mention of one of the city's finest hotels she arched her eyebrow. With hotel rooms at a premium, as well as a four-day minimum stay during the long Mardi Gras weekend, she knew he'd had a battle on his hands even getting a second-rate room. "Should I even ask how many Texas oil wells you had to promise for that?"

He sat down beside her. "You don't think my charm was enough to get us a room?"

The truth was, the man could probably charm the skin off a snake. But then Adam had been charming, too, she remembered. Realizing what she was doing, she shook off the thought. "I'm saying I'm almost afraid to ask how much it cost."

"Six hundred bucks a night."

Lily's eyes widened. "Six hundred?"

He nodded. "Plus I owe a reservation clerk named Dennis another hundred bucks for 'finding' a free room. Check-in time is not for another couple of hours. That should give us time to buy me a change of clothes and a couple of costumes to use for tomorrow."

"I know someone who owns a boutique that carries costumes. His name's Ricardo. He's a customer at the diner. He was in a couple weeks ago and offered to let us get our costumes at half-price."

"Good, then we'll make him our first stop." He stood, held out his hand. "Ready?"

He helped her to her feet. And as they walked to the car, she kept thinking about the plan he'd described to her. He claimed the old adage was true. The best place to hide something or, in their case, someone, was to hide them in plain sight. When he opened the passenger door for her, she paused and looked up at him. "Michael, do you really think this plan of yours will work?"

"Oh ye of little faith. Didn't you ever hear that old story? The one about the cop in a border town who knew this old guy who kept driving trucks across the border every day was smuggling something, but every time he stopped the guy and checked the truck from top to bottom, he couldn't find a thing. All the man had in the truck was a couple of chairs that he had receipts for.''

''I guess I must have missed that one,'' Lily said, unable to believe she was standing here at the lake-front with Michael this way. The place was evidently a popular spot for lovers, given the number of couples she'd spotted holding hands or kissing since they'd arrived. She'd never been on a date, had never been with another man besides Adam. To be here now with Michael so close and looking at her with such warmth—it made her feel like…like a schoolgirl, she thought.

Michael tapped her nose with his finger. ''Pay attention,'' he said. ''I'm trying to make my point here.''

''Sorry. So the man was really stealing the chairs?''

''No. He was stealing the trucks. The border-patrol cop was so busy looking for what was hidden inside the truck that he never looked closely at the trucks themselves. The man wasn't stealing the chairs. He was stealing the trucks.''

''So you're saying that Adam will expect us to try to hide, and by not hiding and making ourselves part of the Mardi Gras mob scene, he won't see us.''

''Smart, as well as beautiful,'' Michael said, and kissed her firmly on the mouth.

When he lifted his head, it took her a moment to focus. Embarrassed by her response, she slipped into the passenger seat and Michael closed her door. After he got in the car, she asked, ''So can we call Gertie now and tell her we're on our way to pick up Timmy?''

Michael's expression sobered. "I think it would be better for Timmy if he stayed put for now."

"No. I won't leave my baby. I—"

"Lily." He said her name in that deep authoritative tone. "My father will be there in a few hours. He'll keep him safe until we can pick him up. I'm just not sure it would be safe for him to be with us right now."

"But—"

"Think about it. It will be a lot easier for Webster to find you if he's looking for a woman with a child. It's only until I can get the two of you out of the city. I've already made arrangements for you and Timmy to stay with a friend of mine."

That came as a surprise to her. "Who? Where?"

"Remember my friend Janie I told you about? The one with two little boys?"

She nodded. "The woman who was married to your partner, the policeman who was killed in some kind of drug bust?"

"Yeah," he said, a haunted look coming into his eyes. "Janie is…was Pete's wife. She and her boys have just moved to Oklahoma, where she has family. Anyway, I've asked her to let you and Timmy stay with her for a while. At least until this mess with Webster is over with."

"And she agreed?" Lily replied, surprised at the suggestion.

"Yes."

"But she doesn't even know me."

"She does know me. And, she knows a little about you."

"She does?"

"She knows you're important to me."

Lily swallowed, unsure of what to say, not sure what to make of all these feelings she had for this man. She'd known Michael for such a short time, and yet here he was risking himself for her and Timmy. It made her feel all the more guilty for not having told him about the disk she'd taken from Adam's safe.

"So, will you trust me on this? Leave Timmy with your friend Gertie until my father can get to them and it's safe for us to go?"

She debated again whether or not to tell him about the disk, and decided against it. As a former cop, and a man who'd lost his partner in a foiled bust, he would want to turn it over to the authorities. And despite everything Michael had done, and was doing, to help her, she couldn't take the risk. She couldn't gamble on trusting him with the disk—not when Timmy's life was at stake. "All right," she told him. "We'll do it your way for now."

He reached for her hand, kissed her fingers and then squeezed them. "I won't let you down. Now tell me where this guy Richard's shop is."

"It's Ricardo's and it's on Saint Charles Avenue."

"Ricardo's?" he repeated as he started the car. "Sounds expensive."

It *was* expensive, Lily realized the moment she entered the shop. No woman could have been married to a man like Adam Webster for seven years and not be able to recognize genuine antiques, priceless chandeliers and silk-moiré wall coverings when she saw them. The Baccarat vases filled with out-of-season blooms alone were worth a small fortune. The champagne being served was a vintage Moet Chandon. And those were just the decorations. One look at the beaded and sequined gowns, the elaborate feathered masks and the Manolo Blahnik and Jimmy Choo pumps and she knew that even at cost, she and Michael couldn't afford to buy a thing. The place was filled with customers of both the female and female-wanna-be gender, all of whom were grabbing things from the racks as if it was a fire sale.

"Your friend has some interesting clientele," Michael commented as they watched a six-foot brunette with an Adam's apple try on a Carmen Miranda–type headpiece.

"Yes, he does."

"Say, what do you think about this one?" Michael asked, holding up a leather outfit with a breastplate and sword that resembled the one worn by the TV actress who had starred as Xena the Warrior Princess.

"I don't think it would look good on either of us. In fact, I don't think we're going to be able to find anything at all here," she told him, wanting to leave the place before Ricardo saw her. "Maybe we should try one of the thrift stores or a Wal-Mart. I'm sure they have costumes."

"Lily," Ricardo called out, and Lily realized she'd

left things too late as he hurried over to her with both arms outstretched. "Lily, darling, it is you." He kissed one cheek and then the other. "I'm so glad you decided to come after all."

"Hello, Ricardo," she said, wondering how she was going to get out of there.

"Darling, introduce me to your friend."

"Ricardo, this is Michael Sullivan. Michael, this is Ricardo..." She flushed. "I'm sorry, Ricardo. I don't know your last name."

"That is because I am like Cher. Only one name is necessary," he declared. "It is so nice to meet one of Lily's friends."

"It's a pleasure to meet you, too," Michael told him.

"Well, I am afraid the two of you have left it a bit late for a costume. Mardi Gras is tomorrow, and, as you can see, the shop has been very busy."

"And we really don't want to take up any more of your time," Lily said.

"You already have a costume for tomorrow's big celebration?"

"Well, no." Lily took a deep breath and decided it was best to be honest. "I'm sorry, Ricardo, but I don't think we can afford any of the costumes you have in here."

Ricardo waved away her objection. "You will come in the back, have some champagne, and we will see what we can do for you."

"But—"

"What is it with you Americans? Always with the

'but.' Phoebe,'' he called to an exotic-looking creature wearing a pink feather boa. ''Bring me the Cleopatra outfit—the size six we special ordered for Mrs. St. Claire that she said was missized.'' He leaned over and said in a stage whisper, ''The lady actually wears a ten, but insisted we order a six.''

He led them into a back room where there were no other customers. Ricardo flicked a switch and Enya's haunting voice came on. By the time he'd offered them each a glass of champagne, Phoebe came in with an ivory and gold box with the name Ricardo's embossed in script across the front. ''Thank you, my dear,'' he said to the woman, and when she exited, he removed the lid on the box. He dug through layers of creamy tissue and removed a flowing white silk dress and gold filigree ropelike belt. ''Ah, this should fit you perfectly.''

''Ricardo, I don't think—''

''No need to think. Just slip behind the dressing screen over there and put it on. I'll get the shoes and the wig.''

Lily put on the dress. The simplicity of the style and cut suited her, and the costume fit as if it had been made for her. By the time Ricardo had outfitted her in the stark black wig, the gold headpiece and bracelets for her upper arms, and had then rimmed her eyes in kohl and applied a berry color to her lips, she was squirming in the chair. Having Michael observe the transformation did nothing to ease her nerves.

''Perfect,'' Ricardo said after finishing her lashes

with black mascara. "Go look in the mirror, and tell Ricardo what you think."

Lily walked over to the mirror and stared at her reflection. The woman looking back at her didn't resemble her at all. She touched her face, just to make sure the striking woman was actually her.

"The transformation is amazing, is it not?"

"Yes, it is," she whispered.

"With those eyes, your skin and bone structure, I was sure you would make a wonderful Cleopatra. And as usual, I was right. You are now every bit as beautiful as Taylor was in the film. Don't you agree, Mr. Sullivan?"

"No," Michael said, all serious as his eyes met hers in the mirror. "She's more beautiful than Liz Taylor ever was."

Lily flushed with pleasure and excitement as Michael looked at her. He wanted her. She had seen desire in a man's eyes often enough to recognize it. She had seen it come into Adam's eyes each time he'd looked at her, each time he'd possessed her. Yet there was more than desire in the way that Michael looked at her now. There was an admiration, a caring that made her feel like a person and not simply a sexual possession to be flaunted and conquered. And just as it had when he'd kissed her, she could feel that liquid heat stirring inside her belly again.

"You are pleased with your costume, yes?"

His question jarred Lily's thoughts back to her reason for needing the costume in the first place—as a means to escape Adam. "Oh yes. I'm very pleased.

It's a wonderful costume, Ricardo. But I'm sure I can't afford it."

"It is my gift."

"But I can't accept this."

"You insult Ricardo by refusing his gift?"

"No, but, I—"

"Then it is done. Besides, it was a special order and nonreturnable. The loss is a small one. But I will allow you to pay me for the makeup, as you must have the makeup for the costume to work properly."

"All right," Lily said, feeling she had truly struck a wonderful bargain.

"And you, Mr. Sullivan. Shall I try to dress you as Marc Antony? I think I have a Roman costume that will fit you. A forty-four long, yes?"

"That's right, but—"

"There is that word again," Ricardo said dramatically.

"A Roman outfit means a skirt, right? I'm not wearing a skirt."

Ricardo tapped his finger against his lips a moment. "What did you think of Russell Crowe in *Gladiator*? Did you think he looked feminine?"

Michael eyed Ricardo as though he suspected it was a trick question. "No."

"Then perhaps I can persuade you to go as a Roman gladiator. The costume I have in mind is perfect for a man with your body," Ricardo said, walking around Michael as though imagining him donned in the garb. "Yes, with your coloring and that fierce look on your face, it will be perfect."

"I don't think so," Michael began.

"We'll take it," Lily said, jumping in before Michael could refuse the man's offer. "But we're pressed for time, so could you just box it up, along with the other things?"

Fourteen

"You don't think people are going to find Cleopatra paired up with a cowboy a little strange?" Lily asked him after they left the thrift shop where he'd purchased himself another pair of jeans, shirt, chaps and a cowboy hat.

Michael adjusted the Stetson on his head. "Have you ever seen some of those getups people wear for Mardi Gras?"

Lily shook her head.

"Trust me, no one will notice."

"But it's such a shame to let that gladiator costume go to waste."

"Forget it. There's no way I'm running around in an outfit with a skirt," Michael told her.

"Russell Crowe didn't seem to mind."

"He's not from Texas," Michael pointed out, pleased to hear the teasing note in her voice. At least the costume excursion had helped to divert her thoughts from Webster.

After stowing their purchases in the trunk, he opened the car door for her, then walked around and got behind the wheel. "I want to make one more stop and pick up a new cell phone, and then we'll head to the hotel.''

"Is something wrong with your phone?"

"I left the charger in my hotel room and the battery's running low," he said, not wanting to tell her that he didn't want to chance Webster being able to use the cell number to track their movements. "It'll just be easier to buy a new one.''

She eyed him suspiciously. "That's not really the reason, is it? You think if Adam got your name from running the plates on your truck that he might be able to find us by your cell phone number."

"Yes," Michael admitted. "It's a long shot. He would need some pretty good connections to get the call logs for my cell and it would take time, but I'd rather we play it safe.''

"Then why the lie? Why not just tell me the truth?"

"Because I didn't want to frighten you," he confessed.

"You mean you didn't want to frighten me any more than I already am, don't you?''

He nodded.

Her lips thinned. "Just because I'm afraid doesn't mean that I'm stupid. I can understand how you would think that, given some of the foolish decisions I've made in my life, but I'm not stupid. And being afraid doesn't mean that I won't do whatever I have to do in order to protect my son. Because I will.''

He touched her face. "I don't think you're stupid. And you don't have to convince me that you're brave,

Lily. I know you are. Hell, considering all that you've been through, I think you're probably one of the smartest and bravest women I've ever met," he told her, meaning every word. "I'm sorry if it seemed otherwise."

She nodded. "I don't need you to protect me from things, Michael. I need to know what's going on so that I'm prepared. All right?"

"All right."

But much to his regret, the lightness of a few moments ago was gone and showed no signs of returning. Even after they'd checked into the hotel, Lily remained somber, preoccupied. And though she'd gone along with them posing as a married couple at the check-in, he suspected she hadn't liked the idea. He also knew from the way she'd been eyeing a toddler in the hotel lobby that she was missing her son.

"Do you think it will be safe for me to tell Gertie where we are?" she asked as they exited the elevator on the tenth floor and headed down the hall to their room.

He paused in front of the door and looked at her. "Go ahead. And give her the new cell number, too." Michael slid the key card into the door. The green light flashed on, and he held the door open for Lily to precede him.

He followed inside, carrying their packages and a small suitcase. While the room boasted thick, silvery carpet, fresh flowers and what he suspected were antiques, there was only one bed. A king-size four-poster with one of those ruffled skirts at the bottom and a pretty duvet in a shiny pale blue, pewter and ivory design. Piles of pillows had been bunched up at the head of the bed. Nightstands with delicate-looking lamps sat on either side. An armoire, which he suspected housed a television set and storage space, took up one wall. A wet bar and a grouping with two chairs, a love seat and a coffee table filled the other half of the room. "Not a lot for six hundred bucks a night, is it?" he remarked as he set down their things, then closed and bolted the door.

"It's kind of small, but nice," she commented, and wandered into the adjoining bathroom. "At least it's clean."

"Listen, Lily, about the bed... I tried to get two doubles, but the king was all they had."

"I assumed as much," she informed him as she walked over to the window. "At least we have a nice view."

Michael joined her at the window and gazed down at Saint Charles Avenue, one of the city's premier streets that boasted some of the most beautiful homes in New Orleans on one end, and a number of seedy joints at the other end. Double lanes of traffic moved in opposite directions while a streetcar lumbered down the center of the grassy boulevard. Already people were lining up with ladders, chairs, blankets and ice chests—ready to camp out and claim viewing space in anticipation of the Mardi Gras festivities that would begin in earnest the next morning. "The reservation clerk said that by sunrise tomorrow there'll be so many people down there on the street, they'll look like ants.''

''And one of them could be Adam.''

Michael felt that kick in his chest again, hated that she was in this situation because of him. ''If he is out there, we'll know and we'll be prepared. After I check in with my dad to see how far away he is, I'll make a few calls, see if I can find out if Webster's in the city.''

She looked up at him. ''How will you do that?''

''I'm going to see if I can reach my brother again. Travis works for the FBI. I'll ask if he can tap a few of his sources and find out if there's been any credit card activity, car rentals, anything that would indicate Webster's in New Orleans.''

''You never mentioned anything about a brother before. In fact, I had the feeling it wasn't easy for you asking your father for his help.''

Michael hesitated. ''My dad and I have been estranged for a while.''

''How sad,'' she said wistfully.

Michael shrugged. ''I suppose.''

''You suppose?'' Lily sighed. ''I loved my grandmother. And I wouldn't have traded those years I spent with her for anything. But still, sometimes I wondered what it would be like. You know, to be part of a normal family with a mother and father, maybe a brother or sister, and all of us living together. I mean, you would always have someone to talk to, to share things with. I bet your house was never lonely.''

Not lonely the way hers had been, Michael realized. "No, it wasn't lonely. A little crazy sometimes, but not lonely."

"Sounds nice."

And it had been, Michael admitted. He couldn't help feeling ashamed at how much he'd taken his own family life and upbringing for granted.

"You mentioned your father was a policeman. Is that why you became one?"

"I guess. My dad was a cop. His father, my grandfather, and his father before him were all cops. It's what the Sullivans do, I guess. Sort of a tradition."

"Your father must have been disappointed when you decided to quit the police force and go to work on the oil rigs."

Uncomfortable with the lie he'd told her, he said, "Let's say he wasn't happy. It's one of the reasons we haven't spoken in so long."

"What happened?"

"It's a long story."

"It seems to me we have time, since we're stuck here at least until tomorrow," she countered.

Michael walked away from the window and sat down in one of the chairs. "Remember that drug bust I told you about—the one that went wrong, where my partner was killed?"

"Yes," she said as she came over and curled up on the love seat.

"It was my fault. I screwed up, and because of me Pete was killed."

"Somehow I find that hard to believe."

"It's true," he insisted, because if he'd been a good cop and checked Giselle out, maybe Pete would still be alive. And the boys would still have their father, Janie would still have a husband.

"Michael?"

He shook off the memory. "Anyway there was an investigation. I was technically acquitted of any wrongdoing, but the blame was mine all the same. My actions...they were an embarrassment to my father. I brought dishonor to the Sullivan name, to him. So I thought it was better for everyone if I just left."

"How could it be better to have someone you love cut you out of their life?" she asked. "To me that would be far worse than having the person die. At least when a person dies they're not leaving you because they want to. I hope that when Timmy grows up I never do something that makes him so angry that he hates me like that."

"I wasn't angry with my father, and I certainly didn't hate him. I did it to make things easy for him," he defended.

"I doubt that he found being cut out of your life very easy."

Was that what he'd done? Had he locked his father out of his life because he'd been angry with him, hated him? No, he'd done it because he'd hated himself, been angry with himself. And he'd been too ashamed to face his father and see the disappointment in his eyes.

"But then, what do I know about family dynamics?

I'm just praying that I can get through this and that Timmy doesn't have to pay for my mistakes.''

"You're going to get through this," he assured her. "And Timmy's going to be just fine."

"Speaking of Timmy, I'd like to call and talk to him."

Michael stood. He unhooked the cell phone clip from his belt and handed it to her. "While you talk to Timmy, I'm going to go downstairs and make some calls."

"But if you need the phone—"

"You keep it. I'll use a pay phone. Besides, I want to check out the hotel security. Come lock the door behind me and put the dead bolt on. And whatever you do, don't open the door for anyone but me."

"I'm sorry, boss, but she gave them the slip," Bernie reported to Webster after speaking with his colleagues in New Orleans. Nervous, he stood in front of Webster's desk where the man was eating one of those disgusting raw fish dishes.

"Elisabeth is only a woman, and a not very bright one at that. And yet she's managed to outwit two professionals. How is that?"

"She had help," he offered. "There's a guy with her, and from the description, it sounds like Sullivan."

Adam snapped the chopstick in two and tossed it on the tray. "I am not happy about this, Bernie. Not happy at all. That's twice now that you've let me down. First by assuring me that Sullivan was the man who could find Elisabeth for me, and now by having your men lose her. You know how much I dislike mistakes, Bernie.''

"I know, boss. And I'm sorry," Bernie said as he stared at the broken chopstick. He couldn't help imagining it as his neck. While he wanted to point out that Sullivan had found the dame, he didn't. Webster had always been a strange dude to work for. He always looked polished and polite on the outside, but he was one cold mother. He'd seen the guy cut a man's throat and leave him to bleed to death while he sat down and finished his dinner. He'd have sworn the man had ice in his veins—except when it came to that bitch he'd married. When it came to her, Webster got that crazed look in his eyes. And since the broad had taken off, he'd seen that look a lot more often than he liked. As much as he hated to admit it, the guy gave him the creeps.

"I'm not interested in your apologies, Bernie. I want Elisabeth found. And Sullivan."

"My guys found the hotel where he was staying. There's no sign of them there, and he hasn't come back for his truck. It's Mardi Gras down there, so they won't have much luck getting a flight out of the city. But I've got people posted at the airport, train and bus stations just in case. We got the license plate number and description of the car they were in just in case they try to drive."

"Did she have the kid with her?"

"No. Just her and Sullivan."

"Elisabeth won't leave without him. Find out where he is," Adam told him.

"We're trying, but—"

Adam slapped his fist down on the desk. "No more excuses, Bernie. Find the boy, and you'll find Elisabeth."

"I'll get my men on it."

"No. I want you to go."

"All right," Bernie said, starting for the door.

"And Bernie?"

He stopped, turned. "Yeah, boss?"

"Don't disappoint me again, because if you do, it will be the last time. Understand?"

"Yeah, boss," Bernie said as he felt the sweat trickle down his spine. He pulled open the door.

"One moment, Bernie," Adam said, and hit his intercom button. "Chantel, get the mayor of New Orleans on the phone for me."

Bernie waited while his boss made small talk with someone in the mayor's office. As he listened, he began to worry the man had lost it. Bernie couldn't help thinking about when that fed had tried to hold him up for more money after delivering the disk with the info on the undercover agents. He'd watched Webster put a knife through the rat's heart and actually smile. Then he'd been smart enough to think of feeding the man to the sharks. The guy had balls and brains, and knew how to tend to business. The only time he ever did anything really screwy and dumb was when it came to that broad he'd married.

No one had dared to say anything when he'd had

that little blonde from the club made over so that she looked like that bitch wife of his. The way he figured it, if the man wanted to screw a woman that looked like his wife, that was his business. But, according to Kit, he'd worked the girl over real good last night and probably would have killed her if Otto hadn't stopped him. She was in the hospital now in a coma and Kitty said she didn't think the cops were buying the story about her being roughed up by some john.

"Thank you. I'd appreciate it if you'd have the mayor call me on my private cell phone," Webster said. "It's a personal matter that I need his help with."

When Webster hung up the phone, Bernie said, "Boss, you don't need to bring a politician in on this. I'll handle Sullivan."

Webster merely smiled at him. "I have no intention of calling in a favor to help you do your job." He picked up the picture of his wife, stroked her face. "Have Sammy get the car ready. Tell him he and I are going to take a little trip."

"Sure thing, boss. Where should I tell Sammy you'll be going?" Bernie asked.

Webster smiled again, and though it shamed him to admit it, even to himself, Bernie couldn't help feeling a little scared at that crazed look he saw in the other man's eyes. He almost felt sorry for the poor dame married to the man. Almost, but not enough to put his neck on the line the way that idiot Sullivan had done.

"To the Mardi Gras."

* * *

Michael exited the room, waited outside the door until he heard the lock shoot into place, then he headed down the hall. Instead of taking the elevator, he decided on the stairs. As he made his way down the stairwell, a check of each floor revealed the doors to each floor remained unlocked. When he exited the last door, he found himself in the lobby beside the elevator bank.

"Can I help you, sir?" a silver-haired gentleman in hotel attire positioned next to the bell captain's stand asked.

"I was just checking things out. I figured that since there's just the one elevator it's liable to get pretty busy tomorrow. So I wanted to be sure I'd have access to the stairs if I need to get to my room."

"Yes, sir. It's a safety requirement that we keep the doors unlocked and the stairwells clear. But seeing how it's Mardi Gras and the hotel's full, we'll be using the service elevator, too. 'Course, you'll need to have one of the hotel employees to run you up in it," he said, the man's southern accent growing more pronounced.

"Thanks. That's good to know."

Michael walked over to the front desk. "Hi," he said to the perky blonde on duty. "My wife and I checked in a little while ago and we were given special tags to wear to let us in and out of the hotel tomorrow. I was wondering if it's possible to get a few extra tags for some friends who are going to try to meet us here for drinks."

"Well, we usually limit access passes to the hotel guests. But I think we should be able to help you. How many tags will you need?"

"Let me get back to you after I find out for sure if our friends are going to be able to join us. I'd hate to take them if we don't really need them."

Well so much for the tightened security, he thought as he checked out the delivery entrance at the back of the hotel. While there seemed to be ample numbers of police out on the streets and near the hotel, all Webster or his men would need to do was claim to be meeting someone in the hotel's restaurant or bar and they'd gain access to the hotel, he reasoned.

After another sweep of the downstairs area and all the points of entrance, Michael headed for the bank of pay phones he'd spied in the corridor leading to the rest rooms. Grateful that the hotel was an older one and that the phones had closed booths to provide some privacy, he stepped inside the old-fashioned cubicle. "Old booths but new phones," he said aloud, and retrieved the prepaid telephone card he'd purchased.

He slid the card into the slot and punched in the number for his dad's cell phone. "Dad, it's Michael. I was just checking to see that everything's all right."

"Everything's fine. Traffic is a bitch, and it's probably going to take me a little longer than I expected to get there. But I'll be there, son. Have you heard anything from your brother yet?"

"Not yet. I'm going to try his cell number again when I hang up. In the meantime, things are starting to get wild in the city. I'm hoping tomorrow morning when the celebration really gets underway, we'll be able to lose ourselves in the crowds and get Timmy.''

''You sure you don't want me to make a call to the police there?'' his father offered.

''I thought about it, but Lily really freaked when I mentioned calling the police. She claims Webster has a lot of them on his payroll in Florida and that his influence stretches pretty far.''

''You know how I feel about dirty cops. But if the man's got enough money to toss around a million-dollar reward to get her back, I guess it's possible he could find one or two bad apples who'd be tempted,'' he said.

''As it is, with Mardi Gras going on, it looks like every cop in the city is working one detail or another. That's why I thought if Travis had a friend here in the Bureau, he or she might be a better bet. As arrogant a bastard as Webster is, I don't think he'd be fool enough to try anything with an FBI agent.''

''Don't count on it. If the man's as obsessed with this woman as you claim, there's no telling what he'll do,'' Big Mike said. ''You just be careful.''

''I will, sir. And thank you.''

''Anytime.''

Lily paced the length of the hotel room, her stomach churning, as she waited for Michael to return. Was she doing the right thing? Was Michael's plan going to work? She thought about Timmy, felt a pang as she recalled his disappointment when she's explained that their trip had to be postponed. And poor Gertie. She knew she'd managed to frighten her. At the tap on the door, she jumped. "Who is it?"

"It's Michael."

She raced to the door, threw back the security bolt and pulled the door open. And she just barely managed to stop from throwing herself into his arms.

His eyes narrowed immediately. He shut the door. "What is it? Did something happen?"

"No. No, nothing happened. I'm just…" She heard her voice break, swallowed hard and turned away, afraid he'd see the tears in her eyes.

He came up behind her, turned her around. "What's wrong?"

"I talked to Gertie and Timmy. I scared Gertie, and she doesn't scare easily. And Timmy…" She swallowed again. "Michael, I want my baby."

He pulled her into his arms, held her, stroked her back. "Just a few more hours. I promise."

Telling herself she was being a ninny, she stepped back. She wiped her face and took a deep breath. "I'm sorry. Maybe it's watching all those people down there, seeing the way they seem to be getting all wound up for tomorrow. It almost seems like some kind of fever that keeps building and building."

"I know what you mean. I guess that's why they call it Mardi Gras madness. There's an energy out there you can't help but feel."

"All I know is that waiting here like this…well, I guess it's driving me a little bit crazy. Anyway, I'm sorry."

"No need to be. I understand. I know not having Timmy with you isn't easy. I talked to my dad. He's only a few hours away. So just try to hang on a little longer. Okay?"

She nodded.

"Tell you what, why don't we go get something to eat. Those sandwiches we had for lunch wore off a long time ago, and I'm starved. The hotel restaurant looks pretty good."

The truth was, food was the last thing on her mind, Lily admitted as they left the room and took the elevator downstairs. And she'd been positive that she'd have a difficult time even forcing a bite of food past her lips. So it came as a surprise when she looked down at her plate—a plate that had been filled with pasta and shrimp in a rich creamy sauce that Michael had insisted she try—and found it nearly empty.

"Feeling better?" Michael asked.

"Yes," she admitted, and took a sip of her wine. For a moment she was struck by how surreal it seemed for her to be sitting at a cozy table sharing dinner and wine with a handsome man as though it was a normal activity for her.

Her dinners with Adam had been so different. While the restaurants and foods varied, the ritual had always been the same. Hours of preparation to make herself beautiful for him, taking care that her makeup was perfect, that the dress she wore was sexy and his latest gift of jewelry displayed. A wave of revulsion went through her as she recalled how he'd liked to parade her through the restaurant, the thrill he seemed to elicit in seeing the way other men looked at her. She'd hated it. Hating knowing what people thought of her. Hated herself for not being grateful to have such a generous husband, for not being able to love him. But what she'd hated the most was when the gleam of lust, of possession would come into Adam's eyes, and he'd take her home to their bed. Lily shuddered as thoughts of that last night came to mind.

"Something wrong with the wine?"

Lily blinked. "No. No, the wine's fine," she told him, taking another sip to prove it.

"Do you want some dessert?"

"No thanks, but you go ahead if you want." She looked at her plate again and laughed. "For someone who wasn't hungry, I did a nice job on that pasta. Thanks for suggesting it."

"Glad you enjoyed it." At the blare of a horn out on the streets, Michael said, "Looks like the natives are getting restless."

"Do you think what the concierge said is true—that this partying is going to go on all night?"

"Probably. I'm told this is only a taste of what it'll be like tomorrow."

When she noted Michael gazing past her toward the lobby, she started to turn around to see what had caught his attention, but he reached across the table and caught her hand. "It's starting to get crowded in here. Why don't we go upstairs?"

Lily didn't argue. Nor did she think anything of his suggestion that they take the stairs. "Shouldn't your father be in New Orleans by now?'' she asked as they began the climb.

"Let's give him another hour or so, and if he hasn't called, I'll try him. I'll also try my brother again.''

Michael didn't have to call either one of them again. They had no sooner returned to the room when the cell phone rang. "Sullivan.'' He paused. "Hey, Dad.'' Several more pauses and all rights, and he said, "I think it might be better if you were to just take Timmy and Gertie and head back to Houston.''

"What? Michael, what are you talking about?'' Lily demanded.

He held up his hand, listened to his father on the other end. "All right. If you're sure you're okay with that. Yes, sir. I'll explain it to her.''

"Explain what? Why is your father taking Timmy and Gertie back to Houston? Why isn't he coming here? Has something happened? Has—''

Michael placed a finger to her lips. "Nothing's happened. I suggested he take them to Houston because I spotted one of the men Webster had tailing us in the lobby.''

"Oh my God.''

Michael took her hands, led her to the bed and sat her down. "You and I are going to leave here in the morning as planned. We're going to go pick up Timmy and Gertie, too, if she wants to come, and we're going to the airport, and you and Timmy are getting on that plane to Oklahoma.''

"Don't worry about me,'' she insisted. "Let your dad take Timmy and Gertie back to Houston now.''

"My dad doesn't think Gertie's up to making the trip. She's pretty stressed out and was having some problems with her blood pressure. It only got worse when my dad suggested taking Timmy to Houston. He's taking her back to her place and is going to spend the night there with her and Timmy. He'll look out for them until we get there."

"Michael, I don't know. If Adam finds Timmy—"

"He won't find him. And even if he does, my dad's a former cop. He can handle himself. He's not going to let anything happen to Timmy. Okay?"

She nodded.

"I'm going to try to reach Travis again," he told Lily. But he hadn't even finished punching in the phone number when another call came through. "Sullivan. Well, it's about time. What have you got?"

While Lily couldn't hear what Travis Sullivan was saying, she did her best to glean what he was saying from Michael's responses. Not that Michael gave much away, she thought.

When he hung up the phone, she asked, "What did he say?"

"He's running some checks on Webster's credit card activity now. He'll get back to us as soon as he knows something. In the meantime, Travis is on his way down here. Because you didn't want me to contact the police, I've asked Travis to try to get someone from the local Bureau to meet us at the airport tomorrow. Normally, the feds don't get involved in something like this."

When Michael fell silent a moment, Lily grew edgy. "What did he say?"

"The FBI has been investigating Webster for some time now. He's been under surveillance for the past few months."

Lily's heart pounded in her chest. She thought about that man she'd seen in his study, the one who'd turned up dead. And she remembered the disk she'd stolen. A part of her wanted to tell Michael what she suspected and about the incriminating disk. But what if she gave Michael the disk, and the FBI still failed to put Adam in jail? What if they put her in jail for not turning it over sooner? Then she'd be helpless to keep Timmy safe. And she'd have nothing to bargain with to save her son. She couldn't take the risk.

"You don't seem surprised."

Lily jerked her attention back to Michael. "I'm not. I've wondered for a while how Adam managed to be so successful with his clubs. When other owners of a club would fail, Adam would buy them out, and within a few months he had another successful hit."

"You thought something illegal was going on?"

"I didn't know, and I didn't ask," she told him honestly. "Adam didn't want me involved in his business."

"No, all he wanted you for was his bed," Michael fired back.

Though the barb stung, Lily kept her eyes on his. "Yes," she said evenly. "That is all Adam ever wanted or expected of me. And if that makes me a whore in your eyes, you're not the first person to feel that way.''

Michael swore and started toward her. ''Lily—''

She held up her hand. ''I'm really tired, Michael. I think I'd like to try to get some sleep. Tomorrow's going to be a long day.''

''I'm sorry,'' he told her.

From the tortured look in his eyes, she didn't doubt the apology was sincere. But she also didn't want to open herself for any more pain from this man. While she might have fantasized about a relationship with him for a few brief moments when he'd kissed her, she knew it was just that. A fantasy. She had to live in the real world. And in the real world, a man like Michael Sullivan would always see her for what she was—a woman who had allowed herself to be bought and used by a rich, ruthless man.

''I'm sorry,'' he repeated. He jammed a fist through his dark hair. ''I don't think of you that way. I never would. It's just that I get a little nuts whenever I think of you with that creep.''

''I hope you're not expecting me to say that I regret marrying him. Because I don't, and I never will—not when it's the reason I have Timmy.''

Michael said nothing, simply stood there with a frustrated expression on his face and a stormy look in his eyes.

Completely drained, she said, ''If you'll excuse me, I'm going to use the bathroom to change and get ready for bed.''

Lily took her time in the bathroom. The soak in

the tub helped to ease some of the tense muscles in her shoulders and neck brought on by the harrowing day. Unfortunately, it did nothing to ease the ache in her heart. Remembering her embarrassment that morning when Michael had seen her in her nightgown, she opted to use the oversize T-shirt as a nightshirt. But now that she had the thing on, she saw that it hit her midthigh. She questioned the wisdom of her decision—especially since it looked as if she and Michael would have to share a bed. Bracing herself, she exited the bathroom and found him staring out the window. "It's all yours," she told him.

"Thanks," he said, and Lily noted how he averted his eyes as he moved past her to the bathroom.

Although it was past eleven o'clock at night, the streets below were packed, and when she saw a crowd gathered round a musician, she unlocked the window and pushed it open. Immediately the lonely wail of a sax filtered through the merriment and drifted up to her. Lily couldn't help thinking of her life, all that had happened and what still lay ahead. And at the sound of the shower being turned on, she wondered how she was going to get through the night.

Fifteen

Michael stood under the cold shower, closed his eyes and tried to erase the image of Lily as she had exited the bathroom with her skin all flushed from her bath, her hair damp at the ends, her legs so silky and smooth. He'd caught one whiff of her scent—that combination of peaches and soap and sunshine—and he'd wanted to kiss her so badly he'd ached. He'd wanted to do more than just kiss her, he admitted. He'd wanted to sweep her up into his arms, carry her to the bed and make love to her until that sad bruised look in her green eyes disappeared.

And because he'd wanted her so badly, he had opted for a cold shower instead. Damn! How had he managed to let her get under his skin this way? If only half of what Travis had told him turned out to be true, Lily and Timmy were in even greater danger than he'd thought. He couldn't afford to let his emotions get in the way. He'd made that mistake once before.

Now here he was doing the same thing all over again. Only with Lily it was ten times—no, a hundred times worse. She was a woman he was attracted to and he wanted her so much he could hardly breathe.

And if you don't start thinking like a cop instead of a man, you could get her killed.

The reminder sobered him. He shut off the shower, dried off and slipped his jeans back on, not bothering with a shirt. Exiting the bathroom, he felt more in control than he had in days. Until he saw Lily.

She stood at the window with her elbows propped up on the ledge, her hands clasped together as though in prayer, her head resting atop them. She'd opened the window and a light breeze ruffled her honey-colored hair. But she didn't seem to notice. She simply tapped her foot in tune with the music that was playing on the street below. When she lifted up on her toes and leaned over to peer at something below, the hem of the green nightshirt rose with the movement, revealing even more of those long silken legs.

He must have made some sound, because she turned her head and looked at him. "It looks like they're having a party," she said.

"Yeah. We probably should close the window or that music will keep us up all night."

"Right," she said, and when she reached out to grab the window arm to pull it in, up went the shirt again.

"I'll get it," Michael told her, yanking it closed. He paused a moment. "Listen, about that crack earlier, I really am sorry."

"I know," she whispered.

Fearful that if she kept looking up at him out of

those big green eyes, he was going to kiss her, Michael said, "Why don't you go ahead and take the bed."

"But where are you going to sleep?"

"I'll pull those two chairs together and sack out on them. I got some blankets and a couple of extra pillows out of the closet while you were in the tub. I'll be fine. You go on to bed."

She looked over at the sitting area and back at him. "Those chairs don't look very comfortable. And I think there's at least a foot too much of you to fit." She whooshed out a breath. "Listen, it's a big bed, and we're both adults."

"Lily, if I get in that bed with you, it won't be to sleep," he told her honestly, watching her eyes widen. He could see she was both tempted and afraid. "That's what I thought. Go to bed, Lily. I'll be fine. Like you said, tomorrow's going to be a long day."

And tonight was going to be even longer—for him.

While she climbed into the big bed, Michael pulled the chairs together and tried to make his long frame comfortable. When after thirty minutes it wasn't working, he tossed the blankets and pillows onto the floor and tried to sleep there.

But every time he closed his eyes, he could see Lily, remember how she had tasted when he'd kissed her. Annoyed with himself and even more annoyed by the fact that just thinking about her had him hard and aching, he punched the pillow and tried counting sheep.

It didn't work. Nothing was working, he finally admitted, and sat up. A look at his watch told him it was well past midnight. He debated whether to take another shower or to just take a walk and see if he couldn't burn off some of this sexual tension.

"Michael?" Lily's voice called out.

"I'm sorry. I didn't mean to wake you."

"You didn't," she said, and sat up in the bed. "I couldn't sleep, either."

Since they hadn't closed the drapes, there was just enough light coming in from outside so that he could see her face. In the soft light, her hair looked as if it had been painted with fairy dust and her skin looked luminescent. Her features were so perfect, they could have been sculpted in ivory, Michael thought. Her mouth—that mouth that he'd been longing to taste again all evening—was the color of a ripe peach. And the eyes that had haunted him from the first time he had seen them stared at him now with such longing, he nearly groaned. "Try to go back to sleep," he told her as he got up, intent on getting dressed and going out for a long run—anything to get his thoughts off her.

"Where are you going?"

"To take a walk, get some air."

"Is that really what you want to do?"

Michael pulled a T-shirt over his head, then looked at her. "No, it's not what I want to do. What I want to do is make love with you. But—"

"It's what I want, too."

Michael froze. A stunned look spread across his handsome face. Mortified that she'd shocked him by being so brazen, Lily wanted to crawl beneath the covers and hide her face. Never before had she been so forward—not even with Adam—especially not with Adam. But never before had she truly felt this ache for a man's touch. No, not any man's touch, she admitted. Michael's touch.

He walked toward the bed and with each step he took, her heart pounded. When he stopped beside the bed and looked at her, she braced herself for his rejection.

"You want to say that again," he said, his voice so low Lily had to strain to hear the words. But she had no trouble seeing the heat that had turned his eyes to the color of steel.

Her pulse jumped. That jittery feeling in her belly spread, moved lower. She swallowed. "I said that I want you to make love to me."

"Are you sure?"

"Yes," she whispered, and pulled back the covers.

Slowly he stripped off his shirt and tossed it to the floor. He was magnificent, she thought as she took in the wide shoulders, the swirl of dark hair that ran down his chest and formed an arrow that disappeared beneath his jeans. With a brazenness that should have shocked her, she never took her eyes off Michael for a second. She simply sat there and watched with fascination as he unfastened his jeans, lowered the zipper. Excitement and anticipation churned in her veins as he shed his jeans and kicked them aside, along with his briefs. In that moment, Lily wished she were a painter or a sculptor so that she could capture him on canvas or in clay. "Tell me what you want, Lily."

"You," she told him because it was true. "I want you to make love to me."

"No," he said, making her heart stop for a moment, but then he joined her on the bed. "I won't make love *to* you, but I will make love *with* you. If that's what you want."

"It is," she murmured, opening her arms to him.

She wasn't an innocent. She'd been married for seven years, had given birth to a child. She knew what sex was, knew the mating ritual of joining her body with a man's. And she thought she knew what to expect.

She hadn't expected the slow, oh-so-slow kisses. Nor had she expected Michael to go on kissing her— first her eyes, then her cheeks, her chin. He kissed her mouth again. More sweet, long kisses at the corner of her mouth, to her lower lip. Kisses that started a fire in her belly and had her sliding her fingers in his hair to bring him closer.

"Open for me, Lily," he murmured, then traced the seam of her mouth with his tongue. She parted her lips, and he took the kiss deeper. His tongue danced with hers, mated, giving her a glimpse of what was to come.

When he broke off the kiss, she whimpered. She hadn't wanted it to end so soon, but she knew that the kissing and cuddling didn't bring the same pleasure to a man as it did to a woman. Still, the kissing had been worth it, she thought. Sitting up, she removed her nightshirt and dropped it to the floor. Then she lay down and waited for Michael to begin squeezing her breasts and thrusting himself into her.

"Lily, what's wrong?"

She snapped her eyes open, found Michael looking down at her, a worried frown creasing his forehead. "Nothing. Why?" she asked, wondering what she'd done wrong, why he wasn't touching her.

He stared at her so intently, she felt as though he was trying to see inside her. "If you've changed your mind and want me to stop, you can tell me. I'm not saying I'll be thrilled about it, because right now—I want you more than I want my next breath. But not if you don't want me."

"But I *do* want you. Why would you think I didn't?"

"Because all of a sudden you looked like you were on your way to the guillotine."

"Oh, Michael. No," she said, stunned. She cupped his face in her hands, his beautiful face with the stubble darkening his cheeks and jaw. "That's not how I feel at all. It's just that I was enjoying the kissing so much, I didn't want it to end. But I know it's different for you. I mean, I know kissing doesn't bring a man the same pleasure. It's all right. We can make love now."

"Where in the devil did you ever get an idea like that?" he asked, and immediately said, "Never mind." He let out a deep sigh. "Listen, I like kissing you. In fact, I like it so much I think I could easily become addicted to it. And if you think I didn't enjoy kissing you just now, you're crazy.''

Her heart seemed to swell in her chest. Afraid she might blubber if she tried to say anything, she threw her arms around him and hugged him.

He caught her in his arms, ran his fingers down her back. A shiver of need raced down Lily's spine. But then he was easing her away from him and looking at her with those too-serious blue eyes. ''I told you, I wanted to make love *with* you, not *to* you. And that's what we're going to do. I want us both to enjoy it. All right?''

Lily nodded.

Then he pressed another of those long, slow kisses to her mouth. And when he lifted his head again, he said, ''But I don't want to just kiss your mouth. I want to kiss all of you.''

And he did.

He kissed her throat, her ear, her collarbone. He trailed kisses along her shoulders, down her arms, to the inside of her wrists. Changing course, he kissed her breast. First one, then the other, laving her nipples with his tongue. By the time he took her into his mouth and suckled, Lily was writhing beneath him. When he closed his teeth over the sensitive tip, she gasped and crushed his head to her breasts.

''Hurry.''

The word became a chant in her blood. She speared her fingers through his too-long hair, drank in his scent—soap and shampoo and aroused male. She moved her hands down his spine, enjoyed the feel of muscle and sinew and heated male flesh. She'd never felt desire like this before, Lily thought as Michael trailed more openmouthed kisses down her rib cage, to her belly, along her hip. He continued the journey moving down her outer thigh, along her calves. Changing directions, he kissed her instep, the inside of her calf, her inner thigh. He repeated the exploration on her other leg, then he moved between her thighs and kissed her center. When he spread her open with his fingers and touched her with his tongue, Lily nearly came off the bed.

"Michael," she cried out, not sure what she was asking for, only that the ache that he had set off inside her with the first kiss had begun a burning need that threatened to consume her.

And then when she thought she couldn't stand waiting another moment, the first spasm hit her, sending an explosion of pleasure through her so intense, she screamed.

"It's all right, love," he said, replacing his mouth with his fingers. He stroked her, sliding one finger inside her, then another. He kissed her mouth, mimicking the movements with his tongue. Lily could feel herself growing damp, knew she should be embarrassed, but then he took her up again, brought her to another peak. And she could barely breathe, let alone think, as she felt her feminine muscles convulsing around his fingers.

Michael tore his mouth free and rolled away from her for a second. "Where are you going?" she asked, suddenly disappointed.

"Needed this," he said, holding up a foil packet. He ripped it open with his teeth and removed the condom.

"Let me," she said, taking the thin covering from him. And then it was her turn to see him shudder as she smoothed the protection over his shaft. "You're so beautiful," she told him.

"That's supposed to be my line," he told her, a smile on his lips as he kissed her again.

But when she reached for him, guided him to her center, the smile disappeared from his lips. "Make love with me," she whispered.

Michael entered her in one deep stroke, filling her, stretching her. Then he began to move. Slowly at first, in and out, nearly withdrawing before thrusting deep inside her again. Then faster and faster until the chant in her head caught fire in her body as she could feel herself reaching flash point again.

Michael caught her hands, twined them with his own, and when he thrust into her again, she arched her back and cried out, "Michael!" The explosion hit her, shattering her, scattering her into pieces. Moments later, she heard Michael's cry as he followed her into the storm.

And as she felt herself float back down to earth, Lily realized she'd made a terrible mistake. She'd fallen in love with Michael Sullivan.

"Pete, look out!"

"Michael. Michael, wake up."

Michael jerked upright in bed, his heart beating so fast he thought it would jump out of his chest.

Breathing hard, he looked around the darkened room to get his bearings. And then he stared at the woman beside him. "Lily." He said her name in a rush and pulled her into his arms.

"It's okay," she soothed. "It's okay. It was just a dream," she murmured while she pressed tender kisses against his neck and stroked his head as though he were a child. "Just a bad dream."

With his back propped up against the pillows, he held Lily close and took comfort in the feel of her in his arms.

"You were dreaming about your friend Pete, weren't you?"

"Yeah. About the night he died."

"You and he must have been very close," she said.

"We were. We grew up together. He was like another brother to me."

"Tell me about him," she urged.

So he told her. About all the good times and the bad. About the two of them going through training together. How he had always looked out for Pete— except for that last time. How he had let his friend down. How his mistakes had cost Pete his life.

"What happened to your friend was tragic, but it wasn't your fault, Michael. He was responsible for the choices he made, not you."

"You don't understand. Pete needed me. He called me that day because he knew he'd messed up and needed me to help him."

"And you tried to help him."

"But I failed him," Michael told her.

She sat up, looked at him with those big, serious green eyes. "No, you didn't. Pete was weak and failed himself. The only thing you're guilty of is thinking that it was your job to save him. It wasn't. And while it was noble of you to want to shield Pete's family, you shouldn't have. It was wrong of you to lie about what happened—especially to your family. You should have trusted them with the truth right from the start. They loved you. They would have understood." She paused. "But then maybe you didn't want to give them the chance to understand because you needed to punish yourself for Pete's death."

Michael knew that much of what she said was true. He should have trusted in his family, should have known his father would have stood by him. But he hadn't, because he had believed he didn't deserve his love. Now he'd made the same mistake again. He hadn't trusted Lily, and now he'd waited too long to tell her the truth about how Adam had found her. Yet if he confessed now, she'd leave and he'd have no hope of getting her to safety. "How did you get so smart?"

"I'm not smart at all. Look at the mess I'm in and the danger I've put Timmy in."

Michael tipped up her chin. "We're going to get through this. I promise. This time tomorrow night, you and Timmy will be safe in Oklahoma."

"What about you? Will I see you again?"

"Count on it," he said, and kissed her deeply, all the while praying that she would want to see him again once he told her everything. When he lifted his head, he whispered, "It'll be morning soon. Let's not waste the rest of the night talking."

"I don't think I'll be able to sleep—not knowing that Adam's men are out there somewhere, wondering if they know we're here, if they know where Timmy is."

"Sleep isn't exactly what I had in mind," he told her, hating that he'd been partly responsible for the worry he heard in her voice.

"No?" she countered, giving him a shy womanly smile. "Then why don't you tell me what it is you have in mind?"

"I'll do better than that, I'll show you," he said, and rolling over with her in his arms, he eased her down on top of him. And as she took him in and began to move with him, Michael felt the last vestiges of the nightmare fade away. She looked like a goddess, he thought as she arched her back and rode him like a stallion. He struggled to hold himself back, nearly lost it when the first climax hit her. Then when she called out his name and her muscles convulsed around him, he felt himself explode. And holding on to her, he followed her over the edge.

Later, much much later as Lily slept beside him, Michael could feel the weight of the past falling from his shoulders. And for the first time in a long time, he allowed himself to think of the future. Maybe he would go back to being a cop, he thought, or possibly even join the Bureau. Lily had been right. Maybe he had been punishing himself all these years because

Pete was dead and he was alive. But whatever role
he'd played in Pete's death, Pete's choices had been
his own. He saw that now.

He looked over at Lily snuggled against him,
asleep. He wanted a future with her, he realized. With
her and with Timmy. God help him, he was in love
with her. The realization stunned him, even frightened
him. And then he imagined what it would be like to
be married to Lily, to come home to her and Timmy
each night, sharing his life with her.

*And what do you think she'll say when she finds
out that you were the one who betrayed her? That
you were the one who unleashed Webster on her and
her son?*

The fantasies dissolved in an instant. Lily would
hate him. And he'd have no one to blame but himself.

Lily paced the hotel room. She glanced at her
watch again and willed the hours to tick past. Edgy,
unable to sit still, she'd been up since dawn. She'd
already donned her costume, done her makeup and
was just waiting for the parades to get fully under
way so that she and Michael could go to Timmy. She
went to the window and stared down for the hun-
dredth time at the spectacle in the streets.

"Lily, try to relax," Michael said, coming up behind her. He slid his arms around her waist.

"I can't. I just want this to be over. I want to see
Timmy."

He turned her around, held her in his arms. "I
know you do. And it won't be much longer."

"He sounded so pitiful on the phone when I talked to him a few minutes ago. Gertie's house is on the parade route and he can see all the people in their costumes and hear the bands lining up for the parades. He doesn't understand why he can't go."

"We'll come back next year and take him," Michael promised.

Lily held on to Michael, held on to the idea that maybe it was possible. Maybe she and Timmy really would be able to come back here with Michael next year. He'd thought she would be upset when he told her that if Travis was right and Adam was convicted of drug and prostitution trafficking, all of Adam's assets would be confiscated and tied up forever. He'd been so sweet, trying to prepare her for the fact that she wouldn't be able to claim any share of their marital wealth. But she didn't care about the money, the houses, any of it. All she wanted was freedom for her and her son.

And Michael. Could he be right? Would she really be able to free herself from Adam and actually have a future with Michael? Oh, she wanted that, she admitted. She wanted it more than she'd ever dreamed.

"Look at that float," Michael said. "There must be at least fifty people on it."

She looked at the monster float, and at the mass of people who stood shoulder to shoulder on both sides of the street with their hands outstretched. "You'd think they would have had enough of this by now. They've been doing this for weeks."

"They don't call New Orleans a party city for nothing."

At the shrill of Michael's cell phone, Lily jumped.

"Take it easy," he told her, walking over and snatching up the phone. "Yes."

Lily held her breath, waiting. From Michael's side of the conversation, she could determine little. He merely seemed to listen, giving an occasional yes or no, and his expression gave away nothing.

"Because I don't have to. I just know, that's how." He scowled. "The minute you find out, call me. Yes, all right. I will," he said. "And Travis, thanks."

When he ended the call, he walked over to her, and Lily knew whatever it was, she wasn't going to like it. "What is it? What did Travis say?"

"Come sit down, Lily."

She jerked away from him. "I don't want to sit down. I want to know what's wrong. Is it Timmy? Has something happened to Timmy?"

"No," Michael said sharply. "Your place was ransacked last night. So was my hotel room and truck. Travis is convinced it was Webster's men. He thinks they were searching for something. Do you have any idea what they might be looking for?"

Lily thought about the disk, considered, once again, telling him about it. But what if Michael's plan fell apart and Adam found her and Timmy? The disk would be her only hope of saving her son, she reasoned, and decided to remain silent. "Maybe they think I still have the money I took from Adam's safe."

"Maybe," Michael said.

"Did Travis say anything more about Adam? Do they still have him under surveillance in Miami?"

Michael said nothing, and an icy fear shivered down her spine. For the first time, Lily thought that she finally understood the adage about someone walking over a person's grave.

"Tell me, Michael. Whatever it is, tell me."

"Webster's in New Orleans."

Sixteen

"Let me go," Lily demanded, and struggled to break free. "I need to get to my baby."

Michael ached for her, hated to see the fear in her eyes. "Think, Lily. Think," he said as he held on to her shoulders and gave her a shake. "Timmy's safe with my father at Gertie's right now because Webster doesn't know about her. We're going to assume his men spotted us last night and know that we're here. If they know, Webster knows. And if we walk out of here now before the time is right, we're going to lead them straight to Timmy."

"Oh God," she sobbed as she fell against him.

He stroked her head. "We're almost there, Lily. We just need to wait a little longer. Once the big parades get under way, there'll be so many people out there moving around in costumes, racing around those floats and bands, Webster would need an army to check out everyone on that street." He pressed a kiss to her temple, held her away from him so that he could see her face. "It's going to be all right. Travis and his men are trying to pick up Webster's trail now."

"But what if they can't find him?"

"They'll find him," Michael assured her. Yet he couldn't stop thinking about his conversation with his brother. Had Travis been right? Was he thinking like a man instead of a cop? If Webster only wanted Lily, why ransack her place? Why search his hotel room and truck? Was Lily keeping something from him? And if she was, could he really blame her? After all, look at what he'd kept from her.

"I want to call Timmy again, make sure that he's okay."

"All right," Michael told her, giving her the phone. "But you just talked to him a little while ago. If he or Gertie knows you're scared, it's only going to make them more nervous. Dad was worried he'd have to take Gertie to the hospital last night for her blood pressure. I'd hate to see that happen today."

"You're right," she said, not completing the call. "I'm just scared."

"I know," Michael told her, and held her close. He could understand her nervousness, because he didn't have a good feeling about this. He didn't like the fact that Webster had shaken the tail Travis had put on the him. And he didn't like the feeling that Lily had been keeping something from him—something that would make Webster take such a huge risk by coming after her like this. He also wished he knew what was behind that call she'd made to Agent Logan. According to what little his brother had been able to find out, the woman who had called Logan had information relating to an agent's murder. But what murder?

Michael thought about his father's refusal when he'd suggested asking Travis to pull a few of the men from his team and send them to Gertie's as backup. He hadn't argued because he'd known his father could handle himself and also he hadn't wanted to pull manpower they needed to handle Webster. But now he wasn't sure he'd made the right decision.

"How about I call Travis back and see if he can send a few men over to Gertie's to help my father keep an eye on the little cowboy?"

"Yes. Yes, I would appreciate that."

Michael made the call to his brother. "Your people will probably have a hell of a time getting there. It's on the parade route. But since we don't know where Webster is, it might be a good idea."

"Mike, about what I said earlier," Travis said. "That crack about you thinking like a man instead of a cop, I'm sorry."

"Don't be. I think you were right," he said, aware that Lily was listening. "I am too close to the situation to be objective."

"She's special, huh?"

"Yeah. And so is the little boy."

"I'm looking forward to meeting them," Travis told him. "And to seeing your ugly puss again."

"Same here," Michael said, and realized it was true. He was looking forward to introducing Lily and Timmy to his brother. And to seeing his father again.

"Give me a call and let me know when your people have them safe."

"Will do."

Michael ended the call and turned to Lily. "Travis is sending someone over to Gertie's now. But it'll probably take a while because of the parades."

"Thank you," she said, and hugged him tight.

Michael held her close, and reveled in the feel of her in his arms. He prayed to God he'd be able to keep the promises he'd made to her. After a moment, he stepped back and said, "Tell you what, since it doesn't look like room service is going to make it up here with that breakfast I ordered, why don't I go down and see if I can rustle us up something to eat? In the meantime, you go fix those tear streaks around Cleopatra's eyes."

Lily touched her face, looked at the black smudges on her fingers. "I probably look like a raccoon."

"Yeah, but a beautiful raccoon," he teased. He dropped a kiss on the tip of her nose.

"By the time I get back and we get some food in our stomachs, those parades should be under way and it'll be time to go." He stared into her eyes. "Is it a deal? You go fix that Queen of the Nile face for me?"

"All right. I'll see what I can do."

"Relax, Bernie," Adam told his fidgety chief of security as they mingled with the other men, dressed in the ridiculous costumes and masks, in the hotel's private dining room. Arranging for a private flight into New Orleans Lakefront airport had made it so much easier than he'd expected. It also made it more difficult for the idiots tracking them to follow.

"Sorry, boss," Bernie mumbled.

Adam scanned the room filled with the costumed riders who had gathered for the ritual breakfast feast. He tried to understand the appeal of climbing aboard the floats and parading through the city to throw trinkets to the fools that had lined up like peasants to see them. The lure of the foolishness escaped him. He watched in amusement as the men returned to the buffet to pile their plates with food guaranteed to bring on a heart attack, then washing it down with gallons of liquor instead of coffee.

It had been a stroke of genius on his part, Adam decided, to hook up with those two idiots in the hotel bar when he'd arrived last night. They'd explained the krewe tradition of gathering for a big breakfast bash before their scheduled parade ride through the city. Apparently the liquor they consumed acted as both a stimulant and warmth if the weather was unpleasant. A stupid tradition Adam thought. But convenient for him. He smiled beneath his mask at his own cleverness. Of course, he'd accepted their offer to go back with them to their room to view their costumes and have another drink. And once he had, it had been child's play taking them out and grabbing their krewe regalia. What better way to go undetected than to mix in with the revelers?

When Bernie started beside him, Adam snapped, "I said to relax."

"Sorry. I guess I keep waiting for one of those feds to walk in."

"And I keep telling you that the authorities aren't going to bother with one of the more prominent carnival organization's preride parties. Certainly not today with all that craziness going on outside. Just keep your mask on and pretend we're just as eager as the rest of these fools to climb up on those floats and parade around throwing beads."

"How are you supposed to eat or drink anything with this mask on?" Bernie asked.

"You hold the mask away from your mouth, you idiot."

"Right, boss."

"And stop calling me, boss," Adam ordered.

"Right, bo— Right."

He really was going to have to get rid of Bernie, Adam thought. While he liked the fact that the man was as strong as an ox and never questioned his orders, Bernie was stupid. Too stupid. After all, it had been Bernie's stupidity in disposing of that agent that had sent the feds to his door. When Bernie reached for another sandwich, Adam said, "Forget about your stomach, and go check in with Deacon. See if he's picked up the boy yet."

Bernie put down his sandwich and left to make the call. "Sure thing, bos— Sure thing."

Yes, he really did need to see about replacing Bernie, Adam decided. As soon as he got Elisabeth and the disk back, he'd see to it that Bernie disappeared. Milling about the room, Adam nodded and pretended to be part of the membership. With the hideous masks on and the amount of liquor being consumed, he doubted most of the fools even knew their own names. He couldn't help wondering how they were going to manage to stand on a float for hours and throw beads.

Bernie returned to the room and hurried over to him. "He's got the kid. But he was bawling like crazy because Deacon left his teddy bear when he snatched him. He gave him a shot of that stuff you said to give him to make him sleep."

"Forget about the boy, you fool." He didn't give a damn about the kid. He never had. The boy was simply a means to get Elisabeth—and the disk—back. "What about Elisabeth?"

"She wasn't there. Just the old lady and Sullivan's father."

"And?" Adam asked impatiently.

"Deacon had to take Sullivan's father out to get to the kid. He couldn't find out from him where she is."

"And the old woman? Did she say where Elisabeth was?"

"Deacon says he roughed her up some, but she swore she didn't know. Just that she was staying at some fancy hotel. She said her and Sullivan were going to come for them this morning after the parades got started."

"That's it? What about the hotel phone number?" Adam asked, impatient with the moron. Feeling as though he was dragging the information out of him.

"No. All she had was a cell number."

"Great. A fancy hotel," Adam fumed. "Do you have any idea how many fancy hotels there are in this city?"

"The old woman said it was a real nice hotel, that your wife promised the boy she'd try to see the King of Rex at his breakfast and get him one of the special doubloons to bring to him."

Adam smiled beneath his mask.

"You want me to have another go at the old lady? See if I can get anything else out of her?"

"That won't be necessary, Bernie. I know where Elisabeth is."

"You do?"

"Yes. If you had bothered to read this morning's paper, you would know that the King of Rex and his krewe members always host a special breakfast on the day of their parade at the Saint Charles Court."

"You mean the place down the street? The br...your wife is just down the street?"

"That's right. Come along, Bernie. I need to make a phone call to my lovely wife."

Lily was trying her hardest not to laugh as Michael returned to their hotel room covered in purple beer and carrying a paper sack of biscuits and jelly.

"I'm not sure purple is your color," she began, and bit her cheek to stop herself from laughing.

Michael gave her a foreboding look, but she saw the laughter in his eyes as he dumped his new cowboy hat into the trash can. When he sniffed at his shirt and blanched, she couldn't help herself. She laughed.

"I'm glad one of us finds this amusing," he said.

"I'm sorry. But if you could only see your face."

"Whoever heard of dying beer purple for Mardi Gras?" Michael muttered. "I could understand if it had been Saint Patrick's Day, and the fellow had wanted green beer to honor his Irish roots," Michael said, a hint of the blarney sneaking in with his Texas accent. "But Mardi Gras?"

"Oh, I don't know. I think it's kind of a nice idea," she teased. "Although beer instead of coffee for breakfast does seem a bit strange."

"Darling, you don't know what strange is until you see some of those outfits down there." He emptied his pockets on the table next to the bar, kicked off his boots and the rest of his clothes. He grabbed a biscuit and started toward the bathroom. "The Rex parade is just getting under way now. Give me a few minutes to take a shower and change, then I'll call Travis and we'll see about heading out."

Not much longer.

Lily could feel the nerves rumbling in her stomach again as Michael disappeared into the bathroom. Walking over to the mirror on the wall, she adjusted her Cleopatra wig and was surprised when she glanced down to see a gun among Michael's things. She knew a moment of unease, then told herself she was being foolish. Probably an ex-cop or Texas-guy thing to carry a gun, she reasoned as she reached up to smooth a strand of dark hair away from her eyes. She was about to turn away, when Michael's cell phone rang. Lily hesitated a second, considered calling Michael, but the shower had kicked on. Remembering that Michael had given his cell number to both Sullivan men, as well as Gertie, she picked up the phone. "Hello?"

"Hello, Elisabeth."

Her heart seemed to stop, and she felt the blood drain from her face as she heard the familiar voice from her nightmares.

"Are you there, Elisabeth?"

"Y-yes. I'm here."

"I've missed you, darling. Have you missed me?" When she didn't answer, he said, "I've grown very tired of this game you've been playing, Elisabeth. It's time for you to come home."

"I'm not coming back, Adam. I'm getting a divorce."

He laughed. "Do you really believe I'd ever let you go?"

"You don't have a choice," she told him. Remembering these past days with Michael, she dug deep within herself for the strength to stand up to him. "You don't own me."

"Ah, but that's where you're wrong, my darling wife. I do own you. And you, better than anyone, should know that I always keep what's mine. Now, be a good girl and come join me in my hotel suite for a little reunion. I'm at the Regent. It's just down the street from the Saint Charles Court."

Lily trembled as she realized he knew where she was. Determined to be strong, not to give in to the fear, she said, "No. I'm not coming, Adam. It's over."

"You'll come, Elisabeth. Otherwise, you'll never see Timothy again."

"You're lying," she said, her heart pounding with fear. "You don't have Timmy."

Adam laughed and the sound chilled her blood. "Did you really think I wouldn't find out about your grandmother's friend Gertie?"

Lily whimpered, pressed a hand to her mouth. Oh my God, she thought. He has Timmy. He has Timmy.

"What was that, Elisabeth?"

"You're lying," she argued, trying not to panic, trying to think. Travis Sullivan's men and Michael's father were with Timmy. They would never let him have Timmy.

"Am I? Regretfully, my man had to dispose of Sullivan's father. And I understand the old woman was quite against the idea of Timothy being returned to his father. But Deacon and Otto managed to persuade her it was the right thing to do. You do remember Deacon and Otto, don't you, darling?"

Lily's stomach pitched as she thought of the Neanderthals that Adam had hired to act as her bodyguards and jailers. She squeezed her eyes shut, feeling sick at the knowledge that he'd had Michael's father killed. She didn't even want to imagine what they had done to Gertie. And worst of all, she knew now that Adam had her son. "Let me talk to Timmy."

"You can talk to him when you get here," he said,

and gave her the hotel room number and instructions. "Come alone."

"All right," she told him after she'd written down the hotel name and the room number he'd given her. She tore the sheet from the phone message pad and tucked it in the waistband of her outfit. Not that she was likely to forget it, she thought.

"And Elisabeth?"

"Yes?"

"If by chance you were thinking about having Sullivan or one of his friends follow you here, don't. There will be someone watching for you as you leave the hotel. Tell me what you're wearing."

She told him.

"Good. And remember, if I see any signs of Sullivan or his brother, I'll kill the boy. Understand?"

"Yes, I understand."

"I was sure you would. Now hurry, darling. You only have fifteen minutes."

"Fifteen minutes? But, Adam, the crowds—"

"Fifteen minutes, Elisabeth. And the clock is ticking. If you're not here, the boy dies. Hurry, darling, I'm anxious to see you again."

"Adam, please. I'll do whatever you say, just don't hurt Timmy. I—"

But the dial tone was already buzzing in her ear. And when she looked up, she saw Michael.

He stood just outside the bathroom doorway, his hair still damp from the shower, a towel draped loosely around his waist. "It's a trap, Lily," he told her.

"I don't care. I have to go. I have to get to Timmy."

"He doesn't have Timmy. You know my dad's there and Travis was sending his men over. If there had been any problem, Travis or my father would have called me."

"Michael," she said on a sob. "He...they killed your father."

Michael's expression grew fierce. "He's lying. There's no way Webster or his men could have taken my dad out. And don't forget, Travis's men are there. It's a trap, I'm telling you."

"Maybe it is. But I can't take that chance," Lily argued.

"Then give me a minute. Let me call my dad."

Unsure what to do, aware of the time, she shoved the cell phone at Michael. "All right. But hurry!"

Michael punched in the number. "Dammit." He punched it in a second time.

"What is it?"

"My dad's phone is going to voice mail, and I can't get through to Travis because the circuits are busy. Let me try the hotel phone. What's Gertie's number?"

But there was no answer at Gertie's house, either. And Lily knew she couldn't wait any longer. "I have to go."

"Then I'm coming with you. Let me get dress—"

"No," Lily told him. "I have to go alone. Adam has someone watching me. If you or anyone follows, he'll kill Timmy."

"I'm not letting you go alone," Michael told her, starting to move past her for his clothes.

Lily grabbed the gun from the tabletop. "You don't have any choice," she said, aiming it at him. Ignoring the tears sliding down her cheeks, she gathered up his ruined clothes with one hand, keeping the gun trained on him with the other. "Hand me the rest of your clothes."

"Lily, don't," he said as he started toward her.

"Stop! I mean it, Michael. I love you, and I don't want to shoot you, but I will if I have to. Now, give me the clothes."

Once he'd handed them to her, she stuffed them in the shopping bag they'd used the day before. She pulled open the closet door, yanked her own clothes from the hangers and shoved them into the bag. Then she backed her way to the door. "I'm sorry, Michael. So sorry."

"Lily, please. Don't do this. Let me help you. Give me the clothes." As she continued to back up toward the door, he said, "Then at least tell me where you're going."

"I can't. I can't. If you feel anything for me…anything at all, you won't try to follow me." Then reaching for the doorknob behind her, she opened the door and backed out into the hall. Not bothering to wait for the elevator, she ran to the door marked Stairs and raced down. When she burst into the lobby, she dumped the bag of clothes in a trash bin and ran out of the hotel.

And as she dodged and maneuvered to fight her

way through the throngs she prayed. Please, God, please. Don't let him hurt Timmy.

Furious with himself and with Lily, Michael slammed the cell phone across the room and heard the satisfying crash as it shattered. Then he swiped the hotel phone off the table. How could he have let this happen? How could he have let Lily go to that monster?

And what about his father? No, he refused to believe Big Mike was dead. He wouldn't believe it. Webster was lying. He had to be.

Bracing his hands against the table, he stared down at the message pad, saw the indentation. He searched the floor for the pencil that had been tossed with the phone, grabbed it and ran it across the blank sheet. "The Regent. Room 502," he read aloud.

He crushed the note into his fist. He couldn't let Lily do this. He had to stop her. Racing over to the closet, he tore through it searching for something, anything, he could wear. When he came up empty, he said, "To hell with it." After knotting the towel more tightly around his waist, he went over to retrieve his boots where he'd left them earlier. And as he bent down to get them, he spied the box with the gladiator costume.

"It beats a towel," he muttered. Ripping off the top of the box, he dug through the tons of tissue and pulled out the studded breastplate and matching skirt and briefs. Within a matter of seconds, he had the thing on, including the sandals. He looked down at the shield and sword inside the box, started to leave them, then thought better of it. They weren't real, but were heavy enough to look like the real thing and could be used as a weapon. He'd have preferred his gun, Michael admitted as he headed out the door. But if it worked for Russell Crowe, maybe it would work for him, too.

He didn't even bother trying the elevator, remembering how slow it had been earlier with the mobs of people in and out of the hotel. He slapped open the door to the stairwell and started down the concrete steps. He didn't bother looking up and ignored the startled gasp as he passed someone else going down. When he shoved open the door to the second-floor landing, he heard a familiar voice yell, "Hey buddy, watch where the hell you're going."

"Travis!"

"Michael! What in the hell's going on?" his brother demanded. He ran his eyes up and down his brother. "And what are you doing in a skirt?"

"Don't ask," Michael mumbled, not bothering to ask why Travis was wearing a security uniform.

"Yeah? Well, while you've been playing dress up, I've been busting a gut to get here. I thought you were in some kind of trouble when I couldn't get you on your cell phone and the hotel said your room phone was out of order."

"Both phones met with an accident." Michael swallowed. "Trav, Webster says his men killed Dad."

"Like hell they did. The kid left his teddy bear at

somebody's house the night before and Dad went to get it. Webster's goons were waiting for him when he got back. Dad got one of them, but the other one managed to get off a shot. Dad took one in the shoulder.''

''Is he all right?''

''He's fine. Just his pride is a little bruised.''

Relieved to know his father was okay, he asked, ''And Timmy?''

''Webster's guys took him. That's why I was trying to reach you,'' Travis told him.

''What happened to your men? I thought you were sending them as backup for Dad.''

''One man. It's all I could manage. And he had trouble getting there with the parade crowds. By the time he arrived, Dad was down and they'd grabbed the kid. They roughed up the old woman a bit, too.''

''How bad is she?''

''She's got a few bruises,'' Travis told him as they raced down the last flight of stairs. ''I think she's more scared than anything. She thought they'd killed Dad, and she's real worried about the little boy.''

She had reason to worry, Michael thought, because he didn't doubt for a minute that everything Lily had told him about Webster was true. The man was sick— sick enough to be jealous of his own son. A knot the size of Texas formed in his stomach as he thought about Timmy and Lily at the hands of that monster. ''Well, Webster has him now,'' Michael said, as he and his brother charged out into the lobby. They nearly ran down a couple dressed as a harem dancer and her sultan as they raced to the doors leading out to the street.

"This way," Michael said, and began pushing his way through the crowd. Not waiting for a break in the marching group, he ran through their ranks to the other side of the street.

"You want to tell me where we're going?"

"The Regent Hotel. It's two blocks over. Webster's there. He's got Timmy, and Lily's on her way to him."

Travis swore. "Why in the hell didn't you tell her to wait—"

"Because he threatened to kill Timmy unless she came."

They hit a bottleneck of bodies as the parade stopped for a toasting along the route. Travis used the delay to alert his team and order them into position at the Regent.

"Come on," Michael said, and they barreled their way through to the corner.

A police officer stopped them. "You gentlemen need to step back and wait."

Travis pulled out his badge. "FBI. I need to get through." When the officer looked at Michael in his gladiator costume and hesitated, Travis said, "He's working undercover."

The policeman nodded. And like Moses at the Sea of Galilee, the policeman parted the crowd. As they took off at a run down the street, Michael looked at his brother's badge and said, "Nice touch. Maybe I ought to get me one of those."

"Maybe you should," Travis said. "But you'll need to get rid of the skirt first."

Michael acknowledged the joke with a nod, but his thoughts were already on Lily and Timmy, and what he intended to do to that bastard Webster if he had laid a finger on either of them.

When they reached the hotel Michael said, "Webster told Lily he had someone watching her to make sure she wasn't followed. I think it's a bluff, but I don't want to take any chances. Tell your guys that whatever they do, make sure they stay out of sight. No false moves. Since Webster knows what I look like and probably knows what you look like, too, we should go around the back way."

"You think he'd recognize you with that outfit on?"

Michael looked down at his attire again. "Maybe not."

"Why don't you go in through the front, and I'll take the back. I'll call for backup—make sure my men are in place."

"All right. Thanks, Trav."

His brother nodded. "Mike?"

"Yeah?"

"Did you ever find out what it is she's got that Webster is after?"

"No. And the truth is I don't care. He wouldn't have either one of them if it wasn't for me. The only thing I care about now is making sure Lily and Timmy are okay. I can't lose them, Trav. I can't."

"You're not going to. You got your gun?"

"No," Michael admitted. "Lily has it."

His brother arched his eyebrow, but said nothing. He reached into his boot and gave him his spare. "Now let's go get your lady and kid."

Seventeen

When the door to Adam's hotel suite opened, Lily shoved past Deacon and went inside. "Where is he? Where's Timmy?"

"Darling, is that any way to greet your husband?" Adam asked. "Come let me fix you a drink."

"I don't want a drink. I want to see my son."

"Deacon, leave us alone, please," Adam said in that suave lord-of-the-manor voice of his.

Lily couldn't help but wonder how she had ever thought him a charming gentleman. He was a vile, despicable human being, and whatever she had to do to remove Timmy forever from his grasp she would. No matter what the cost to her.

Once Deacon left the room, Adam set down his glass and walked over to her. "You make a quite fetching Cleopatra, darling."

He circled her, and Lily knew he was checking her appearance for flaws. He always checked her appearance, noticing each mark, each ounce, anything that didn't meet with his image of how she should look.

When he came back to face her again, he said, "But I think I prefer you as a blonde." Then he ripped the wig and headdress off, tearing out strands of her own hair with it.

Lily said nothing, simply stood there while he stared at her chopped and dyed hair.

He made that annoying tsking sound. "What a mess you've made of your beautiful hair," he said, running his fingers through the shortened strands. "But don't worry, once we're home I'll see that it's taken care of, and it'll be just as beautiful as it was before."

"Adam—"

He curled his fist into her hair and took possession of her mouth. She wanted to scream at the pain he was causing by pulling her hair. But if she had to choose between the pain in her head and suffering his kiss, she preferred the pain. She would endure this, she told herself, at the invasion of his whiskey-laced tongue shoving between her lips. She would endure whatever she had to if it meant Timmy's safety. But when he ran his free hand down the front of her body and cupped her breast, Lily nearly gagged. She pulled her mouth free and gasped in a breath.

"I've missed you, darling," Adam told her. Releasing her head, he pulled her to him, rubbed his erection against her. "You don't know how lonely I've been without you," he said, his voice taking on an animalistic pant.

Lily could feel the bile rising in her throat. She was sure she was going to be sick. Adam caught her face, turned it to him and started to kiss her again, but she pushed him away. "I want to see my son."

For a moment Lily thought she had gone too far when she saw the black fury in Adam's eyes. Then just as quickly, his expression changed and the debonaire gentleman was back. "Very well, Elisabeth. You want to see Timothy. Come see him," he said. He walked over to an adjoining door and opened it.

Lily rushed to the door and looked inside where Timmy was curled up, asleep on the bed. She started to go in to him, but Adam caught her around the waist and held her back. "You said you wanted to see him. You've seen him."

"But he's so still," she said, worried he wasn't breathing. "Timmy's a restless sleeper."

"Deacon gave him something to help him sleep."

A white-hot rage pumped through her. She jerked away and spun around to face him. "You let him drug my son?"

Adam waved her concerns aside. "Unfortunately, in his haste to return *my* son to *me*, Deacon left the boy's teddy bear behind. Timothy was hysterical and was making himself sick."

"But he loves his teddy," she complained, her heart aching as she imagined how frightened Timmy must have been. "He's never without it."

Adam pulled the door closed.

"Please, Adam, let me go to him. Just let me make sure he's all right."

"Of course you can go to him," he said, an evil grin snaking across his lips. "But first you have to give me what I want."

Lily swallowed. "What do you want?"

"Why, the same thing I've wanted from the moment I first set eyes on you when you were fifteen years old. I want you. Naked and in my bed," he whispered as he ran his thick fingers down the side of her cheek.

Lily turned her head away, repulsed by his touch, sickened by the very thought of him ever invading her body again.

He caught her chin and forced her to look at him. "And," he whispered, the stench of whiskey on his breath strong as he spoke. "I also want the disk that you stole from me."

"You can have the disk," she told him, praying that she could use it as her bargaining chip. "I'll give it to you," she promised. "All you have to do is let Timmy and me go."

"Elisabeth. Elisabeth." Adam repeated her name as though he were addressing a child. "Do you really think I would ever let you go after I went to so much trouble to get you in the first place?"

Bells went off inside Lily's head at his statement. Suddenly she got a dreadful feeling deep in her soul. A part of her didn't want to ask the question, but she knew she had to have the answers. "What do you mean you went to so much trouble to get me in the first place? I came to live with my mother because my grandmother died."

"Yes, but your mother died. Such a tragedy, her being so careless about her insulin and overdosing the way she did."

"It was an accident," she argued. "You and my

mother were good friends. You loved her. I know you did. That's why you agreed to let her name you as my guardian in her will.''

''Of course, I loved your mother. But I loved you more.''

''It was an accident,'' she said, wanting, needing to believe that.

''So naive, my darling. Who do you think arranged for her to take that accidental overdose and go into a diabetic coma?''

''No,'' Lily said, horrified. ''You couldn't. You wouldn't. She was your friend. You loved her.''

''Yes, but I wanted her daughter. Unfortunately, she had begun to realize my feelings for you weren't that of an honorary uncle. She was going to ship you off to some convent school where I wouldn't be able to see you anymore. I couldn't allow her to do that. Not to us. So I had to take care of the problem,'' he said as calmly as if he were describing a decision to get rid of an old car and replace it with a new one. ''Don't you see, darling? I did it for us. So that we could be together.''

He was insane, Lily realized. Truly insane. She had to get Timmy and get out. ''I know what's on that disk, Adam. I know about the man who was in your study that night, the one you said was a business associate. I know he was some kind of federal agent and that you had him killed.''

''Is there a point to this, darling?''

''The point is that I'll give the disk back to you,

and I won't say anything to anyone about it. But you have to let me and Timmy go.''

"Enough of this nonsense," he said, clutching her by the arm so tightly that Lily knew she would have bruises. ''You'll give me the damn disk if you want to keep that brat in there alive. As for you, you're not going anywhere.''

Terrified, Lily yanked free and started toward the bedroom where Timmy was. Adam grabbed her by the hair, dragged her back and shoved her down onto the sofa.

"In fact, it's time you starting acting like a wife again," he told her as he stood over her and began unbuckling his pants.

He was going to rape her. Lily knew it. She knew it, and this time she wasn't going to suffer in silence. Not now. Not ever again. He came at her, and when he started to rip the dress from her, Lily fought him. Striking out, she punched and kicked and fought for all she was worth.

When she hit his mouth, Adam's eyes blazed furiously. ''You bitch,'' he yelled, and slapped her face so hard, she saw stars. She could taste blood in her mouth, and she heard bells ringing in her ears.

"What in the hell—"

Only the bells weren't just ringing in her ears, Lily realized. They were ringing in the hotel. ''It's a fire alarm,'' she said aloud, identifying the sound. She scrambled up from the couch.

Someone pounded on the door. ''Hotel security. Open up. The hotel's on fire.''

"It's the hotel security," she shouted at Adam when he failed to respond.

"Hotel security. Open up or we'll break the door down. The hotel's on fire. Everyone must evacuate."

All the while the alarms continued to scream throughout the hotel. She could hear people squealing and running down the halls. "Adam, let them in. We have to get out."

When Adam went to answer the pounding on the door, Lily raced to the bedroom to get Timmy. "Timmy, it's Mommy. Wake up, sweetie."

"Mommy?"

"Yes, baby. Mommy's here."

"Mommy, Teddy's lost."

"He's not lost," she told her groggy son as she scooped him up into her arms. "Remember, he has his special ID tag that Michael gave him? He's waiting for us at home."

"Want to go home," Timmy whimpered.

"We will, baby. We will soon," she promised, and hurried out of the bedroom with Timmy in her arms just as a fireman and a hotel security officer entered the room.

The sirens continued to scream, and Lily could hear the chaos erupting outside the suite. While Adam began demanding to know what was happening and questioning the whereabouts of his own security people, a man in a hotel security uniform came over to her and said, "Why don't you give him to me, ma'am? I'll take him down and make sure he's safe."

Lily put Timmy down, but he clung to her. "Want to stay wif you, Mommy."

"That's all right. I'll take him with me," Lily said, smoothing a hand over her son's head. She started toward the door, praying that with the chaos she could somehow get Timmy and herself out—and away from Adam.

But as she started to move past him, Adam caught her arm. "Stay where you are. We're not going anywhere, Elisabeth." He released her and turned back to the two men he'd been arguing with and said, "I don't care what the manager is doing. You get him up here. I don't see or smell any smoke. For all I know, some kid pulled the alarm as a prank."

"It's no prank, sir. Now, if you'll just let us get you and your family out of here."

Adam jerked away from the fireman and continued to put up a fuss, when a second man in a hotel security uniform approached her. She saw what looked like sympathy in his eyes as he gazed at her torn dress. Lily clutched the fabric together.

"It would really be better if you let one of us take your little boy out for you, ma'am," he said. "It's kind of wild out there right now. He might get hurt."

"All right," Lily said, and she thought there was something familiar about the man. "It's all right, Timmy. Go with the officer. Mommy will be right behind you."

"Come on, buddy. How'd you like to see a real fire truck?"

"A weal one wif hoses and wadders?"

"You bet," he said, and began to lead Timmy from the suite.

"Wait a minute," Adam said when they started past him.

"Let him go, Adam. He's frightened by the noise already," she said, determined to get her son away from Adam to safety even if it meant that she couldn't be with him. "You don't want Timmy to start crying again, do you? You know how much it annoys you when he cries."

"All right. Take the boy out," he said.

"You'll need to come, too, sir," the fireman told him.

"I'm not going. Now get out," Adam said, shoving the smaller man out the door.

"You really need to come with me, ma'am," the other officer said. "It's not safe for you in here. I'll see that you're brought to your son."

"But my husband," she began, knowing Adam would never let her just walk out this way.

"Someone will see that your husband is taken care of," he said, his blue eyes meeting hers evenly. He took her by the elbow and began nudging her toward the door.

In that instant, Lily realized who he reminded her of. Michael. Her heart beating fast, she said, "All right, Officer." And she started to go with him.

After locking out the fireman, Adam whipped his attention back to her. She watched the rage come into his eyes as he saw the officer trying to hustle her toward the exit. "Get your hands off my wife," he told the blue-eyed officer, and he grabbed her by the arm, jerking her to his side.

"For God's sake, Adam. The hotel's on fire. We have to get out of here."

"We're not going anywhere. And I want you to get out of my hotel room," he told the officer.

"I need to get you and your wife out of here, sir," the man said. "Ma'am," he began, and started to take her by the arm.

Not trusting Adam and unsure of what he would do to Michael's brother, she shook her head. "It's all right, Officer. You should go."

"But, ma'am—"

"You heard my wife," Adam said. "Get out."

The man hesitated and began to open the door.

Sensing a trap, Adam grabbed a silver-handled walking cane from the stand next to the door and raised it.

"Look out," Lily screamed as Adam rushed the man, striking him in the back and shoving him through the door. Still holding the cane, Adam shoved his weight against the door and tried to slam it closed.

Lily stood there horrified as she heard shouting in the hall, and saw a man's muscled arm come through the door with a gun in his hand. "Look out," she yelled again. But Adam brought the cane down on the arm and sent the gun flying to the floor.

She heard a grunt, watched the door give slightly and then saw Michael come barreling into the room. As Michael stumbled forward and fell to the floor, Adam slammed the door shut, locking them inside.

"Open up, Webster," someone yelled, and pounded on the door.

"Michael," she cried out at the sight of him in his gladiator costume, sprawled out on the oriental rug. She rushed to his side. "Are you all right?"

"Yeah. Damn shoes," he muttered as he shoved himself to his feet.

Suddenly Lily remembered the gun she had in her purse. She hurried over to the couch, found the clutch and tore it open. But the gun was gone.

"Is this what you're looking for?"

She looked up and saw Adam holding the gun, aiming it at Michael. "And don't bother trying to get to your weapon, Sullivan. I have it, too," he said as he patted his waistband where the gun was tucked. "Now tell your friends out there to leave. Or else I'll put a bullet right between your eyes."

"Go to hell."

"The only one who'll be going to hell, Sullivan, is you—unless you do as you're told." He released the safety on the gun. "Do it."

"Michael, please," Lily begged.

"Travis," he shouted. "Call your men off."

"But, Mike—"

"Do it, Travis," Michael commanded. "He's got a gun."

"All right. We're going," Travis yelled out, and Lily could hear footsteps retreating.

"Very good, Sullivan. Now, Elisabeth, step away from Mr. Sullivan."

"No," she said, throwing her body across him.

"I'm not going to let you kill him. Let him go, Adam. He has nothing to do with this."

Adam laughed. "Oh Elisabeth darling, that *is* a good one. You honestly believe he has nothing to do with this? Who do you think told me where to find you in the first place? Sullivan works for me."

"You're lying," she said. "You're lying."

"If you don't believe me, ask him."

"Michael?" she said, turning to him. When she looked at his face and saw the guilt reflected in those blue eyes, pain slashed through her with the swiftness of a laser. She hadn't thought it possible for a heart to actually break, but in that moment she felt her own heart shatter, then crumble into tiny pieces.

She knew Adam was telling her the truth.

Michael watched the emotions race across Lily's face. He thought he had known guilt and self-hatred after Pete's death. It was nothing compared to what he was feeling now. "Lily, I can explain."

Something, some spark, died in her eyes. "Then it's true. You work for him."

Frustrated, and at a loss as to how to make her understand, he answered honestly. "Yes, he did hire me to find you. But I walked away from the job because I fell in love with you. I love you, Lily," he said, and wished he had told her before now. "I wanted to tell you the truth. I planned to tell you everything when I came to your house yesterday, but you were getting ready to bolt. And I was afraid if I told you then, you would have run and refused to let me help you."

"You dare to fall in love with my wife, Sullivan?" Adam asked, his fury evident by the dark expression on his face. "I ought to shoot you for that alone."

"Adam, don't," Lily screamed.

"What does it matter to you if I kill him? He's nothing to you. He's a bounty hunter I hired to find you. He's served his purpose. It's time to dispose of him."

"You think you can shoot me and just walk out of here?" Michael countered, buying time. If he'd had any doubts before about the man's sanity, he no longer did. Adam Webster was insane. "My brother's a federal agent. He may not be right outside that door, but he won't be far away. You won't make it out of the hotel."

"I'll make it out of here the same way I made it in. With my costume. And, of course, Lily already has hers."

"It'll never work."

"Won't it? Do you really think your brother or anyone else will be able to find us among the hundreds of thousands of people partying out there in the streets right now? I think not."

"I found you, didn't I?" Michael reminded him.

Webster glared at him. "And you think that makes you clever, Sullivan? I should have realized that Elisabeth would be foolish enough to leave a trail even a Boy Scout could follow.''

''I'm not a Boy Scout. And I was clever enough to find your wife when you couldn't.''

Webster glared at him. ''Yes, but I hope you aren't expecting to collect the rest of that fee I promised you.''

''I don't want your money. And if you want to go on breathing, you'll put down that gun and let us walk out of here.''

''Us? There is no 'us' except for the one in your fantasies, Sullivan. Elisabeth is my wife. She belongs to me. Come over here, Elisabeth.''

Lily hesitated a moment, then obeyed him. He slid his arm around her waist, yanking her back so that her body was pressed against him.

''She's not a piece of property, Webster. You don't own her.''

''Ah, but that's where you're wrong. I do own her. And she knows it. Don't you, darling?'' he asked, and slid his hand up from her waist, closing it over her breast.

Michael shook with rage as he saw the revulsion and shame come into Lily's eyes. ''Let her go, or I'll kill you with my bare hands,'' Michael warned him.

Webster smiled. ''Such gallantry, Sullivan. I do believe you've taken on the character of your costume quite literally,'' he said. ''She's mine, and I'll do whatever I want to her,'' he spat out and then he crushed the nipple of Lily's breast between his fingers. Lily whimpered.

"You bastard," Michael raged as he started to come at him.

"Don't," Webster said, raising the gun. "One more step, and I'll pull the trigger."

"Adam, please. I'll go with you. Just let him go."

"You know I can't do that, darling. Not now."

"No," Lily screamed, and shoved at Webster's arm, causing the gun to misfire.

Quickly Webster swung the weapon back and aimed it at him, prepared to fire. Lily threw herself in front of Michael.

"Lily, no," Michael said, holding her, trying to move her out of harm's way. When he looked up, he saw Webster watching them. Saw the speculation come into his dark eyes. Saw the blinding rage as realization dawned.

"You've fucked her," Webster spit out the words. "You've fucked her, haven't you?"

Michael remained silent.

"Answer me, you bastard! Did you fuck her?"

"No," Lily answered as she came to her feet. She hiked up her chin, faced him defiantly, and in that moment, Michael realized he'd never known anyone more beautiful or brave.

"Fucking a woman is what *you* do, Adam," she told him. "He and I made love. For the first time in my life I actually made love with a man. A real man. Not...not some animal!''

"You filthy whore. I gave you everything. Everything," he ranted. "I clothed you, fed you, educated you. I even got rid of that worthless mother of yours and married you. And this is how you repay me? By allowing this scum to touch what's mine?''

"You bought me," Lily told him. "And the price I had to pay was too high.''

Webster backhanded her, knocking her to the floor. "You worthless bitch.''

"You bastard," Michael shouted, and lunged at Webster.

Webster fired, and Michael felt the bullet graze the flesh at his temple, felt the trickle of blood seep down near his eye.

"Adam, stop," Lily screamed, once again placing herself between him and Webster.

"Lily, don't," Michael said, trying to urge her to move aside, not trusting Webster.

"You're right, Adam," Lily told him. "I don't know what got into me. You've been so good to me all these years. You gave me everything and I should have been grateful. I can see now how wrong I was," she continued. "Please, let's go home. Let me try to make it up to you.''

"Do you really think I want you now?" Webster asked. "Now that I know he's had you? You're nothing to me now. Just another worthless cunt. The only thing I want from you now is that disk.''

''What disk?'' Michael asked, his gaze going from Lily to Webster and back to Lily again.

Webster laughed. ''What's this? She allowed you to screw her brains out, but she never told you about the disk she stole from me? Why do you think I was willing to pay you so much money to find her?''

''I thought you wanted her back,'' Michael answered honestly.

''I did want her back. After all, I'd invested a great deal of time and money in her. But I knew I had to get the disk back since there was, let's say, some damaging information on it. Naturally, I couldn't allow Lily to make a mistake and have it get into the wrong hands.''

Michael thought of his conversation with his brother, how Travis had been convinced Lily was hiding something. While he'd eventually suspected as much himself, he hadn't believed Travis was right at first. Because he hadn't wanted to believe he was wrong. Just as he hadn't wanted to believe he was wrong all those years ago about Pete.

''I'm not surprised she didn't tell you, Sullivan. Elisabeth has always been one to keep secrets. Even from me—despite everything I did for her.''

But he could hardly blame her for not trusting him, Michael thought. Because he hadn't trusted her, either. He'd kept his own secrets because he didn't want to lose her, didn't want to come clean about his own deception. He could see that now—now that it might be too late. Even if they got out of here, the chances of her ever speaking to him again were slim. After all, it was because of him that she was in this mess now. Somehow, he had to make it right.

"But none of that really matters now, does it? I'm through with both of you. All I want now is my disk." He turned his gaze on Lily. "Where's the disk, Elisabeth?"

"Don't tell him," Michael told her. "You tell him where it is and he'll kill us both."

"I'll kill you right now if she doesn't," Webster countered, aiming the gun at Michael again.

"No," Lily told Webster. "Don't shoot him."

"Forget about me. Think of Timmy. Don't give him the disk."

"Where is it, Elisabeth?" Webster demanded.

She hesitated, her gaze bouncing between Webster and him.

Suddenly Webster grabbed her around the neck, held the gun to her head. "Tell her to turn over the disk, Sullivan. Tell her, or I'll shoot her. I swear it!"

Michael bunched his hands into impotent fists. He wanted to rip the man apart, but couldn't afford to risk him shooting Lily. As it was, Webster's gun hand was anything but steady. The arm he had wrapped around Lily's neck was so tight, Michael feared he would crush her windpipe. From the way her fingers clutched at that arm, he suspected she was having trouble breathing. Worst of all was the look in Webster's eyes.

"All right," Lily told him, her voice strained. "But I don't have it with me. I have to take you to it."

"You're lying," Webster shot back.

"I'm not," she said, and coughed. "I swear, I don't have it here. I hid it. It's someplace safe. But I—I'll have to take you to it."

After a moment, Webster loosened his hold around her neck. "All right. But no tricks, Elisabeth. You double-cross me and I'll not only kill you—I'll kill that brat you love so much. Understood?"

She nodded.

"Lily, don't do it. He can't hurt Timmy. Timmy's safe. And he'll kill you the minute you give him the disk."

"I've had about enough out of you, Sullivan."

"No," Lily protested. "I'll take you to the disk, but you've got to leave Michael here alive."

"You're not in a position to bargain, Elisabeth," Webster snarled.

"Yes, I am," she insisted. "Michael's right. You might kill me, but you won't get Timmy. I know he's safe where you won't be able to touch him. If you want the disk, you'll let him live."

"What's to stop me from just killing you both now?"

"Because you don't know where the disk is or in

whose hands it will end up. You need me to take you to it."

Webster studied her a moment, appeared to weigh his options. "All right. I won't kill Sullivan. But he's going to place a call to his brother, and have him and his minions let us pass."

"And if I refuse?" Michael replied.

"Then I'll kill her right now. And we both know that while you might not be afraid of dying, you don't want her death on your conscience. After all, you already have your partner's death on your head." Webster laughed. "And we both know that you'd rather die than have to live with the guilt of knowing you caused another death."

"I'll make the call," Michael told him, hating that his Achilles' heel was so apparent, and even worse, knowing that it was true.

"I thought you would," Webster said. "And tell Agent Sullivan that if anyone so much as approaches us when we leave here, I'll kill her on the spot."

Webster tossed Michael the cell phone, and he placed the call to his brother. "All right, it's done. When she gives you the disk, don't add a murder wrap to your sins. Let her go, Webster. She doesn't deserve to die."

"Giving me orders, Sullivan?"

"Making you a promise. You harm a hair on her head, and I swear to God, I'll hunt you down like a dog and kill you."

"You know, I do believe the man loves you after all."

"I do love you, Lily," he said, willing her to look at him, but when she did all he saw was the pain of betrayal.

"Come on," Webster told her. He tightened his arm around her neck again and began backing up toward the door. "Unlock the door," he ordered.

And once she had done as he'd ordered, Webster took the gun away from Lily's head. And he aimed it at Michael.

"Adam, no!"

He fired, striking Michael in the leg.

Lily screamed. She struggled to break free of Webster. "You promised," she accused as he shoved her through the door.

"And I kept my promise. I didn't kill him. I'm just making sure he's in no condition to play hero and come after you."

Eighteen

"Jesus Christ, Mike, let me get you to a doctor," Travis argued as he met him on the stairs of the Regent Hotel.

"I'm all right," Michael insisted, ignoring the pain in his leg as he hurried down the last flight of stairs.

"You're not all right. You've got a bullet lodged in your thigh, and that damn thing wrapped around it isn't going to stop it from bleeding if you keep moving like this."

Michael swung around, met his brother's concerned gaze. "I've got to stop him, Travis. If I don't, the minute she turns that disk over to him, he'll kill her."

"I've got a team of men following them. He's not going to get away."

They exited the hotel to a city that had fallen under the spell of the Mardi Gras. The crowds, partying and parades showed no signs of slowing down. If anything, it appeared to have grown more wild and crowded during the last hour. "Your people know to stay back—not let Webster see he's being followed?"

"Are you kidding? In this crowd, Webster could

have a whole battalion following him and he wouldn't know if they were after him, or just more of these nuts out looking to party.''

Michael tried to find some comfort in his brother's explanation. It was true, he reasoned. The crowds and celebrations were so massive, he couldn't help but worry they would work in Webster's favor. "Which direction did they head in?''

"Back down toward the Saint Charles Court where you were staying,'' Travis told him. "You have any idea what's on that disk?''

"No, but I think it might have something to do with the federal sting that was going down in Florida—when that agent was killed. It's the only thing that makes any sense. You said Logan told you the woman who called him had information about the murder. Maybe there's something on the disk that can tie back to Webster. Why else take this kind of risk? It has to be something that would put him in the pen for a long time.''

"Could she have hidden the disk at the hotel without you knowing it?'' Travis asked.

Michael thought about it, recalled the hours he'd spent there with Lily, making love, talking, laughing. Then he recalled how frantic she'd been when he'd come out of the bathroom and seen her on the phone with Webster. Her movements had been too panicked for her to remember something like that disk. "I guess it's possible, but I don't think so.''

"Any ideas where she's hidden it?''

Michael tried to think as they moved along in the

crush; people laughing, dancing and drinking while beads, cups and doubloons were landing all around them. Holding his leg, Michael managed to get through a group dressed like space monsters. He thought about the car they'd left in a garage. "Your people went over everything in her car?" Michael asked, remembering how she'd hurriedly packed her belongings yesterday. Yesterday? God, had it only been a day ago that they'd escaped Webster's goons? He felt as if he'd known her and loved her for a lifetime.

"Nothing there that we could find."

If Lily had had the disk in her car, she wouldn't have agreed to abandon it in the parking garage as she had—not without at least insisting they go back for her clothes or Timmy's. "What about her house?"

"Nothing."

With effort, they made it past one street corner. As they did so, Travis flipped out his cell phone. "This is Sullivan. I need an update." When he ended the call, he said, "They're three blocks ahead of us. They've passed the Saint Charles Court and are headed toward Canal Street."

Someone bumped into his leg, and Michael groaned, seeing stars as the pain shot through him.

"Mike, your leg's bleeding again. Let me get you to a hospital. My guys will follow Webster and Lily. He won't get away."

"No," Michael told him. "I can't take that chance. I've got to get to them before something happens to her. I have to do this, Travis. I have to."

"All right. But let me lead for a change, and see if I can't scare our way through this madness."

And as Michael allowed his brother to bulldoze through, he couldn't help thinking it felt good to connect with his family again. He just wanted the chance to make things right with Lily. Webster had been right. If anything happened to Lily, his conscience would make his own life a private hell.

"Quit stalling, Elisabeth," Adam commanded, and dragged her up from the ground when she stumbled. He closed his fingers around her arm like a vise and pulled her with him along the street.

"Adam, wait. My shoe," she protested.

"Hurry up," he told her and loosened his grip just enough so she could retrieve the sandal she'd deliberately thrown off in her efforts to stall him. "Put the damn thing on, and let's go."

She did as he ordered, but continued to hang back, despite Adam digging his nails into her upper arm until it was raw. She still didn't know what she was going to do, or how she could possibly escape. She only knew that she wasn't going to meekly give him the disk and allow him to kill her.

Not now. Not when she had so much to live for. Her heart ached as she remembered Michael's face when he'd told her that he loved her. She'd wanted to tell him she forgave him, that she'd understood why he had done what he had. But with Adam watching her closely, she'd known if she had even given

Michael so much as a look of understanding, Adam would have made good on his threat to kill them both.

"How much farther?" Adam shouted as he pulled her along the sidewalk where the crowd wasn't quite as thick.

"About six more blocks."

"Where are we going?" he asked.

"If I tell you, you'll have no reason not to kill me."

He made a face at her. "All right. I'll play your little game for now. But I'm warning you, I'm growing tired of it. Now let's go."

He yanked her again, and this time Lily really did stumble. She fell to the pavement, scraping her knee and tearing the white dress that Ricardo had taken such pride in giving to her.

"Get up," he ordered, and hauled her to her feet. "You're filthy," he told her, noting her hands and dress were now stained with God-knows-what mixture of drink, food and bodily fluids that the Mardi Gras revelers had discarded onto the streets.

She tried wiping the sticky wet stuff down the skirt of her dress. Adam grabbed her by the arm again and started pushing his way through the sea of bodies.

They made it another block before everything came to a complete halt. "What in the devil is going on up there?" he demanded.

Straining to see, all Lily could make out were the overhead trucks and flashing lights at the corner. The parade passing in the street itself had come to a stop, as well. Marching bands, dance teams and drill units all marched in place. She even spied several of the flambeau carriers, the torchbearers established when there were no streetlights or car lights to show the way and who continued to march during the evening parades, holding their unlit torches as they danced in place in the street. People were running up to the floats. Women and children were riding atop shoulders, holding their hands up, begging for more throws.

"Why aren't we moving? Why has everyone stopped?" Adam demanded to no one in particular.

"Rex is toasting at city hall," a guy next to him said. "Probably Zulu or the mayor. It's tradition. The rest of the parade has to stop while the kings and queens make their toasts."

"How long does it take?" Adam asked.

The guy shrugged. "Not long. You've probably got time to take your lady friend up to the float and get her some nice beads."

"I don't like this," Adam muttered. His gaze darted to the right, to the left, looking all around as though expecting a trap. "Let's go."

Lily tugged back. "Adam, there's nowhere to go. We can't get through. You heard the man. Everything stops until the toasts are over."

Adam's eyes narrowed. He spun around, looking behind him. "No. We can't wait any longer. I don't trust Sullivan and his brother. They're out there. I know it. If we stay here, they'll get me."

Lily knew in that moment that Adam's sanity—if he still had any left—was now hanging by a thread.

So many people crowded the streets that there was no way he would be able to pick out Michael, his brother or anyone else.

"Let's go."

"But we can't move."

"Yes, we can," he told her, shoving her forward.

She rammed into the back of a man and elbowed another. "I'm sorry," she murmured, continuing to offer apologies that no would could hear above the thundering noise of the bands and people shouting for throws.

Adam urged her toward the curb. "We're going to cut across, take the back streets where there aren't any parades."

Lily knew that once he had her away from the crowd, she would have no further chance to escape. Even if she were to bring him to Gertie's and retrieve Timmy's teddy and give him the disk she'd sewn into the stuffed toy, it would not stop him from killing her—possibly Gertie, too, if she was still there. She couldn't let that happen. And she wasn't going to die.

"Come on," Adam said, pulling at her arm again.

Lily stared up ahead. The big overhead truck with its flashing lights started to move. Maybe if she could somehow break away from him when the parade started to move again she could escape.

She thought she heard someone shouting her name and glanced behind her. Had it been Michael? Had he somehow managed to come after her despite being shot?

"I said come on," Adam ordered. He grabbed her

arm again and shoved her toward the corner, not noticing the curses and complaints his elbowing was generating.

When they reached the curb, Lily pretended to stumble again. Only this time when she fell, something seemed to snap in Adam. "Get up, you troublesome bitch," he said, grabbing her by the hair and yanking her to her feet. He pulled out the gun and pointed it at her chest. "I've had enough of these stalling tactics."

Stunned that he'd pulled the weapon out in the open, Lily looked about her. She was surrounded by people—people dressed like Keystone Kops with toy guns, prisoners from jail in their striped outfits, gangsters in striped suits and fedoras with machine guns, make-believe soldiers with rifles—but not one of them was paying any attention to her and Adam. No one realized his gun was real.

"Where's the disk?" Adam demanded.

"Lily! Lily!"

She looked back, positive now she had heard Michael's voice above the din. But she couldn't depend on Michael to save her. She couldn't depend on anyone to save her now, but herself. She scanned her surroundings, tracked the progress of the parade. The floats had begun to move again. So had the marchers. She could see a gap in the parade—thought she saw one of the monster-size floats coming.

Adam shoved the gun beneath her breastbone. "I said, tell me where the disk is, or I'll shoot you right now."

Lily held her breath a moment as she waited for the float to come closer. She gauged her options, deciding she had none. She had to try it. Praying her timing was right, she said, "All right. I'll tell you. Just put the gun down, Adam."

He lowered the weapon, but continued to hold her arm. "All right, where is it?"

"I hid it. It's in…" She yanked her arm free, pretending to fall backward into the street where the floats had been passing.

"Bitch! You're not getting away from me," Adam yelled, and lunged toward her.

As he tried to grab at her in an effort to keep her from escaping, Lily reached out and caught Adam's arm. She pulled him forward instead, sending him sprawling into the street in front of the giant float.

Adam screamed, and Lily turned away as the tractor pulling the float hit his head first, then dragged his body beneath the massive tire wheels, unable to stop. She didn't bother looking back to see if he'd survived. Lily knew no one could have survived that kind of blow to the head.

"Lily! Lily," Michael called out.

Stunned, sickened by what she had done, she looked up and saw Michael shoving his way through the crowd of horrified people. He limped toward her, his leg wrapped with a bloodied bandage, blood streaked at his temple. The fleeting thought that went through her mind was that he really did look like a gladiator—one who had just survived a battle.

Then he was standing in front of her, pulling her

into his arms, kissing her head, stroking her back, holding her. "It's over, Lily. It's over."

Suddenly other people were surrounding them. Some of the men she'd seen dressed as Keystone Kops and soldiers were holding very real-looking weapons and making official noises as they ordered people back, trying to maintain order amid the chaos.

When she lifted her head to look at Michael, she said, "I killed him, Michael. I killed him."

"Webster killed himself. He was sick, Lily. A sick man who would have killed you. All you did was save your own life."

"Timmy?" she asked.

"He's safe. And Gertie's fine. So is my father. Everyone's okay. Thanks to you. You're the hero here, Lily. You saved us all."

Lily didn't argue with him. She didn't bother telling him that it was his love that had made her strong, had made her believe in herself. He'd made her want to live not just for Timmy, but for herself.

Michael continued to hold her close, murmuring reassurances. She didn't know how long he held her. It might have been minutes. It could have been hours. And then the blue-eyed security officer was tapping Michael's shoulder.

"I need to get a statement from her, Mike."

"Not now," Michael told him.

"It's all right," she said, extricating herself from Michael's arms. "You must be Travis Sullivan."

"Yes, ma'am," he said, and flashed her that same charming grin that belonged to Michael.

"I'm please to meet you, Agent Sullivan."

"Travis, ma'am. And I hope it's all right if I call you Lily. I have a feeling we're going to be seeing a lot of each other."

She certainly hoped so, Lily thought. But when she looked at Michael, she saw those dark clouds, that same self-recrimination she'd seen the night he'd told her about his friend's death.

"If you'll come with me, I'd like to get a statement from you."

"Of course," she told him.

"Mike, you coming?"

"No. You go on and get Lily's statement. I'm going to see about this leg."

Seated across from his brother in the temporary office he'd been assigned to use at the Bureau's office in New Orleans, Michael listened as Travis gave him a report on what had transpired the previous evening after he'd taken himself to the emergency room to have the bullet removed from his leg.

"With the stuff on that disk," Travis began, "Webster would have been facing a life behind bars—maybe even the death penalty.

"Talk about a smart lady," Travis went on. "She sewed the disk into her son's teddy bear. She knew Webster couldn't stand the kid, and she figured if he did find them, he wouldn't bother with the boy's favorite stuffed toy."

"Lily's a lot smarter than she gives herself credit for."

"She's also very brave. From what I gather, the guy has had her under his thumb and in his control since she was a kid. It couldn't have been easy for her to walk out on him like she did. And she took a big risk stealing that disk—that took a lot of guts. Hell, I know men who wouldn't have had the nerve to do what she did."

"Lily's a lot stronger than she thinks."

"All I know is with that disk and Webster out of the way, she saved a lot of agents' lives last night. With the information Webster had, our agents would have been sitting ducks."

"I hope you told her what a difference she made," Michael said.

"Sure did," Travis said as he sat back in his chair and kicked his feet up on the desk. "That's some woman you've got there, bro. I'm happy for you."

"She's not my woman," Michael corrected. Lily didn't belong to him or anyone.

"Funny, I got the impression you thought that she was," Travis said, swinging his feet back down to the floor. He eyed him closer, leaned forward a fraction. "And from what you told me, the lady risked her own neck to save you from taking a bullet in the head last night."

"What's your point?"

"My point is, I doubt the lady did that unless she thought there was something between you, too."

"She's better off without me."

"That what she said?"

"It's not her decision," Michael said, and stood.

"I'm not sure it's yours, either."

"What's that supposed to mean?"

"It means you can't decide what's best for everyone, Mike. Lily has a say in this, too. You took off and shut everyone out when Pete got killed because you thought it was your fault. Now there's this thing with Lily. So you were the one who led Webster to her. You're also the one who helped her to fight him."

"I didn't help her. I almost caused her to be killed. That monster would have killed Timmy, too," Michael pointed out.

"But he didn't. They're both alive, and they're fine."

"No thanks to me."

"All right, you made a mistake by not telling her up front about Webster hiring you. You're human, Mike. We humans make mistakes. You get over it and move on."

"I'm not sure I can."

"You'd better," Travis insisted. "Because if you don't, and you walk away from that lady, you'll be making the biggest mistake of your life."

Nineteen

"Timmy, you stay here and take care of Gertie while Mommy answers the door. Okay?"

"'Kay."

The doorbell sounded again. "I'll be right back, Gertie."

"Go on and answer the door," Gertie told her. "You've been fussing over me worse than a mother hen ever since those nice agents brought me over here last night. Timmy and I will be fine. Right?"

"Wight," Timmy said, and went back to munching on the bowl of popcorn that sat between him and Gertie while they watched a new Disney video.

Relieved to see Gertie relaxed after the fright she'd had, Lily rushed from Timmy's room through the length of the house to reach the front door. "Coming," she called out as she drew closer. She pulled open the door and saw Michael.

"Hi."

"Hi," she said, drinking in the sight of him. She noted the bandage near his temple, saw the cane he leaned on, the dark shadows beneath his eyes.

"May I come in?"

"Of course," she said, holding the door open for him to enter. She felt a little blip in her heart as she watched him limp inside. "Would you like to sit down?"

"Thanks," he said with all the politeness of a stranger as he sat down in the big stuffed chair adjacent to her couch. "I guess I probably should have called first instead of just showing up like this."

She smiled at him. "It does seem to be one of your faults," she teased, immediately regretting the remark when he didn't smile in return.

"Travis tells me Timmy and Gertie are both okay."

"Yes," she said, growing more uneasy by the second. Any thoughts she might have harbored that Michael had come here to declare his love for her faded like yesterday's revelry had with the dawn of Ash Wednesday.

"Is that Timmy I hear laughing?"

"Yes. He's in his room with Gertie. Your brother was kind enough to have one of his agents bring her over. I didn't want her to be alone after what had happened," she explained. "But she seems fine now. She and Timmy are watching a new Disney video. They're halfway through their second bowl of popcorn, too."

"Sounds like you're spoiling them."

"After everything that they've been through, I figured they deserved to be spoiled."

"So do you," he told her.

"I don't know about that," she told him, remembering the role she had played in the tragedy last night. "I'm not sure I'll ever be able to forget what happened, knowing I'm responsible for Adam's death."

"You have nothing to feel guilty about, Lily. The man was insane, and if you hadn't done what you did, he'd have probably killed you."

"I know that. But it doesn't absolve me of all blame. Running away like I did seven months ago…it was a mistake. And the rest of my life I'm going to have to live with the knowledge that had I been stronger and stayed and fought Adam for what was right as I should have, he might still be alive."

She swallowed, searched for the words to explain to Michael the conclusions she had reached during the night. "I know I'm also going to have to face Timmy one day and answer his questions about his father and how he died."

"You'll find the right words," he told her.

"Yes, I will."

He gave her a fleeting smile. "You sound confident. I'm glad."

"I am confident, because I learned a few things about myself these past few days. I learned that I'm not weak or stupid or helpless."

"You never were."

"But I didn't know that. I thought I needed someone to rescue me, to save me and Timmy from Adam."

"You saved yourself," Michael pointed out.

"Yes. I did. And now I know that whatever happens in the future, I'll be able to handle it."

"I never doubted that you would. You deserve to be happy, Lily. I hope you will be."

"Why does that sound like a goodbye?" Lily asked, her heart heavy.

"Because it is. I came to say goodbye to you and Timmy. And to give you this." He reached inside his shirt pocket and removed a photograph, handing it to her.

Lily stared at the snapshot of her and Timmy. "But how?" she began.

"Margie Schubert asked me to give it to you."

Pain and anger sliced through Lily, a reminder of Michael's betrayal.

"I'm sorry for my part in what happened. The minute I realized that the situation wasn't what Webster had claimed, I should have told you who I was and that he had hired me to find you."

"Yes, you should have."

"I'm more sorry than you'll ever know," he said, and shoved his hands through his hair. He kept his head down for a moment, and when he looked up at her again, he looked like a man who had lost his soul. "I hope you believe me when I tell you that I never meant to hurt you."

"I believe you," she told him. "But your deception hurt, Michael. You should have told me."

"I realize that now. But at the time, I thought I was doing the right thing."

"You could have trusted me to understand," she said.

But hadn't she been guilty of the same thing? Lily asked herself. She hadn't told him about the disk because she had been afraid to trust him, too.

"I should have. But I was afraid you'd run away from me, and I wanted to protect you, to keep you safe. Of course, thanks to me, you were nearly killed."

"But I wasn't killed. I'm alive, Michael. Probably more alive than I've ever been, because for the first time in a very long time, I'm not afraid. I'm actually thinking about the future."

"I'm happy for you," he said as he picked up his cane. He stood. "I hope someday you'll be able to forgive me. If it's okay with you, I'd like to say goodbye to Timmy."

"Of course," she told him, hurt beyond words that he could walk away from her so easily. "I'll get him for you."

And while she stood back and watched Michael steal both her son's and Gertie's hearts, her own heart ached because she loved him, and she knew the stubborn man loved her. It also infuriated her that he could throw what they had away because he was suffering a mountain of guilt.

Lily looked at him, realized he was about to walk out that door and out of her life. She'd made so many mistakes in her life already because she'd been fearful of the outcome. She didn't want to make another one now for the same reason. If Michael rejected her, at least she would have the satisfaction of knowing she'd tried. Letting him walk out the door without telling him what was in her heart was a mistake she refused to make. If there was any chance for them to be together, she had to know. She drew in a breath. "Gertie, would you take Timmy into the kitchen for some cookies and milk. I'd like to talk to Michael a moment before he goes."

"Come along, Timmy," Gertie said.

"Michael, what about us?" she asked once Gertie and Timmy had left the room. "I love you. And last night you told me that you loved me. Was it the truth? Or did you just say that so I wouldn't feel like a fool when I found out you were the one who told Adam where I was?"

His mouth tightened. "I never did tell him. But he figured it out."

"You never answered my question. Was the part about loving me a lie?"

"No, I do love you," he said, practically spitting out the words.

They were a soothing balm to her heart. "Then why are you leaving me?"

"Jesus, Lily! How can you ask me that?" He limped over to the window, turned back. "Look at what I've done. A man is supposed to protect the people he loves. Instead of protecting you, I nearly got you and Timmy killed."

"But you didn't," she pointed out. She went to him, cupped his face in her hands. "I'm fine, Michael. We're fine. And I love you. So does my son."

He turned his face away. "I don't deserve your love or his. You're both better off without me."

"And what about you? Are you better off without us?"

"That doesn't matter. I want the best for you and Timmy. And, trust me, I'm not it. I'm not even close."

Hurt and growing angrier by the second over his stubbornness, she asked, "And what gives you the right to decide what's best for me? I've spent the last seven years of my life with a man who decided what I wore, what I ate, what I was supposed to think. Do you honestly think I would settle for that again?"

He narrowed his eyes. "That's not what I'm doing."

"Isn't it? You have this idea that I need someone to take care of me, to rescue me when I get in trouble. Well, I don't. I can take care of myself and Timmy. And I don't need anyone to rescue me. I can rescue myself." She drew a breath, decided to lay it on the line. "I want a partner, Michael. Someone I can share things with. Someone who can share things with me. I want a man who will love me for who I am and forgive me for my mistakes. The same way that I'll love him for who he is and forgive him for his mistakes. I want you, Michael."

"You deserve better, Lily. I've made enough mistakes. I'm not going to make an even bigger one by staying around and screwing up your life."

Lily realized in that moment that she'd lost. "So

you're going to run away again?'' she tossed at his retreating back.

"I'm moving on with my life. The same way you should move on with yours.''

"Lie to yourself, Michael, but don't lie to me,'' Lily told him. She pressed a fist to her breast to ease the ache in her heart. "You're running away—again—the same way you ran away from your career as a policeman, the same way you ran away from your family. And while you might want to think you're doing it for us, you're not. You're doing it to punish yourself for not living up to this superhero image you have in your head of what you think you should be.''

"Goodbye, Lily,'' he told her, and opened the door.

She followed him out onto the porch and blinked back tears, determined not to cry—at least not in front of him. "Haven't you heard anything I've said?''

"I heard every word.''

"And you're still determined to leave.''

"It's for the best.'' He kissed her gently on the lips and stepped back.

The tears began to fall. "Go ahead, run away then,'' she said, sobbing. "But I've got news for you, you'll never be able to run far enough, because the person you're really running from is yourself.''

Michael looked down at the letter he'd been struggling to write to Timmy for the better part of an hour. He read the "Hi Cowboy— How are you doing?''

but the rest of the page remained blank. Sighing, he left the letter—or what there was of it—on the table in his parents' den and walked over to the window.

He looked out at the familiar surroundings, the place where he'd grown up. Home. He still wasn't sure what had made him change his destination from Florida to Texas that day when he'd left Lily's and gone to the airport. He'd only known that he hadn't been able to get the things she'd accused him of out of his head. And when he'd gone up to the ticket counter at the airport to check in, he'd booked a flight to Houston and come home. It felt good to be home, he admitted. It felt good to heal the wounds he'd caused to his family and himself five years ago.

So why did he still feel so miserable?

Because of Lily, he admitted. He still couldn't erase the image of her from his mind.

He stared out at his mother's garden. The trees were thick with leaves of green already, and he spied a bird's nest at the top of an oak. Spring was almost here, he thought. And as he stared at the flowers, he remembered that first day he'd gone to Lily's house and had seen her and Timmy planting a garden in that tiny strip of a backyard.

Would her flowers be blooming now? he wondered.

He missed them both so much it was making him crazy.

So what are you waiting for? Why haven't you gone back?

"Hey, Mike," his brother said, sticking his head in the den.

"Hey," Michael said, glad for the distraction.

"Writing a letter?" Travis asked as he came into the room, plopped onto the couch.

"Trying. I'm not having much luck."

"You wouldn't happen to be writing to Lily, would you?" Travis asked nonchalantly, but Michael knew there wasn't anything nonchalant about the question.

"To Timmy. I promised him I'd write."

"Cute kid," Travis said. "And his mom's not bad, either."

Michael scowled at him. "You going somewhere with this, bro?"

"Just making conversation. Mom said to tell you dinner's ready," Travis said as he pushed up from the couch. He paused at the door. "And in case you're interested, I saw Lily this week when I was in New Orleans doing some follow-up on the Webster case."

"How is she?" Michael asked, unable to stop himself. He knew he'd done the right thing by walking out of her life. He had meant every word he'd said about her deserving someone better. But damned if it had helped make it any easier for him to stop thinking about her, missing her, wanting her.

"She's good. She's working at the diner again. At least for now."

Michael's head snapped up at that. "What do you mean, at least for now?"

"Well, I got the impression she was thinking about

moving away. She said something about maybe moving southwest, maybe Texas.''

''Don't try playing matchmaker, Trav. You're no good at it.''

''Hey, Texas is a big state. Besides, I'm just telling you what the lady said. She claims that boy of hers has really taken a liking to cowboys. Naturally, when people think of cowboys, they think of Texas.''

Michael thought of Timmy, felt that warmth inside him again as he remembered the little boy hugging him and saying he loved him. ''They'd do well out here.''

''That's what I told her,'' Travis said. ''I also told her if she decided to come out this way that some man was going to scoop her up and marry her, because most Texans aren't as dumb as my brother.''

Michael pitched the pen at him, which Travis caught easily.

''Why the woman wants someone as mule-headed as you when she could have me, I'll never know. But she loves you, Mike,'' Travis said, all serious now. ''She's a special lady and she's been through a lot. She's not going to wait forever for you.''

''I don't want her to. That's why I left. So that she would move on with her life.''

''And what about you, Mike? When are you going to move on? When are you going to stop beating yourself up whenever you make a mistake? You keep cutting people out of your life every time you mess up because you're afraid of hurting them, and pretty soon you're going to be all alone.''

''That's not what I'm doing,'' he argued.

''Isn't it? You've got this thing about trying to fix things for the people you care about. You did it with me when we were kids. You sure as hell did it with Pete. I grew up and learned to clean up my own mistakes, but Pete never did. He depended on you to do it for him. And, of course, you always came through. Until that last time. That last time, when he really screwed up and got himself killed, you weren't able to clean up his mess. So you took on Pete's failure as your own failure—as your mistake. It wasn't,'' Travis told him. ''It was Pete's mistake. And when you tried to cover for him and that backfired, you punished yourself by cutting everyone out of your life.''

''I didn't.''

''Yes, you did. You shut me out, Dad, Mom. You quit a job you loved. You even gave up thoughts about going into the Bureau.''

''I had to look out for Janie and the boys,'' he defended.

''No, you felt guilty because you couldn't save Pete from himself. Helping Janie and the boys wasn't for them. It was for you. It was a way to remind yourself that you weren't the superhero you thought you should be. And that's why you walked away from Lily. You're punishing yourself because you weren't the one to save her. She saved herself. And the sad part about that is by cutting her out of your life you're not only punishing yourself, you're hurting her. The same way you hurt Dad when you walked away from here five years ago. Lily's had enough hurt to last a lifetime. She doesn't deserve to be hurt again.''

Was that what he had done? Michael wondered. Had he really been so intent on punishing himself for what he saw as his failures that he was hurting the people he loved?

''You better come on, Mom's got dinner on the table,'' Travis told him and exited the room.

Michael looked at the letter he'd been writing to Timmy, balled it up and put it into the trash.

''Mikey!''

At his father's shout, Michael hustled into the kitchen. ''Sorry to keep you waiting,'' he said as he took his seat at the table.

His mother beamed at him. ''You don't know how nice it is to have both of my babies here at the dinner table again,'' Katherine Sullivan said.

''Katie, your babies are grown men now,'' Big Mike pointed out.

''I know, but they'll always be my babies.''

Michael smiled and served himself up some of the mouthwatering corn bread.

''I understand from Finney that you were in the department this week,'' Big Mike told him.

Michael looked up at his father. "Still got your spies at H.P.D., I see," he joked.

"Michael Patrick Sullivan, tell me you haven't been spying on the boy."

"Now, Katie, don't go getting all worked up. I just happened to see Finney for coffee this morning, and he mentioned he'd seen Mikey in the new police chief's office." He slanted a glance at his son. "Pass me some of your mama's corn bread."

Michael winced at the childhood name Mikey and passed his father the bread basket. He hadn't said anything to his family as yet about the offer he'd been made to come back to the department.

"So you thinking about going back to being a copper?" Big Mike asked casually as he buttered his bread and took a bite.

Travis looked up from the meal he'd been inhaling and said, "Don't count on it, Pop. He was also talking to the Bureau."

"That true?" his father asked.

"I'm weighing my options," Michael said.

"Well, I suspect it all hinges on what Lily says," Travis said, and dodged when Michael tried to kick him beneath the table.

"Lily?" Katherine Sullivan said, her eyes bright and alert. "Isn't that the woman with the little boy on that case your father and brother helped you with in New Orleans?"

Travis started to open his mouth, but stuffed another piece of corn bread into it instead when Michael shot him a silencing look.

"Yes."

"So is she the girl you came home to brood about?"

"I didn't come home to brood."

His mother patted his hand. "Yes, you did. But it's okay. Now, why don't you tell me all about her."

Michael told his mother all about Lily and Timmy. And when he'd finished, she was beaming. "She sounds wonderful."

"She is," Travis said. "Just wait until you meet her."

"And when is that going to be?" his mother asked Michael.

"Just as soon as I can talk her into marrying me."

"Lily," Gina called out, sticking her head inside the door leading to the kitchen. "Hon, you got a customer."

Lily groaned. Her feet were killing her. The day had been a killer, and she'd been just about to sign out and go home. "I don't suppose I could talk you into taking care of the table for me, could I?"

"Honey, believe me, this is one you want to handle yourself."

Lily looked up. There was something in Gina's tone, and that mischievous look in her eyes, that Lily didn't quite trust. Since Michael had left she'd been moping so much that Gina and Nancy Lee had made a campaign out of cheering her up. Of course, their answer to everything was a new romance. And they had gone out of their way to steer every halfway nice guy that came into the diner to her table. "All right, who is this one?"

"Who is what one?" Gina asked innocently.

"I mean, is this another truck driver or oilman? Or maybe he's another banker. Wait, you haven't shoved any stockbrokers at me this week." She sighed. "I appreciate what you're doing, but the guy could be the king of England and I wouldn't be interested."

"Hon, all I'm telling you is that you've got a customer at your table. You don't want to wait on him…well, Nancy Lee won't like it," she said with a shrug of her shoulder. "I'll just tell him to come back tomorrow."

"All right," Lily said. Scooping up her pad and pencil she went charging into the diner. Tired and cranky, she was halfway to the table by the window, when she faltered. Great, she thought, Nancy Lee was standing in front of the table talking to the man and blocking her view of him. Wondering if the guy was complaining about the slow service, Lily started to hurry over to get his order when she caught a glimpse of his feet. He was wearing cowboy boots. She sliced her gaze to the chair across from him and noted the cowboy hat.

"Good seeing you," Nancy Lee said, and walked away.

Suddenly Lily's heart began to swell with hope, with love, as she looked at Michael with the crossword puzzle and pencil in his hand. As though sensing her gaze, he looked up and gave her one of those knee-weakening smiles.

Clutching the pad to her chest, she approached his table. "Would you like to hear the specials?" she asked him, just as she had that first time.

"Sure," he said, and she went through the list of the day's specials and took his order. "How are you with puzzles?" he asked.

"Lousy," she told him.

"This one's not too tough. How about giving it a try?"

"All right," she told him.

"Okay. Here's the clue. It's a tough one. Two parts. The first one is a man's name. He's stubborn, thick-headed and he's made a lot of mistakes and is probably going to make more in the future. His biggest mistake, though, was that he walked away from the woman he loves because he didn't think he deserved her. The truth is that he loves her so much he can't see straight, and more than anything, he wants a life with her. He wants to be her partner. And he wants her to be his partner. He wants her to allow him to be a father to her son. And he wants to make more babies with her."

"And that's the clue?"

"Yes, that's the first part."

"How many letters?" she teased.

"Seven."

"Michael."

"Right," he said, grinning.

"Now here's the really, really tough part. Will you marry me?"

"How many letters?"

"The right one—the one I'm hoping you'll give me has three."

Lily smiled at him, and taking her pad, she wrote out the word "y-e-s" and handed it to him. "How about this one?"

"It's perfect," Michael said, and pulled her into his arms and kissed her.

New York Times **Bestselling Author**

JOAN JOHNSTON

CHARITY

Nothing could have prepared beautiful, bold Charity for meeting
identical twin sisters Hope and Faith Butler at Hawk's Pride—
and seeing a mirror image of herself.

HOPE

The stunning discovery that she is a triplet cannot distract
Hope Butler from her heartbreak—the man she has loved all her life
is about to marry someone else.

FAITH

Guilt stricken by her sister's abandonment, Faith Butler vows to see
her sisters happy, no matter what it takes. Even if she has to
break up one wedding, arrange a couple more…and seize her
own chance for happiness.

Three sisters. Three lives. Three hearts.
Reunited in a brand-new story of passion and secrets.

SISTERS FOUND

Available the first week of December 2002 wherever paperbacks are sold!

METSY HINGLE

66826 THE WAGER   ___ $5.99 U.S. ___ $6.99 CAN.

(limited quantities available)

TOTAL AMOUNT	$_____
POSTAGE & HANDLING	$_____
($1.00 for 1 book, 50¢ for each additional)	
APPLICABLE TAXES*	$_____
<u>TOTAL PAYABLE</u>	$_____

(check or money order—please do not send cash)

To order, complete this form and send it, along with a check or money order for the total above, payable to MIRA Books®, to: **In the U.S.:** 3010 Walden Avenue, P.O. Box 9077, Buffalo, NY 14269-9077; **In Canada:** P.O. Box 636, Fort Erie, Ontario, L2A 5X3.

Name:_____

Address:_____ City:_____

State/Prov.:_____ Zip/Postal Code:_____

Account Number (if applicable):_____

075 CSAS

  *New York residents remit applicable sales taxes.
  Canadian residents remit applicable GST
  and provincial taxes.

MIRA®